"YOU HAVE EXACTLY SIXTY SECONDS TO ASK HOW YOUR CHILDREN ARE."

"Victor? For God's sake, where are you?"

"If you ask me that, I'll hang up."

Donna felt herself panic. She tried to keep her voice from cracking. "How's Adam? How's Sharon?" she asked, obeying his instructions.

"They're fine," he said coldly. "Sharon doesn't miss you at all." Donna thought of her little girl, saw her soft brown curls and pale blue eyes. Those extraordinary eyes which registered everything like an instamatic camera. She will not forget me, Donna thought. She will not forget me. "Adam asked about you."

Donna's heart was beginning to race. "What did you tell him?"

"That you didn't want to see him anymore. That you'd found another family you liked better."

"Victor, you didn't say that! My God, you didn't really tell him that!" He knew. He always knew her worst fears.

"Your sixty seconds are up, Donna. Goodbye. . . ."

KISS MOMMY GOODBYE

"IMMENSELY ENGROSSING AND FULFILLING!"
—*Indianapolis News*

D0905694

KISS MOMMY GOODBYE

A Novel by
Joy Fielding

[signature: Joy Fielding]

A SIGNET BOOK

SIGNET
Published by the Penguin Group
Penguin Books USA Inc., 375 Hudson Street,
New York, New York 10014, U.S.A.
Penguin Books Ltd, 27 Wrights Lane,
London W8 5TZ, England
Penguin Books Australia Ltd, Ringwood,
Victoria, Australia
Penguin Books Canada Ltd, 10 Alcorn Avenue,
Toronto, Ontario, Canada M4V 3B2
Penguin Books (N.Z.) Ltd, 182–190 Wairau Road,
Auckland 10, New Zealand

Penguin Books Ltd, Registered Offices:
Harmondsworth, Middlesex, England

Published by Signet, an imprint of Dutton Signet,
a division of Penguin Books USA Inc. This is an authorized reprint of a
hardcover edition published by Doubleday and Co., Inc.

First Signet Printing, June, 1982
22 21 20

Part One
THE PAST

Chapter 1

"Could you be a little more specific when you say 'erratic behavior'?"

"Specific?"

The lawyer smiled with well-practiced patience, perfectly pitched understanding in his voice as he elaborated.

"Yes. Could you give us some *examples* of what you describe as your wife's erratic behavior over the last few years."

"Oh, yes. Certainly," the man nodded.

Donna Cressy sat in the straight hard-backed chair, her back rigid, not touching the wood, and watched the man in the witness stand, the man to whom she had been married for six years, Victor Cressy, age thirty-eight and five years her senior, continue to grind what was left of her self-image into fine flecks of ash (human remains from the cremator's oven), to dissect every phrase she had uttered during their life together, every tone, every nuance until there was nothing left but his interpretation of how it had been. She almost smiled—why should their divorce be any different than their marriage?

She looked at his face and wished she could be like some of those women she had often read about who, when they looked at a lost or former lover, wondered what they could have seen in him in the first place. But it was all still there to see—the conventionally handsome, even kind face, with its brooding blue eyes and almost black hair, the sensitive yet commanding set of his fea-

3

tures, his full mouth, the imperious yet curiously respect-ful tone of his voice.

"She stopped driving the car," Victor said, almost won-drously. Obviously something beyond his comprehension.

"What do you mean? She just stopped?" the lawyer probed. "Had she had an accident?"

His lawyer was good, Donna admitted to herself. Victor had said he was the best in Florida, which hadn't sur-prised her. Victor had to have the best. It was a quality she had first admired, then learned to despise. Funny how the things you loved could turn so quickly into objects of scorn, she thought. Funny how a road-weary lawyer with a well-rehearsed client could still manage to make every-thing sound so spontaneous. Her own attorney had told her that a good lawyer never asked a question for which he didn't already know the answer. Her lawyer was also considered to be good—though not as good as Victor's.

"No. She never had any accidents in all the years I knew her," Victor answered. "She'd been driving since she was sixteen and as far as I know, she'd never so much as dented a fender."

"And when you were first married, did she drive often then?"

"All the time. In fact, I bought her a car, a little Toy-ota, for our second anniversary. She was thrilled."

"And she just stopped driving one day?"

"That's right. Suddenly, she just refused to get behind the wheel."

"Did she offer any explanation?"

"She said she didn't want to drive anymore."

Victor's lawyer, a Mr. Ed Gerber, raised his eyebrows while simultaneously furrowing his brow and pursing his lips. Donna thought that must be hard to do. "When ex-actly was that?"

"About two years ago. No. Maybe a little more. It was around the time she got pregnant with Sharon. Sharon's sixteen months old now, so, yea, I guess it was about two years ago." His voice was deep. Thoughtful.

"And she hasn't driven since?"

"Not to my knowledge."

"And to the best of your knowledge, nothing happened to cause this decision?"

"That's right. I—" he hesitated, as if debating with himself whether or not to continue. "I once saw her get behind the wheel of the car, about a year ago when she thought I was still asleep—"

"Still asleep? What time was it?"

"A little after three A.M."

"What was she doing out at three A.M.?"

"Objection." Her own lawyer. Mr. Stamler. The same height and weight as Mr. Gerber. Approximately the same age. Interchangeable, except that Victor had told her Mr. Gerber was better.

"Sorry. I'll rephrase that. What was your wife wearing at the time, Mr. Cressy?"

"Her nightgown."

"And where were the children?"

"Asleep. In the house."

"Would you describe exactly what you saw that morning."

Victor looked perplexed. Donna could see his confusion was sincere. Forgive them, Father, she found herself thinking, for they know not what they do. Victor had sworn to tell the truh. And he was telling it—as he saw it. As he knew it. His truth, not hers. Her chance would come later. Her last chance.

"I heard the front door close and I looked out the window to the carpark and I saw Donna unlock the car and get inside. I remember being astounded that she would even be thinking about driving again, and then even more surprised that she would be going anywhere at three in the morning. That was long before I found out about her relationship with Dr. Segal, of course."

"Objection. There is no proof that Mrs. Cressy had any intention of going to meet Dr. Segal that morning."

"Sustained." The judge. The same height and weight as both Mr. Stamler and Mr. Gerber. Perhaps twenty years older.

"Did Mrs. Cressy, in fact, go anywhere?"

"No. She put the key in the ignition and switched on the motor, and then she just sat there like she couldn't move. And then she started to shake. All over. She just sat there and shook. Finally, she turned off the motor and came back inside. I went into the living room to see if she was okay, and I could see she'd been crying. I asked her what was wrong."

"And what was her answer?"

"She told me to go back to bed. And then she went back to her room."

"Her room? You had separate bedrooms?"

"Yes."

Victor looked deeply embarrassed by the admission.

"Why was that?"

"It was what Donna wanted."

"From the beginning?"

"No. Oh, no." He smiled. "We have two children, remember." Mr. Gerber smiled in consolation. It seemed even the judge smiled. Only Donna remained unmoved. "No, she, uh, told me she wouldn't sleep with me anymore on the day she found out she was pregnant with our second child."

"Did you consider that announcement strange?"

"Only a little. She'd been saying no for quite a long time by that point. Except for the odd occasion." His smile was puppy-dog sad. Donna wanted to punch him in the mouth.

"So your wife refused to have sexual relations with you?"

"Yes, sir." Almost inaudible.

"Did she give you a reason?" Why was he so concerned with reasons? Donna wondered.

"At first, she used to say she was just too tired, what with looking after Adam—he's four now." Donna stared at Victor with disbelief. He had once told her he could sell sand to the Arabs, and it was true he had been Prudential's top insurance salesman for the past five years running. But before her eyes she had just witnessed the almost total transformation of a Yankee from Connecticut transplanted to Palm Beach, Florida, only eight years ago, into a born and bred good ole boy from the South, his voice even hinting at a mild Southern drawl, and she had actually believed in this new identity. "She used to say she was just too tired, what with looking after Adam"—she heard his voice silently repeating. "What with looking after Adam"! Victor Cressy had never used the term "what with" in his life before. And that final little sentiment— "he's four now," tacked onto the end of the thought like so much country molasses. And she had fallen for it! The way she recognized the judge was falling for it as well. For a moment, she felt panic and looked around her shoulder for Mel. He was there. He smiled but he looked as puzzled as she felt, and as she turned back to face the witness stand, she felt something she had not allowed herself to feel since she had decided to leave Victor—that he might win after all. Not the divorce suit—she didn't care who was granted the divorce, being branded an adulteress didn't bother her (she had committed adultery, after all), but what had suddenly traveled from Victor's mouth to her ears in that mellifluous near-Southern drawl was the very real possibility that she could lose her children, the very things that had sustained her these last trouble-filled years, the only things that had kept her sane.

Sane?

Not according to Victor. "Then, of course, she was sick so often."

"Sick?"

"She seemed to have one cold after another, and when it wasn't a cold, it was the flu. She'd be in bed for days."

"And who would look after the children?"

"Mrs. Adilman from next door. She's a widow, she would come in."

"Was Mrs. Cressy seeing a doctor?"

Victor's smile was a neat mixture of irony and regret. "At first she was seeing our old family doctor, Dr. Mitchelson. Then he retired and she wasn't seeing anyone except for her obstetrician, Dr. Harris. Until she met Dr. Segal. Then suddenly he became the family practitioner."

"Dr. Melvin Segal?"

"Yes."

"He began treating your wife?"

"And my children."

"They had no pediatrician?"

Victor's voice raised itself in anger for the first time that morning. It was very effective. "They had a perfectly good pediatrician. The best. Dr. Wellington, Paul Wellington. But Donna insisted, and she was very adamant about it, that Sharon and Adam go to see Dr. Segal."

"Did she offer an explanation?" Again he wanted explanations.

"None that was satisfactory."

The lawyer paused. Like the wanderer in a poem by Robert Frost, he had come to a fork in the road. He had been offered two paths to follow and he could choose only one. He could travel the road to adultery, or the more erratic, as he had earlier phrased it, trail of Donna's behavior. He opted for her sanity, or lack of it, as he hoped to prove, since he had already started out in that direction, and unlike the poet, he recognized he could always double back later.

"I'd like to return to Dr. Segal in a few moments, Mr. Cressy," Mr. Gerber continued, unfurrowing his brow and doing something weird with his lips. "Right now I'd like to concentrate on those of your wife's actions you found strange. Can you give us a few more examples?"

Victor looked over at Donna, then lowered his head. "Well," he began slowly, "there was the period just after Sharon was born that she hated the way she looked and decided to change the color of her hair."

"That's not so unusual, from what I understand about women," Mr. Gerber said, chuckling lightly with condescension. Victor was smart enough not to join him. He tolerated his lawyer's well-timed interruption, then continued with his story, the narrative picking up gradual speed as it rolled to its conclusion.

"No," Victor agreed, "it wouldn't have been unusual, and at first I didn't think anything about it, except that I always preferred it long and natural, and she knew that." Pause. Let it sink in. She deliberately altered something that was already preferred. "At first, she just put streaks in it, so that it was still brown but with a few blonde highlights. That wasn't bad, but after about a week, she decided she didn't like that any better than plain brown, so she had it frosted, which made it almost all blonde streaks with just a little bit of brown. Then she decided that if she was going to have long hair, it might as well be all blonde and so she had it done really blonde, almost white. But then she complained that the sun kept turning it yellow, so she had it turned strawberry blonde, and then a few weeks after that, she changed it to red." He stopped to catch his breath. Donna remembered the red. She had hoped to look like Tina Louise. Instead she came out looking like Little Orphan Annie. "The red didn't last any longer than any of the others, so she had it done auburn and then black. By then her hair was such a disaster in terms of the condition it was in from all the bleachings and colorings that she had to have it cut. So she cut it to just above her shoulders, and put it back to its natural color, like how she has it now, and she looked terrific, and I told her so, and the next morning, she came down to the breakfast room and at first I didn't recognize her. She looked like an inmate of a concentration camp—she'd cut her hair herself so that there was practically nothing there, and she was so thin." He shook his head in bewilderment.

"What did her friends think of all these changes?" his lawyer asked.

Her lawyer sat poised to object at the slightest hint of hearsay.

"By this point," Victor continued carefully, "she really didn't have many friends. Certainly, none that ever came to the house." Effective pause. Surreptitious glance at Mel. "Mrs. Adilman *did* ask me if Donna was all right once."

"Objection. Hearsay."

"Sustained."

Victor waited to be led; his attorney readily, though subtly, did the leading.

"What did *you* think of all these changes, Mr. Cressy?" his lawyer asked.

"I just kept hoping that it was something she was going through after the birth of the baby. I'd heard that women sometimes went a little crazy after—"

"Objection, your honor. Really—"

"Sustained. You're on dangerous ground here, Mr. Gerber."

Mr. Gerber was suitably humbled. He lowered his head and asked his next questions without raising it.

"Did things improve with time?"

"No. They got worse."

Donna felt her foot going to sleep. It's always darkest before the dawn, she remembered her mother once telling her. She shook her foot, felt the nerve ends tingling, and smiled with the recognition she still had nerve endings that could tingle, that she was still alive. She saw Victor's eyes narrow—he had seen her smile and he was questioning it, disapproving of it. Fuck you, she thought, wishing she could yell it aloud, knowing she couldn't. Not if she wanted to prove herself a fit mother, to be able to keep and raise the children she had watched come into this world.

Victor's voice was droning on about some real or imagined slight she had done him, humiliations she had wrought. She refused to have people over, to entertain any of his associates or prospective clients, and when they went out to parties, she was often sarcastic and rude, putting him down unmercifully. Either that or she would go to the other extreme and not say anything all night. It was a nightmare; he never knew how she was going to react. Neither did anyone else. And then there was that business about cleaning the house.

Victor made the story sound as if he were hearing it for the first time himself. "It started after Sharon was born and she had to get up in the middle of the night to nurse her. Sharon would cry around two A.M. and Donna would feed her and then put her back to bed, but instead of going back to bed herself, she'd start to tidy up. She'd clean the living room, the dining room, the kitchen, even the kitchen floor sometimes. When Sharon gave up the two A.M. feeding—which she wasn't long in doing—Donna still got up every morning around two or three and cleaned the house for at least an hour. Once, I went into the kitchen and she was standing there washing the dishes." He stopped, then continued sadly, "And we have an automatic dishwasher."

Who was this crazy lady they were talking about? Donna wondered. Because undoubtedly Mrs. Victor Cressy had been a crazy lady.

She suddenly found herself thinking back to the first time the concept of hell had become a reality for her. She had been about twenty-six, living on her own, dating a lot of men, relishing her freedom and independence. A group of the people she worked with at McFaddon Advertising had decided on a Fourth of July picnic weekend at the beach-front home of the parents of one of the employees (his parents summered in the North), and she had been included, having a wonderful time until she was assigned to the kitchen clean-up crew and spent the hours from midnight till two A.M. washing dishes in the sink, the automatic dishwasher having decided to get in the holiday spirit and take the weekend off like everybody else. As she had stood there, her hands shrinking in the hot water and overabundance of suds, watching the revelers return with yet another armload of dishes just when she had thought she was through, she had been reminded of a book she had studied in college, and one she had recalled often since, Albert Camus' *The Myth of Sisyphus*. According to the ancient Greek myth, Sisyphus had angered the gods for reasons which had escaped her then as they did now, and he had been condemned to spend the rest of eternity pushing a large and monstrously heavy rock up to the top of a huge hill, only to have it roll back down to the bottom just as he was reaching the summit. Camus had asked the seemingly ridiculous question, was Sisyphus happy? More ridiculous still, he had concluded that yes, Sisyphus was indeed happy because he knew in advance that the rock would never reach its destination, that he would always be forced to carry it just so far and then watch it backslide, that there was no hope of his ever succeeding. And in abandoning hope, he had gained his salvation; by knowing and accepting his fate, he became superior to it. Donna had pondered these existential theories of existence as her hands went in and out of the water, and she had decided as yet another sinkful of dishes emerged from beneath the bubbles, that if, in fact, there was a hell, and each person were assigned his or her own particular and private hell, then hers would undoubtedly be eternal kitchen duty. The thought of having to spend forever at the kitchen sink, coming to the end only to find another load waiting, brought home to her the concept of Hell, its possible reality, in a way that no amount of Sunday sermonizing could ever have hoped to accomplish. For the first time in her life, Donna Cressy had feared death.

And now here she sat in the starkness of the courtroom and heard herself described, accurately she had to admit, at least superficially accurate, as some maniac for cleanliness who woke herself up in the middle of the night in order to wash the dishes her automatic dishwater was perfectly able to handle. Did she sound like a woman in control of her life? Did a woman whose hair coloring traveled from Gloria Steinem to Lana Turner to Lucille Ball to Dorothy Lamour to Mia Farrow—anybody but herself—in the space of a few months have any right to supervise the development of two young children with perfectly healthy heads of hair?

Not according to what she had just heard. And there was more, much more to come, she knew. They hadn't begun to talk about Mel, about her immorality. They had thus far avoided any detailed mention of the children themselves. Victor was only the first witness to be called.

There was doubtless a long string of witnesses to follow, all to condemn her in tones varying from outrage to pity. She had only herself. Once again she found herself smiling ruefully—why should their divorce be any different from their marriage? Then she noticed the judge was staring at her, silently questioning her smile, so incongruous under the circumstances. He thinks I'm crazy, she said to herself, as the judge banged his gavel and adjourned the session for lunch.

Victor was standing beside her before she could even think of rising from her chair, his face full of gentle concern.

"Can I talk to you for a few minutes?" he asked.

"No," she said, standing up and pushing her chair back. Her lawyer had already moved to the back of the courtroom where he was talking to Mel.

"Donna, please, don't be unreasonable."

She looked genuinely surprised. "How can you expect me to be anything else? You expect the lady I just heard described by your very own sincere mouth to act with reason? As usual, Victor, you expect too much." She began to scratch at the top of her left hand above the thumb.

"Rash back?" he asked.

She stopped scratching. "Something you forgot to mention this morning. Oh, well, the day is still young. I'm sure you'll get around to it." She wanted to stop but couldn't. "Oh, and you forgot to tell him I have hemorrhoids from reading on the toilet despite all the times you warned me against it." She slapped her hand. "Bad little girl."

He grabbed her hand. "Donna, please. Look what this is doing to you."

"Please let go of me."

He let go reluctantly. "I just want to spare you any further pain and humiliation this whole mess is going to cause you."

"Are you going to drop the custody action?"

He looked genuinely distraught. "You know I can't do that."

"You don't seriously believe I'm not fit to raise my children?" she almost shouted. Mel and Mr. Stamler looked in her direction, Mel instantly moving toward her.

"They're *my* children too," he reminded her, "and I'm only doing what I feel is right." Mel was at Donna's side.

"You won't win, you know," Donna said with more conviction than she felt. "The judge will hear my side of the story. He won't let you take my children away from me."

Victor looked from Donna to Mel with undisguised hatred. When he looked back at Donna, any concern his face had once held had vanished. His voice had lost any trace of Southern gentility, was unabashedly Northern and cold like a biting Chicago wind. "I promise you," he said, spitting the words into the air between them, "that even if you win, you'll lose."

"What's that supposed to mean?" Donna asked, but his back was already to her, and seconds later he was gone from the courtroom.

Chapter 2

She had let the phone ring three times before it became obvious that no one else in the office was going to answer it. "McFaddon Advertising," she said clearly, picking it up. "Donna Edmunds speaking. Just a minute please. I'll see if he's here." She leaned across her desk to the one directly beside hers. "For you, Scott," she said, placing the caller on hold. "Are you here?"

"Male or female?"

"Definitely female," she said, smiling.

"Sound sexy?"

"Definitely sexy."

"Then I'm definitely here." He pressed the correct button on his desk phone and Donna replaced her receiver as Scott Raxlen uttered his first breathy hello. "Oh, yes, of course, Mrs. Camping. Could you hold on just one minute please," he said, quickly pressing another button and turning angrily in Donna's direction. "Thanks a lot. You didn't tell me it was a client!"

"You didn't ask."

"Nice person! You know I have a headache."

"A hangover."

He smiled. "Hell of a party," he said, turning back to his desk and resuming his conversation with Mrs. Delores Camping.

"How late did you stay?" Irv Warrack asked, coming up behind Donna. "What's that you're working on, anyway?"

"I left before you did," she reminded him, showing him a sketch she was preparing for a design layout. "For the Petersen account."

"That's good. McFaddon's going to like that." He waved a mock cigar between his fingers. "You got a great future here, kid." She grimaced. "You're not happy?" he asked, obviously surprised.

Donna put down the pen she'd been sketching with. "I'm happy enough, I guess. I don't know. I'm not sure this is really what I want to do with the rest of my life—" She looked into the kind eyes of her co-worker. "Guess I'm going through a sort of—transitional phase at the moment. Sound pompous?"

He smiled. "Just a bit. Honey," Irv Warrack continued, conspiratorally leaning against her desk, "anyone who can write copy like 'The Mayflower Condominiums—An Original Concept—For Original Americans' has found what she should be doing for the rest of her life. Understand?" She laughed. "Gotta go," he said, straightening up.

"Where are you going?"

"Home. I'm beat. Aren't you beat?"

"It's not even lunch time!"

"That late?" He walked toward the door. "Gotta rest. I'm taking out your friend tonight."

"Susan?"

"That's the one. Great girl. Cover for me, okay." He opened the front door. "Did your friend ever show up again, by the way?"

"What friend?"

"Last night. The guy you kept looking at."

Donna was momentarily startled. Had she been that obvious? "I left before you did, remember?"

"Oh, yea. Well, have a nice weekend." He walked through the door and was gone.

"Warrack take off?" Scott Raxlen asked, finished with his phone call. Donna nodded. "That's a good idea." He stood up and stretched. "Think I'll go home too. Take care of my headache."

Donna looked around the fast-emptying office. "What's with everybody? We have one little party to celebrate the end of a successful campaign—"

"Mayflower Condominiums—An Original Concept—For Original Americans—"

"And the whole place falls apart the next morning. Rhonda doesn't even bother to show up; Irv takes off five hours early; you're about to do the same—"

"Who was the guy?"

"What guy?"

"The one Warrack was asking you about?"

Donna shook her head. "I don't know how you do it. You have two sets of ears?"

"Who is he?"

"I don't know. We were introduced, then he disappeared."

"The best kind. Take my word for it, Donna, it's better that way."

"Go home, Scott."

He walked to the door. "He was that good-looking, huh?"

"Go home, Scott."

"Cover for me?"

Donna waved him out the door. She returned to her design layout, but her pen remained poised without moving. Maybe she should just get up and go home like everybody else. No, she couldn't do that. "Why do I have to be such a Goody Two-Shoes?" she asked herself out loud. Always have to stay to the bitter end. Except at parties. Then she usually left early. Her mind drifted back to last night's festivities, sponsored by the satisfied client. Immediately, she saw the stranger's face. What a face, she thought, picking up the phone, feeling a sudden need to confide in someone. "Susan Reid, please. Thank you." She waited several seconds. "Oh, all right. I'll hold." Why not? It was becoming obvious to her that she would get nothing much else accomplished today. She looked around. "Great," she said into the receiver. "I'm the only one here. What? Oh, sorry. No, I wasn't speaking to you.

Will she be much longer? Thank you." Almost five minutes later, Susan Reid finally came onto the other end. "Boy, you're a hard lady to get to talk to. I've been holding on for ten minutes. I'm a busy person, you know." She stopped. Her eyes stared straight ahead at the large picture window which looked out onto picturesque Royal Palm Road in the fashionable heart of fashionable Palm Beach. "What? Oh, sorry. Look, Susan, I have to go. I can't talk to you now. No. What? No. Listen, I have to go. He's here. He! Him! This gorgeous guy I met last night. He's standing outside the front window with what looks like a bottle of champagne, my God, it's champagne, and two glasses. I don't believe this. My heart is pounding like a drum. I have to go. He's coming inside. I really don't believe this. I'll talk to you later. Goodbye."

She hung up the phone at the precise moment Victor Cressy walked in the front door.

"Hi," he said casually, placing the glasses on her desk and promptly uncorking the champagne.

"Oh," she said loudly as the cork shot across the room, and then tried to sound as casual as she could. "Good shot." He smiled, his crystal-clear blue eyes fastening on hers, themselves blue though several shades darker. He poured the champagne, which Donna couldn't help but notice was Dom Perignon, and then slowly put one glass in her hand before picking up his own. They clicked glasses together while Donna fought the sudden fear her stomach might start to rumble. It was almost lunch time and she hadn't eaten breakfast.

"To us," he said, his eyes laughing. Is he making fun of me? she wondered.

Donna felt the desperate need to go to the bathroom.

"I'm Victor Cressy," he said, still smiling, this time with his whole face.

"I remember," she said.

"I'm flattered." He took a long sip of his champagne. Donna followed his lead.

He should only know how well I remember, she

thought, thinking back quickly to their brief introduction of the night before.

"Donna, this is Victor Cressy, probably the best insurance salesman in the southern hemisphere—" And then he was gone. Dangled before her eyes like so much bait to a starving fish and then quickly pulled away again, led back into the chaos of Florida pinks, greens and baby blues—lost in the maelstrom of elderly bodies, drinks in one hand, newly signed documents of ownership (Mayflower Condominiums—An Original Concept—For Original Americans) in the other.

That was it, she realized with a start. An entire night of fantasies carved from a few brief words. Though she had tried as hard—and as subtly—as she could, to position herself as close to him as possible at various times throughout the evening, they had never exchanged another word. He never approached her, never tried to enhance *his* position with regard to hers and after several furtive glances at what she decided was an exquisite profile on an extraordinary face, she had lost sight of him altogether. When she had finally worked up enough courage to question someone as to his whereabouts, she was told he had left the party.

And now here he was. Just the way her past evening's fantasies had promised.

She watched his mouth as he spoke, his tongue now and then appearing with almost snakelike precision to remove any excesses of champagne from his decidedly sensual lips, the upper lip being somewhat fuller than its bottom counterpart, giving him the pouty look of a spoiled rich graduate of an all-boys' prep school. It was a look she found almost painfully attractive though she couldn't discern why—arrogance and insolence had never been high on her list of commendable attributes. His voice was forceful but not forbidding—a man who obviously was in good command of his own life, who seemed to know what he wanted. He had an easy control of his words, made commendable small talk, steering the conversation effortlessly to the party, his immediately positive impression of her when he spotted her amid the fuschia prints and blue hair, her own naturally brown hair resting just above the understated lilac of her dress. Understated lilac, his term.

"Always this busy?" he asked. She smiled, realizing she had barely said two words since his arrival, preferring to watch him while he talked instead. "Can you take the rest of the day off?" he asked suddenly. She looked around the office, and promptly rose to her feet. That's right Donna, she heard a voice say. Play hard to get.

Immediately, he stood up beside her. "We better hurry then."

She followed his fast pace to the door. "Why are we hurrying?" My God, she speaks!

"I thought we'd go somewhere special for dinner."

"It's not even noon," she said, fumbling with the keys to lock the office up for the weekend. She hadn't left a note or anything, what if someone came by?— There was nobody left to cover.

"We'll have lunch on the plane."

"Plane?"

"The restaurant I'm taking you to for dinner"—he paused, not without a touch of smugness, opening the door of his light blue Cadillac Seville and waiting while she maneuvered herself inside—"is in New York."

"Is this what you call being swept off your feet?" she asked as they clicked yet another glass of champagne together and continued to stare into each other's blue eyes.

"I'm just sorry dinner has to be so early. I'd forgotten that return flights like to land well before midnight."

"Oh, this is wonderful," she assured him quickly. "Something very civilized about eating before six P.M." They laughed. "I don't really believe I'm here." She laughed again. Why was she so nervous? He obviously had made no hotel reservations; they weren't planning on spending the night. She had nothing to worry about except possibly the fact that he had made no hotel reservations and they obviously weren't planning on spending the night. Why weren't they? Had he decided on the drive to the airport that he really didn't find her as attractive as he had originally? No, that was impossible. He wouldn't have ordered another bottle of Dom Perignon if he didn't find her attractive.

"So, you don't make a habit of this sort of thing?" she ventured, moving her hand around in a vague sort of semicircle, hoping he would understand what she meant by this sort of thing.

"Only for special people," he said, telling her in four short words that she was special, but then so had others been. Just enough of a tease.

"Kind of an expensive way to make an impression, isn't it?"

He laughed. "Well, I guess that depends on your philosophy." He paused, then continued. "You see, some people want to leave a million dollars behind when they die. I want to die *owing* a million dollars."

She laughed. "I like your philosophy the best." She lowered her eyes.

"What are you staring at?" he asked suddenly.

"Your hands," she said, surprised at her answer.

"Why?" There was just a hint of a laugh in his voice.

"Because my mother always told me to look at a man's hands."

"Why?" he repeated.

"Because she always said that that's what a man makes love with." Goddamn, she thought. Why had she said that?

His face broke into a grin. "Your mother sounds like an interesting woman. I'd like to meet her."

Donna smiled at the sudden image of her mother's beautiful face in front of her. "She's dead," she said quietly. "Cancer."

He reached across the table and took hold of both her hands. "Tell me about her."

She shook her head. "No."

"Why not?"

She shrugged. "Just seems like kind of heavy stuff for a first date. That's all."

"I think I've just been insulted," he said, though he made no move to withdraw his hands and his face was still smiling.

"Oh no, no. Really. I didn't mean—it's just that I usually end up in tears when I talk about her, even though it's almost ten years ago. I know it's silly—"

"I don't think it's silly. I won't mind if you cry."

Donna paused. Her mother was smiling at her.

You'd like this man, Mom, she thought.

"She was so lovely," she began. "She really was this incredible woman. I could talk to her about anything. I can't tell you how much I miss her." She stared hard into his eyes, trying to block out the new image that had suddenly interfered with the old, pushed the smiling healthy lady aside and replaced her with a figure less than half her former size, her skin translucent and crawling with minute malignant monsters, changing the smile in her eyes to eyes that saw only pain. "I'd give anything to be able to talk to her again."

"What would you say to her?"

She looked up at the ceiling, trying to keep the tears she felt forming from falling. "I don't know." She laughed suddenly, feeling the tears recede, seeing only Victor in front of her again. "I'd probably just ask her what to do."

"About what?"

"About everything." They both laughed. "I don't know, I just always felt that if I couldn't decide something for myself, if I didn't know what was the right thing to do, or even what I should wear one day, silly things like that, that she'd always be around to tell me what I needed to hear. Sometimes it's just really nice having someone make your decisions for you. Am I making any sense?"

"Is that why you let me order dinner for you? And yes, you're making perfect sense."

She looked around the very dim restaurant. Her eyes were only now beginning to make out the small tables and chairs clustered about the small room. She noticed that even at this hour most of the tables were full. "I just thought that you would probably know what item on the menu was best," she said smiling, thinking that any man who would fly for several hours and spend hundreds of dollars only to fly back that same evening, had to have a dish he especially liked. "Why did you specify that the lobster had to be boiled exactly seven and a half minutes?"

"Something I learned from an old college professor. Don't ask me how it came up, but I still have this clear picture of him standing behind his podium exclaiming, 'Never boil a lobster for a period any shorter or longer than precisely seven and a half minutes.'"

"Why is that?"

Victor smiled. "Beats the shit out of me."

It was the first time Donna had heard him swear and it caught her off guard. She laughed long and loud.

"It was a math course of some sort," he continued. "He must have been talking about precision, I suppose. Who knows? It's a long time ago. About the only thing I remember about his class actually—except for the seven and a half minutes—is that every time we had a test or an exam, I used to intermingle verses of haiku poetry—my own—amidst the cut and dryness of the arithmetic."

Donna was surprised. "Haiku poetry?"

"Yes, you know. The Japanese style verse that's only seventeen syllables long. The key is to create an entire image, produce something of vivid clarity, a thought painting a picture, inside a very rigid structure."

"Why did you do that?"

He thought, smiling. "I'm not sure. Maybe to show the old guy that poetry could be every bit as precise as mathematics. I don't know. Maybe for my own recreation." He paused. "Why are you smiling?"

"It's just so nice to have a real conversation with someone," she said sincerely. "Most guys I've gone out with lately don't really talk about anything, let alone haiku poetry. They just always seem to be steering the conversa-

tion over to sex." She stopped, realizing that in the last
several minutes, she had done precisely that. Twice.

"Are you from New York originally?" she asked.

"Connecticut."

"Your family still there?"

"My father died of a heart attack when I was five."

"So did mine—but I was twenty-three. Your mother?"

"Dead."

"Two orphans," she said, smiling sadly. "I have a sister. Joan. She's at Radcliffe."

"Only child," he responded.

Their lobster arrived, overspilling the plate. They ate in
long silences punctuated by short, staccato bursts of conversation and much laughter.

She: "Do you live right in Palm Beach?"

He: "I have a house in Lantana. You?"

She: "An apartment in West Palm."

More silence. More champagne.

She: "How come you have a house?" Breathholding
pause. "You're not married, are you?" Of course, that
was it. He was married! That was why he had to be back
that night. Goddamn! Of course! He was married.

He: "No, I'm not married."

She: "Are you sure?"

He: "Very."

More silence. Dessert. Coffee. Check please.

He: "Why do you pick at your cuticles?"

She: "Nerves."

He: "What are you nervous about?"

She: "Life."

Much laughter. Much hugging on the way to the airport. Sleeping—half-sleeping on each others' shoulders on
the plane ride home. Crawling into his Seville at the West
Palm Beach airport. Driving quickly to the ocean. Parking
the car and listening to the roar of the waves. Was any of
this real? Had any of it actually happened? She looked
into his beautiful face. I could love this man, she realized
with some sense of panic. I could really love this man.

She hadn't necked in a parked car in years, more years than she could remember. Donna tried to picture who the boy had been, her mind careening back through at least ten casual lovers rolling over on assorted beds back through time, pausing long enough to single out one or two who had approached love, perhaps overtaking it only to see it slide backward, rolling slowly into a steady decline like Sisyphus' mythical rock until it hit bottom. Rock bottom.

This time was nothing like those.

Victor's lips were gentle, not urgent. His kisses were the kisses of a romantic, not a horny teenager. His mouth was open but not devouring, knowing exactly when and how, and how much. Her mother had been right—he had good hands.

"Why are you stopping?" she heard a voice ask. Her voice. "Who said that?" she laughed, trying to joke, surprised at her own eagerness, her own willingness not to be coy.

"As much as I love the ocean," he said quietly, his head lowered against hers, his breath gently whisking against her chin, "I've never been one for making love in the front seat of a car—or the back seat, for that matter."

The revelation came as no surprise. She fought the urge to ask, your place or mine?, and remained quiet until he resumed speaking several seconds later.

"Besides," he continued, "I don't like starting anything I can't finish."

"Why can't you finish?" she asked, again surprised by the urgency in her voice and the disappointment she heard creeping in. They both laughed.

"Because I have to be up very early in the morning," he answered, taking her hands and intermingling their fingers.

"Going somewhere?" she asked, hearing a loud voice inside her saying, "I knew it was too good to be true; he's leaving to join the Peace Corps in darkest Africa first thing in the morning!" The voice was so loud and insistent she almost didn't hear what he actually said in the following instant. "You're going where?" she shouted, Africa quickly becoming the preferred place to be, as she permitted his voice to penetrate the one now screaming inside her.

He said it again simply, with even a hint of a smile. Almost, in fact, if it was possible, eloquently. "To jail," he repeated, and then neither said another word.

Chapter 3

She picked him up in front of the West Palm Beach jail-house at seven P.M. on Sunday night. He was smiling, looking none the worse for wear for his two-day incarceration—if anything, he looked even better than she remembered, dressed casually in blue jeans and an open-neck shirt. He was already waiting for her—they had released him some ten minutes ahead of schedule.

"Time off for good behavior," he joked, getting into the passenger seat beside her and immediately cradling her in his arms, his lips tasting better than a good brandy as they touched lightly down on hers.

"Honest to God," she began, starting the ignition, "I don't believe this whole thing." Especially the way my heart is thumping, she thought. She pulled away from the curb into the middle of the street. For some reason, the West Palm Beach jail was situated on one of West Palm's main streets just next to a used car lot. From the outside, it looked like just another reasonably run-down store front, West Palm Beach separated from its easterly counterpart, Palm Beach, more by a gulf of dollars than by the inland waterway that physically divided the two territories. West Palm had a decidedly lived-in aura; nothing in Palm Beach proper betrayed any signs of use or age—except possibly its population.

"Do you always pull away from the curb like that?" Victor asked casually. "You'll ruin the tread on your tires." Donna smiled, finding it very difficult to concen-

trate on anything other than the few black hairs she had
seen escaping the top of his pale blue shirt.

"Well, I've certainly learned my lesson," he said
solemnly, pausing dramatically. "I'll never run a stop sign
again."

"I thought you said you didn't run that stop sign."

"They said I did."

"But you said you didn't and that's why you chose two
days in jail rather than pay the stupid ticket. A question-
able move, even if you were innocent! Now you say you
were guilty?"

"As charged, yes," he agreed, nodding his head. "But I
couldn't let them know that, not after I made such a fuss.
The principle of it all, you know." He laughed.

She laughed as well, although she wasn't sure why. In
her mind, she was trying to come to quick terms with a
man who would choose two days in jail rather than pay a
parking ticket he could well afford for an offense he now
admitted he was guilty of committing—and still refer to it
as a matter of principle.

They crossed over a bridge and headed onto South
Ocean Boulevard. "So, how was it?" she asked. "Rough?"

"You better believe it. Two days in solitary confinement!"

"Solitary confinement?"

"There was no one else there."

"You were the only prisoner?" He nodded. "Then you
weren't raped," she stated more than asked. Why was she
always talking about sex?

"I was hoping we'd save that for tonight," he said, their
eyes freezing on each others'. "Watch the red light!"

Her foot moved immediately to the brake, slamming
down hard, jerking them both forward. They were a good
fifty feet from the stoplight and there were no other cars
in the vicinity.

"Sorry," he said immediately. "I just saw it out of the
corner of my eye and I thought it was closer."

Donna's heart was racing. "That's okay. I shouldn't
have taken my eyes off the road."

"Would you be insulted if I asked you to let me drive?" he asked, suddenly.

"You want to drive?" she repeated.

"If you wouldn't mind." He paused, smiling. "For some reason I feel a little nervous tonight, and I usually find that I can relax behind the wheel of a car."

"I wouldn't mind a bit," Donna said earnestly.

Victor opened his door and Donna slid over into the place he left vacant while Victor walked around the front of the red Mustang and proceeded to occupy the driver's seat Donna had given up.

"That's better," he said, and she immediately agreed. He advanced the fifty feet to the stoplight which turned green precisely upon his arrival. A good sign, she thought.

He looked over at her briefly, the thin lines around his eyes relaxing into creases which, she thought, actually seemed to be smiling. His voice was very soft. "Home?" he asked, and then turned his attention back to the road without waiting for an answer.

Donna couldn't believe what was happening to her.

She had been prepared for him to be a good, even an excellent lover (although she had also spent the previous two days convincing herself that he would probably not be—something was bound to go wrong somewhere—not even fantasies were as good as this reality). She had not been prepared, however, for just how good, how truly excellent he was. Beyond excellence. Into the realm of the fantastic.

She had never had a lover who was so willing to do anything—everything—to make her feel good. His dedication—a strange word to use, she realized, but she could think of none better—was all-encompassing. He wanted only to make her happy. He wanted nothing from her except for her to lie there smiling. She was simultaneously passive and delirious.

They had walked quickly and silently from the car into his moderately large bungalow and once inside, he had taken her hand and led her through the hallway, past the living and dining rooms and the kitchen, all of which Donna noted in passing were neat and tasteful, and back to the rear of the house where the bedrooms were situated.

Donna guessed there must be three, possibly four bedrooms, by the length of the hallway. He led her into the first room, a room of soft blues and beiges ("surf and sand," he joked quietly, leading her to the double bed and starting to kiss around her mouth).

He undressed her without saying a word, letting his hands, his fingers, do all the talking. When she reached over to unbutton his shirt, he moved just out of her reach, pulling back the bed covers and guiding her inside them. "Let me," he said, his voice very low, his fingers moving to unbutton his shirt. "Let me do everything." Donna had never heard anything as sexy as those four words sounded.

She watched as he took off his shirt and slipped out of his shoes and socks. Donna felt she should perhaps avert her eyes as he lowered his jeans and shorts but she didn't, couldn't. He was the most beautiful man she had ever seen.

He crawled into bed beside her and immediately took her in his arms, his lips moving softly over hers. They kissed for what seemed like an incredibly prolonged period of time and yet simultaneously felt like no time at all.

Everything he did was more than she had hoped. The way he touched her, moved her, stimulated her, while demanding nothing in return. At one point, she had moved to take him in her mouth, but he had caught her hair with his hand and brought her body over his, positioning her open legs directly above his waiting mouth and lowering her slowly down.

"Let me—" she whispered later, using his words.

"No," he said, again moving just out of her reach and sliding his head down her body, his hands remaining on her breasts. "I want it all," he said as his tongue moved slowly down her skin. "I can't get enough of you."

When he finally entered her, she felt she was beyond

further orgasms, her entire body soaked with perspiration, her hair clinging wetly to her head, sticking against her cheek. "I can't come any more," she breathed, feeling his hands rotating her hips against the rhythm of his own.

"You'll come," he said, shifting their positions, lifting both her legs over his shoulders, high into the air, raising himself onto his knees.

"Oh my God," she shouted, feeling him penetrate deep inside her. "Jesus Christ!" She could barely catch her breath.

Minutes later, he brought her legs down and turned her so that they lay moving together on their sides. Slowly, very slowly. His lips tentatively moved away from hers. She opened her eyes to find him staring at her.

"Would it upset you very much," he asked, "if I told you I think I'm falling in love with you?"

She began to cry, realized she was indeed coming again, and hugged him so tightly against her that she found it hard to distinguish where he left off and she began.

They decided to get married two months later over mushroom burgers at Hamburger Heaven.

"When?" she asked, as she drove him back to his office after lunch was finished.

"As soon as I can make all the arrangements," he said, his body suddenly tensing.

"What's the matter?"

"Sorry, honey," he said, sounding genuinely contrite. "It's just that I get very nervous when you hold your hands on the wheel like that." She looked at her hands; they were resting with a moderate degree of casual abandon at the bottom of the steering wheel, a position they often maintained when she was driving. "If something were to happen," he continued, "you know, if some idiot did something stupid and you had to move fast, you'd never get your hands back on the wheel in time to get out of his way. You'd be a goner." Her hands moved to the proper position on either side of the steering wheel.

"Your're right," she said, "I better start being more careful with myself."

She pulled the car to a halt in front of his office, a large stucco building of appropriate canary yellow. A stocky man of medium height walked past their parked car and into the building's imposing front door.

"Wasn't that Danny Vogel?" she asked. He nodded. "Haven't you patched up that silly squabble yet?" He shook his head. "I thought he apologized."

"He did." Victor got out of the car and leaned back inside. "You decide who you'd like to invite. Make a list. As far as I'm concerned, the less people the better."

He started to close the door. "Victor?" He pulled it back open and stuck his head inside. "I love you," she said.

"I love you, honey," he answered, closing the door gently.

Donna watched him walk inside the large white door. He didn't look back. It seemed he never looked back. About anything. He was so sure of everything he did. "Oh, God, Mother," she heard herself suddenly exclaim, realizing how little she really knew this man, feeling an advance onslaught of pre-nuptial jitters, "please tell me I'm doing the right thing." But the only voice she heard was the Dee Jay on the car radio telling her it was two o'clock and time for a look at the news.

She had been sitting for well over an hour just staring at the name. Lenore Cressy. Beside it, printed neatly in the same even black-inked hand that had penned the multitude of other names, addresses and phone numbers in the small black leather bound book, was a Connecticut address and phone number. Lenore Cressy. Donna continued to stare.

He had told her there was no wife; his mother was dead; he'd been an only child. Who then? Perhaps an aunt or a cousin. Obviously a relation. She looked away from the address book, debating with herself what to do. Their wedding was less than two weeks away and so far he'd only asked her to do two things for him—arrange for the flowers and the photographers. It meant two phone calls, and yet here she was, already sidelined by an irrelevancy. She tried to assign herself to the task at hand. They had decided on white and yellow roses, and since he mentioned that he also loved daisies, they had been added to the decor. She looked around the room, suddenly very glad he had thought of having the wedding here, at his home, the home that would soon also be hers.

His list of the people he wanted to invite consisted only of five names which brought the total number of guests to twenty people. She'd sought out his address book, not to deliberately spy on him, but to find the phone number of the florist he had suggested she call after telling her he knew it to be superior to the one a friend of hers had recommended. Carnation Florists, right there under the letter C. Seven listings above Cressy, Lenore.

She picked up the phone and dialed.

The woman's voice was nasal and Floridian. "Carnation Florists," she said with a marked degree of boredom.

"I'd like to order some flowers," Donna told her, her mind not on flowers at all.

"Yes. What would you like?"

Donna quickly explained, and then had to repeat, that the flowers were for her wedding, yes, her own wedding, and that she wanted enough white and yellow roses to fill a fourteen by sixteen foot living room, the roses to be interspersed with daisies, as would be her bouquet. She had decided to wear the simple white silk dress Victor had seen in the window of Bonwit Teller on Worth Avenue rather than the pale blue one she herself had spotted across the road at Saks, so that detail was all taken care of. It took another twenty-five minutes to work out the details with the nasal voice from Carnation Flowers, but once done, it left only one item not already arranged: the photographers Victor had mentioned as being the best in Palm Beach. Messinger-Edwards, he had said, and he had their number listed in his address book as well. Donna went to turn the page but couldn't. She was stopped by

Lenore Cressy. Her fingers played with the dials. Who was Lenore Cressy? One phone call and she would certainly find out. And then what? She would discover a faceless, long-lost, long-ignored cousin of sorts who Victor never talked about and obviously did not want at the wedding or he would have included her name on his list. To pick up the phone and dial this woman would be tantamount to the same kind of invasion of privacy she, herself, detested. She quickly flipped to the M's. There was still time to find out who Lenore Cressy was, and in a far more honest, direct way. She would simply ask Victor about her later on.

Chapter 4

The fight began almost imperceptibly, neither party able later to recall at exactly what moment their discussion became something more, moving from something vaguely unpleasant to something distinctly unpleasant, progressing—or deteriorating—from a discourse to a disagreement to an argument, growing into a debate soon out of control, mushrooming into a full-fledged all-out honest-to-God fight. Their first.

"I called the florist," Donna said.

"And?"

"Everything's arranged. White and yellow roses. And daisies. Like you said."

"I thought that was what you wanted," Victor said genuinely.

"It is," she smiled. White and yellow roses would be lovely. And daisies. Victor was a man of determined good taste.

"We can have white and pink roses if that's what you'd prefer," he offered.

"No." She said, remembering that had been her first choice, but after all, it was his wedding too. "White and yellow is fine. It'll be beautiful."

He smiled. "Well, I just thought, with the room being the color it is." Donna took a moment to reassess the room. It was very Florida-sunny and bright. White walls pierced by colorful modern lithographs, an Estève beside the pale yellow wet bar, Jim Dine's series of hearts behind

the canary yellow swivel chair, an imposing Rosenquist
over the green-and-white floral sofa, itself flanked by a
pale ice-green love seat, a black lamp on a glass table between them, to highlight the soft mint of the plush carpet-
ing. It was a beautiful room. Victor had a lovely, almost
innate sense of design. It was something he was deeply interested in—not just the fact that something worked, but
why it worked. The same with art—he was not simply a
trendy collector; he had made it a point to be as
knowledgeable as the people he was dealing with when
purchasing art work. He studied; he planned. He rarely
made mistakes.

"Anything else?" he asked.

"I called the photographers."

"Which ones?"

"Messinger-Edwards," Donna answered. Victor smiled.
"They'll be here at four."

"Why four?"

The question caught her off guard. She stumbled. "I
just thought four would be a good time. An hour before
the ceremony. You know, get some shots of us . . ." she
trailed off. "Why? Isn't four o'clock a good time?"

He nodded. "Sure." He paused. "I wouldn't have done
it that way, but sure, it's fine."

"How would you have done it?"

He shook his head. "Four o'clock is fine."

She changed the subject. "I bought the dress at Bonwit's. I drove in today and tried it on and it looked great.
You were right." He smiled.

"You'll be sitting around in it for a long time, you realize, since you've called the photographers for four
o'clock."

"You want me to change the time?"

"No. Four o'clock is fine. You just have to recognize
certain consequences, that's all. The dress might look a
little wilted by the time the ceremony starts."

"When would be a better time? Five?"

"We're getting married at five." He laughed softly.
"Forgetting our anniversary already?"

"Well, when? Later?"

"No. We'll be too drained later to pose for formal pictures."

"Well, when, then?" she repeated.

"I told you. Four o'clock is fine."

"But you said you wouldn't have done it that way."

"I changed my mind. I recognize you were right. I agree with you."

"So what's all this about recognizing certain consequences?"

"What do you want from me?" he asked, his voice lowering in direct proportion to the rise in hers. "I said I agree with you."

She wasn't sure exactly why she felt so frustrated; she only knew she felt like smashing him over the head with the Milo lithograph that hung on the wall near where he was sitting.

"Who is Lenore Cressy?" she asked, realizing instantly that her timing was all wrong.

The look on his face told her immediately that there would be no such thing as a right time.

"Where did you hear about Lenore Cressy?" he asked, the question not quite a demand. "Did she phone while I was out?"

"No." Donna found herself more and more uneasy. The woman, whoever she was, was obviously more than a much-neglected cousin. You didn't get out of your seat for a forgotten maiden aunt. Victor moved toward her.

"You didn't answer my question," he said, his voice remaining calm.

"I just saw her name in your address book," she explained. "When I was trying to find the number for Carnation Florists. Why are you upset? Who is she?"

"Did you call her?"

"No, of course not. I'd never do that." She wanted to add that she'd been tempted, but decided it was information she'd do better keeping to herself. "Who is she?"

There was a long pause. Victor's face relaxed. "I guess you wouldn't accept 'nobody special' as an answer at this point, would you?" She smiled, feeling the tension ease, and shook her head. "My mother," he said flatly and returned to his seat.

For a few seconds, Donna was too stunned to say anything. "Your mother?" she finally heard herself ask, the question dangerously close to a shriek. "Your mother? I thought you said your mother was dead!"

"She is," he replied, his voice the same even flat monotone it had been seconds before. "As far as I am concerned."

"What are you talking about?" She suddenly found herself standing up.

He stood up again as well, and began moving away from her voice. "I said that as far as I'm concerned, my mother is dead. She has been for more than three years now."

"What is that supposed to mean?"

"Why are you getting so upset?"

"Why? Why? We're supposed to be getting married in a few weeks and suddenly I find out you lied to me about your mother being alive!"

His face turned angry. "Now just a minute. Watch out before you start calling names."

"What names have I called you?"

"You just called me a liar. I've never lied to you."

"You told me your mother was dead!"

"She *is* dead as far as I'm concerned."

"Then why is her phone number in your little black book?"

There was a long silence. Donna felt a constriction in her throat, felt tears forming behind her eyes.

"I don't know," he said finally. "I don't know."

Donna sank back into the love seat behind her, its warm ice tones suddenly cold. "I think you better tell me just what's going on," she said.

"There's nothing going on. Whatever happened, happened more than three years ago. It's dead and buried." He stopped; she was staring at him expectantly, making no move to wipe away the tears which were now falling at an even clip down her cheek.

"You'll run your mascara," he said gently, almost timidly.

"Tell me," she said, her hands frozen at her sides.

He sat beside her and took her hands into his. She offered neither resistance nor acceptance. Her hands moved as if they were inanimate objects. Lifeless.

"I love you," he said.

She laughed. "Now you're going to tell me you also have a wife who's legally alive, but that that's all right too, because as far as you're concerned, she died with your mother." She looked frantically into his eyes for some sign that her feeble attempt at humor was just that—a bad joke. His eyes made no denial. "Oh, no," she said, trying to free her hands, to stand up. He wouldn't let her. "Oh, no," she kept repeating. "I can't believe this. I just don't believe it."

"Listen to me," he said, his voice rising. "Just shut up for a few minutes and listen to me."

"Don't tell me what to do."

"Shut up," he yelled. "I *am* telling you what to do. That is, if you're interested in hearing the truth."

"It's a little late for truth now, isn't it?"

"Is it?" he shrieked. "Is it? Is that what you're telling me?" He let go of her hands almost violently, getting up and moving around the room, a grenade whose pin has been pulled.

"You're not interested in hearing the truth? You don't mind hearing lies or half-truths; you don't think anything about calling me a liar, but when it comes to hearing the truth, you're not interested!"

"Don't you dare twist this thing around!" Donna yelled, jumping to her feet. "Don't you dare make this sound like somehow it's my fault, that I'm the one to blame."

"The ball is in your court, Donna," he continued. "Nobody's talking about blame. Who said anything was anybody's fault? Why do you have to assign blame? We're talking about truth. Either you're interested in hearing it or not."

"I don't believe how this has gotten twisted!"

"What are you going to do, Donna? Are you going to hit the ball back or are you going to just walk off the court?"

"Christ, spare me the metaphors."

There was a moment's silence. "What are you going to do, Donna?" he repeated. "It's up to you."

"Me," Donna said under her breath, jerking her fist against her chest. "It's up to me."

"I'm prepared to tell you the truth if you're prepared to listen."

"If I'm prepared to listen," she repeated numbly, sitting back down. For several minutes, no one said a word. Then Donna lifted her head and looked directly at Victor. Still not saying anything, she indicated she was ready to listen.

Victor took a deep breath. "Thank you," he said. Another long pause. "A little more than five years ago, maybe closer to six," he began, trying to choose his words carefully, tripping over them several times in spite of his efforts, "I met and married a girl named Janine Gauntley." Donna took a deep inhale of air, praying she wouldn't faint, feeling her stomach begin to heave. "Listen to me," he continued, aware of her acute discomfort, of the growing blankness in her eyes though she continued to stare directly at him. "We're divorced," he said quickly. "I swear to you. We're divorced. We have been since I moved down here. The marriage was a disaster—I honestly have no idea why—it just didn't work, and so after almost two years we gave up on it and I moved out. We had no children. There didn't seem to be any complications. But there was one." He paused, not without a flair for the dramatic, even in moments of crisis. "My mother." Donna released an almost silent breath of air, the food in her stomach moving up and down as if on a seesaw. She said nothing, waited only for him to continue. "I told you I was an only child," he went on, quickly adding, "and that's true, I am. My parents weren't able to have any more children. My mother had several miscarriages after I was born, one of them when she was almost six months pregnant. It was a little girl and, obviously, she didn't survive. My mother never really recovered from that, and I know this is going to sound like a cliché, but Janine became just like that daughter to her. They were very, very close. Too close." He stopped. "Whenever Janine and I had problems, she always took Janine's side. It was really like Janine was her child and I was the in-law. And rightly or wrongly, I resented it. But I accepted it, resigned myself to it; it was something I could live with, as long as Janine and I were together. When we split up, I knew my mother would take it very hard, but what I didn't know was that even after I'd moved out, into my apartment, my mother continued to see Janine, to speak to her every day the way she always had." He stopped, looking to Donna for a glimmer of understanding. He saw only puzzlement, a slight furrowing of her eyebrows. "It was like—like she threw all her support behind the woman who'd made my life miserable for two years. Maybe I'm not explaining it right. I don't know, but I felt, I really felt, betrayed. Yes, betrayed. That's the word, I just couldn't stand that the two of them should stay friends. It was over with Janine and me. I wanted her out of my life." His voice grew more intense with each recollection. "Finally, I offered my mother the choice. Janine or me—her son." He shook his head. "It may sound petty or childish now, I don't know. But it was something that was very important to me at the time, and that's the main thing. Not how important or trivial it was to anyone else, but how much it meant to me." He stopped again, finding it increasingly difficult to persist. "I—uh—I told my mother how I felt; I told her I thought her choice was clear, but—well, it wasn't even that she chose wrongly, it was—" He stopped for a full second then continued. "She hesitated." He stopped again, obviously still unable to grasp the psychology behind what had taken place. "I offered her a choice between her own son and someone

who'd come into her life only two years before, and she
hesitated. So I said that as far as I was concerned, she
had obviously made her choice; there was nothing more
for either of us to say, and that I would clear out of her
life. And I did. I quit my job; I packed my bags and I
moved to Florida." He looked lovingly at Donna. "Close
your mouth," he said gently. "A bee will fly in."

She ignored his attempt at levity. "You just picked up
and left everything," she said, amazed.

"I left nothing," he said. "Not everything. There was
nothing there to leave."

"You haven't seen your mother since?" He shook his
head. "Does she know where you are?"

"She knows."

"And?"

"Nothing," he said. "She's phoned a few times, but I
have nothing to say to her."

"After all this time?"

"Some hurts don't die."

"Mothers do," Donna said flatly. "Is what she did really so unforgivable?"

Victor shook his head in bewilderment. "I thought so,"
he said. "Maybe I'm wrong. I just know I'm still not
ready to see her again." He sat down beside Donna. "I
know that it was never my intention to lie to you. When I
told you she was dead, I had no idea I'd be proposing two
months later. By that time, especially after hearing so
much about your own mother, how you felt about her, I
didn't know how to tell you the truth. I knew you'd never
understand." He shook his head again. "For a man who
prides himself on his common sense, it was an uncom-
monly senseless way to handle things."

Donna nodded her head in silent agreement. "And your
ex-wife?"

"What about her?"

Donna felt her anger returning. "Why didn't you tell
me you'd been married before?"

"As far as I'm concerned, the present was all that
was—is—important."

"Stop saying that," Donna said, standing up.

"Saying what?"

" 'As far as I'm concerned,' " she repeated. "You keep saying that! Unfortunately, your 'concerns' aren't the same as the facts. Don't you think I had the right to know?"

"No," he said, rising and standing beside her. "No. I didn't see how a previous marriage had anything to do with us. There were no children involved. I haven't had any connection with Janine in years. I'm certainly not planning on seeing her again in the future." He moved around. "I didn't see—I don't see," he emphasized, "how a discussion of my previous mistakes could have any bearing on our lives together." Donna groped for words to refute him. "Have I ever asked you anything about your past? About old boyfriends?"

"It's not the same thing," Donna protested. "I was never married before!"

"Did I ask you that?"

"You didn't have to. I told you everything about me anyway. I didn't wait to be asked."

"Well, I'm different than you are. Is that so awful? So wrong? That I'm different than you are?"

"That's not the point."

"What, precisely, is the point?"

"The point is you should have told me." She collapsed back into the love seat. He moved slowly toward her, eventually stopping in front of her, lowering himself to his knees.

"Would it have made any difference?" he asked. "Would it have changed your feelings for me if I'd told you I'd been married before?"

"Not then," she answered.

"And now?" he asked, his eyes becoming instantly cloudy, catching Donna by surprise. She had not been prepared for his tears. "Does it make a difference now in the way you feel about me?"

Donna shook her head. "I don't know." She paused. "I

just feel like someone's come along and kicked all the air out of me."

His hand moved in soothing strokes down her arm. "I'm so sorry," he said. "I was wrong. I was very stupid. I can't explain it any other way." He moved up to sit beside her. "I guess I'm not used to making mistakes, and when I do, I don't like to talk about them."

She looked into his eyes, his tears seeming to mimic the path of her own. "But why? Mistakes only make you more human."

"Don't you think I'm human?" he asked. "Oh God, I love you so much."

They collapsed sobbing into each other's arms, Donna's mind such a jumble of confusing thoughts and instincts, she barely knew where she was anymore, or who she was.

"Please tell me you love me," she heard him say.

She shook her head. "I love you," she acknowledged tearfully. "I love you." She extracted herself. "I just don't know if we should—"

"Should what?"

"Maybe we should postpone things for a while," Donna said.

"What for? Either you love me or you don't."

"Maybe love just isn't enough."

"What else is there?"

"Trust," she said simply.

Instantly, she felt him withdraw. Where were his arms? She wanted them back around her. Where were the soft, soothing words of apology? She wanted to hear them. The words of reassurance, telling her he loved her, that he would make everything all right again. He opened his mouth to speak; she waited to hear the soft, soothing assurances.

His voice was cold, distant. "There's nothing I can do about that," he told her. "I've explained everything as best I can. I've apologized. All I can. All I'm going to. You can accept my apology or not. I love you. I want to marry you. But if you feel you can no longer trust me, well, then, there's nothing I can do. Trust takes time.

More than that, it takes a certain amount of blind faith. You either have it or you don't. I can tell you that I love you, that from now on I'll answer all your questions as honestly, as openly, as I can. I can promise you I'll never lay a hand on you in anger, that I'll never cheat on you. Ever. I can swear it. But I can't prove it. You have to trust me. You have to be prepared to give one hundred percent all the time."

"I thought marriage was a fifty-fifty affair," she said quietly.

"Who told you that?" he asked, trying to smile. His voice was gentle again. "Certainly no one with any brains." He touched her face. "You try meeting someone halfway and see where it gets you. It gets you halfway." She laughed quietly through her tears. "And if the other person doesn't come out his half of the way," he continued, "you have a choice. You can either stay where you are—halfway—which is nowhere, and fail, or you can go the other quarter distance or thirty percent, or maybe even, God forbid, the whole rest of the way over to his corner and put your arms around him and tell him you love him. Even if he's still insisting he's right and you're wrong, even when you know he's full of shit, because chances are he knows he's full of shit as much as you do, even if he's not prepared to face it just at that moment." He paused. "Come out the extra percentage, Donna," he pleaded. "Trust me. I know I'm full of shit. But I love you. Please don't postpone our wedding. Go forward, not back." He took her head between both his hands. "Marry me," he said.

The photographers arrived at fifteen minutes after four. Donna had been dressed and waiting for more than three quarters of an hour. Despite the air conditioning, she was beginning to feel exactly the way Victor had predicted—wilted. She kept checking her image in the mirror, adjusing and readjusting several stray strands of hair that refused to cooperate. Victor kept telling her to leave her hair alone, she was only making it worse, he said, and greasy as well. When she finally got the hairs in place he stared at her and said, "What'd you do that for? I liked it better the other way." She took guarded, though frequent, glances at her underarms until Victor told her that the more she worried about perspiration, the more likely she was to perspire, and then her glances became more guarded though no less frequent. The tops of her hands began to itch; Victor told her not to scratch. It was just her nerves, he said. She wanted to tell him that the only thing wrong with her nerves was the fact that he was getting on them. She wanted to tell him to shut up and go back to Connecticut. She wanted four, maybe five, good stiff drinks. She wanted to wreak chaos through the flower-filled room which, despite its sunny festivity, was beginning to feel like a funeral parlor with herself the freshly laid-out sweat-stained corpse. She wanted to kick off her shoes, tear off her dress, destroy her veil, burn her bouquet, and run like hell.

How did Victor feel? she wondered. Then the doorbell rang. It was four-fifteen and the photographers appeared, full of apologies, making excuses, setting up equipment, snapping pictures, the bride alone, the bride and groom, a formal sitting, a candid shot, some guests arriving early, the caterers and their crew arriving late, full of the same apologies, the same excuses, setting up equipment, setting the tables, more guests arriving, much mingling, congratulations, the telegram arriving from Donna's sister once again apologizing for not being able to attend, making excuses (make-up exam and all), wishing her the best of luck, the justice of the peace arriving with his clerk, on time, no excuses, no apologies. Just smiles, hellos, introductions, best wishes. Being moved into appropriate places, sudden bursts of silence as loud as the noise they interrupted, the justice of the peace talking, saying something about the solemnity of the occasion, the joyousness of what they were about to undertake. Undertakers, she thought, watching his lips move, not hearing what he was saying through the buzz in her ears, feeling the perspiration starting to stain her dress, the rash on her hands beginning to itch again, hearing familiar voices saying "I will," wondering why they hadn't said "I do," feeling Victor's lips brushing gently against her own, hearing the happy squeals all around her and knowing it was all over. Over. What precisely, she wondered, was over? What precisely was beginning?

She looked over at Victor, beaming at her with proud satisfaction. How did Victor feel? she wondered.

"I was just wondering," she asked him later between mouthfuls of food and the persistent congratulations of their inebriated guests, "about, you know, about how you just packed up and left everything and everybody back in Connecticut . . ." She'd had those four, maybe five drinks.

"What about it?" he asked without a trace of rancor, having himself imbibed a similar quantity.

"Well, I was just wondering what would happen to me if we didn't work out. I mean, would you just pack up and leave the great state of Florida? Would you simply declare me dead and depart for parts unknown?"

He smiled at her, his face a mask of love, his voice soft and caressing, sending familiar tingles through her body. "I'd obliterate you," he said tenderly. Then he kissed her. The new Mrs. Donna Cressy spent the better part of her wedding night in the bathroom throwing up.

Chapter 5

Donna watched the man as he rose from his seat near the back of the courtroom and walked past her—an uneven, unsteady sort of jaunt which never quite coordinated with itself—to take his place in the witness stand. She stared at him hard, this man who was about to testify against her. He was of medium height and middle age. In fact, everything about him shouted middle—middle age, middle class, middle America, middle of the road. Middle. Donna smiled at the silent sound of it. Middle. When you kept repeating it, it began to sound somewhat absurd, like a child's nonsense word. Middle . . . middle.

He had brown hair which was neatly combed over to one side to cover a budding bald spot. Again she smiled at her choice of words. How could anything that was balding be described as budding? Why not? she asked herself. She could do anything—she was crazy. At least she was sure that was the way she was about to hear herself described. Donna Cressy, occupation: crazy lady. Unfit to raise her two small children. All smiles vanished. Damn this man, she found herself thinking. Whoever he was.

The sudden realization that she didn't know who he was, this man who was about to lend credence and support to Victor's portrait of her, made her very nervous. She turned quickly to Mel, who now sat just a few rows behind her in easy view, and raised her eyebrows, asking him silently if he was familiar with this man. Mel responded with a subtle shrug of his shoulders—two secret bidders at an art auction at Sotheby's. He, too, had no idea.

Donna returned her gaze to the witness stand. The man about to be sworn in had no distinguishing features other than that his skin seemed almost too lose for him, as if he had put on someone else's overcoat. While it was the right color and suitably healthy looking, it just seemed to hang on him. Other than that, the man was neither good-looking nor bad, neither kind nor menacing. Neither. Nor. The type of man often passed over for key promotions because one simply forgot he was there. In the middle.

His voice was quiet. Pleasant. Donna edged forward in her seat. It was important that she hear what this man had to say. The clerk instructed him to state his name, address and occupation.

"Danny Vogel," the man said, trying hard not to look in Donna's direction. "114 Tenth Avenue, Lake Worth. I'm an insurance salesman."

The judge instructed Danny Vogel to speak up and Danny Vogel nodded without speaking.

She recognized the name. Danny Vogel. Gradually, the rest of him came clearer and clearer into focus, rather like a Polaroid picture in the process of self-developing. His address felt familiar. She had been there. Had driven there. She shuddered. She was remembering. He worked with Victor. Of course she knew this man, although he'd lost a considerable amount of weight since she'd last seen him. That would explain why his flesh seemed so rootless, why she had failed to recognize him.

What it didn't explain was what he was doing here, why he had been called. She couldn't remember the last time he'd been in her home; she had no recollection of him ever being around her children. How could he testify as to what kind of mother she'd been?

"How long have you known Mr. Victor Cressy?" Victor's lawyer, Mr. Ed Gerber, was asking him.

In a loud, even voice which showed he had listened to

the judge's instructions, Danny Vogel responded, "About eight years. We work in the same office."

"Would you consider yourself a good friend of Victor Cressy?"

"Yes, sir," he nodded, looking at Victor for confirmation. If Victor moved at all, Donna was unaware of it.

"And Mrs. Cressy?"

"I knew her less well," he stated, still looking at Victor. Less well, Donna thought, he didn't know me at all. We were acquainted. At various social functions, we maybe said hello, goodbye, yes, I'll have another drink. Less well! The presumption inherent in those words! You weren't even present at our wedding, her eyes screamed at him, trying to force his gaze in her direction. And why weren't you there? Ask him that, Mr. Gerber, Florida's finest, ask Mr. Danny Vogel why he wasn't at his good friend's wedding even though the woman his good friend married, this woman he knows "less well," had asked that he be included.

"What is your impression of Victor Cressy?" Ed Gerber asked.

"In what respect?" the witness asked. Donna found herself smiling in spite of herself. Not an easy question to answer, Mr. Gerber, she thought, understanding Danny Vogel's need for a qualification.

"In general," the lawyer elaborated. "As a man, a friend, a coworker."

Donna could see Danny Vogel making an invisible list inside his head. He was a man obviously well used to listening and carrying out his client's instructions. "As a man," he began somewhat slowly, "Victor Cressy is strong, forceful, even dynamic. He's intelligent, grasps things easily, knows all the details. He's demanding, I would say, but no more so of anyone else than he is of himself. To me, he has always come across as fair, disciplined and in control." He stopped. Donna helped him draw the imaginary line through Victor Cressy, man in control. "As a friend, he's loyal, honest—if he has a beef with you, believe me, you know it. He tells you exactly what he thinks, which obviously leads to some ups and downs." Obviously, Donna concurred, but does Victor ever really tell you exactly what he thinks, or do you just think he does? "He's very private, isn't usually the type to confide his problems to anyone, so when he does, you know they're pretty serious. But he's always there to help you with any problems you might be having." Cross a line through Good-Old-Always-There Victor Cressy, friend. "As a co-worker, no question about it, he's the best insurance salesman in the office. He works hard, he's a real perfectionist, and," Danny Vogel looked around the courtroom as if he expected a suitable adjective to come forward and loudly proclaim itself, "he's just the best." On that suitable superlative, cross out Victor Cressy, coworker. Well done, Mr. Vogel.

You weren't at the wedding because Victor Cressy still hadn't gotten around to forgiving you, valued coworker, for allegedly interfering with one of his prospective clients, a slight you weren't even aware you'd committed and for which you spent almost a year apologizing before Victor, intelligent, fair man that he is, felt you had been punished enough, and deigned to speak to you again. You have everafter felt you were entirely in the wrong and that Victor was not only right in his initial assertions but in his subsequent treatment of you. Your "good friend" is a master manipulator. His genius lies in not only convincing others that he is right all the time, but in having long ago convinced himself, thereby giving credence to even the most ludicrous of his actions. He's the one who's wrong, and yet everyone else feels guilty! Donna looked from the witness over to Victor Cressy. Such talent had to be a gift from God.

"And your impressions of Mrs. Cressy?"

"The first few times I met her, I was very impressed," he allowed. "She was lovely, seemed to have a nice sense of humor . . ."

Why is he talking about me in the past tense? Donna wondered. Had she passed away suddenly? Was her hell to be this courtroom and not a sink full of dirty dishes, after all? Listening to an endless litany of witnesses denounce her every move and motivation—Sisyphus pushing the giant boulder—until she collapsed under the weight of it all, shouting, "Yes, you're right. It's all my fault."

". . . she seemed to change," Danny Vogel was explaining.

"When was that?"

"It's hard to pinpoint exactly because I only saw her on rare social occasions and they got rarer all the time." He paused, collecting his saliva and then swallowing it. "But when I first met Donna she seemed fairly outgoing, and through the years she just seemed to get more withdrawn. She stopped having company over to her home—"

"Objection," Donna's lawyer said, rising. "This witness is not in a position to state who did or who did not come into the Cressy's home."

"Sustained."

Danny Vogel looked confused.

"Mr. Vogel," Ed Gerber continued, picking up the dangling thread, "how many times were you, yourself, invited to the Cressy house for either dinner or any type of social gathering?"

Danny paused to reflect. "In those first few years of their marriage, I'd say several times a year. After Adam was born, maybe once. After Sharon, not at all. Once," he began, looking toward Ed Gerber, who, obviously knowing what the witness intended to say, indicated that he was to go on, "she came by to pick Victor up from work, and Victor and I were waiting on the street—she was late—and I leaned in the car to say hello, and Victor suggested that Renee and I come over for a barbeque dinner at their place one night the next week and she said no, it was absolutely out of the question. Victor looked very embarrassed. Needless to say, *I* was embarrassed."

"Did she offer an explanation?"

"No. That was all she said. It was very strange."

"Did you notice anything else that was 'strange'?" Ed Gerber asked, repeating and emphasizing the final word.

Danny Vogel shook his head. "Not really. Oh, except her hair. It was a bright carrot red. I'd just seen her the previous week at a party and it had been blonde."

"So you did have occasion to see Donna Cressy at various social functions?"

"Oh yes. We moved in roughly the same circles. Our office was a friendly one. Someone was always having a party."

"Over the years, was there any discernible change in Mrs. Cressy's behavior at these functions?"

"Well, like I said, she was becoming more withdrawn. It seemed each party, she said less and less. She hardly ever smiled. She had a lot of colds. There always seemed to be something wrong with her—"

"Objection." Mr. Stamler sounded ineffably disgruntled.

"Sustained," the judge said. "The court will draw its own conclusions, Mr. Vogel."

Danny Vogel seemed genuinely upset he had caused the court any problem. "I'm sorry, your honor," he said quietly, then, mindful of his previous admonition, repeated it in a louder voice.

"Did you ever have one of those parties in your own home, Mr. Vogel?" Ed Gerber asked, knowing he had.

"Yes, sir."

"To which the Cressys were invited?"

Again, a positive reply.

"When was that?"

"A little more than two years ago," Danny Vogel answered. "My fortieth birthday."

Donna knew the date precisely. It was twenty-five months ago. Nine months exactly before Sharon was born. The night Sharon was conceived.

"Could you describe precisely what happened from the time the Cressys arrived at your party?"

Donna thought back to the party. What could he possibly have to say?

"Well, they were late. The last ones to arrive. But Victor was very friendly, cordial. Donna kind of hung back.

She didn't smile when she came in; she seemed distracted.
I just figured she was in another of her moods—"

"Objection."

The objection having been ruled on and sorted out, the
witness continued with his testimony. "Anyway, she didn't
say much that I was aware of. Every time I looked over
in her direction she was just standing off by herself. She
just stood like that, I don't think she moved, with a drink
in her hand, nursing it and sniffing—she had a cold, and
I remember her nose kept running. She always seemed to
have a Kleenex in front of her face."

They're going to take my children away from me because I used a Kleenex to wipe my nose? Donna wondered in disbelief. Kleenex user unfit to wipe her
children's noses! Damn them, she uttered into herself, she
was the one who had gotten up at three in the morning to
wipe their noses when they cried. ("Mommy, the nose,
the nose," Adam had always yelled at the slightest
dribble.) She had wiped their noses and their tears and
their glorious little round butts. But it was somehow
wrong for her to wipe her own nose—even when she had
a cold.

But, of course that was the whole point. She had another cold. Victor had already mentioned her fondness for
the affliction. This was merely what they termed corrobo-
rative evidence. They weren't going to damn her because
she had used a Kleenex to wipe her nose, they were going
to damn her because she had another cold.

"I went over at one point to speak to her," Danny
Vogel continued, unaware of Donna's silent interruption,
"but the coversation was pretty much one-sided."

"Can you recall any of it?"

"I told her she looked lovely." He chuckled. "She
agreed with me."

Now, it was crazy to agree, Donna thought.

"Her voice was very husky. She seemed to be suffering
from laryngitis, which she got quite frequently, and so I
concluded it must be painful for her to talk, especially af-

ter I tried to ask her a few questions and she didn't answer."

"What kind of questions?"

Danny Vogel shrugged his shoulders. "I asked her about her son—Adam. How he was, if she was planning on sending him to nursery school. She didn't answer. She just looked at me, I remember, and she looked almost—afraid—"

"Afraid? Of what?"

"I have no idea. She didn't say anything."

"Your honor," Donna's lawyer, Mr. Stamler, said rising from his seat, "I fail to see the point of this witness' testimony. If he is to be a character witness for Victor Cressy, that's fine. Let him confine himself to that type of testimony, but so far anything he has had to say regarding Mrs. Cressy has been totally irrelevant. Because the lady failed to answer his questions to his satisfaction, Mr. Vogel seems to imply that there was something amiss in her behavior. Donna Cressy had a cold; she had laryngitis. Does that qualify as unbalanced behavior? Does that make her an unfit mother?"

"If I may beg the court's indulgence," Ed Gerber interjected before the judge could speak. "We intend to prove the relevancy of this testimony immediately."

The judge looked appropriately skeptical, but allowed the lawyer to continue.

Ed Gerber twisted his mouth unattractively, until the next question was formulated in his mind and ready to be spit out.

"Did Mrs. Cressy's subsequent behavior at the party do anything to, let us say, arouse your suspicion as to her state of mind?"

"About halfway through the party," Danny Vogel answered, choosing his words carefully, "there was a total transformation in her behavior. It was like Dr. Jekyll and Mr. Hyde. Or Mrs. Hyde," he added, laughing meekly at his joke. No one joined him, although Ed Gerber did smile. "One minute, she was sniffing and not talking to anyone and the next minute, she was yelling, and I mean yelling, in a perfectly clear voice, one that had absolutely no traces of a cold in it anywhere, and that's how she was for the rest of the evening." He paused, waiting for someone to object. No one did. Donna looked at the judge. His interest had been rekindled. He was listening intently.

"Did anything happen that you were aware of to occasion this change?"

"Donna was standing across from the bar—in the same position she'd been in since their arrival—when Victor walked over to her to offer her a Kleenex. I saw it in his hand, and then suddenly she slapped his hand quite loudly, knocking the Kleenex out of his hand, and pushing his arm against one of the other guests who spilled her drink—I believe it was Mrs. Harrison—down her dress. Donna got very belligerent. She raised her voice and kept it raised until they left. Every time anyone started to have any kind of a conversation, she interrupted, giving them her opinion, which always seemed to be the opposite of what everyone else was thinking. She insulted several of the guests and used obscene language on several occasions. And she was merciless with regard to Victor. Every time he opened his mouth, she made some sarcastic reply. She kept putting him down, outlining all she felt was wrong with him. Mimicking him. It was very embarrassing. Finally, Victor indicated it was time they left and she made another disparaging comment about her master's voice, or some such remark, and then they left. I must admit we all breathed a large sigh of relief."

Ed Gerber took a long, smug pause. "Mr. Vogel, to your knowledge, could this sudden shift in behavior have been due to Mrs. Cressy's consumption of alcohol that night?"

Danny Vogel looked delighted he had been asked that question. He confided the answer as a schoolboy might, having been allowed to release a secret too long contained. "No," he almost squealed. "Like I said, she just stood off to one side, directly across from the bar, and nursed that one drink I had originally brought her. She didn't move. I never saw her get another."

"You said earlier," Ed Gerber continued most carefully, "that Victor Cressy was a man who rarely confided his problems to other people."

"That's correct," the witness agreed.

"Now tell me, but be careful, I don't want you to tell me anything that was actually said because that would be hearsay," Ed Gerber said with a sly smile to Mr. Stamler, "but without going into any actual conversations, did Victor Cressy ever confide in you that he was worried about his wife's behavior?"

"Yes, he did. On numerous occasions."

"Did he ever express concern for his children?"

"Yes, sir."

"What kind of father was Victor Cressy?" Ed Gerber asked. Once again, Donna noted the tense. Had Victor suddenly passed away as well?

"From all I could see, he was a wonderful father. He was very concerned about his children, right from the time he first learned Donna was pregnant. He read all the books, went to prenatal classes with his wife—both times—and knew all the breathing exercises. He stayed with Donna all through her labor, and with Adam I think it was close to twenty-four hours—"

Twenty-six hours, you clown, Donna's eyes screamed. And it was me who was in labor, not the jerk doing all the breathing. I was the one in pain. How lucky you are to have such a considerate husband, the nurses had told her. Especially after Sharon's birth, that one nurse who had beamed so glowingly at Victor. Bitch, Donna had wanted to shout, ask him about the way she was conceived!

"He was very insistent that Donna eat all the right foods. He was thrilled when she decided to nurse both children. He felt that was healthier. He was very proud of his children. He'd bring them to the office occasionally. You could just see how crazy he was about them."

"And did you ever observe Donna with her children?"

Danny Vogel shook his head. "No." Somehow he made it sound like a condemnation.

Donna's lawyer was quick to take the offensive when it was his turn to cross-examine.

"Mr. Vogel," he began, his voice clipping off his words as a typewriter dispenses letters, sharply, crisply, with determined speed, "are you by any chance a trained psychologist?"

Danny Vogel smiled and shook his head. "No, sir."

"Have you had any extra training in any of the behavioral sciences?"

"No, sir."

"A psychology major at the university perhaps?"

"No, sir." The smile had vanished.

"So that you have no real qualifications, shall we say, for assessing Mrs. Cressy's behavior?"

"Just my eyes and ears," Danny Vogel retorted, the snake cornered and frightened, coiled to strike.

"Eyes and ears can be deceiving, Mr. Vogel, as we all know. No outsider to a marriage can ever fairly or fully assess what goes on inside that marriage, wouldn't you agree?"

"I suppose so." He paused. "But Donna's behavior was more than—"

Mr. Stamler cut the witness off abruptly. "Would you say you're especially qualified to comment on female behavior? How many times have you been married, Mr. Vogel?"

Danny Vogel squirmed visibly. "Twice," he admitted.

"Your first marriage ended in divorce?"

"Yes, sir."

"And your second? A happy one?"

"We're separated," he said, keeping his voice clearly audible while lowering his head.

"So you're really not much of an authority on women, are you, Mr. Vogel?" the lawyer asked sarcastically, then continued on immediately.

"You stated moments ago that you never observed Mrs. Cressy with her children, is that correct?"

"Yes, sir."

"So then, you're really not in a position one way or the

other to comment on Mrs. Cressy's abilities as a mother, are you?"

"No, sir, but—"

"Thank you, that's all, Mr. Vogel."

Danny Vogel hesitated momentarily before stepping away from the witness stand. He looked at Victor who continued to largely ignore his presence, still carefully avoiding Donna's glance as he ambled back to his seat.

Mr. Stamler—did he have a first name? Donna suddenly wondered, realizing she had never called him other than Mr.—patted her hand reassuringly. He obviously felt they had won that round. The witness had admitted he was in no position to comment on Donna's capabilities as a mother—"So then, you're really not in a position one way or the other to comment on Mrs. Cressy's abilities as a mother, are you?" "No, sir," the witness had agreed. "But—" Her lawyer had quickly terminated the testimony, but the word remained in the records. The court had heard it. She had heard it. The judge had certainly heard it. But.

She repeated it over in her mind—but, but, but, but—until, like the word middle, its meaning was reduced to an absurdity.

"Tell me a story."

Donna looked over at her young son, just four years old, who sat less than an arm's reach away, rubbing his nose with the bright blue blanket that covered his bed. "Adam, I've already read you three stories. I said that one was the last. We agreed that when it was over, you would get under the covers and go to sleep."

"I am under the covers," he said, crawling swiftly inside his bed.

"Good." Donna stood up, feeling tired and drained, yet reluctant to leave his side. Immediately, Adam sensed her indecision.

"Please—" he said, his face already a huge grin of anticipation.

Donna sat back down on the bed next to his pillow.

Adam immediately propped himself up beside her. "All right, which story do you want me to read?"

"Not read. Tell."

"Oh, honey, I'm so tired. I can't think of—"

"Tell me a story about a little boy named Roger and a little girl named Bethanny—"

Donna smiled at the mention of the two names—Adam's latest friends from nursery school. "Okay," she said. "Once upon a time, there was a little boy named Roger and a little girl named Bethanny, and one day they went to the park—"

"No!"

"No?"

"No. They went to the zoo to see the giraffes!"

"Who's telling this story? You or me?"

Adam took a second to recollect his thoughts. "Tell me a story," he persisted, "about a little boy named Roger and a little girl named Bethanny and they went to the zoo to see the giraffes. Would you tell me that one?"

"Okay," Donna said, chuckling to herself. "So they went to the zoo—"

"No! From the beginning. Once upon a time!"

"You're pressing your luck, kiddo!"

"Tell me a story about a little boy named Roger and a little girl named Bethanny, and they went to the zoo to see the giraffes. And they took some peanuts with them. But the sign said 'Do Not Feed The Amiuls.' "

"The what?"

"The amiuls," he replied impatiently.

"You mean, the animals?"

"Yea." Of course, what's the matter with you, Lady? Can't you hear good? "Would you tell me that one?"

Donna took a deep breath. "Once upon a time there was a little boy named Roger and a little girl named Bethanny, and they went to the zoo to see the giraffes. And they took some peanuts with them. But the sign said 'Do Not Feed The Animals.' Okay?" Adam nodded. "And so—"

"And so?"

"And so they ate up all the peanuts by themselves," Donna said quickly, "and had a wonderful time and went home to their mommies and lived happily ever after." Donna kissed him gently on the forehead, stood up again and switched off the light.

"Where's your mommy?" the small voice asked, catching Donna off guard.

She stumbled for several seconds. It was the first time he had asked her that particular question, and she wasn't sure how to answer him. As simply as possible, she decided, hearing her voice soft against the semidarkness. "She's dead, honey. She died a long time ago."

"Oh." Long pause. Donna turned to go, feeling she had said the right thing. That wasn't so hard, she thought. "What's died?" he asked suddenly. Donna stopped. Did they really have to get into this now? She looked at Adam's face. Yes, they obviously had to go into it now. She sat back down on the bed, her mind searching to recall what Benjamin Spock had advised in this regard.

"Uh—let me see." You certainly couldn't tell a child who was about to go to sleep that death was like going to sleep, and somehow she choked on the thought of the word Heaven. Damn, she thought, can't you wait a few days and ask then. That way, if Victor wins his suit he can deal with this little matter. "No, I will tell you," she said aloud, Adam looking at her with sudden surprise. Victor would not win his case. He would not take her children away.

"Why are you yelling?"

"Oh, sorry." She suddenly recalled Dr. Spock's advice. "Everybody dies, sweetie," she explained. "It happens to everything that lives—flowers, people—amiuls. It's very natural and it doesn't hurt or anything. We just stop living. But it usually doesn't happen to people until they're very old." Adam was staring at her. "Do you understand? Is that okay?"

He nodded, wordlessly, crawling deep inside his covers. Again, Donna kissed his forehead.

"I love you, sweetie-pie."

"Good night, Mommy."

Donna walked the few steps down the hall to Sharon's room and peeked inside. Sharon immediately sat up in her crib.

"What are you doing up?" Donna asked her.

The little girl said nothing, pulling herself up in the darkness and holding her hands out toward her mother. Donna walked over and pulled Sharon out of the crib, holding her warm little body against her own.

"You're supposed to be asleep, you know."

Sharon stared deeply into her mother's eyes. Gently, slowly, with almost deliberate precision, Sharon lifted her right hand and brought it down in a gentle caress across Donna's cheek. Donna hugged the little girl tightly against her. "Go to sleep, little one. I love you, my angel. Go to sleep, baby."

Sharon laid her head on Donna's shoulder and quickly drifted off to sleep.

"Mommy!" Adam's voice penetrated the stillness.

"I'll kill him," Donna said aloud, moving Sharon back to her crib and lowering her gently inside.

"Mommy!"

Donna stepped out into the hall, moving quickly back to Adam's room. "What is it, Adam?" she asked, a hint of annoyance in her voice. Adam was once again sitting up in his bed.

"I want to ask you a question."

Please don't ask me what happens when you die, she pleaded silently. I'll buy you a copy of Elizabeth Kubler-Ross in the morning! "What is it, honey?"

"Who made me?" he asked.

Oh no! Donna thought. Not now. Not life and death both in the same night. Not after a day full of divorce. She sank back onto his bed. "Mommy and Daddy made you, honey."

He looked at her with great curiosity in his eyes. "Out of—?" he asked, waiting for her to complete the sentence.

"Out of a lot of love," Donna answered after a silence of several minutes, hoping, even as the words fell out of her mouth, that Sharon would never ask her the same question.

Chapter 6

"You're not breathing properly."

"I am so."

"No, you're not. You're supposed to be doing level A breathing. That's supposed to come from down low in your stomach. You're doing level B."

"I'm supposed to be smelling a flower."

"No, you're not. Smelling the flower is level B. We're practicing level A right now."

"I'm tired," Donna said testily, pulling herself slowly and with some difficulty into a sitting position. "Let's call it a night."

Victor was adamant. "If we don't practice the breathing every day, there's no point in going through with this." His face was dangerously close to a pout.

"*Now* you decide there's no point?" Donna questioned, trying not to laugh, "now that I've already put on twenty-five pounds and I only have two more months to go." She struggled to her feet. "Not fair, Victor, not fair."

"You're the one who's not being fair," he chastised. "To the baby."

"Oh, Victor, lighten up. What's happened to your sense of humor? You're so funny when we're in class." She waddled over to the wet bar and poured herself a glass of ginger ale. "They should see you when you get home."

He looked stricken.

"We'll practice tomorrow, Victor. One day isn't going

to kill us—or the baby . . . if we miss doing the breathing one day."

"Suit yourself," he said in a tone he adopted for all unsuitable occasions. "It's you who'll regret—"

"Oh, spare me, Victor." She shook her head, trying to keep from getting angry. She felt a fight approaching and she wanted to avoid it, sidestep it before it became too large to get around. "I wonder what women did before they had prenatal classes."

"They suffered," he said simply. "A lot," he added for emphasis.

"But they survived," she reminded him.

"Some."

His smugness was starting to rile her. Her patience, she was discovering, was decreasing in direct proportion to the increase in her belly. The larger the load, the shorter the fuse.

"Victor, my survival will have nothing to do with whether or not I tune-tap during transition." (Two terms they had learned the previous week.)

Victor shrugged his shoulders and leaned his head to the side. Then he turned silently and walked out of the room. Donna watched the seat of his pants as he moved away from her. Despite the anger she was feeling—out of proportion to the situation, she recognized—she still wanted him, would offer no resistance if he were to turn around, drop his pants and move toward her, lower her to the floor and—sure, she thought, looking down at her exorbitant girth. Sure thing.

That was the way their fights had usually ended in the past. Not precisely the scenario, of course. The only time Victor had ever actually dropped his pants after a fight, he had ended up hopping the entire distance of the room over toward her, and by the time he had reached her they were both laughing so hard his erection was gone and she had cramps in her stomach. Still, when they were finally able to struggle free of their clothes, their lovemaking was as good as it always was, their soaked bodies melting into each other on the living room floor.

Maybe that was the trouble now, the reason their fights seemed to be increasing. They hadn't made love in almost a month. Despite the fact that the books said you could, and their doctor said they could, Victor was increasingly concerned he might hurt the baby, and the simple fact of it was that it wasn't very comfortable, no matter what anybody said. She smiled with the image of Victor above her, his body perpendicular to hers, his arms twitching frantically in an effort to keep as much weight off her as possible. "You get on top," he had said, trying to roll them both over. "I think I'm getting a hernia," he muttered a minute later, still trying with no success to reverse their positions. Finally, both laughing and exhausted, she had landed with a thud on his belly. "The Americans have landed!" he shouted.

Donna found herself standing alone in her living room laughing. No matter how vicious the argument, if he wanted to, Victor could always joke her away from her anger. Unless, of course, *he* was still angry. Then it was a different story altogether.

It had been like this almost from the beginning. After a brief honeymoon in Key West, which he loathed and she loved ("to tacky, too many queers," he had said; "lots of character; they're artists," she had responded; the truth, they both concurred later, lying somewhere in the middle, a truth that existed regardless of their opinions), they returned to Palm Beach and a series of dilemmas that were not so easily resolved. Donna was never quite sure where the source of the arguments began. She knew only that something that would begin as an ordinary discussion, perhaps a mild disagreement, would minutes later erupt in a series of violent explosions, building in intensity, until each word was a potential mine and stepping even near it meant possible death, certain wounding.

She: "What's the matter?"

He: "Nothing."

"Something is obviously bothering you. Why don't you tell me what it is."

"There's nothing bothering me."

"Then why haven't you spoken to me since dinner?" she asked.

He looked peeved. "All right, there *is* something bothering me. But it's no big thing. Just leave it alone and it will go away."

"You don't want to talk about it?"

"No. Just drop it. Please."

And so it, whatever it was, would be dropped. But not quite.

"What did you do to your hair?" Victor asked.

"What do you mean, what did I do? Nothing. I just combed it differently."

"Then why did you just say 'nothing'?"

"Because I didn't do anything to it. Just ran a comb through it," Donna answered, defenses raised.

"Differently," he said flatly.

"So what?"

"So, just yesterday I told you I liked your hair the way you had it."

"So?"

"So you felt compelled to change it. Naturally. Every time I tell you I like something, you change it. Heaven forbid we do something that Victor likes."

"What are you talking about?"

"I'm talking about how I shouldn't tell you if I like something around here because that's the last I'll see of it." His voice was rising.

"I don't believe this," Donna found herself uttering. "Come on, Victor, we can't be arguing about the fact I combed my hair differently."

"Why can't we?"

"Because—because it's so trivial!"

"Trivial to you, maybe. Maybe it's not so trivial to me. Did that ever occur to you? The fact that something that might be insignificant to you might have some importance to me. That I might have feelings that are different to those of Donna Cressy."

"You're seriously upset because I combed my hair with

a part in the middle instead of off to one side?" she asked in total disbelief.

"You're not listening to me."

"What did I miss?"

"Forget it. There's no point."

"You seem to feel there is. Tell me. What did I miss? What didn't I hear?"

"The hair is just one thing. It's everything. *Anything* I like around here gets changed."

"Everything? Anything?" Donna questioned angrily. "You're the one who's always telling me not to use words like always when we're having an argument."

"I didn't say always."

"You said everything. It's the same thing. A complete generalization."

"It's not the same thing."

"Why are there always two sets of rules—one for you and one for me?"

"Now who's generalizing?"

She shook her head. "I can't win."

He was quick to pounce. "That's precisely your problem. You always think in terms of winning and losing. Not how to solve something. Just how to win."

"That's not fair."

"True though."

"No, it's not true."

"Did you or did you not say, I can't win?"

"I don't believe this!"

"Rant and rave all you want. It won't change things." His voice was suddenly, irritatingly steady and calm. Donna tried to collect her thoughts, her emotions, to tie them into a neat bundle. Like so much garbage.

"This is ridiculous," she said more to herself than to Victor although he heard and agreed. "What is it we're arguing about here?" She paused, trying to remember how it had all started. "You said everything around here that you like I change."

"No, I didn't."

"What did you say then?"

"I said that everything around here that I like *gets* changed."

"Gets changed? By whom? Obviously, not by you or there wouldn't be a discussion here—"

"If you say so."

She stopped. "What's that supposed to mean? That *you* change these things, whatever the hell they are?"

He shook his head. "You have to swear, don't you? You can't even let me *agree* with you gracefully."

"What are you talking about?"

"I agreed with you that *I'm* not the one who changes things—"

"You agreed with me? 'If you say so'? That was agreement?"

"You cut me off."

"What? When?"

"Before. Look, what does it matter? You've made your point."

"What point?" She was yelling.

"Stop yelling. You're always yelling about something."

"I'm *always* yelling? There you go again with your generalizations."

"Well, listen to you. My voice isn't raised."

Donna took several long, deep breaths. "You said everything gets changed. Right?" He didn't answer. "You don't do it. Everything obviously doesn't change itself. So that leaves me, right?"

"If you say so."

"If I say so. That's an agreement?"

"If you say so."

"All right, I say so."

"Okay. Just so we know where we stand."

"I'm so confused I don't know if I'm sitting or standing or lying down," she said. "But I would like to get to the bottom of this."

"No matter what it costs."

"Why should it cost anything?" She felt her frustration growing.

"Because it always does whenever we have a fight."

"But why should it? Why can't we just discuss our problems like two normal people? If something is bothering you, tell me. I can't second guess you. I can't read your mind. If you're mad at me for something, tell me specifically what it is you're mad about."

"I did. You didn't like what I told you."

"My hair? We are really fighting about my hair?" He smiled smugly. "But you said everything? What else do I change that you like?"

"Let's drop it."

"No. Let's get it out in the open and then get rid of it."

He was furious. She could see the ice reflecting in his eyes. "All right. I mentioned about a month ago that I really liked that shepherd's pie you made; we haven't had it since. I told you I thought you looked terrific in that red dress; you haven't worn it since—"

"It's too short. It's out of style. Nobody wears dresses that short anymore—"

"You're interrupting me. Did you want to hear what I have to say or not?" She nodded silently. "The other night," he continued, "I told you I liked creamed cheese—"

"We *had* creamed cheese."

"What we had was creamy cottage cheese, which I hate. I told you I liked creamed cheese, but as usual, you don't listen to me. You get what *you* like."

"That's not so! I thought I had gotten what you like. Is that what you were so upset about the other night?"

"What other night?"

"The night you didn't say a word to me after dinner? The night you said something was bothering you but to leave it alone, it would go away?"

"But you wouldn't leave it alone, would you? You never do. Like now."

"*Now* is happening because I left it alone then! It didn't go away at all. It just festered and got worse." She was getting really angry now. "I don't believe it. I don't believe you would actually get upset because I made a mistake and got you the wrong kind of cheese! I don't believe we're actually having a fight about it two days later."

"It wasn't a mistake."

"What's that supposed to mean? That I did it on purpose?"

"No. Not on purpose. Subconsciously."

"Subconsciously?"

"Don't yell."

"What the hell is that supposed to mean?"

"Don't swear."

"Don't tell me what to do!"

"Let's just drop it."

"No! Let's settle it once and for all. I feel like I'm drowning in a sea of trivialities."

"Trivial to you."

"Yes!" she screamed. "Trivial to me! And they should be trivial to you! Shepherd's pie, a red dress, cottage cheese, my hair. I can't believe those are issues worth fighting over! These things are symptoms of a deeper problem. My God, they can't be the problem itself!"

"If you say so."

"I say so!"

"Then why ask me what I think? Why bother?"

"You really believe I deliberately bought you the wrong kind of cheese?"

"Subconsciously, I said."

"There's no room for honest mistakes in your world?"

He was suddenly very quiet, his tone unmistakably patronizing. "Honey," he said, taking her hands in his, "I don't say you mean to do these things. But don't you think it's funny that you always manage to do the things that you like the right way and somehow the things that I like either never get done or get done wrong?"

She shook her hands free of his with a force that surprised them both. "Goddamn you," she shouted, "you s.o.b., I never heard such a load of crap in my entire life. You stand there like some little dictator and tell me what I should do and not do, what I don't do, what I do subconsciously. I never heard such bullshit."

"If you're going to swear, I'm going to go in the other room."

"Don't you dare go anywhere."

"Now who's telling who what to do?"

"You rat!"

"Sure, now start with the insults. First, I'm a dictator, a 'little' dictator I believe you said, you seemed to put special emphasis on the word 'little,' why, I'm not sure. Then you called me an s.o.b., and now I'm a rat. Go on, what further damage can you do?"

Donna was crying hard now with frustration. "What about the damage that you do?"

"I haven't called you any names. I haven't sworn. I asked you to drop this whole discussion. You wouldn't. Now you're insulting me, calling me names. What's on the game plan next, Donna? Do you throw darts?"

He started to walk from the room. "Don't you walk out on me," she called after him as he continued to walk away from the living room and into their bedroom.

"Leave me alone, Donna," he said wearily. "Haven't you said enough?" He flipped the remote control unit which turned on the television set.

"Please turn it off," Donna said quietly.

"What, so you can yell at me again? No, thanks."

"Please."

"No." His eyes were glued to an episode of "All in the Family." She recognized it as one they had already seen.

"I just want to get this settled."

"I don't want to talk to you anymore tonight, can't you understand that? Can't you get that through your thick skull?"

Donna began crying again. "Now who's being insulting?"

"Oh, okay. You got your way. Now I've insulted you too. We're even. I'm the world's worst husband. I'm a rotten person."

"Nobody said you were a rotten person. Nobody said you were a bad husband." She paused. "Please turn off that damn TV."

"Here we go again with the swearing."

"Oh come on, Victor. Don't be such a prude."

"That's good, Donna. Keep it up. Now I'm a prude. Go on, what else can you call me?"

"Will you turn off that TV?"

Surprisingly, he pushed the button and the television flipped off. "All right, Donna. It's off. Go on, but go on only when you understand that you take full responsibility for whatever happens from here on out. I asked you to drop it. I have begged you to drop it. No, you're intent on doing real harm here. Okay, you've bruised me so far, but I can still walk. You have five minutes to finish me off."

"Why do you say it that way? Nobody's trying to hurt you."

"I guarantee that within five minutes you'll have carried this fight into an arena I can't even imagine yet. But go on. Say what you want to. I'll listen for five minutes." He looked at his watch.

Donna frantically tried to organize her thoughts into words. They refused to unjumble, becoming clogged at the roof of her mouth, sticking to the sides of her gums like peanut butter, emerging as a confused rehashing of what she had already said.

"I just don't understand how we get into these stupid arguments," she began feebly, impotently.

"We get into them because you won't let go. You push until it's too late."

"I don't think I do."

"Obviously. What would you call what you're doing right now?"

"I'm trying to get to the bottom of this."

"The bottom of this is that you don't really like me very much."

"That's not true. I love you." He raised a doubtful eyebrow. "I do." She had raised her voice and immediately checked herself. "I'm sorry."

"Sorry that you love me, I know."

"Not sorry that I love you," she yelled, "sorry that I yelled."

"Please don't yell at me anymore, Donna. I've had enough. Really, you don't have to yell at me anymore."

He sounded like a prisoner-of-war being tortured by the enemy.

Donna looked to the ceiling. "What is going on here? Somebody help me."

"Is this how we're going to spend the next five minutes. Because if it is, I'd rather watch 'All in the Family.' At least their fights are funny."

"Damn you," she cried. "You tell me to talk, and then you don't let me. You interrupt. You manipulate the conversation until I'm so mad I'm screaming."

"That's all you ever do, Donna."

"And in the end I never get a chance to say what I want to say."

"Just what is it you want to say, Donna? Do you really know?"

"It's just that you seem to have such a low opinion of me."

"*I* have a low opinion of *you?*"

"Yes. You always assume the worst."

"*Always?*"

"That I change things that you like, deliberately, subconsciously. However. You seem to feel I'm always against you. But you won't give me a chance to defend myself. Half the time I don't even know you're upset because you don't tell me what's bothering you—"

"Why should I? You just dismiss it as trivial anyway."

"Shit, we're just going around in circles."

"And you're still swearing. Tell me, does it give you an extra charge to swear because I've told you how much I object to it. Because you know it bothers me?"

"Why do you have to take everything so personally? Why, if I say 'shit' out of sheer frustration do you automatically assume I'm saying it to upset you."

"Because you are."

"That's paranoid, Victor!"

She had gone too far. She knew it as soon as the words were out of her mouth. He had held out the gun and she had supplied him with the necessary ammunition. He had been waiting for the slip, pushing for it, the one word he could use to blow them both to smithereens. Her five minutes were up and she had given him his word. Paranoid.

His voice was quiet.

"Well, you finally said what you wanted to say, didn't you, Donna."

"I just meant—"

"I don't want to hear anymore of what you have to say. You've said it all. You've hurt me enough. Do you want to see blood? Is that what you want? You've taken a simple little disagreement, a stupid little statement I made, for which I apologized—"

"You apologized? When did you apologize?"

"You don't listen to me, Donna. I keep telling you that."

"You never apologized!"

He suddenly screamed. "All right, I never apologized! If you say I didn't, then you must be right because, God knows, you're always right. I thought I did. But I guess I was wrong. Again." He paused. "What difference does it make?"

"It makes all the difference. If you'd apologized, this whole fight wouldn't have happened."

"Of course it would have, don't you see? You were so determined to tell me what a rat I am, how *paranoid* I am, how wrong I am, you would have found a way regardless of whatever I did or didn't say. I think I apologized. You say I didn't. It doesn't really matter. What's important is what you said later."

Donna tried to clear her head. Something was wrong with what he was saying, but she was just too confused and tired to figure it out.

"I don't understand."

"No, you never do," he said sadly.

Donna felt the pangs of guilt beginning to congeal inside her stomach. Why didn't she understand? Why did she always yell? Why did she have to swear so much? She knew he didn't like it. She knew he liked shepherd's pie—why didn't she make it more often? Had she deliberately, subconsciously, bought him the wrong cheese? No, damn it, she thought suddenly, no, she hadn't.

"You're always so intent on being right," he said slowly and with such quiet conviction that Donna, already struggling with her guilt, felt compelled to listen. "You don't understand that it doesn't matter ultimately who's right or who's wrong. What's important is what's said in the interim. You didn't hear *me* insulting you."

"You don't call telling me I deliberately change everything you like insulting?" she exclaimed.

"You're interrupting again."

"Sorry, I thought you were finished."

He raised his hands in the air in mock surrender. "Okay, if that's what you say."

"No, please, Victor. Go on. I didn't mean to interrupt."

"You'll let me finish what I have to say? You won't interrupt?"

"What is this? An organized debate or something? People have discussions; they interrupt each other."

"But you do it all the time. You never let me finish a thought."

Donna bit down hard on her lower lip. "All right," she said slowly. "I won't interrupt again."

He took a dramatic pause. "The reason we go around in circles is simple, Donna. You ask me what's bothering me. I already know what's going to happen if I tell you—*this* is going to happen; *tonight* is going to happen, because you really don't want to hear what I have to say. You just want the opportunity to tell me I'm wrong."

"That's—"

"You're interrupting."

"Sorry."

"Look at tonight, Donna. It wouldn't have happened if you hadn't pushed it. I asked you to drop it. Whatever's bothering me would eventually go away. But no, you have to drag it out so you can tell me how stupid it is, how trivial it is, how wrong I am. About it. About you. About everything. If you don't want to hear what I have to say, then don't ask me what's bothering me. But a funny thing happens in all our fights, Donna. You always ask me what's bothering me and yet somehow all that ever really gets said is what's bothering you. And I get called all sorts of lovely little names that I can still hear in my head long after I've forgotten what the fight was all about." He paused. "It's your mouth, Donna, you just don't know what damage you do with your mouth. You start in on me and you don't let go."

"*I* start in on *you?*"

"You can't help but interrupt, can you?" Donna's shoulders slumped under the gathering weight of guilt. She wiped a tear away from her eyes and said nothing. There seemed to be a lot of truth to what he was saying. Why couldn't she just shut up when he told her to? Why couldn't she just agree with him about things? Everything was always fine as long as she agreed with him, as long as she let him make all the decisions. Why did she always have to push for a solution? In the end, nothing was ever solved. Just as nothing that was bothering him ever really went away. She sighed. Nothing dropped, nothing solved. A sort of married nothing ventured, nothing gained.

In the end, she spent half of what was left of the night apologizing, begging forgiveness, chastising herself while he looked on with silent approval. Still, somewhere in the back of her mind she could hear her mother's voice— "Don't let anyone bamboozle you. Speak up." She felt somewhere down deep in her gut that there was something specious in his arguments. But they contained enough truth, just enough truth, to serve as the necessary bait to snare the fish, and once the sharp hook had torn into her tender cheek, she was consigned to—(resigned to)—her place at the bottom of some boat and left flopping and desperate for breath—a fish out of water.

The other half of the night would be spent making love and Donna was always surprised to discover that their performance outside of bed had no effect on their subsequent performance once inside it. If anything, their lovemaking was that much more intense.

It was always the same. Each argument brought the

same results. If her apologies were not immediately forth-
coming, they always hobbled along several days of chill-
ing silence later. And with each fresh apology, her
mother's voice deep inside her became quieter and quieter.

It would be the same tonight, Donna had known as
soon as her husband had walked wearily out of the room,
his back hunched as if he'd been lashed. Except there
would be no lovemaking. Nothing to dull the mind by release of the body. Why had she started up? Would it have
hurt to do the stupid breathing exercises? God, she was
lucky he took such an interest in her pregnancy. Some
husbands didn't care about any of it. Victor was as interested in her condition as if it were happening to himself.
He just wanted to be a part of it, to share it with her.
And his concern about the breathing exercises was
concern for her and for their baby. Why did she begrudge
him so? Concern—or control? the voice inside her asked.
She shoved the voice aside and walked into the bedroom.

"I'm sorry," she said. "Really."

He looked more hurt than ever. "You always are. But
it never changes anything.

"I'm just irritable tonight. I feel a cold coming on."

"Another one?"

She shrugged. "I have that awful post-nasal drip. You
know."

"You didn't take anything for it, did you?" Again,
concern for her pregnancy, their unborn child. Why did it
sound so much like an accusation?

"Of course not." She paused. "You want to do the
breathing?"

He checked his watch. "It's eleven o'clock. It's too
late." He grimaced with invisible pain.

"Something wrong?"

"My stomach has a hard time with your rampages."

Donna said nothing, feeling the sudden weight of Sisyphus' rock descending on her shoulders. She sat down on
the bed and started to remove her clothes. There was
silence while he used the bathroom, a silence which was
only broken by several loud blows of his nose.

"You shouldn't do that," she said when he came out of the bathroom. "You'll destroy the fibers in your nose."

He said nothing. She went into the bathroom. Why did she always feel much worse *after* she apologized.

She crawled into bed beside him. He lay on his back looking up at the ceiling, his hands folded under his head. Donna spent several minutes looking at him before she spoke. "I love you," she said, watching his mouth, waiting for him to reply.

"It's okay," he said, moving an arm out from under his head and moving it toward her, her signal that she was finally being forgiven and it was all right to approach him. She moved into the half-circle his arm created, resting against his chest, running a hand up and down his body while his hand absently stroked her back.

"Why do you give me such a hard time?" he asked softly. Somewhere in her gut, in muted, muffled cries, the voice inside her began screaming.

Chapter 7

"You made this a different way," he said.

"It's the same way I always make shepherd's pie."

"No, it isn't. Something's different. I can taste it."

"Nothing's different. You say that every time."

"Every time it's different."

"It's the same way I always make it. Don't you like it?"

"It's all right. Not as thick as usual."

He rose from the table.

"Where are you going?"

He opened the cabinet door under the sink.

"What are you doing in there?"

He had his hand in the garbage bag.

"I thought so," he said triumphantly, pulling out an empty tin of tomato sauce.

"You thought what?" Donna asked, her finely tuned tentacles sensing a response she would not like.

"Tomato sauce. I thought the recipe called for tomato paste."

"The recipe calls for tomato sauce," she said testily. "Are you going to come back to the table before it gets cold?"

"Let me see the recipe book."

"Don't you believe me?"

"Can't I see the recipe book? No one said I didn't believe you! Jeez, Donna. A little paranoid, aren't you?"

Donna put down her fork and got up from the table. "You know, if I said something like that to you, you'd be furious." She reached into the shelves over the phone where she kept her assorted cookbooks and handed him the well-worn copy of *Second Helpings, Please.*

He took the book from her hand and let out a deep sigh. "Are you going to start something because I asked if I could see the cookbook?"

She looked down at her enormous belly. The doctor had said the baby could come any time now. Her due date was only two weeks away and it was, at best, an educated guess. "No, I'm not trying to start anything."

She watched with growing irritation as he flipped through the pages.

"What's it called?" he asked.

"Hamburger Shepherd's Pie," she answered, walking back to the kitchen table and sitting down. "And it's getting cold."

He read the list of ingredients. "Well, you're right. Tomato sauce is what it says."

"Thank you."

He returned the book to its shelf. "I always thought you used tomato paste."

"I usually do," she said, then immediately wished she hadn't. His eyes shot to hers with lightning speed. She continued quietly. "I made a mistake once and used the tomato paste, and when you said you liked it—"

"You changed it."

"No! I used it. Except today I didn't have any tomato paste so I used tomato sauce which is what the recipe calls for in the first place."

"Then why did you tell me you hadn't changed anything?"

"Because I didn't want to have precisely this conversation."

"We wouldn't be having it if you had told me the truth. I'm not stupid, you know. I knew something was different."

"It tastes the same to me."

"But not to me! I knew right away there was something different."

"Do we have to continue this discussion? We sound like one of those commercials on TV! 'That's not Heinz,' " she mimicked.

"Here goes the mouth."

"Oh, come on. Victor. Does everything have to be such a big deal?"

"You're the one who made it into a big deal. Why did you have to lie about it?"

"I wasn't lying."

"You said that nothing was different."

"Oh God, Victor. Let's just drop it!"

"Sure. Whenever you want to drop something, it just gets dropped."

"You really want to fight about the tomato sauce?"

"It's just your attitude, Donna. It's the same old thing. What's important to Victor is of no consequence. It's too trival to discuss. Every day it's the same damn thing."

"You're swearing," she reminded him.

"Oh, I forgot. Only you're allowed to swear."

"Jesus Christ, Victor," she burst out, "you make me so mad! 'Every day it's the same damn thing!' " she said, going over his words.

"If that's what you say."

"That's what *you* said! Word for word. You said, 'Every day it's the same damn thing.' "

"I don't remember saying that."

"Well, you did. Then I told you you were swearing."

"Oh, yes, I forgot. I'm not allowed to swear. Just you."

"Nobody said that." She was crying.

"Get a Kleenex, Donna."

"No."

"Fine. Don't get a Kleenex."

Silence.

"Aren't you going to finish your supper?"

"I'm not hungry."

"Oh, fine. I make shepherd's pie especially for you—"

"Don't do things especially for me, Donna. It's not worth the price I have to pay."

"I like to do things especially for you," she found herself pleading.

"Maybe. But somehow they never come out the way I like them, do they?"

Just enough truth. She felt the sharp tug at her cheek.

Later, with the apologies still fresh in the air, his following hers ("I'm sorry, too," with such world-weary resignation), his arm around her shoulders, lying side by side in bed, her eyes almost closed to sleep, he spoke. "I don't understand how you could run out of something like tomato paste. Didn't you just go shopping the other day?"

"I forgot to get some." She moved away from him and flopped onto her left side like a giant whale.

"How could you forget? Didn't you make a list?"

"No, I never make lists." Please let me get some sleep.

"No wonder you never have anything! No wonder you're so disorganized!" Eureka. I have found it! "How can you not make a list?"

"I'll make a list," Donna said. "Now please, let me get some sleep."

"How could you not make a list?" he repeated. Even with her back turned and her eyes closed, she knew he was shaking his head.

At 3 A.M. her water broke and the bed was instantly soaking wet. Victor leaped frantically from the bed. "Jesus Christ, what did you do?"

Donna simply smiled at him, her smile a mixture of excitement and perverse satisfaction. Serves him right, she thought, and then immediately felt guilty.

In the end, she had to have a Caesarian section. The doctor had prepared them for that possibility a month before, telling them that the baby was in a breach position and while there was still a good possibility that it would turn itself around, they should be prepared for surgery if it became necessary.

Donna spent twenty-six hours in labor before the doctor decided it was necessary. She and Victor had more than enough time to get her breathing down to perfection, with Victor breathing along beside her the whole time, telling her jokes, encouraging her, wetting her lips with the sponge he had remembered to bring (part of their prenatal instructions), rubbing her back almost constantly.

Donna coped quite well, the excitement she was feeling being sufficient at first to take her mind off the pain. After fifteen hours in labor, no food and no sleep, she began to feel less excitement, more pain. "I'm getting a little tired of this," she announced to Victor. He kissed her forehead and continued to rub her back.

At the end of twenty hours she was becoming increasingly belligerent. "This is ridiculous," she moaned, looking around the small labor room. "Why don't they put a television in here?" The room itself was very pleasant, one wall freshly papered in green and white, bright-colored closets and a Kandinsky print directly across from her bed. "Do I really need all this stuff around me?"

"It's monitoring the baby's heartbeat," Victor said of the large gray computer they had hooked up to her body by means of a special belt that went around her stomach. It traced the baby's heartbeat and seemed to those who know nothing of computers, to work along much the same lines as a lie detector. It also monitored and took note of her contractions.

"Oh, you're having another contraction," Victor stated, obviously startled at its coming so soon after the previous one.

"Thanks for telling me," she gasped.

"A big one. Look at it, honey."

"I don't have to look at it! I can feel it! What do you think I'm doing here?"

"It's very exciting."

"Good—then *you* have the contractions and I'll watch the bloody machine. That's it, I've had enough."

"You must be in transition," he said happily. "Trish said you'd get very irritable during transition."

"Where is she? I'll kill her."

Victor was behind her again rubbing her back. "You should be happy," he said. "Transition means it's almost over. Just another couple of hours."

Only a man could say something like that, she thought.

A woman in one of the next labor rooms let out a piercing, agonizing cry, followed by an enviable string of four letter words. "My sentiments exactly," Donna said. "Look, I've given it my best shot, but I've had enough. It's your turn. I'm going home."

Donna tried to pull herself off the bed. "Donna, for God's sake—"

"Call me when it's over," she said, disconnecting the machine.

"Donna, please—" Victor urged helplessly.

"Call me a taxi, Victor."

Victor called the nurses.

"Spoil sport," she said.

Two hours later she was delirious.

"Twentieth Century-Fox," she exclaimed.

"I beg your pardon?" Victor asked.

"Dr. Harris asked me a question," Donna said impatiently. Dr. Harris had by this time joined them and was sitting at the foot of her bed. "He asked me what movie studio made *The Seven Year Itch* and I told him."

"Jesus."

"That's my line." Suddenly she was crying. "Victor, please, could they give me a shot of something?" She knew he had hoped she could do without any drugs.

"Sure," he responded immediately. "Dr. Harris?"

Dr. Harris administered a shot of demerol, which Donna was disappointed to discover did nothing to ease the always intensifying pain of the contractions. It only made her groggy.

"I don't think the baby's going to drop anymore," she heard Dr. Harris say from afar. The baby, he had told her, was standing straight up. "We better operate. We've waited long enough."

After that everything happened very quickly. She was wheeled into the operating room and placed on the table.

The I.V. unit to which she had been hooked up since she entered the hospital stayed right with her, as did Victor, two lifelines of support. They told her to lie on her side in a fetal position and not to move—not an easy request when one is into hard labor, she realized—and she was given two more shots, the first one a local anesthetic to relieve the subsequent pain of the second one, the epidural, which was to then take away any feelings altogether. She grimaced and gasped loudly as she felt the fluid from the epidural shooting through her spine. It felt as if she were being pounded all along her back with a hammer. Trish, their darling prenatal instructor, had neglected to mention the pain that accompanied an epidural. She had spoken only of the glorifying numbness. The nurse put an oxygen mask over Donna's nose and she felt herself being strapped down and a green sheet being placed in front of her so that the actual operation would be hidden from her sight. Victor was given a seat beside her head. He held her hand and talked to her reassuringly.

"I can feel that," she said suddenly, aware that her flesh was being tampered with though she couldn't tell just how. "I can't breathe."

The anesthetist assured her that she was breathing just fine.

"My nose is all stuffed."

"That's a natural reaction," he told her, then went on to explain why. She didn't hear a thing he was saying. All she heard was the delicious sound of a healthy nine pound five ounce baby boy crying loudly as he was pulled from her stomach and lifted above the sheet so that they could see him.

"Hello, Adam," she said, feeling the tears fill her eyes.

"He's a little tank," Victor said with unmistakable pride.

"It was all those buttertarts you told me not to eat."

He laughed. "I love you," he said.

She smiled into his tearing eyes. "I love you too," she said, feeling a little like the couple in the movie on natural childbirth they had seen at their class. ("Saying I love you at a time like that is so cliché," they had told each other at its heartwarming conclusion.) And yet it was all she really wanted to say. "I love you," she repeated, "I love you."

Adam cried for the next three months. He cried before feedings, after feedings, between feedings, all day and all night. Donna worried that she didn't have enough milk; the doctor assured her Adam was putting on weight; Victor told her to persevere. Donna worried that maybe she should put Adam on a bottle. Dr. Wellington, her pediatrician, told her to do whatever made her the most comfortable; Victor told her to persevere.

Adam cried when he was put in his crib; he cried when he was lifted out. He cried when he was rocked and when he was carried. He cried in the car and in his carriage. His little face turned red and his fists turned white. Sometimes by the time Victor came home from work, Donna's face was as white as Adam's hands and her eyes as red as his face. Both would be crying.

"You're not holding him right or something," Victor said.

"Then you hold him," Donna stated quickly in return, putting the shrieking infant into Victor's arms. Adam screamed harder.

"I wouldn't have done that," Victor said. "You've just disturbed him worse." Victor shifted the baby into another position.

Adam stopped crying. Victor smiled, trying not to look too smug. "There, I told you it's all in the way you hold him."

Adam started screaming again. Donna smiled in spite of herself. Good boy, she found herself thinking.

"I told you you shouldn't have moved him," Victor said angrily, putting the baby back into Donna's arms. "Is it time to feed him?"

"I just fed him an hour ago. And two hours before that."

"Maybe you're feeding him too much," Victor suggested.

"Why don't you ask him?"

"Have you changed his diaper?" he persisted.

"It doesn't bother babies to be wet."

"That's not what I asked you."

"I changed it an hour ago, after I fed him and he pooped all over me."

"Change him again. He's probably uncomfortable."

"Why don't you change him?"

Victor looked sheepish. "He's too little for me to change, Donna. I'll do it when he's older."

"Sure."

"Oh, please, don't start in on me. I've had a hard enough day without getting a hard time from you when I get home."

Donna changed Adam's diaper. It was perfectly dry. Adam kept screaming.

At two in the morning, Donna fed him again. At three he was still screaming. Donna walked into the bedroom.

"It's your turn," she said to Victor who was pretending sleep.

"You want me to feed him?" he demanded angrily. "Tell me how and I will."

"Is this why you were so anxious that I breast feed?"

"Goodnight, Donna," he said, turning on his side and facing away from her. "The baby's crying."

"Then go hold him. I've already held him and I just finished feeding him. *You* can walk him around for a while."

"Donna, I have work tomorrow!"

"What do you think that I do? Sleep all day? With that racket! I have to listen to it all *day*, too."

"Get Mrs. Adilman to come in. She said she'd love to."

"I have. But she's not exactly a spring chicken. There's only so much she can take."

"Meanwhile the baby's still crying."

"He's your son, too," Donna said in a tone which told

Victor there would be no further discussion. She crawled into bed. Victor angrily stalked out.

Three hours later, Adam was still screaming; Victor had not come back. Donna walked into Adam's bright yellow and white nursery. Adam was screaming in his crib; Victor was asleep beside the crib on the floor.

The first time that Adam stopped crying and actually slept through the night, Donna was convinced he was dead. Mrs. Adilman peered in through the kitchen window at Donna who sat at the white round kitchen table slowly savoring her morning cup of coffee. She indicated to Mrs. Adilman that she was welcome to come in.

"Victor went to work early?" Mrs. Adilman asked. It was just eight A.M.

"He had to go to Sarasota for a couple of days. Business."

"And the baby? Sleeping?" she asked, incredulously.

Donna put down her cup of coffee. "I think he's dead. I'm too afraid to look."

Mrs. Adilman looked stunned. "What?"

"He was crying when I went to bed, but he must have stopped sometime in the night when I was asleep. I woke up about half an hour ago. The house is so quiet I can't believe it."

"You haven't checked him?"

Donna looked Mrs. Adilman right in the eye. "I know this is probably going to sound awful," she began, "but I really felt like a cup of coffee this morning, and I knew that if I went in there and he was dead, then I'd never get my cup of coffee, and there'd be nothing I could do anyway so I might as well have my cup of coffee first and then look." Mrs. Adilman stared at her with total disbelief. Victor couldn't have done it any better himself. He had probably called her from Sarasota and asked her to come over.

They checked the baby together. He was sound asleep.

Donna went back into the kitchen and poured herself a second cup of coffee.

Chapter 8

Donna started making lists. Every morning when she woke up, she made herself a list of the things she had to do that day. Now that she was no longer working and Adam had adjusted comfortably to life in the southern United States, she had much more free time. Time to do the laundry, clean the house, pick up clothes at the cleaners, go grocery shopping (for which she had a separate list), go to the dentist, the doctor, the bank, the hardware store, organize small dinner parties, run some necessary errands for Victor and of course, be there to feed Adam, who since the night he'd stopped crying had miraculously put himself on a three-feedings-a-day schedule and given Donna even more time to tend to the things on her various lists.

One day, she made two lists: the things she had to do and the things she hated to do.

She hated:
1. housework
2. cleaning
3. taking the dishes out of the automatic dishwasher and putting them away
4. doing the bills
5. calling the people whom Victor instructed her to complain about various malfunctions around the house
6. "Search for Tomorrow"
7. her hair

8. her clothes
9. the way she looked
10. her body, still not back in shape
11. exercising.

(Items 6 through 10 she realized, were not things she hated *to do*, but since they were things she hated and it was, after all, her list, she decided to write them down anyway.)

Donna made a list of the things that Victor said to her each morning. At the end of each week, she made a separate list of her daily favorites:

1. Your mascara's all over your face. Did you forget to wash it off last night?
2. You snored again. That's a nasty habit you picked up while you were pregnant.
3. You feel all right? You don't look so hot.
4. What's the matter? Are you in a bad mood?
5. Should you be giving him that much pablum?
6. I think you're wrong.
7. No, I don't have time for breakfast. If you'd get me out of bed on time—
8. Did you burp him properly? I didn't hear him burp. Are you sure?
9. Don't scratch your hands. That's why you got the rash in the first place. Honestly, Donna, you're worse than the baby.
10. I don't always criticize you, for God's sake. Are you starting again so early in the morning?
11. No, go ahead. Finish what you have to say. Make me late.
12. What did you do with my keys?
13. You threw out that envelope I asked you to save! Oh no, here it is.
14. I wouldn't dress him that warmly. No, you're the mother. You do it the way you want. You know best. I just don't think he needs to be, well, no, you decide.

15. Do you have anything to do today?
16. I don't know, Donna, I think eight for dinner is more than you can handle.
17. Why aren't you eating a bran muffin? I told you I wanted you to eat a bran muffin every day. That way maybe you won't get so many colds.

She made a list of the things they fought about:

1. the fact he was always criticizing her driving
2. the fact he was always criticizing her appearance
3. the fact he was always criticizing the way she ran the house
4. the fact he was always criticizing the way she was bringing up Adam (spoiling was the word he used most often)
5. the fact that he was always criticizing her. Period.

which led to fights about:

6. the fact that she was always generalizing
7. the fact that he couldn't say a word to her without her accusing him of criticizing her
8. the fact that she was always starting in at him over something
9. the fact that she never gave him enough emotional support
10. the fact that she was always criticizing him. Period.

They never fought about: 1) In-laws (there were none, so to speak); 2) Money (there was enough); 3) Sex (there was plenty and it was still always good, although lately Donna was beginning to feel too worn out under the weight of all their other fights to feel much like participating—a relatively new development).

While Donna sensed that this last area was rife with potential, thus far Victor was either too proud or too much the gentleman to call it to issue. Perhaps because they both sensed it was too major an issue to explore—

they only fought over minor things after all, never over anything of real import, sensing possibly that their life together could not tolerate a rift of larger proportions. Besides it was pretty hard to get mad at your wife when she was always sneezing or throwing up, and Donna seemed to have developed a continuing sort of cold-flu bug in the last couple of months which, while seeming to disappear for a week or two, always returned. She attributed it to a low resistance brought on by fatigue. Victor told her that as long as she continued in her poor eating habits, she was bound to catch all sorts of assorted bugs. She told him her eating habits were fine and to bug off, which led to another fight to add to her continually growing list.

She made two other lists. One of all the things she liked about Victor, one of all the things she didn't. She put them side by side.

The Things I Like	*The Things I Don't Like*
1. His sense of humor	1. He pouts
2. His perseverance, drive	2. He never lets up
3. His take-charge attitude	3. He has to be in total control
4. His arrogance	4. His arrogance
5. He wants the best of everything	5. He expects too much
6. His intelligence	6. He thinks he knows it all
7. His judgment	7. He has to be right all the time
8. He does anything he sets his mind to do well	8. He's a perfectionist
9. He has great theories	9. He has great theories

To her list of likes she added three points: he loved Adam (although she wished he'd spend more time doing the things with Adam he was always telling her to do); he loved her (despite his constant criticism of her, it was, strangely, something she never doubted); and he was still the best lover she'd ever had. She took count. The positives still outweighed the negatives.

"Where are you taking that?" Donna's voice was sharp, as it often was when she was caught off guard.

"Don't get excited. I'll put it back when everybody leaves," Victor answered, smiling.

"But I liked it where it was. Where are you putting it?"

"In the closet. You know I hate all these little things cluttering up the place."

"Victor, my mother gave me that doll. It's from Mexico."

"I know, honey, and I promise I'll put it back in the living room tomorrow, but can't we, for one night, put it in the closet? It won't break."

"But I like it."

"And I don't." Impasse. "Donna, we've had this discussion a hundred times at least since we've been married. I hate a million little do-dads all over every room; you like it—"

"They make the place look homey."

"According to you. According to me, they make it look messy. Now, I know how much a lot of these pieces mean to you and I usually don't say anything, now be fair, do I?"

"No, but—"

"So, I don't think it's out of line for me to ask you for one night, just one night, to do things my way." He walked with the small cloth doll to the hall closet.

"What else have you moved?"

"I just straightened things up a bit."

Donna walked from the kitchen into the living room. "My, my," she said, "but you've been a busy little boy."

"The place was a mess, Donna. I noticed you hadn't gotten around to doing anything about it yet, and there *are* two couples coming over for dinner—"

"I just vacuumed this afternoon."

"Please don't raise your voice."

"Where did you put the dry flowers?"

"They're in the linen closet. Don't say it—I know you like them. Just for tonight, Donna. Please?"

Donna bit down on her lip and walked back into the kitchen. Victor followed close behind.

"Now please don't pull one of your moods," he cautioned.

"One of my moods?"

"You know what I mean." He looked around. "Oh, you made the chicken, huh?"

"Yes. Something wrong?" Donna asked.

"No, that's just fine. I thought I told you I preferred roast."

"No. You didn't."

"I did, I'm sure. Oh well, chicken it is."

"You *like* my chicken with cumberland sauce!"

"I know. Just that I like your roast better. That's all, honey. The chicken always comes out a little dry, that's all."

"Since when? You never said that before."

"I always say it. You don't listen." Victor smiled and raised his eyebrows. It was something he did often. Every time he did it, she wanted to chop his head off with an ax.

"What else are you serving?"

"Potatoes, green beans with pine nuts—"

"Again?"

"The last time I made green beans with pine nuts was over a year ago and it wasn't for the same people."

"You're sure?" She turned her back to him and walked to the fridge. "No soup?" he asked.

"Sorry, I forgot to mention it. Cold cucumber soup. Does that meet with your approval?" She lifted the large terrine of soup out of the fridge.

"That's fine. What are you getting so defensive about? Can't I be interested?" She shrugged. "Here, you're going to drop that." He rushed over and took it from her hands. "Where do you want it?"

"On the counter," she said. On your head, she thought.

"Jesus Christ, what's all over this floor?"

Donna looked at the floor. "Oh," she said, remembering. "Adam spilled some apple juice this afternoon. I thought I'd cleaned it all up."

"It's so sticky. Did you use the mop?"

"No, I got down on my hands and knees and wiped it up."

"You need the mop. This way it stays sticky and you track it into the carpets. No wonder the rugs are starting to look so dirty."

"Oh, Victor, lay off, will you?"

"Look, Donna, we really shouldn't be having company. It's too much for you. Look at you. You're a nervous wreck. I can't say anything to you without your getting all upset. The place is a mess. I'm not angry or anything. I understand you don't have time to clean the whole house while you're looking after Adam, but I told you we didn't have to have anyone over. You're the one who insisted."

"I just said I thought it would be nice. And I still do—if you'd stop picking on me—"

"Picking on you—?" They heard Adam crying. "What's he doing up?"

"I think he's coming down with something."

"I told you to wear a mask around him when you have a cold."

"Victor, the doctor said that wasn't necessary. I asked him. Besides I don't have a cold."

"This week." She walked back to the fridge and opened it, taking a small bottle of medicine out. "What are you doing?"

"I'm going to give him a few drops of Tylenol." She started to walk out of the kitchen.

"The kid cries and you're going to give him medicine?"

"He has a slight fever. I'd like it to break before it gets worse. I called Dr. Wellington. He said to give him Tylenol."

"You know there have been reports that Tylenol can cause liver damage."

"God, give me strength," Donna whispered. "You won't let me give him baby aspirin—"

"Sure, you want him to start bleeding internally?"

"Oh Christ, Victor, does everything have to be a major debate? Can't I do anything without taking it to a vote? Can't I make even one little decision all by myself?"

"You make *all* the decisions around here. When has my word ever counted for anything?"

"Your word always counts."

"Oh, it does? Are you going to give him the Tylenol?"

"He has a fever, Victor. The doctor—"

"Are you going to give him the Tylenol? Yes or no?"

"Yes."

"Of course, we always do everything your way."

Donna felt her eyes filling with tears.

"Why are you crying, Donna?" he taunted. "We're doing what you want to do. We're doing things your way. We're giving Adam the medicine; we're having chicken for dinner; we're having the Vogels and the Drakes over tonight. We're doing everything you wanted. Why are you crying?"

"You're twisting everything all around!"

"You're crying all over your makeup." He checked his watch. "They'll be here in ten minutes. You timed that beautifully. Sure, answer the door with your eyes all teary. Make me the heavy."

Donna tried to wipe her eyes.

"You're smearing your mascara," he said.

"Damn you," she muttered. "Why do you always have to spoil everything?"

"That's good, Donna. Keep it up. Let's really start something here."

Adam began to shriek. Donna turned and walked out of the room.

Dinner started out a strained affair. Donna was very tense. Aside from the odd phrase, she said little for much of the first part of the evening, trying to busy herself in the kitchen, smiling instead of talking, feeling her muscles tightening with the strain. Victor seemed perfectly normal; to his company, he was friendly and talkative. He told several very amusing anecdotes, one of which Donna was loathe to discover, as the evening progressed, she was tempted to laugh at, and would have had she not been so angry. In fact, she had to bite down hard on her lip to keep from laughing and Victor, who noticed everything, took note and smiled. He had obviously decided not to stay angry—why was it always up to him? Perhaps the dinner was better than he'd expected, although she'd burned the pine nuts and the green beans were a touch overdone. After he smiled, Donna felt lighter, less hostile. She realized how much she didn't want to be angry, how pleasant it was when they were nice to each other. Besides, if she didn't signal an appropriate response, she would only be accused of prolonging the fight, of being the one who insisted on war when he had indicated a willingness for peace. And he would, of course, be right. She smiled directly at Victor. The air was starting to clear.

"I love you," she said later, because she needed to feel love.

"I love you," he answered, because it was the expected response.

The rest of the evening was a dramatic change. Donna was gregarious, chatty, even overly friendly. She was pushing, she knew, but it just felt so good not to have someone mad at her. When the evening was over and the Vogels and the Drakes had gone home, Victor checked Adam and found him sleeping like the baby he was. Even at fifteen months, they still almost always referred to him as a baby.

"Sound asleep," Victor said, crawling into bed beside Donna, his arm encircling her immediately. "I checked his head. It feels cool."

"That's good," Donna said. She was so tired. He leaned over her. "Please, Victor, can we just go to sleep tonight? I'm really tired."

He looked hurt but moved back to his side of the bed. "Turn over," he said simply. "I'll hold you."

Donna turned over, moving into the warmth of his curved body.

"I love you," he said, because he needed to feel love.

"I love you," she answered, because it was the expected response.

Several minutes went by and then she spoke again. "Last night I dreamed you had an affair," she said.

"Oh?"

"Yea. Except you were really big and fat."

"Oh, well, that explains it."

"What?"

"I always get big and fat when I have an affair."

She laughed, and the tensions which had remained despite the truce finally disappeared. She turned toward him, feeling suddenly not tired at all and his arms moved quickly around her. She desperately wanted everything to be all right between them. So, she suspected, did he.

"I love you," he said, because he meant it.

"I love you," she answered, because she wanted to mean it.

Chapter 9

"How long until you're ready?" he called from the living room.

"Just another couple of minutes. Why don't you have a drink in the meantime?"

"I'm already having my second. Do you want me drunk before we even get there?"

"I'll be there in a minute."

Donna checked her appearance in the mirror, liked what she saw, put a final brush of color on her cheeks, fluffed out her hair and walked into the living room. Tonight was going to be different, she had resolved earlier. They would not fight. She would not bait him or otherwise goad him; she would be agreeable and charming. She would support him, compliment him, often and sincerely in front of the other guests at Danny Vogel's party, and she would try desperately hard not to cough, sneeze or otherwise indicate to anyone that she had a cold, despite a deepening case of laryngitis. She would also not discuss Adam unless absolutely pressed because Victor always hated when other people talked about their children. In short, she would be the perfect wife; she would give the one hundred percent Victor was always lecturing her about—no, that was wrong. Definitely getting off to a bad start if she kept that attitude up. He didn't lecture her; he only made conversation, and eminent sense at that. Whatever happened, whatever was said or done, they would not fight. Their fight of the other evening (she really couldn't remember how it started or what it was about although she suspected sexual tension was the ultimate culprit) had been enough to convince her that these endless battles had to stop. They simply couldn't keep screaming at each other the way they did, not just because of themselves, for their own sakes, but for Adam who was now past two years old and beginning to be affected by the things he saw and heard around him. After the other night, when Adam had been begging them to stop yelling at each other and they had merely ignored his pleas and kept on, it had been somehow frightening to watch him turn his little back and start playing right along side them, ignoring them entirely, blocking them out as if they really weren't there. She had decided that night that there would be no more fights. Maybe she couldn't control Victor's temper, but she could control her own, and it took two to make a fight. She would not allow herself to be drawn into one again. She would not be responsible for creating a scene; she would not contribute to its survival.

And they had to start making love again on a regular basis. Their sex life had always been wonderful; now it was becoming nonexistent. This was her fault more than his, she knew. But increasingly, she couldn't bring her mind or body to make love when the only emotions she was feeling were resentment and even hatred. Worse than hate—despair. She couldn't play the whore—a two-cent whore, at that, because lately that was all she felt she was worth. If she allowed him to make love to her, to crawl over her, to enter her, she feared she would disappear altogether, lost under his crushing weight, bruised beyond recognition, if she was ever found at all.

She stopped herself. If she was going to make tonight work, she had to stop thinking like that. All other nights were in the past. Today was the first day of the rest of her life and all that malarky.

She walked up behind Victor. "Hi. I'm ready."

He turned. "Is that what you're going to wear?"

Immediately, she felt her resolve start to crumble. Immediately, she stopped herself, coached herself, what was the matter with her? Couldn't he ask a simple question? He couldn't be expected to know what she had been thinking. He was entitled to say what he wished. She shouldn't have expected him to say exactly what she wanted to hear. There it was again—her expectations. Always getting them into trouble. If only she had no expectations, she would be much better off. They would both be a lot happier.

"Don't you like it?"

"I've never liked it before," Victor said. "Why would you think I'd suddenly start liking it now?"

"I thought you did."

"No, Donna." He put down his drink. His voice was calm, not at all unpleasant. "But what does it matter what I like? You're going to wear it anyway."

Donna tried to smile. "What would you like me to wear?"

"Forget it, Donna," he said, checking his watch. "It's late."

"There's time. I'll hurry and change. Just tell me what you'd like me to wear."

"What about the blue dress?"

"Blue dress?"

"Forget it."

"Wait a minute, what blue dress?"

"The one with the little flowers on the sleeves."

"Flowers on the sleeve—Oh! Oh! That's not blue, it's pale green."

"So sue me, I got it wrong. I made a mistake. I'm sorry." He bowed in mock supplication.

"You don't have to apologize. It's just that I didn't know which dress you meant when you said blue—"

"You've made your point."

Donna felt herself about to respond angrily, stopped herself just in time, and took a breath.

"I'll go change."

"Don't do it for me," he called after her.

Several minutes later, he followed her into the bedroom. The red and black dress she'd had on lay discarded on the bed. She stood in front of the full-length mirror adjusting the pale green dress she had replaced it with.

"What do you think?" she asked. She had to admit, it did look better.

"Not bad," he said. "But the makeup's wrong."

She turned abruptly back to the mirror. "What's wrong with it?"

"Too obvious. It was fine for red and black, but it looks cheap with the green."

"Cheap? Don't you think you're going a bit overboard?"

"Suit yourself. I'm just telling you the dress looks great but your face looks bargain basement."

Donna looked at the floor. She would not cry, she repeated to herself, she would not lose her temper. His sexual frustration was talking now, not him, and she was the one responsible for that condition. "How do you think I should do it?"

"However you want. It's your face."

"Please, Victor, I'm asking your opinion."

"I'd just tone it all down. Be as natural as possible."

"I really don't have very much on."

"Are you kidding? You're wearing enough to make Emmett Kelly jealous."

Donna walked quickly into the bathroom and washed her face. She redid her makeup, applying only a cream under her eyes (to disguise the bags) and around the sides of her nose (to disguise the peeling—her nose was raw from blowing it), a touch of blush-on and some mascara. She sneezed just before Victor could give her his final seal of approval.

"Jesus, what did you do that for?" he asked.

"I didn't exactly do it on purpose, Victor."

"Go clean your face," he said, and Donna returned to the bathroom to wash the mascara off her cheekbones.

"I don't know how you managed to get another cold," he said on their way out to the car. They had called Mrs. Adilman as they were leaving and she had come right over. "Thank God *someone* around here gets places on time."

She ignored the latter remark, answered the former. "I get them from Adam," she said. "Now that he's in nursery school two mornings a week, he brings home lots of colds. They call it Nursery Nose."

"Maybe you should be sending him somewhere else."

They got into the car.

"It would be the same thing," Donna said, continuing the conversation. "Besides, there is nowhere else. I checked all over. This is the only place where they'll take him only two mornings a week."

"What about Montessori?"

"He'd have to go every day."

"What's wrong with that?"

"He's a little young yet, Victor, he's only two and a bit. How many years of school do you want him to have?"

"You've got to let go some time, you know," he cautioned, putting the key in the ignition.

"It's not a question of letting go—"

"Are you going to start?"

Donna immediately stopped talking. "I'm sorry," she said quickly. "I really wasn't trying to start anything."

"You don't have to try," he said, then immediately added, "you better drive. If a policeman stopped me, I'd never pass the breathalyzer test."

"Back to jail," she said, trying to stir what she now thought of as fond memories.

"You'd like that, wouldn't you," he answered. They changed seats. She started the car. The radio came on immediately, flooding the space between them. Donna turned it down. Victor quickly turned it back up. Neither spoke. She backed out of the carport.

"Wave goodbye to Mrs. Adilman," he instructed. They both waved at the plump, graying woman who stood at the door waving them good night as she had obviously done years before with her own children.

"Do you think she'll get mad at us if we're out past midnight?" Donna asked, trying to joke.

"Be careful, you almost hit that garbage can."

Donna checked her rearview mirror. "I'm nowhere near that garbage can."

"Are you going to drive? We're already half an hour late."

"It's a party, Victor, no one is going to arrive exactly on time."

"If they were your friends, we'd be there on time, you can bet on it."

"That's not fair, Victor. And it's not true."

"Oh really?"

"Besides, I don't have any friends."

"My fault, I suppose."

"No," she said, feeling somewhat that it was. "You can't help it if you're not comfortable with any of them."

"You could still see them on your own."

"It's a little difficult when they work all day and I'm at home with Adam."

"You're saying you want to go back to work?" he asked.

"No. Not yet."

"What do you mean, not yet?"

"I may go back next year part-time while Adam's in nursery," Donna said, voicing these thoughts for the first time.

"Oh, I see. When it's convenient for you, then Adam's not too young anymore."

"Next year he'll be three years old! That's when all kids start nursery!"

"You're raising your voice."

Donna was surprised to realize that she had. "I'm sorry. How did we get on this topic anyway? All I wanted to say was that it's a little difficult for me to see what few friends I have when they work all day and you won't socialize with them at night."

"So, it's all my fault," Victor concluded.

"I'm not saying that."

"What are you saying?"

"Forget it."

"Incidentally, do you know where you're going? We passed the turn-off three blocks ago."

"Well, why didn't you tell me?" She stopped the car.

"You were too busy yelling at me." She turned the car around, found the right street and made her turn.

"You always turn corners that fast?" he asked accusingly.

"It wasn't fast."

"Took the curb off the sidewalk. How fast are you going anyway?"

"Victor, who is driving this car, you or me?"

"I just asked how fast you were driving. Can't I ask you a simple question? Jeez! Starting with your mouth already. Can't help yourself, can you? I mean it would really kill you to have one nice evening."

"I don't believe this," Donna muttered, feeling the tears start behind her eyes.

"Christ, Donna," he yelled, as she slammed her foot on the brakes inches before a stop sign. "Where are you looking? You almost drove through that stop sign!"

"I didn't though, did I?"

"You trying to kill us?"

"I stopped," she said, starting again.

"What were you thinking about?!"

"Victor, you're making me a nervous wreck, will you please shut up!"

"Oh, it's my fault you almost missed the stop sign!"

"Nobody said it was your fault!"

"You're yelling."

"You're driving me crazy! Will you just let me drive?"

"What—so you can kill us the next time?"

"I'd be fine if you'd just shut up."

"Stop yelling at me!" he shouted.

"Shut-up!" she screamed in return, the words exploding upon impact with the air. "Shut-up! Shut-up! Shut-up!"

She drove through a red light.

"Jesus Christ, are you crazy?! You *are* trying to kill us," he yelled. "Pull over. Did you hear me? Pull over!"

"I didn't see it! I didn't see it!"

Victor reached over her, grabbed the wheel and steered the car to the side of the road. "Get out of the car."

"Victor," she cried, the tears she had been pushing back erupting now with double force. "I didn't see the lights!"

"I know. And you didn't see the stop sign. And it's all my fault."

He pulled her out from behind the wheel. She shook his arm free. "Don't touch me," she said, trying to wipe her eyes.

He looked at her, suddenly calm. "Oh, is that what this is all about?"

"What are you talking about?"

"You didn't have to almost kill us to get out of sleeping with me tonight. I'm getting used to the word no."

Donna couldn't believe what she was hearing. Over and over in her mind she replayed the words. She still couldn't get them to make any sense.

"I didn't see the red light!" she cried out in desperation. "You were yelling at me about the stop sign and you wouldn't drop it and I started yelling and got so upset I missed the stoplight! It had nothing to do with sleeping with you!"

"It's all my fault," he said sarcastically, shaking his head. "I'm the one who drove through the stop sign and the red light."

"I didn't say that."

"Oh? So you're willing to concede that *you* were driving. Interesting."

"I was trying to."

"And I wouldn't let you. Is that it? Get in the car, Donna. Or do you want everyone who drives by to think I'm beating you up? Is that part of the plan?"

They walked around the car in opposite directions and got inside, Victor now behind the wheel, Donna, shaking, at his side.

"You *are* beating me up," she said as he started the car. "Just that the bruises don't show."

"You're crazy," he said to her. "Sometimes I really worry about my son's safety."

"What?"

The word came out in a hoarse whisper, Donna's voice finally giving in to battle fatigue and shell shock. She started to cough and continued until Victor pulled the car to a sudden halt.

"What are you stopping for?" she asked through her tears.

"We're here."

"Here? You mean we're still going to the party?"

"Well, I don't know about you, but I certainly am. Late though we are."

"I look a mess."

"Par for the course these days."

"Victor—"

"Don't start in on me. I've had enough for tonight. Now," he paused, choosing his words deliberately, "I am going inside. You have two choices. You can either come with me and try to have a good time, abhorrent though I know that thought is to you, or you can stay out here and sulk like a little girl. I'll be embarrassed, of course, but I'll deal with it. Either way," he added, getting out of the car, "I'm going inside."

Donna felt herself being lifted out of the car by the force of her own panic. Maybe she *had* been trying to kill them. Who knew anymore? Certainly anything would be better than this. Certainly at this moment, she wanted to die. Then she thought of Adam. Her beautiful little boy. And she knew she didn't really want to die at all. She wanted Victor to die.

The realization made her gasp for air.

"What's the matter now?" he asked her.

No, please, please. I didn't mean it. I didn't mean it. "Victor, please can we talk?"

"You've said enough." A familiar refrain.

"Please."

"Wipe your eyes." They reached the front door and Victor rang the bell.

Danny Vogel, looking every one of his forty years and more, answered, a drink in his hand, his beer belly protruding over his obviously new Gucci belt.

"Gotta lose weight," he said instead of hello. "You're late. We were starting to think you might not make it."

"Wouldn't miss it."

Donna kept her head down as they walked inside. She kept in Victor's shadow, reluctant to show her face. It felt puffy and streaked. Not until she caught sight of herself in one of the hall mirrors and saw that despite the swelling around her eyes and her newly red nose, she looked presentable, did she lift her head.

"Happy birthday," she said huskily, then cleared her throat.

"You have another cold?"

Donna nodded. Victor reached in his pocket and handed her several Kleenex.

"Can I get you a drink?"

"Gin and tonic," Victor answered.

"Scotch and water," Donna said, wondering why, since she rarely drank scotch and water.

"Coming right up," Danny said smiling. "Mingle, children, mingle."

Victor took his cue immediately and disappeared into one of the groups of well-wishers. Donna looked around her. There were about thirty people there, she calculated quickly, not one of whom she wanted to talk to. She didn't know at least half the people there and had exhausted whatever she'd had to say to the others at the last party they attended.

Whatever happened to those wonderful teenage parties? she found herself thinking as she walked absently through the people, settling finally on a place not far from the bar, where she could observe and yet not have to participate. The kind of parties where you played records and danced and then turned off the lights and necked with whoever was closest by and prayed his braces wouldn't get caught with yours, and someone always told the story about the two dogs that were "doing it" and got stuck together until someone finally came out and threw cold water over them. Whatever happened to those parties? Why did they always have to grow up into the kind of party where everyone stands around with a drink and a phony smile complaining about their work and their kids and their lives? Was everyone as unhappy as she was? Was that what married life was all about?

"Scotch and water," Danny Vogel said, suddenly beside her. She took the drink and said nothing. "You should see the cake that Renee made for me," he said proudly. "She shaped it like a giant penis." He waited for her reaction and continued when he got none. "That's not supposed to be flattering," he explained. "She said it's because I'm a big prick!" He laughed, flattered nonetheless.

"Why do men always feel complimented when women tell them they're pricks? I don't understand, is there a special prize for hurting women?"

"Uh, excuse me," Danny Vogel said, and retreated quickly.

Donna took a long look around the room. It reminded her of the room in which Anne Bancroft had tried to seduce a wary Dustin Hoffman in *The Graduate*, a movie she had seen three times. Anne Bancroft had sat on a bar stool very similar to the one just to her left and lifted her knee provocatively into the air. Dustin Hoffman had stood rather nonplussed a safe distance away. It was that kind of a room. Most of the funiture had been cleared away to make room for the guests; what remained was of the white-and-black vinyl variety, modern and cold. The Vogels' sense of art was restricted to waterfalls and big-eyed children. Somehow their choice of friends seemed to suit the room perfectly.

She took a small sip of her drink, realized immediately that she hated the taste and wondered who she was to feel so superior to everyone here. Was misery in any way superior to enjoyment? Had she really become a martyr to the cause? If so, what was the cause?

She looked at some of the faces around her. Some were deeply tanned, most were not, native Floridians being much more careful of the sun than those who came only for a vacation. Most of the faces were smiling; some were openly affectionate. Arms intermingled, hands touched, the odd kiss on the cheek was extended. There was obviously a place somewhere for warmth.

But not with Victor.

From time to time, various people approached her. She said nothing to their small talk. Eventually they went away. Danny Vogel made another attempt, muttered something about his child and Montessori schools and finally excused himself when she made no response.

What had happened to them? She took another slow sip of her drink, remembering back to that first drink of Dom Perignon they had shared together. She remembered their whirlwind flight to New York. The lobster boiled precisely seven and a half minutes. She had let him order for her even then.

How exciting it had all been. How attracted she was to him. So excited, so attracted, she'd married him despite growing doubts, the knowledge he had lied to her about his mother.

Her own mother had once advised her to watch how a man treated his mother; it was indicative of how he would behave to a wife. She shuddered, then shook her head slowly, realizing how long it had been since she had even thought about her mother, how long it had been since she'd had time to think about anything except Victor. She was always so on guard. Everything she said; everything she did. What did she say? What did she do?

She didn't read anymore, at least nothing more demanding than a magazine—magazine mentality, Victor described it. But she simply lacked the concentration to tackle even a Gothic novel, let alone an author like Albert Camus.

She never went to movies. Victor hated them—he boasted often that the last movie he had seen was *High Noon* although he watched *The Magnificent Seven* every time it came on television. At one point in her life, Donna had gone to a movie at least four times a week. Now, there was just no time.

She had given up her job, although that had truly been her decision. She didn't want anyone else bringing up her child. She wanted those first three years at home, then she would go back to work. No, it wasn't Adam's existence she begrudged in any way. He was her salvation. She may occasionally have tired of his demands, of his whining, of his assorted schedules, of not even being able to go to the bathroom without him sitting on her lap, but she enjoyed him, she always loved him.

She no longer loved Victor.

It was that simple.

For a long while she had been telling herself that if she didn't love him deep down (why not up front instead of deep down?), then she wouldn't get so angry at him, that love and hate were flip sides of a coin and that if she was capable of the kind of loathing she at times felt for him, she must also be capable of that kind of love.

But that was a convenient rationalization, an easy excuse.

When was the last time they had talked without arguing? When was the last time they had discussed haiku poetry? Probably the first time. When was the last time they had looked at each other with trust, not had to search every utterance for possible misinterpretations before speaking?

He was probably as unhappy as she was.

They were both miserable, and they were making their son miserable. Adam, she thought. Victor had been wonderful throughout their son's birth.

Of course he'd been wonderful, she snapped at herself. Everyone can be wonderful for twenty-four hours out of a lifetime! That wasn't fair, she knew, but who cared. She was tired of trying to be fair. All right, Victor wasn't a monster—he had his fine moments, he was kind to old ladies and stray dogs—and he was even a decent man most of the time. Just something was wrong with the two of them. Together. Perhaps it had been the same way with his first wife, she didn't know. It really wasn't important. What was important was the way he was to her, and no matter how you tried to judge it, how far you bent over to be fair, the fact was that their marriage was a disaster. If he was to blame, she was crazy to stay. If she was to blame, it meant the same thing. Whoever was at fault, him, her, both of them, the plain truth was that they were making each other miserable, and she was too young to throw away the rest of her life because she didn't know what else to do. She knew what else to do.

She had to leave Victor.

The massive rock lifted from her shoulders. For the first time all evening, her nose felt clear, her throat unrestricted.

Victor was walking toward her.

"Are you going to stand here all night? Not talk to anyone?"

"I've been thinking," she said.

"What about?"

She shook her head. "I'll tell you later. Now isn't the time."

"It's as good a time as any."

She looked up into his eyes. They were very blue, surprisingly soft. Maybe this was the right time after all. When he was relaxed, when she couldn't be accused of acting out of a fit of pique. She didn't know. Surprisingly, she didn't care. He had asked, pushed for an answer. He would get it.

"I think we should get a divorce." The words were soft yet strong. Forceful, without being loud. The kind of quiet conviction that comes when one is absolutely certain one is doing the right thing. He understood that quality in her voice immediately, and so he asked for no repetitions or clarifications.

They shared several seconds of absolute silence.

"I love you," he said at last.

"You don't," she responded.

"Please don't tell me how I feel," he asked, a slight edge to his voice.

"I'm sorry," she said. Four exchanges and already she was sorry. Of course he was right. She hated to be told how she felt; she shouldn't be doing the same thing to him. Oh, Goddamn it, did she really have to go through this tortuous thought process every bloody time she said something? "I'm sorry, Victor, this isn't the time to discuss it."

"Then why bring it up? A hell of a time to drop a bomb like this on me!"

"You asked."

He shifted uneasily, keeping one eye toward the other guests and one on her. "You really want to embarrass me, don't you?"

"No," she stated simply.

"It doesn't matter how I feel about you?"

"Feel about me? Victor, you told me you loved me not two minutes ago and already we're fighting, the accusations are flying. Maybe you *do* love me, maybe you don't. It doesn't really matter anymore how we feel about each other. What's relevant is that we can't live together. We can't, and you know it."

"I don't know it."

She shrugged, about to say "I'm sorry," but stopped herself and said nothing.

"What about Adam?" he asked.

Immediately, she felt a sinking feeling in the pit of her stomach, a buzzer like a smoke detector ringing endlessly in alarm behind her ears. Just as a horse senses when its rider is afraid, so she knew had Victor intuitively felt her fear. Though her voice remained soft, it had lost its strength, its conviction was now forced.

"What *about* Adam?" she asked in return.

"You're planning on divorcing him as well?"

"Of course not. I'll take Adam with me."

"Oh?"

She stared hard at Victor. This was just a gambit, she told herself. He was using her fear of losing her son to make her stay. But he would never follow through.

"I wouldn't leave my son," she said.

"What makes you think that *I* would?"

Donna felt herself beginning to panic again. She fought for control.

"We'll discuss it later," she said, knowing it was futile.

"No, you're the one who insisted we discuss it now. Let's finish it."

"We'll talk about it at home."

"Oh? You're still going to let me come in the house? Very kind of you considering it was mine to start out with."

"Victor, please—"

"Let me tell you one thing, little lady, so you better listen. No one—not you, not some fancy lawyer, not the courts, no one, is ever going to take my son away from me. I'll fight you till there's nothing left of you. And in case you have any doubts that I'm telling the truth, remember that I'm the guy who spent two days in jail rather than pay a parking ticket—"

"A stop sign," she said numbly.

"What?"

"The ticket was because you went through a stop sign." The irony of the entire evening hit her like a sharp poke in the ribs, and she coughed up a flood of tears.

"Jesus," Victor said, trying to block her body with his own.

"Something wrong?" asked a woman nearby, approaching quickly.

"My wife has a cold," Victor said hastily. "Here, wipe your eyes." He handed her a Kleenex. Donna ignored it, continuing to sob.

"Donna, sweetie," Victor soothed for his gathering audience, "come on, honey. It'll be all right. It's a terrible cold," he explained. There were about five people gathered around them now. Donna sniffed loudly. The small gathering quickly began to disperse. Victor held a Kleenex in front of Donna's nose. "Blow," he commanded.

Inside her, Donna felt the scream beginning to build, and waited for the sound. Instead, she was surprised to see her right arm shoot up from her side and slap whatever part of Victor was closest at hand with such force that it caused his drink to fly from his outstretched arm and spew its contents down the backside of one of the ladies who had only minutes ago been so solicitous.

Victor was like an octopus—he quickly had the drink wiped up, the dress restored, his glass recovered, and the guests convinced an unruly sneeze had been the culprit. Donna saw from the faces of several of the guests that they would not be fooled. From their distance they had seen what had actually occurred. Seen Victor's hand outstretched, offering a Kleenex to his ever-sickly wife, seen her own hand shoot out in full attack, seen the results. They heard nothing. Victor's wife—just one of her moods. Poor Victor. Well, what the hell, if that was what they wanted—

Victor leaned over her. "If you don't start smiling and taking an active part in this little celebration, I'm going to have you committed," he said with the same quiet force her voice had earlier contained.

—that was what they were going to get.

Donna took the proffered Kleenex, blew her nose loudly and then walked boldly into the center of one little clique which had hastily regrouped after the little glass-spilling episode had been resolved.

"We were just talking about a neighbor of ours," one of the women informed her, moving to include her into the conversation. It was a nice gesture but Donna was no longer in the mood for nice gestures, preferring to turn a critical eye on all those around her. The woman was maybe ten years older than Donna and her hair was several shades of yellow, although Donna realized even as she criticized that the woman was undeniably attractive. "He had a nervous breakdown a number of years back. The doctors said he was a sadomasochist with homosexual tendencies. Apparently, they were able to cure his masochism and reorient his tendencies very quickly, but he remained a sadist for some time."

"I think sadism is so much healthier than masochism,

don't you?" Donna asked, not altogether sure if she was serious or not.

Neither were the people present who responded to her query with uneasy laughter.

"Anyway," the woman continued, "he's out now and working at a respectable job. All straightened out, it seems."

"What sort of job?" somebody asked.

"He designs underground parking lots," Donna shouted, this time not waiting for anyone else to laugh before she broke into gales of laughter of her own.

The other guests began to turn slowly away from whatever conversations they were engaged in and follow Donna's progress around the room.

Donna continued. "I heard someone over here talking about what a lot of bees there are around this year. Isn't that the truth?! I've never seen so many bees."

"I've never seen so many flowers," said another woman somewhat smugly.

"Oh God, couldn't you puke!" Donna roared. If anyone had not been watching her, they were now. "That's like saying, 'When fate hands you a lemon, make lemonade!' People who say things like that make me want to throw up," she looked at the woman, the smugness obliterated by shock. "No offense meant," she added.

She saw Victor walking toward the front door. Oh well, if he was going to have her committed, she might as well go down in a blaze of glory. "Did any of you see 'Sesame Street' the other day? I'm sure some of you are young enough to have small children. No one watches 'Sesame Street'?" If anyone did, no one was saying so. "Well, it's practically a religious experience around our house. Adam and I watch it every day." Victor was shaking his keys, something he always did to indicate when he was ready to leave. She ignored him. "Well, the other day, and I tell you this in peril of my life because Victor hates to talk about children, he says it's boring to other people—hah! I can see you're certainly not bored. Well, they did this take-off on 'Masterpiece Theatre'—you know, they always do little things that the kids don't catch but the adults all appreciate—and they called it '*Monster*piece Theatre.' And the host was Allister Cookie, the cookie monster, of course doing Allister Cooke. And the play they did was *Upstairs, Downstairs*. And all it was was Grover running up and down the stairs, you know, to illustrate the concept of up and down. You all know who Grover is—"

"Donna," Victor called, the shaking of the keys having failed to move her, "I think we better go."

"My master's voice," Donna said, dripping with sarcasm.

He walked over to her. "You really shouldn't drink when you're taking antibiotics."

"Oh, hello, Victor. Congratulations. I didn't realize your medical certificate had arrived in the mail." She turned to the other guests. "You send in two boxtops from Preparation H—"

The rest of what transpired was pretty much a blur. It took several more minutes of cajoling, reasoning and bullying before Victor was able to get her out of the house. She remembered shouting some vague obscenities—nothing as specific as she would have liked—and wondering why she was behaving this way and then thinking it didn't really matter—nothing did, and soon she was sitting in the car beside a Victor so silent, she could actually feel his rage inside her own body, growing and about to implode. She closed her eyes.

She was surprised to discover, as the car pulled to a halt under their carport, that she had actually slept all the way home.

She walked almost dreamlike past Mrs. Adilman, heard Victor thank her, pay her and show her out before she reached Adam's door. Out of habit, she opened it and checked on her sleeping son, then she walked across the hall to the bedroom she shared with Victor. All she wanted to do was go to sleep. She had never felt so exhausted in her life. The only night that had in any way approximated the way she was feeling now was the night her mother had died, a night she had sat up by the telephone, knowing it would ring, praying it would not. And when it had, at about 3 A.M., she had been startled nonetheless. Oh my God, no! It's the hospital, the nurse had said. You better come, your mother's very low. Is she—? She's very low. Donna had called a cab, not trusting herself to drive. Her father was already at the hospital, her sister was with him. Only Donna had come home, hoping perhaps irrationally that by not keeping a deathwatch, death would go elsewhere where he received greater attention, thinking how strange it was that when humans assigned death a human form, it was always male whereas life was always a woman. Her mother.

Donna sat down on the bed and began unzipping the back of her green dress. In front of her she saw the back of the cab driver, his black hair slick with cream. She had told him where she was going and to please hurry. Are you a nurse? he had asked, trying to make conversation. No, she had answered, my mother is dying.

Donna stood up and stepped out of her dress. Absently, she picked it up and threw it over a chair. There had been no further conversation. The cab driver had stepped on the gas pedal and gotten her to the hospital in record time. She walked inside, found the proper elevator and somehow made it up to the eleventh floor. She saw her sister as soon as she turned the corner. Joan's face was bloated and red and her knees were obviously about to give way beneath her. She stood alone in the middle of the hallway. Nurses passed her; no one noticed that she was about to collapse. Donna rushed toward her, encircling the child in her arms, realizing even as she did so that when your mother dies, you're not somebody's little girl anymore. Immediately, Joan's knees gave out, wobbling toward the floor. She held onto Donna as if Donna were made out of granite. Who is holding *me* up? Donna wondered, as the two sisters stood in the center of the sterile corridor and sobbed.

Donna walked into the bathroom and splashed some

water on her face. The effect was negligible. She spread
some toothpaste on her toothbrush and brushed her teeth,
then she rinsed her mouth and walked back into the bedroom, discarding her bra, panties and shoes on her way to
the bed. She pulled down the covers and crawled inside.

When they had let her go into the room, the first thing
she felt was the stillness. Her father sat numbly on the
bed, slouched over and motionless, almost like a piece of
sculpture by George Segal, white papier-mâché instead of
flesh, an overabundance of feeling so strong that it became no feeling at all. Frozen in time.

Donna closed her eyes, aware now that Victor had just
entered the room. She would not see him.

Her eyes moved from her father who sat at the foot of
the hospital bed, up to the body of her mother. Funny,
she thought, how quickly it becomes "a body." But that
was precisely what it was, she thought. It wasn't her
mother. Most assuredly not her mother. The face was so
thin, the body beneath the white sheet just a skeleton, the
lines of her hips and bones so painfully evident. Her eyes
were closed, her mouth open. Someone had hurriedly af-
fixed her wig and it balanced somewhat askew atop her
head, too large for her. Donna had walked past her father
and stood by her mother's face, looking at it without
searching for any answers, knowing there were only facts.

She had leaned over and kissed her mother on the forehead, her flesh in the middle ground between warm and
cold. What amazed her was the total absence of breath.
Of life. What had been her mother, truly been the essence
of her mother, was gone. And so, she realized, what she
was kissing was not her mother at all. She was kissing a
memory: the memory of her mother's back as she walked
up a flight of stairs, of the time she made a chicken pie
and forgot to add the chicken, of the laughter they had
shared when Donna, at age eight, had come home from
school and told her first dirty joke ("and the thunder
rolled over the mountains and the little boy ran in the
cave"), of her anger so healthy and honest, of her arms,
of her eyes, of her smell, so soft and reassuring. When she

held you and you felt her arms around you, her smell encircling you, and you knew you were safe—you're nobody's little girl anymore—

Donna tried to move.

She couldn't

The smell.

A different smell. Donna tried to move.

She couldn't

She opened her eyes.

He was on top of her and he was a stranger. She opened her mouth to speak, but his hand quickly covered it. "Just shut up for a change, Donna," he said. He was moving her legs, trying to force them apart. The weight of his body was fully on her own. She couldn't move. She could barely breathe. "Open your legs, dammit," he shouted, though his voice stayed below a whisper. She tried to twist away, but her arms were pinned down at her sides. He prodded her with angry fingers; she glared at him with frightened eyes, more frightened than she had ever been, of anything, of anybody. God, please just let me die, she wished as he moved her body into position, boring into her as if he were a drill, scratching at her insides, inflicting all the pain he could manage. She was dry and unresponsive; when he was inside her and pounding against her, she thought only of the son they had somehow created together, from this same act. No, not this same act. There were no similarities.

When he was finished, he moved without apologies away from her and into the bathroom. She remained motionless, her eyes closed, her mouth open, her hair a loosely fitting wig. She knew only a few things, but those things she knew for absolute certain. Her mind created an imaginary list, bold-faced black type over a white corpse.

1. She could never leave Victor. He would never let her. He had proved that tonight.
2. She would never let him touch her again. If he did, she would kill him.
3. She would never yell at him again. She would do

whatever he wanted as long as he agreed never to touch her. But he would get no more arguments from her. Nothing was important enough to fight over. Not anymore.

4. She would never again drive a car.
5. She was dead. As dead as she would ever be.

Chapter 10

Mrs. Adilman looked grayer and plumper than when Donna had last seen her. Unlike most of the other witnesses who carefully avoided looking anywhere in her direction, Mrs. Adilman had smiled and said hello as she walked past Donna to take her place on the stand. Donna was surprised to learn the woman's first name was Arlene, something she had never thought to ask her. She was surprised also to discover that the woman was only fifty-six, a fact well suppressed by the cotton housedresses and comfortable walking shoes she always wore. Mrs. Adilman seemed to Donna, then and now, as the epitome of the kindly grandmother, the one who brought you cookies and could always be persuaded to read just one more bedtime story. The kindly grandmother who was about to whip off her false front and reveal the wolf underneath. Why Grandmother, what big teeth you have!

They dispensed with the unarguable facts quite quickly. She had met Donna when Donna had first married Victor and moved into his house (stress possession of house); they had become better acquainted with the passage of time and especially with the birth of Victor's son (an interesting interpretation, Donna thought). Donna was a very sweet girl (thanks a lot, lady) but very susceptible to colds and flu bugs. (Must we sit through this again?) This was especially true after Sharon was born. Mrs. Adilman seemed to be there at least two days a week while Donna was in bed. Her behavior became increasingly strange (that word again). Objection. Overruled. Moving rapidly from the realm of the unarguable. She would often see the lights on at all hours of the night. Once, when she had to get up to go to the bathroom, she noticed the lights on in the Cressy house and Donna up washing the living room walls. It was almost four A.M., and Donna had spent the day sick in bed. She knew that because she had come in to look after the children. After that, whenever she had to get up in the middle of the night, which she often did, her kidneys subject to infections easily, you know, she always looked to see if the lights at the Cressy's were on. They always were. Donna was always up. Cleaning.

And as a mother?

Donna held her breath. The lady could hurt her.

"She was pretty good with Adam," Mrs. Adilman began. The lady was going to hurt her. "But I do remember one peculiar incident." She looked apologetically at Donna.

"Please tell us about it," the lawyer encouraged.

"Well," she said, "I was out watering the flowers—I hadn't been able to sleep that night so I was up early—and I noticed Donna sitting in her kitchen. She was drinking a cup of coffee and so I went over to say hello. Victor was out of town on business, and I asked her if the baby was sleeping. Adam was a bit colicky as a baby. He used to cry a lot and that particular morning it was so peaceful."

"And what was her reply?"

"She said she thought he was dead." Donna missed the next several exchanges while she watched the judge's face. It looked appropriately shocked. Way to go, Arlene, Donna thought. "She said that if she checked him and found out he was dead, she'd never get her cup of coffee."

Ed Gerber pretended to think for several minutes—Donna could tell now when he was only pretending because he always brought the third finger of his left hand to the tip of his nose and crossed his eyes in the process. It was very difficult to think when you were so busy

crossing and uncrossing your eyes. This was done to allow
the witness' testimony time to sink in. This pretense continued for only several minutes, however, because any
longer and the humor of it all might emerge from the
midst of this horror.

"Don't get me wrong," Mrs. Adilman added (how
could we possibly get you wrong? Donna wondered), "I
think Donna loved her little boy. I think she loved him."

Thank you, Arlene. Actually, I still do.

"Did Mrs. Cressy inform you when she was pregnant
with her second child?"

"Yes."

Donna closed her eyes.

"Could you tell us about it, please." More a statement
than a question.

"Objection."

"On what grounds, Mr. Stamler?" asked the judge.

"I fail to see the relevance, your honor."

"I assure you," interjected Mr. Gerber, "we will show
relevance."

"Objection overruled."

"Please tell us about that conversation, Mrs. Adilman."

Donna prayed for a thunderbolt to strike the woman
dead. None came. Her lawyer looked over at her. "Well, I
tried," he said, patting her hand.

"I was out in my garden as usual," Arlene Adilman began, obviously fixing the scene in her own mind. "Donna
came home. Yes, she'd been out—Adam was at nursery—
and I remember the taxi brought her home—"

"Taxi?"

"Yes. I hadn't seen her drive her car in a couple of
months. She took cabs all over. I assumed something was
wrong with the car."

"So, the taxi brought her home," Mr. Gerber reiter-
ated, stressing the word taxi and getting the witness back
in the right lane.

"Yes. And she looked very upset—"

"Objection."

"Well, she'd been crying," Mrs. Adilman said, lodging a protest of her own. "That much was very obvious."

"Overruled. Witness may continue."

"She walked over to me and I said hello and asked her if she was feeling all right. She told me she'd just been to the doctor and that she was pregnant."

"And what did you reply?"

"I said that that was wonderful. That there was nothing sadder than an only child."

"And her response?" Gerber asked.

"She said she didn't want the baby."

"Didn't want the baby?"

"She said it was a terrible mistake and that she just couldn't have this baby."

"Couldn't have?"

Did he have to repeat everything? Was he hard of hearing?

"Did she elaborate?"

"She just kept repeating that she couldn't have it, that she didn't want it, and then she begged me not to tell Victor that she was pregnant. I told her he'd find out soon enough anyway."

"And what did she say to that?"

"She said he might never have to find out about it at all." She paused and looked directly at Donna. "When it occurred to me what she had in mind—"

"Objection. The witness has no way of knowing what was in Mrs. Cressy's mind."

"Sustained."

"Just tell us what was said, Mrs. Adilman," the lawyer advised.

"Well, after she said that, about Victor never finding out, I said, oh no, Donna, you can't mean that. You wouldn't do anything to hurt that helpless baby, would you? I mean, I just couldn't believe that she would actually do anything like that, kill her own—"

"Objection, your honor."

"Sustained."

Donna's eyes filled with tears. I didn't do anything, did

I? she screamed silently at the woman on the stand, who
for the first time, seemed embarrassed and averted her
eyes. I didn't abort my baby. I went through that whole
mess again. I got fat; I went to more classes even though
the odds were I'd have to have another Caesarian. I went
through the operation again with Victor at my side. I had
my little girl. And you, you old witch, you were right. I
couldn't kill my child, no matter how it was conceived,
even though I wanted to, wanted to as much as now I
want to hold onto her. Because that little life is my life,
and no matter how much I've managed to mess up my
own life, that little girl is a happy, gorgeous, well-adjusted
little angel, and I'm the one who's largely responsible for
that fact. While you're up there telling them about my
changes of mood and hair colors, and all my sneezing and
cleaning and crying, would someone please point out that
in the interim I somehow managed to produce two glori-
ously beautiful, well-adjusted children! Would someone
please put in a kind word for me? No, Donna answered
herself silently. It's not your turn yet.

The next witness identified himself as Jack Bassett. He
was tall, slim and blond, with the look of a slightly over-
the-hill beach bum. He ran a sporting-goods shop and
had known Victor, he explained, albeit on a fairly casual
basis, for several years. Victor had, in fact, sold him a
policy one day while in the shop looking at fishing reels
with his small son. Several weeks later, he had run into
Victor and his wife and son as they were walking in the
Palm Beach Mall. Donna was pregnant at the time, he
said.

Donna remembered no such meeting and no such man.
He stood—or sat, she corrected herself—before her,
about to condemn her with his responses, and she had no
idea why, or what he had to say. Had she stepped on his
toe when they were introduced? Had she giggled inappropriately or asked for a Kleenex?

"Did you see Mrs. Cressy on any other occasions?" Ed
Gerber asked.

"Only once."

"Would tell us about it, please?"

Jack Bassett smiled. His teeth were white and straight. Donna wondered what other memorable meeting they had shared. "I'd taken my cat, Charlie, to the vet, a Dr. Ein, over on South Dixie near Forest Hill." Donna felt a slow ache in the pit of her stomach. Though she still had no recollection of this witness, she knew now the area into which they were moving. At last, Mr. Gerber had returned to the fork in the road. He was beginning his journey down the other path. Donna quickly looked behind her. Mel smiled reassuringly. Jack Bassett's all-American voice pulled her eyes back to the witness stand. "I parked in the lot and took Charlie inside."

"This is a parking lot for clients of the veterinarian?"

"For the Animal Clinic, yes, and for several other medical offices on the other side of the lot."

"What happened when you came out of the clinic?"

"Well, I was feeling a little at loose-ends. Dr. Ein had said he'd have to keep Charlie overnight and I love that cat like I love my kids—"

Everyone smiled approvingly. And she was the one who was supposed to be crazy?

"Anyway," he continued—

Anyhow, Donna mouthed.

"I went back to the parking lot. There were a lot more cars parked there now—I'd been in the vet's about an hour—and I couldn't remember where I'd put the damn thing—excuse me, I'm sorry for the language."

The witness was duly pardoned and asked to go on. Get on with it, Donna urged silently. Get to the good stuff. We know it's coming. You saw something, didn't you? When you were looking for your car. Something you didn't expect to see. Tell us all about it. Why did everyone feel they had to build suspense? Didn't anyone just want to mind his own business anymore? Where was all that marvelous noninvolvement she kept reading about?

"Anyway—"

Anyhow.

"I looked around and then I saw this little white MG. You know, one of the old classics. A beautiful little car. I thought I'd go take a look at it. I honestly didn't realize anyone was inside it." He seemed embarrassed. "I bent down and peered in the window."

"Someone was inside?"

"Yes, sir."

"Did you recognize anyone?"

"Not at first. At first I just saw what I thought were a couple of kids necking."

"You saw two people kissing?"

"Yes, sir. Quite passionately."

"And?"

"And I think that was all they were doing. I really couldn't see."

"Objection."

"No need to object, Mr. Stamler," Mr. Gerber followed with quickly. "The question was misinterpreted. I didn't mean 'and what else were they doing,' I meant simply and what happened next."

"Strike that last answer from the records," the judge instructed.

"And what happened next?" Ed Gerber repeated clearly.

"I guess they caught sight of me and they pulled apart."

"Did you recognize them at that point?"

"Not really. She looked a bit familiar, but it wasn't until they got out of the car a few minutes later that I recognized who she was. Her hair was very different from the last time I'd seen her."

"And who was she?"

"Mrs. Donna Cressy," he said, smiling inappropriately at Donna.

Surprise! she wanted to yell.

"And the man she'd been kissing?"

"Dr. Mel Segal."

"Why is it dragging on for so long?"

Donna sat next to Mel inside the classic white MG she had heard described earlier that afternoon. They were parked in front of the house she was currently renting.

"Victor has a lot of witnesses," Mel said, by way of an explanation.

"One for each grudge."

"Apparently."

"They all say the same thing." He nodded. She turned abruptly toward him. "Do you think I'm crazy?" He put his arm around her. "I don't know," she continued, shaking her head. "I sit and I listen to them. Can they *all* be wrong?"

Mel smiled gently at her. "They're *all* wrong," he said.

She leaned her face against his. "Thank you."

"What are you going to do tonight?"

She looked toward the house. "I thought I'd take the kids over to McDonalds. God, what would Victor do with that one? Letting my children eat junk food!"

"Victor would never be stupid enough to touch something like that. If he attacks McDonalds—he's attacking an American institution!"

She laughed. "You want to go get Annie? Come with us?"

He shook his head. "No. You go. Just you and the kids."

She patted his hand and unbuckled her seat belt, smiling. "What kind of a man has seat belts installed in a classic old sportscar?"

Mel laughed. "Only us vile seducers of pregnant crazies," he answered, leaning over and kissing her.

Donna put one hand on the door handle and stopped. "You know I'm kind of afraid to go in there!" Mel looked at her, the question implicit in his eyes. "Just that Adam got into a big discussion on life and death last night," she explained. "I'm not sure I'm up to it again tonight. It was a very strange thing," she continued. "I wanted to tell him that my mother had gone to Heaven, but I just couldn't get it out."

"Why is that?"

"I'm not sure. I guess because I don't really believe that there is a Heaven."

Mel's voice was soft and reassuring. "Do you have to believe everything you tell him?" he asked simply.

The truth of Mel's question caught her off guard. Suddenly, she found herself laughing. "Of course not," she answered, images of Santa Claus, Cookie Monster and the many other creatures of Adam's fertile imagination—an imagination she actively encouraged—passing instantaneously before her eyes. "Thank you," she said, nodding her head, feeling things regain their proper perspective. She opened the door. "You'll always be here, won't you?" she asked, looking back at him before getting out of the car. "Whenever I start taking myself too seriously and things—"

"What things?"

She smiled. "I love you."

"Aw, you say that to all us vile seducers."

She closed the door and leaned through the open window. "You bet your ass I do." Then she turned and walked quickly up the pathway to her front door.

Chapter 11

He had been staring at her for the better part of an hour.

At first, she had assumed he was staring at someone else; then she had changed her mind and concluded he was staring at the wall behind her. Now, she had definitely decided he was staring at her. She moved an imaginary hair away from her right cheek, lowered her chin and simultaneously lifted her eyes in the manner she had heard Lauren Bacall describe as "The Look" she had once made famous. Donna wondered if the bearded man across the room thought she looked like the young Lauren Bacall. She lowered her gaze.

Fat chance, she said to herself, coming face to face (face to stomach?) with reality. She was eight months pregnant. Of course, with all the people between them, it was quite possible he couldn't see her whole body. From the breasts up, she didn't look pregnant at all. If anything, she had lost a lot of weight everywhere but in her stomach. Most people at the party seemed surprised, in fact, at how much weight she had lost in the last few years. She, in turn, was surprised at their surprise, having not realized herself how thin she had become. Maybe it was her hair, she thought suddenly, pulling on it. Maybe she should do something about it—trim it, cut it, maybe even color it. It was making her look too thin, too haggard when she was supposed to be blooming. Blooming—sure thing.

He was still staring at her.

Donna didn't know who the man was. She knew most

of the people at the party, although it had been several
years since she had seen them. They had been largely *her*
friends, after all, and somehow she and Victor had lost
contact with most (if not all) of her friends in the last
couple of years. She looked around the room: there were
former friends from McFaddon Advertising ("they're so
boring," Victor had said, "all they ever talk about are
their ad campaigns"); a few girlfriends she used to lunch
with ("I don't know how you can stand them, Donna. All
they ever talk about are movies. They're so frivolous. You
have more substance than that."); some old boyfriends
("I don't like to know about your past. It's none of my
concern."); and her good friend, her former good friend
and confidante, Susan Reid, whose party she was now at-
tending. ("All she ever talks about are men and wild parties. Definitely not a good influence, Donna.") Also
present were a number of Susan's friends that Donna
recognized but did not know, and some she did not recognize at all. Including the man with the sandy moustache
and beard who stood over by the patio door staring at
her.

"Who's that man over there?" Donna asked her hostess
as Susan was about to walk by. "The one with the beard."

Susan pretended to be looking around the room. She
lifted her drink to her mouth and talked from behind its
protective shield, her gaze now floating absently without
establishing any unnecessary eye contact. "Oh, him.
That's Mel Segal. He's a doctor. Divorced, I think. Has a
little girl. Kind of cute, huh?"

Donna shrugged. "Not my type." Then she laughed.
"Look who's talking about type; I'm eight months pregnant, for God's sake."

"Where is Victor, anyway?" It was the first time in the
two hours Donna had been at the party that anyone had
even asked.

"He's out of town on business. Sarasota."

"Everything all right with the two of you?"

"Oh, sure. Fine. Why do you ask?"

Susan shrugged. "I don't know. Just that you look, kind of—I don't know."

"Tell me."

"You just don't look like you!" she blurted out.

Donna instinctively did not want to understand what Susan's observation implied. "Well, I *am* pregnant," she replied.

"Yea," her friend concurred. "I guess that's what it is."

The two women stared at each other with fond regard. Donna thought of all the phone calls they had shared, the laughs and agonies over assorted lovers, the movies they had seen together, the gossip they had exchanged. Until her wedding. Susan and Victor had simply never gotten along; their personalities were diametrically opposed. No one ever said anything, but gradually, Susan's visits had become less and less frequent and Victor was always finding an excuse not to go to one of Susan's many social get-togethers. (The one time in the last few years he had run out of excuses, he had stood around most of the evening waiting to leave and had finally jangled his keys in Donna's direction at ten P.M.) Donna knew that the only reason she was here at all tonight was because Victor was out of town. Thank God for Sarasota, she thought.

"Can I get you another drink?" A man's voice. Donna looked up, surprised to discover that Susan had gone and that Dr. Mel Segal had taken her place. She handed him her glass.

"Ginger ale," she said, when she couldn't decide what else to say.

She watched him angle his way through the crowd. He was a nice looking man, she decided. Fair complexion, a lot of hair. A good muscular body which probably had to struggle to keep in shape. He looked like an overgrown kid, Donna concluded, as he moved back toward her, a drink in each hand. He had brown eyes, and dimples when he smiled.

"A ginger ale for the pregnant lady," he said, handing it to her.

"Thank you."

"You want to go out on the patio?"

Donna found herself startled. Why did he want her to go out on the patio? Did he have a thing about pregnant women? She'd read that there were men who did.

"Any special reason?" she heard herself ask.

"I'd like to talk to you," he answered.

She wanted to ask him what about, but decided she might not like his answer, and by now she had decided that she *did* want to go out on the patio with him. He motioned for her to lead the way.

"Have we met before?" she asked him as they walked past the other guests on the cement patio and over to a section of lawn that was unoccupied.

"No."

They stopped.

"I'm all ears," she said.

"I was hoping you'd do the talking."

"Me? You're the one who said you wanted to talk."

There was a long silence. Finally, after obvious deliberation, he spoke.

"This is none of my business."

"What is? Isn't," she corrected.

"You."

"What are you talking about?"

Another long silence.

"Look, this isn't like me at all. I usually never interfere with someone's private life. I'm very easy-going; I believe in letting sleeping dogs lie and all that—"

"What are you trying to tell me?"

"That you are the most unhappy-looking woman I have ever seen."

Donna was too surprised to react.

"I'm sorry. It's a hell of a thing to say to a complete stranger, I know. Just that I've been watching you, and I keep hearing people go by saying 'what's happened to Donna? She used to be so pretty,' and, to be honest, well, I think you're still pretty, but you're obviously so desperately unhappy—"

"You said that," Donna was beginning to react. She felt the tears filling up her eyes.

"Oh, no, please don't cry. I'm a total disaster when a woman cries." He moved his arms around her and walked with her to the far end of the garden. The tears were becoming sobs, her shoulders were starting to heave. Minutes later, the rest of the guests had deserted the patio area and Donna sat on the far grass, curled in the doctor's arms, crying as she hadn't cried since that night almost nine months ago. Mel sat beside her, his hold never weakening, until the last sob wrestled free of her body.

"I shouldn't cry," she said at last. "It's not good for the baby."

"Start worrying about what's good for the mother," he answered. "Usually what's good for Mommy is good for the child."

Donna tried to smile. "I forgot you're a doctor." She paused, wiping her nose carelessly with the paper napkin from around her drink. "Where's your office?"

"South Dixie. By Forest Hill Boulevard."

She nodded her head. "In one of the clinics?" His turn to nod. "General practice?" He nodded again. "You like it?"

"Very much."

"Susan told me you had a daughter—"

"Yes. Annie. She's seven. Going on twenty-four." Donna managed a weak laugh. "Kid's been through a lot the past few years." He stared into her eyes. The tears hung precariously on their lids, waiting for the slightest provocation to fall. "I guess Susan also told you I'm divorced."

"Yes."

"Amazing girl, that Susan. She's learned the art of staring right at you, saying all sorts of nasty things about you, smiling at you all the while, and you don't even see her lips move. Great talent."

"She didn't say anything nasty about you."

"Divorce is always nasty—especially when there are kids."

"Why did you do it then?"

"I didn't—it was Kate's decision. She felt cheated, I think—"

"Cheated?"

They moved so that they were no longer locked in each other's arms and now sat side by side, two separate entities sitting with their knees up and parallel, leaning forward, their hands moving almost rhythmically to pick at the grass around them.

"Typical story," he shrugged. "We married right out of college; she worked to put me through med school, gave it up when I graduated. We had a child. I worked hard. I was never home. She was always home. She resented it. Then she resented me. She joined a few women's groups. Next thing I knew, she announced she was leaving to start a new career—she wants to be a lawyer—and that was that."

"And Annie?"

"She's with me. Kate gets her holidays and summers."

Donna felt her whole body tense. Why you? she wanted to ask. Why did you get custody? Instead she said, "And Kate?"

"She graduates in a year's time. Actually, I think she'll make a fine lawyer."

"You're not bitter?"

He shook his head. "No. Listen, it was at least as much my fault as hers. Basically, she didn't see me for about nine years, and when you're only married nine years, it doesn't make for much of a marriage." He paused, throwing a long blade of grass up in the air. "It's funny, though, how things work out. I mean, ever since she left, I stopped working so hard. I suddenly realized I had a kid to raise, and so now I'm never home later than six P.M. and I always wait with her till the bus picks her up in the mornings. I never work weekends except in emergencies. All the things Kate was after me about when we were married." He looked at Donna. "Why do we always do things so ass-backward?"

"Why do you have custody?" Donna asked suddenly, no longer able to hold the question at bay.

"Kate thought it would be better for Annie. Law school's a hard place for a four-year-old. Or even now that she's a precocious seven."

They looked straight ahead toward the house.

"You want to talk now?" he asked.

"No," she answered.

"Why? Don't you trust me?"

"If I start to talk, I'll cry."

They continued to stare straight ahead, almost afraid to look at each other.

"What are you hoping for, a boy or a girl?"

"A girl. I already have a little boy. Adam."

"Any names picked out?"

"Sharon, if it's a girl. My mother's name was Sharon."

"My mother's name was Tinka."

"Tinka?"

He laughed. "Picture three little girls, if you will, ages five, seven and nine, arriving by boat from Poland. Their names are Manya, Tinka, and Funka."

"Funka?"

"See? Tinka doesn't sound so bad any more, does it?"

She laughed. "What happened to them?"

"The usual. They grew up, got married, had children and died. Except for Manya. She's still hanging on. I think she's about eighty-six now—she lies about her age." He laughed. "In the interim, they changed their noses and their names. Manya became Mary and Funka became Fanny. Only Tinka stayed Tinka." He smiled and shook his head. "A hell of a woman."

"Are you an only child?"

His laugh was loud. "Are you kidding? I have four sisters and two brothers. We're scattered all over the country. From Vermont to Hawaii."

"I have a sister," Donna ventured. "She's living in England now."

"And your husband? What does he do?"

Donna stood up and wiped the grass off her skirt. She

was surprised to see that Mel remained sitting where he was.

"I'm kind of tired," she said, looking down at him. "I think I better go home."

"All right," he said, still not moving.

"Could you give me a ride?" she asked, surprising herself.

He got to his feet very quickly. "Sorry," he apologized, "I just assumed you had a car."

"I don't drive."

"Oh? Unusual."

"I used to drive."

He said nothing.

"If and when you decide you want to talk," he began, after the silent drive to her house, "you know where my office is. Please come and see me."

She smiled, opened the car door and crawled out of the small white sportscar. "Thank you," she said.

He waited until she was safely inside before he drove away.

Sharon was three months old before Donna walked into Dr. Segal's office.

"I didn't recognize you for a minute," he said, standing up to greet her. "You've changed your hair."

Donna's hand automatically moved to her almost carrot-colored hair. "Do you like it?"

He laughed. "Yea," he said. "It's cute."

"You sound like you mean that."

"I do."

"Victor hates it."

"Victor?"

"My husband."

"Is that why you're smiling?"

"What do you mean?"

"The first time you smiled since you walked in was when you said that Victor hates your hair."

"Am I that transparent?"

"Only when you want to be."

She smiled again. "The only problem is that I hate it too."

"The only problem?"

"I also hate Victor." She suddenly started to laugh, and for the next five minutes her laughter was as strong as her sobs had been some five months before. "There, I said it out loud. I hate him." The laughter changed abruptly to tears. "My God, I hate my husband. And I hate myself."

Mel couldn't have stopped her from talking now if he'd stuck a gag in her mouth and taped it closed. The words raced from her throat, vomited into the space between them. She'd barely have time to clean one story out of the way before her body was throwing up others. All the stories. Her almost six years of life with Victor. All of it, including the night of Sharon's conception.

"He keeps trying to make up for it, I guess," Donna was saying. "He's very attentive; he's always making a big fuss about Sharon—he's very good with her. He helps out a lot. He's always buying me little presents, taking me out to nice places for dinner. He never tries—" She looked at Mel to see if he understood what she was about to say without her actually having to say it. He did. She continued. "But even when he puts his arm out to help me out of the car, it makes me want to be sick."

"Maybe because you don't need any help getting out of the car."

Donna looked up into Mel's chocolate-brown eyes. He was sitting on the edge of his desk; she was sitting about a foot away. She swallowed hard, as if she were trying to digest what Mel had just said. "He makes me feel so inadequate," she said, looking around the office. "At first it was kind of nice having someone take charge, make all the decisions. But after a while it—you know what it does to you?" she asked, coming up with the answer for the first time, herself, in precise verbal terms. "It turns you into a child again. It robs you of your adulthood. After a little while you start to act just the way you're being treated—like a child! You become totally dependent. I'm thirty-two years old! I have two children. I shouldn't be dependent on anyone but myself. I don't understand how this all happened to me!" She groped for words, her hands at her neck. "I can't breathe! He doesn't give me any air. He decides everything; he questions everything—the most minute, stupid, inconsequential little things. He has to be a part of everything." She threw her hands up in the air. "And you know what's really frightening lately?"

Mel walked around behind his desk. "What?" He sat down on his chair.

"He thinks everything is getting better between us. He thinks there's hope for us! He said so this morning. 'We don't fight anymore,' he said. 'You've learned to compromise. I actually think you're starting to grow up. Except for what you did to your hair, of course!' " She screamed. A simple, loud, straightforward yell. "Compromise! I hate the word! You know what compromise means, Dr. Segal? It means giving in. The reason we don't fight anymore is that a year ago I decided I'd never fight him again. I just go along with whatever he decides. That's his idea of compromise. If I say blue and he says green, so I turn around and say green, then we're compromising." She stood up and began pacing. " 'Growing up,' he said. I'm starting to grow up! I'm starting to die! Is that the same thing? His idea of a grown-up is an obedient child. That's all I've become. Except that like most children who spend all day obeying their parents, I've become spiteful, resentful. Mean. It's like if I can draw blood, I know I'm still here. Is this making any sense at all?" She stopped pacing.

"Probably the best sense you've made in six years." He got up and moved toward her.

"I just feel like I've lost control of my life. I'm always sick. I'm afraid to do anything because I might make a mistake and do the wrong thing. I'm afraid to say anything, to have an opinion because it might be the wrong opinion." She shook her head. "I'm afraid to be myself because I haven't a clue where I went." She paused, looking up into Mel's kind face. "The only time I feel at all in charge of what I'm doing is for a few hours in the middle of the night." Mel looked at her quizzically. "I put on my little cotton cap and get out my bucket and mop and pretend I'm Carol Burnett. I clean that fucking little house until it glows."

Dr. Mel Segal laughed out loud.

"You're not offended?"

"By what?"

"I swore. I didn't mean to."

Mel obviously had to rethink what she had said. "Fuck?" he questioned. "You call that swearing? My seven-year-old uses worse language than that."

"It doesn't bother you?"

Mel shrugged, indicating it didn't.

"Victor would hate it. He doesn't even like me to swear."

"I have seven words to say to you," he said, counting them silently on his fingers.

"They are?"

"Leave that motherfucking son-of-a-bitch."

The room was absolutely still.

"I can't."

"Why, for God's sake? Can you name me even one positive thing about the man?"

Donna moved away from Mel and began pacing the room again restlessly. Then she stopped. There was a question mark in her voice. "He's good in emergencies?" she volunteered.

"How many emergencies have you had lately?" Mel leaned back against his desk again. "Donna, anyone can rise to an emergency. It's the day-to-day business of living that gets you, the little things. He's killing you."

Donna shook her head. Now that someone was finally on her side, finally saying the things to her out loud that she had been saying to herself in silence, she found herself in the weird position of trying to defend the same man she had been prosecuting.

"It's not all his fault. I mean, I know I've made this whole thing sound like it's all his fault, but you have to remember you're only hearing my side of the story. I haven't exactly been an angel. I've said terrible things to him in front of other people, insulted him, hurt him. I know all the vulnerable spots, remember. I know just where to stick in the pins!"

"Why are you making excuses?"

"Excuses?"

"For not leaving him."

"We have two children!"

"You think they're benefiting from the kind of example you're setting? You want Sharon to grow up into a Barbie doll? You want Adam to get his idea of what love is all about from the two of you?"

Donna's eyes filled with tears. "I'm afraid he'll take them away from me! Don't you understand? I know Victor. If I try to leave him, he'll take my babies away from me."

Mel walked over to Donna and surrounded her with the steadiness of his body. His arms engulfed her, pressing her to his chest. His voice was soft.

"You can fight him, Donna. You used to fight him. You can do it again. If you don't, you'll be losing a lot more than just your children."

"My children are everything."

"No," he said, pushing her away from his chest but keeping his arms resolutely around her. "They're a large part of your life but they are not the sum total of your life. There is still a person in there named Donna who exists quite apart from everyone else."

Donna shook his head. "No," she said. "I told you. I lost her a long time ago."

"No, you didn't," he said, looking above her eyes to the top of her head. "Anyone who can color her hair bright carrot-orange has not totally abandoned her claim to individuality." They both tried to smile.

"Is that what I'm doing?"

"I'm not a psychiatrist."

"What are you?"

"A friend."

She lowered her head and let him hug her against his chest once more.

"Thank you," she said. "I think that's what I need."

Chapter 12

Donna sat with one arm around Adam and one hand on Sharon's tummy. They sat on the sofa in the far bedroom, a room which served as a den by day and had about a year ago been turned into Donna's bedroom. The blue print sofa was a pull-out bed, and Donna now sat in the middle of it, Adam to her left and Sharon lying squealing on her back to her right. Every now and then, Adam reached over Donna's lap and pinched his sister's toes.

"Adam, don't do that."

"I don't like her."

"That's fine. Just don't hurt her."

"Tell her to be quiet."

"She's not making any noise. You're the one who's talking. Now, do you want to watch 'Sesame Street' or not?"

"Yes."

"Fine. Then watch."

For several seconds Adam's gaze returned to the television in front of them.

"I don't like her," he said again, stealing a furtive glance in the baby's direction. "I don't want to look at her."

"Then don't look at her."

He stood up and walked over to the baby. Sharon's eyes followed the path of her older brother. Donna sat ready for any sudden moves. "I don't like you," he said loudly. "I will never like you. I don't love you. I will never love you."

"All right, Adam, that's enough."

The litany continued.

"Not when you're bigger. Not when you're older. Never. Ever."

"All right, Adam, I think she got the message."

Adam turned to go back to his seat. On his way he managed to bring the palm of his hand down hard on the baby's forehead. Sharon looked startled but did not cry.

"All right, that's it," Donna said, flipping the remote control unit on the large color TV and watching Big Bird disappear. She picked Sharon up and carried her into her room, putting her on her back in her crib, and starting the musical mobile over her head. Sharon cooed and wiggled her appreciation. "You're such a sweet thing," Donna said, patting her daughter on the stomach. The child never cried. She couldn't have hoped for a better baby.

"And now, you," she said, returning to the den where Adam was screaming and frantically trying to find his way back to "Sesame Street." "Give me the remote control unit. Come on, Adam, you'll break it. That's right. I want to talk to you." She sat the crying youngster on her lap. "Stop crying. Come on, honey. I want to talk to you." Adam stopped his squirming and stared at her; his piercing blue eyes exact replicas of his father's. "I love you," she began. "You know that. I love you more than anything in the world."

"Don't love Sharon," he begged.

"I do love Sharon."

"No!"

"Yes, I do, honey. That's a fact of life you're just going to have to get used to. She's your sister, and she's here to stay. Now I know that's not an easy thing to accept when you're three years old, but that's just the way things are."

"But I don't like her."

"That's fine. You don't have to like her. But you can't hurt her. Do you understand that? She's a baby and she can't defend herself. Would you like it if someone bigger came up to you and hit you on the head?"

He felt his head. "No," he answered.

"Well, she doesn't like it either. So, no more hitting. Do you understand?"

"Yes. Can I watch 'Sesame Street' now?"

"On one condition."

"What's condition?"

"A condition is the basis of an agreement." She stopped. Oh sure, wonderful explanation to give to a three-year-old. Clears everything right up. "Let me put it this way—You can watch it if you let me bring Sharon back in here, and no hitting."

Adam gave the matter serious consideration. "All right," he said. Donna lifted the boy off her lap and put him in his original position on the sofa, then she stood up and walked to the doorway, flipping on the TV as she did so. From her position at the door, she heard Adam mutter as Big Bird snapped back into focus, "But I don't like her though."

Donna smiled at her young son. You better relax, she wanted to tell him. It doesn't get any easier.

Victor had been trying not to say anything about her hair for more than an hour. Donna could actually feel the effort involved. She found herself enjoying each minute, knowing he was dying to tell her what he thought of it. She could see the questions as they formed behind his eyes—"For God's sake, Donna, what did you do to your hair *this* time? You know I've always hated black hair unless it's natural. Otherwise, it looks so phony. What are you trying to do to yourself anyway? You want to look like Wonder Woman?"

What was the matter with her? What was happening to her? Donna felt herself begin to panic. What had she let happen to herself? Was she really the kind of person whose only enjoyment came from watching another person's pain? Had she really turned into that kind of a monster? Better someone else's pain than my own, she heard herself respond. "I think sadism is so much healthier than masochism, don't you?" Jesus. When had she said that? The party. The night of Danny Vogel's party. The night—

She looked over at Victor. He smiled at her, lowering the book she knew he was only pretending to read.

"How was your day?" he asked.

"All right."

He had asked the same question at supper earlier. She had given him the same answer.

"What did you do?"

"Well, obviously I had my hair done."

"Yes, I see."

"Do you like it?" The question was pointed and carried traces of a smirk.

"No. You know I don't like dyed black hair."

"Your hair is black."

"My hair is natural."

"My hair's natural too. Just the color isn't."

"Is that supposed to be funny?"

"I thought so."

No, she didn't. Not really. Neither of them had any humor left anywhere inside them.

"What else did you do today?"

She knew how hard it must be for him to carry on a polite conversation. What he really wanted to do was drag her by her newly blackened split ends back to the hairdresser and have at least the top of her head made normal again. But he stayed in his seat. He stayed where he was and listened to her reply.

"I took Sharon in for her six-month check-up. Then I watched 'Sesame Street' with Adam. Sharon kind of watched."

"Dr. Wellington?"

"Hmm? Oh, no, Dr. Segal. I told you I was changing doctors."

"Dr. Wellington is the best pediatrician in—Palm Beach."

"He's also the busiest. He doesn't know if my children

are black or white, male or female. Besides, Dr. Segal is
my doctor, and this makes things a lot easier."

"Who is he, anyway? A nobody family practitioner."

"I like him."

"That doesn't make him a good doctor."

Donna had said everything she intended to say on the
subject. She stood up.

"Are you going to make some coffee?"

"I was going to go to bed."

Victor checked his watch. "It's only nine o'clock."

"I'm tired."

He stood up. "Please, Donna," he said, his hands tentatively reaching out for hers. Immediately she tensed and
withdrew. He pulled his hands back to his sides.
"Couldn't we just sit and talk for a while?"

"I'm really tired, Victor."

"Don't you want to hear about my day?" She could
hear the pleading implicit in his voice.

Donna stood as if she had been overcome by nerve gas,
unable to move. She didn't know what to do with her legs.
They felt paralyzed. She wanted to run; somehow she
couldn't get her feet to understand. Victor took this as a
sign that she would listen to him. "I sold a staggering life
insurance policy. You want to know to whom?"

No, she thought. "Who?" she asked.

"One of the men who bought into The Mayflower."
Donna regarded him blankly. What the hell was he talking about? "He was actually at that party the night we
met." Oh, that Mayflower. An Original Concept—For
Original Americans. She wished she'd never heard of the
damn place.

"I'm going to bed, Victor."

"Your room?" he asked suddenly.

Donna hoped she didn't look as startled as she felt.

"Of course," she said, trying to keep her voice calm.

"I thought maybe—"

"Goodnight, Victor." She walked past him and out of
the room.

It was almost midnight when she heard him come out of
the bathroom and go in to check on Adam and Sharon.
He did that every night. Then he would turn around and
walk back to his own room and go to sleep. Except that
this time she didn't hear his footsteps receding. She heard
them approaching. Immediately, she retreated far down
under her covers.

She didn't have to see him to know he was standing in
front of the open door. She could feel him moving softly
toward her.

"Donna?" She said nothing. "Donna, I know you're not
asleep." Go away, her silence screamed. I am not here. I
am not here. "All right, you don't have to say anything.
But you *will* have to listen. I'll do it this way, if this is the
way you want it."

This is *not* the way I want it! I want you to go away
and leave me alone. I don't want to hear any of this. If
we were doing what I wanted, you wouldn't be in here. I
wouldn't have to listen to any of this.

His voice was soft. "I love you, Donna. I've always
loved you. You know that. I've made some mistakes, I
admit it. I've mishandled certain things. I did them out of
love." Do I have to hear this? Do I have to listen to this?
"I've tried to be patient, Donna. I've let you sleep here,
alone, undisturbed all this time. During your pregnancy, I
didn't want to do anything that might hurt the baby, and
after, I've waited till I thought things were starting to improve between us. For a while, we seemed to be getting
along. I kept hoping you'd turn up at our bedroom door,
but—" I am not here. I am not here. I am not hearing
any of this. "Donna, there's nothing I can do about that
night. It's over. It happened a long time ago. I'm really
sorry it happened the way it did, but you have to understand what you were doing to me. You kept on at me;
you humiliated me at the party; you don't even realize
what you're doing sometimes, but you just—" Is this supposed to be an apology? I'm sorry, but you made me do
it? I'm sorry, but be reasonable Donna it was all your

fault? I am not here. I am not hearing any of this. "Look, it didn't turn out all that badly after all, did it? I mean, we have Sharon. And I love you, Donna. We're a family. I didn't mean to hurt you, Donna. Come on, now, be honest. I really didn't hurt you. Did I?" You're right, Victor. You didn't hurt me. You only put five years of marriage on the end of your prick and rammed them home to me the best way you knew how. I am bursting with the residue of what you left inside me. "Please, Donna. I can't do any more than say I'm sorry. I can't make that night go away. It happened. But we can't let it destroy us. It's gone on long enough. It's time we started living in the present, enjoying what we have." I think I've heard this speech before. Something about the ball being in my court. Play or get off the tarmac? "I just want things back the way they were between us before that night." Back to the way things were between us before that night? Are you crazy? You want things back to the way they were before? Don't you realize that that night was *exactly* the way things were before? You just used a different approach! "Please, Donna, I want my little girl back again."

Donna felt her body starting to heave. She quickly threw back the sheet and raced to the closest bathroom where she emptied her dinner into the toilet. Then she sat on the cool of the tile floor, her hair matted at her forehead, tears streaking her cheeks, hugging the side of the toilet bowl, until she heard him walk back down the hall and close his door behind him.

She awoke at precisely three A.M., as she did every morning. Then she got out of bed and walked toward the kitchen. The counters were dirty, she had noticed while making dinner, and the outside of the appliances. Adam's fingerprints were all over them. She would give them all a good scrubbing. Make everything shine.

She walked into the kitchen and turned on the kitchen light, then she flipped on the small transistor radio very quietly and got out her Ajax, her Fantastik, and her handiwipes, and started to work. She always worked to the beat of the music. The beat goes on, she thought, applying the Fantastik to the white countertop. Victor had once caught her using Ajax—don't you know it destroys the finish?—and they had spent a good couple of hours thrashing out that important issue. Yes sir, nothing was too unimportant to discuss ad nauseum in this marriage.

She felt the beat change. Obviously, another record. She adjusted her tempo accordingly.

"—first I was afraid
Then I was petrified—"

She recognized the song. Gloria Gaynor, she said to herself proudly.

"Kept thinkin' I could never live without you by my side—"

It gets faster in a minute, she thought, her hand poised and ready to wipe. Any time now, just another few bars—

"—and I learned how to get along—"

Now.

The song took off. Donna's hands danced along the countertop.

"And so you're back—"

Rubbing. Rubbing. Cleaning. Till it shines. I will make you shine.

"—if I'd a known for just one second
You'd be back to bother me—"

The music building. And building. Clean, Donna, clean!

"Go on, now Go! Walk out the door!"

Donna stopped abruptly.

"Just turn around now
'Cuz you're not welcome anymore."

She stared at the small transistor. Then her eyes moved to the kitchen door.

"—think I'd crumble? Think I'd lay down and die?
Oh no, not I—I will survive—"

Donna's hand dropped the handiwipe onto the floor.

"As long as I know how to love
I know I'll feel alive—"

She moved to the phone. Victor always kept the keys to his car in a dish under the phone.

"I've got all my life to live
I've got all my love to give
And I'll survive. I will survive—"

She picked them up and walked out of the kitchen toward the front door.

"Hey—hey—"

Donna felt the cool night air hit her body and realized all she had on was a thin nightgown. It didn't matter. She was just going out to start the car. She'd come back inside and throw something on after she got the kids. But first she had to start the car. Something she hadn't done since—

She wouldn't think about it. She would simply get into the car and drive. She had always been a good driver. Before Victor— She stopped. Had she ever done anything on her own before she met Victor?

She opened the car door and got behind the wheel. The image of Victor was right beside her. "Watch that trash can," it said.

"I will not listen to you," she said aloud, putting the key in the ignition. "You are not here." The radio blasted into the small space. She had forgotten that Victor never turned it off. It was always there as soon as the ignition was started.

The radio was turned to the same station as her small transistor. Gloria Gaynor had only just started the second verse. That's good, Donna thought, keep telling me. Keep telling me.

"—not to fall apart."

I will not fall apart. I will put this car into reverse and back out onto the street. Then I will go inside and get my children.

"And I've been oh so many nights
Just feeling sorry for myself—
I used to cry
But now I hold my head up high—"

Donna felt her head raise. She tried to put the car into reverse. Her hand wouldn't move. She could actually feel Victor's invisible hand on top of hers.

"Do you know where you're going, Donna? You passed the street three blocks ago."

Get out of my car, Victor. You are not here.

"You're straddling the white line."

I am not.

"*—And you see me*
Somebody new
I'm not the chained-up little person
Still in love with you—"

"You almost missed that stop sign."

I didn't.

"*—Go on, now go*
Walk out the door
Just turn around now—"

"For Christ's sake, Donna, are you trying to kill us!"

I didn't mean to, I didn't see it—

"*—weren't you the one who tried to break me with—*"

"Just shut up for a change, Donna."

Don't do that! Don't do that! Get off me. Do you hear me? Get off me. I will not be violated. I will not be violated this way!

"Are you trying to kill us?"

Bad little girl. Bad, bad little girl.

"Just shut up for a change, Donna."

You must be taught a lesson. You must be taught a lesson.

"*—Oh, go on, now go*
Walk out the door—"

Donna felt her hand begin to shake. Then her whole body.

"*—You think I'd crumble?*
You think I'd lay down and die?"

She couldn't stop the shaking.

She couldn't stop the shaking.

"*—And I'll survive. I will survive—*"

Donna reached up and turned off the ignition, then she lowered her head to the steering wheel and cried.

How could she survive? she wondered ruefully. She'd forgotten she was already dead.

Chapter 13

"My God, what happened to you?"

"You don't like it either, huh?"

Dr. Mel Segal stood up behind his large wood desk and walked around to where Donna was standing.

"Victor calls it my early-Auschwitz period."

Mel smiled. "The man always had a way with words."

"But you don't like it either?"

Mel took a long pause. "I'm not crazy about it, no."

Donna let out a sharp exhalation of air. "I did it myself," she said, running her hand through what remained of her hair. "Last night."

"What brought that on?"

"Victor said I was starting to look more like my old self again. I would have shaved it right off but I didn't have the guts."

"You came close."

"Victor says I look like a starving Peter Pan."

"Leave it to Victor."

"Are you going to tell me to leave him?"

"No."

"Why not?"

"I told you that the first time you walked in here. You're an adult—I figure I only have to tell you something once. The rest is up to you."

"Ah, come on," she teased. "Tell me to leave him."

His face was suddenly very serious. "I can't."

Donna turned toward the door. "Nuts," she said. "Why do I always have to get involved with men of integrity?"

"Involved?"

Donna turned back to face Mel. She was caught off guard by the choice of her words. "Well, you know what I mean."

He said he did, but she could see he didn't. For that matter, neither did she.

"It was really nice of you to see me without an appointment."

"Since when have you needed an appointment?"

"You have a waiting room full of people."

"Why did you come?"

"I'm not sure."

"The kids okay?"

"Fine."

"You?"

"Fine. I feel—fine. Actually, I feel about as good as I look." She laughed. "You think they have a bed at the nearest hospital I could use?"

"You don't look that bad."

"I do."

"Personally, I've always thought Peter Pan was kind of cute."

Donna smiled and walked toward him. "He's always spoken very highly of you, too," she said, her hand reaching up to touch Mel's face, feeling his beard brush against her hand.

"How's Annie?" she asked, withdrawing her hand.

"Great. She's very heavy into masturbation at the moment."

They laughed.

"What do you do about it?" Donna asked.

"Do? Nothing. Let the kid enjoy herself."

Donna and Mel stood staring at each other for several long seconds without saying a word. Then Donna heard a voice break the silence.

"I better go," the voice said quietly.

"Okay," Mel answered, even more softly.

"I want you to kiss me so badly I can't stand it," the voice continued. "Oh, my God," Donna said aloud and turned quickly and walked out of the room.

He was right behind her. She heard him make hurried excuses to his visiting patients—he'd be back in a minute, a sudden emergency—and seconds later she heard his footsteps behind her on the stairs. When she reached the bottom, he was right at her heels.

"My car's in the lot," he said, taking her elbow and moving her toward it. She recognized the little white MG. "Goddamn, it's locked," he said, fidgeting in his pocket for the keys. "Here they are." After a few fumbles, he found the right key and opened both doors. Donna climbed in the passenger side and Mel got behind the wheel. They closed the doors.

"Where are we going?" she asked.

"Nowhere," he answered, his arms immediately wrapping themselves around her, his lips sealing themselves across her own. Donna had never kissed a man with a beard before. She liked it. She liked everything about him.

"This is incredibly unprofessional," he said, moving his lips from her mouth to her eyes.

"I couldn't ask for better treatment."

Their lips moved back to their previous positions. They remained huddled that way for several minutes, kissing frantically, grabbing at each other, touching each other's cheeks, finally pulling apart and staring into each other's newly awakened eyes. He moved his right hand up to her head and rubbed it across her cropped hair.

"How can you kiss a woman with a crew-cut?" she asked.

"Watch," he said. And did.

"I can understand why I'm attracted to you. But I'll never understand what you find attractive about me."

"I like your eyes," he said gently. "Your nose, your lips." He kissed each in turn. "Your ears." They laughed, as he kissed each one. "Your neck." He leaned forward.

"Careful, I don't think there's room in this car for you to like any more of me."

"Where are the kids?"

"Adam's at nursery. Sharon is with Mrs. Adilman."

"Can you wait while I finish up upstairs?"

"Yes."

He leaned toward her again. "I have wanted to kiss you," he said, "since I first saw you at Susan's party, looking like a pregnant walking stick."

She laughed. "Ah, yes. My Biafran refugee period. One of my favorites." She looked at him seriously. "What will you think, I wonder, if you ever meet the real me?"

"Well, let me see," he said, drawing an invisible line down her cheek with his finger. "I've liked you pregnant, I've liked you streaked, frosted and blonde. I've liked you skinny and teary-eyed. I've even liked you skinny and smiling. Not to mention I liked you as a redhead, a carrot and a raven. I even like your natural shade, what's left of it. Somehow, I suspect I'll like you when you're old and gray, if I'm lucky enough to still be around you by that time."

"I'm the lucky one," she said, tears filling her eyes. He promptly kissed them away, and then brought his lips back to her own. "My God," she said suddenly, pulling away. "Who the hell is that?"

Mel quickly opened the door of his car. Donna looked over, half-expecting to see Victor, but instead found herself staring at a tall, blond, almost careless looking man who had been leaning against the car window, peering in at them.

"Sorry," the man said, moving backward, his eyes on Donna. "I was just admiring the car. I didn't realize anybody was in it."

Donna opened her door and got out as Mel did the same on his side. Mel waited as Donna walked around the car and then took her arm. Donna noticed the blond man's eyes were still on her as she and Mel were walking away. When she turned around again as they were about to go back inside the clinic door, she saw that he was still staring.

Their lovemaking was a disaster. Perhaps because they were so nervous. Perhaps because they were so eager to be good for each other. Whatever the reasons, they simply failed to connect, their perspiration more the sweat of effort than of passion. Though they brought in all the latest techniques, everything they did seemed forced, as if they still had one eye to the textbook. There was much grunting, much motion and very little joy.

He found it difficult to achieve an erection, and once achieved, impossible to maintain. She was too dry, too sore, too scared. Both were anxious. They fumbled with each other's bodies as if they were opposing players on a football team, and finally let the ball drop.

"I'm sorry. I'm so dry," she said, trying not to cry. "It's just that I haven't made love in almost a year and a half. And since Sharon was born, I guess it's still kind of sore in there. From lack of use."

"I feel like a spastic kid," he said. "You know, like the first time you do it and you're worried sick that you're not gonna find the right place." He looked down at his limp penis. "Not that I'd have anything to put in it at the moment."

Suddenly they were both laughing.

"God, we were awful," she said.

"The pits," he agreed.

Their laughter grew and reverberated throughout his home.

"Do you think we'll improve?" she asked.

"Can't get any worse."

"When does Annie get home?"

Mel looked over at the clock which sat on the end table by his bed. "In an hour. She has ballet after school today."

"Think we can get it right by then?"

"I'd sure like to give it a try."

Donna looked into his lap. "I think the general shape of things is improving," she said, feeling very wicked to be saying such things (Victor had never liked it when she tried to put a rating on their sex together, nor had he approved of this kind of dialogue), feeling very wicked to being here at all. At the same time, she realized, she was feeling something else as well. Donna smiled up at Mel, whose body was moving over her own. As the familiar stirrings began filtering through all the right places, Donna was feeling that there just might be some hope left for her after all.

She was packed, and waiting for Victor on the sofa when he finally got home. He looked around the living room, saw her suitcases, and walked over to the bar to fix himself a drink.

"You want one?" he asked.

"No, thank you."

He poured himself a tall glass of scotch and walked back to where Donna was sitting. "I take it this is some sort of goodbye scene," he said.

Donna's voice was quiet. "I'm leaving you."

"I kind of thought that's what you were going to say." He took a long swallow of his drink. "The children?"

"They're with Susan."

"Susan?" He shook his head. "I should have known she'd be behind this."

"Susan had nothing to do with this. I called her this afternoon when she got home from work and asked her to look after the kids for a few hours till I spoke to you." She paused. "She was very surprised."

"But delighted, I'm sure."

"I don't want to argue about Susan, Victor."

"I don't want to argue at all."

"Good." Donna stood up. "I'll call a taxi."

"I'll drive you."

"No."

He put his drink down on the glass coffee table. "You won't let me do anything for you?"

You've done enough, she wanted to say, but didn't. "I can do things for myself."

"No one said you couldn't."

You really don't understand any of this, do you Victor?
You have no idea why this is happening to you.

"Can we talk about it?" he asked.

"I have nothing left to say."

"Do you think you're being fair?"

"I think so. Yes."

"Six years of marriage and you have nothing to say?"

"I'm sure we've said it all, Victor."

She moved toward the phone. He grabbed her hand.

"Donna, please. What can I say?"

"Nothing, Victor. There's nothing you can say."

"I've said I'm sorry. Christ, how many times have I
said I was sorry? I'd do anything to take back that
night—"

"It wasn't that night, Victor." He looked surprised. "I
thought for a long time that it was. But it was only a small
part of everything else. Maybe even the least of it, I don't
know."

He obviously had no idea what she was talking about.
"Is there someone else?"

Donna looked into Victor's blue eyes and saw images
of Mel. "No," she said. She and Mel had not seen each
other in several months. By mutual choice, they had decided that if she were to end her marriage, it would be because it needed ending and for no other reason. Mel had
been the catalyst, but he was certainly not the cause.

She was walking out on her marriage because the hope
she had felt rekindled inside her body that first afternoon
with Mel had flatly refused to be buried again under Sisyphus' mighty rock. If an endless challenge with no hope
for the future was Sisyphus' idea of a good way to spend
eternity, well, that was fine. To each his own. But she
wasn't dead, after all, she had discovered, and she was
getting out of Hell.

"I'll let you know when I'm settled," she said. "You
can come see the kids. We can try to work out what's best
for everyone."

"What's best for everyone is for us to stay together."

"No. That's not best."

She called for a taxi. Victor was surprisingly quiet.

"It won't be easy by yourself, you know," he said, finally.

"I know."

"I don't think you do."

Donna shrugged.

"You can change your mind," he said. "Think about it. If you decide you want to come back—"

Donna nodded her head but said nothing.

"You'll call me soon?" he asked.

"Tomorrow."

"I love my children, Donna."

She felt the tears starting. "I know you do."

"I just don't think we should do anything rash or sudden—"

"I won't."

"You'll call me."

"Yes."

They heard a car pull up outside and honk.

"I love you, Donna," Victor said quickly.

Donna lowered her head. "I know you do, Victor." She took a deep breath. He moved toward her suitcases. "No, please," she said, her voice stopping him. "I'll do it."

"They're heavy," he cautioned.

She walked over to where the two medium-sized pieces of luggage sat on the floor and picked them up. "No, they're not," she said. A minute later, she was gone.

Chapter 14

Donna asked for, and received, a glass of cold water. Her throat was feeling very dry. She had been testifying all day. All morning, and now for more than three hours this afternoon. It was finally out, all of it. The marriage of Victor and Donna Cressy. According to Donna Cressy, of course. Testifying in her own behalf, she had spoken slowly and deliberately. Usually, she looked at her lawyer as she answered his questions; occasionally, she spoke directly to the judge. Surprisingly, she sometimes glanced at Victor, hoping to see even a glimmer of understanding in his face, something that said, "Ah, hah, now I see what you mean. I understand. Your honor, I withdraw my custody action. The woman is obviously in excellent control of all her faculties." But all she saw were shakes of his head, a commitment to his side of the story only.

Ed Gerber waited for her to finish her drink of water. He had been hammering away at her for the last hour and a half. Unlike her own attorney, who had been gentle and supportive, Mr. Gerber was sharp and angry. Outraged, from the sound of it. What she had done to the institution of marriage, the foundations of the family! My God, would Motherhood ever recover sufficiently well to carry on?

Donna's voice stayed level throughout his cross-examination. Despite her inquisitor's attempts to force her into the mold he had already sculpted for her, she remained steady, she did not cough or sneeze, her nose did not run, she did not scratch her hand and she had not had to ask for even one solitary Kleenex. She *had* asked for a glass of water, but no one had seemed to view this particular request as unusual.

"And so your husband made several, numerous attempts at a reconciliation?"

"Yes."

"You rebuffed them all?"

"Yes."

"When did these efforts of Mr. Cressy cease?"

"When I told him I was in love with someone else."

"With Dr. Mel Segal?"

"Yes."

Why was he going over this? She had already admitted her infidelity.

"Where are you living now, Mrs. Cressy?"

"I've rented a house in Lake Worth."

"And Dr. Segal?"

"He has a home in Palm Beach."

"You don't live together?"

"No."

"Why is that? Would you say it's against your moral code?" He almost choked on the words.

"We don't live together," Donna said coolly, "because I needed time to be alone with my two children. I did not leave one marriage so that I could rush into another relationship. I needed time to stand on my own two feet."

"But you still see Dr. Segal, is that correct?"

Donna looked over at Mel. "Yes," she said.

"And you intend to keep on with this relationship?"

"Yes."

"Until you tire of it as well, I suppose. Kind of like hair coloring—"

"Objection, your honor."

"Sustained."

Donna looked from both attorneys to the judge and then back to Mr. Gerber.

"Tell me, Mrs. Cressy," he continued, "what kind of a father is Victor Cressy?"

Donna looked over at Victor. "He's a good father," she said softly.

"I'm sorry. I couldn't hear that, Mrs. Cressy. Could you say that again, please?"

"I said that Victor is a good father," she repeated loudly.

"Concerned?"

"Yes."

"Attentive?"

"Yes."

"Interested?"

"Yes."

"Did he ever abuse his children?"

"No."

"Did he ever beat them?"

"No."

"Did he, ever, in fact, raise a hand to either of them?"

"No."

"Would he, in your opinion, take good care of them if the Court were to award him custody?"

Donna felt her saliva turning to dust inside her mouth. How she wanted to lie, to tell gross tales of perversion and wilful cruelty, to give Victor the horns and tail she wished the others could see. Except that there were none. He had none. Victor was never a monster, she realized. Only a man. The wrong man.

"Victor would always take good care of our children," she said.

"Has Mr. Cressy ever been unfaithful to you?" Ed Gerber asked suddenly.

"Not to my knowledge."

"He has always supported you well?"

"Yes."

"Provided a good home for you and his children?"

"For *our* children, yes."

"Oh, of course, excuse me. Thank you, Mrs. Cressy. That will be all."

It was over.

Donna sat motionless for several minutes, reluctant almost to give up the seat she had been occupying all these hours, feeling a little like a Queen for the Day now being forced to abdicate her throne. She looked toward the judge. I am a good mother, she wanted to say. Just because I admit that Victor is a good father does not in any way negate my contribution. Because he is concerned, attentive and affectionate doesn't make me any the less so. I'm the one who carried them, who bore them, who nursed them, bathed them, rocked them, changed them, cleaned up after them, played endlessly with them. Loved them. Love them still. Oh, how I love them. Please, please, don't take my children away from me. I don't think I could live without them. Don't take my babies away.

Instead, she said nothing but a simple thank you and stepped out of the witness stand, moving quickly to her lawyer's side.

The judge spoke as soon as she sat down. "Since it's Friday afternoon," he said in tones so solemn Donna found it hard to comprehend exactly what he was saying until he had already finished and had left the courtroom, "we will adjourn till Monday morning, at which time I will inform you of my decision. Have a pleasant weekend."

Donna waited until everyone had cleared the court. Mel was waiting for her in his car; her children were with Annie, and Mel's housekeeper. In a few minutes, she would get up and walk out, let Mel drive her home to what could be her last weekend as a full-time mother. A pleasant weekend, the judge had wished them. The only way this weekend could be anything but torturous would be if she were to sleep right through it, and she already knew she would get no sleep at all.

Donna looked around the now empty room. For three days, she had sat and listened to the Donna Cressy Story. As told to—a court full of strangers. As told by—Victor Cressy, his friends, neighbors and various confidantes. She had finally told her version—the only authorized version—as well. They had all given their précis of the Myth

of Donna Cressy, and like the eye-witnesses at the scene
of an accident, their descriptions varied with each individual accounting. There were no liars here.

Donna looked up at the now vacant judge's seat. He
looked like a kind man, a man who would try to be fair.
Fair—what was fair? Donna lowered her head to the long
table in front of her, covered her head with her hands and
cried.

Donna sat inside the crowded wicker and orange living
room, Sharon squirming restlessly on her lap, and listened
to the sound of the rain pouring down outside. Pouring
was hardly the correct word, Donna thought. Deluge
seemed more appropriate. The great flood, back by popu-
lar demand. Donna shifted her daughter wearily to a more
comfortable position. The child immediately shifted back.
The weekend was obviously not about to proceed according to Donna's plans.

First, the rain had put an abrupt end to any thought of
parks or beaches. It left them stuck indoors, and in
Adam's case especially, it left him restless and almost
hostile. Secondly, any new hopes for a quiet, perfect time
alone with her children were shattered when she was reminded that her children were neither quiet nor perfect.
Noisy, normal children did not make for quiet, perfect
times. To complete the pleasantries, the weatherman was
forecasting a similar day for tomorrow. Donna sighed
wearily—she had already exhausted all the ideas from her
book on creative play for preschoolers; she had already
allowed them more TV time and candy than was their
daily ration; Sharon had already taken her afternoon nap;
Donna's hands were tired from coloring, pasting, painting
and cutting out; and her voice was almost hoarse from
reading aloud everything in the house but the last issue of
Playboy magazine that the house's previous tenants had
left behind.

Adam walked back, sulking—his Saturday sulk, she
called it—into the room. If I have to tell him that story
one more time, she thought, thinking of the little boy

named Roger and the little girl named Bethanny. She had told it in all its possible variations at least twenty times since the morning. She didn't want to tell it again.

"Tell me a story," he whined, as if he could read her thoughts.

"Not now, Adam." Sharon squirmed again, pressing hard against a nerve on Donna's leg. Donna shifted her over; Sharon shifted back again.

"Tell me a story about a little boy named Roger and a little girl named Bethanny and they went to the zoo to see the giraffes. Tell me that one."

Donna looked impatiently at her son. "I can't right now, Adam. I'm reading Sharon a story. You can listen too, if you want."

Adam grabbed at the book. "That's my story," he said.

"It's your book," Donna conceded.

"She can't read it!" he shouted.

"I'm reading it to her."

"No!" He began pulling the book out of Donna's hands.

"Adam, you'll rip it—"

"She can't read it. You can't read it to her!"

"Adam, stop it!"

"It's my book! She can't read it!"

Sharon reached over and grabbed the book. "No!" Adam screamed, and started twisting Sharon's fingers, trying to pry them away from the book. "Get your hands off my book!"

"Adam—"

"She can't touch it!"

"Let's not get silly—"

"She can't touch it!" He started pushing at Sharon's shoulders.

"Adam, she'll fall!" Donna heard her voice raising.

"I want her to fall. I want her to get off you. I want my book!"

"You haven't looked at that book in two years!"

"I want to look at it now."

"Of course."

"I want it!" He pushed hard on Sharon's chest. Sharon, reasonably quiet up to this point, started to scream.

"You're going to get it!" Donna yelled, standing up abruptly, hearing the book fall to the floor, feeling Sharon wiggle out of her arms, seeing her two children tumble to the floor on top of each other, kicking and screeching all the while. When Donna heard the knock on the door some five minutes later, all three were nursing their assorted wounds and crying.

"Who is it?" Donna asked, walking slowly toward the front door.

"Terry Randolph," the woman called from the other side. Donna immediately opened the door. Terry Randolph and her young son Bobby jumped inside out of the rain. Adam came running over. "I'm sorry, did I catch you at a bad time?" the woman asked, noticing Donna's troubled expression and teary eyes.

"Rainy Saturday Blues," Donna answered.

"Exactly why I came over," Terry Randolph said cheerfully, showing a mouthful of teeth.

"Can I get you a cup of coffee—?"

"Oh, no, no," the woman said. "We're not staying. I guess I could have just phoned but Bobby's so rangy being cooped up all day, so I thought a little rain wouldn't hurt us. It's only two houses away, after all."

What did this woman want?

"We were just sitting around telling stories and stuff," Terry Randolph continued, "and suddenly Bobby piped up how he'd like to have Adam come on over and play—"

Oh, no, Donna thought. Not this weekend.

"Oh, can I, Mom?" Adam chirped enthusiastically.

"We thought he could play and have supper and then sleep over. Weatherman says it's going to rain all day tomorrow too."

"Oh boy! Oh boy! Can I, Mom?"

"Sweetie," Donna said, trying to collect her thoughts, thinking about her perfect weekend, possibly her last weekend with her children, seeing it vanish into the tor-rent outside and Terry Randolph's overbite. "Honey, I thought that we could—"

"I want to go! I want to go! Please." His eyes were beginning to cloud over.

Give it up, she said to herself, feeling a mild panic building inside her.

"Please—"

She swallowed hard, forcing the panic back down. This wasn't the end, she told herself. Don't get silly about this. Her voice was barely audible. "All right," she said.

"Wonderful," Terry Randolph squealed, looking as delighted as the two four-year-olds.

"I'll go get my pajamas," Adam yelled.

"I'll come with you," Donna volunteered, following quickly down the hall after her young son. When she got to the door of his small room, he already had his pajamas in his hand. "Don't forget your toothbrush," she said.

"It's in the bathroom," he answered, trying to get past her.

"Adam, are you sure you want to go? I mean, we could tell stories. I could tell you the story about a little boy named Roger and a little girl named Bethanny and one day they went to the zoo to see the giraffes—"

"I want to go to Bobby's," he wailed, interrupting her.

Donna straightened her shoulders. "Okay, okay. You go to Bobby's." But don't you dare be a good boy, she wanted to call after him. You be rotten, you hear me? You be a rotten kid! Then maybe she'll send you home.

After the door had closed behind them, Donna gathered her daughter into her lap again and picked up the discarded and long forgotten book on farmyard animals. "Well, it looks like it's just you and me, kiddo," she said.

Sharon brought her hand gently across her mother's cheek, her enormous eyes locked into Donna's. Then she sank back against Donna, refinding the painful nerve in Donna's leg and pressing down hard against it. Donna shifted her daughter once again to a more comfortable position. Once again, the child immediately shifted back.

The judge looked tired, as if he had been wrestling all weekend with Solomon's ghost. Would he suggest slicing her children in two? she wondered as the court was instructed to stand and then sit down again. Donna felt her knees shake with each successive motion. Oh God, please, please, she muttered silently. Her attorney covered her hands with his own. The judge spoke almost immediately.

"In the case of Cressy versus Cressy, I have given both the divorce and custody suits very careful consideration. I have reviewed the evidence in each instance and have reached my conclusions. As to the divorce action initiated by Mr. Victor Cressy against his wife, Donna Cressy, I find in favor of Victor Cressy. Divorce is granted on the grounds of Mrs. Cressy's admitted adultery."

Donna felt her heart beginning to sink despite her prior knowledge that Victor would most assuredly win this part of the suit. Still, just hearing the words, "I find in favor of Victor Cressy," made her feel vaguely sick, forced her to keep her eyes lowered and sightless, staring very hard at nothing at all.

"As to the custody suit," the judge continued, "this was not by any means as clear-cut an action. The court heard evidence for three days which was largely intended to support Mr. Cressy's contention that his wife is an unstable woman and hence, an unfit mother. Mrs. Cressy, herself, made no attempt to deny either her affair with Dr. Mel Segal or her often, shall we say, peculiar behavior." Donna held her breath. "But I find that while the evidence suggests a deeply unhappy woman, it does not support Mr. Cressy's contention that his wife is unbalanced or, in any way, unfit." Donna raised her eyes to meet the judge's. He continued to speak. "While it is obvious to the Court that both parents love their children, what must be considered here is the welfare of these children, and the Court feels that due both in part to their tender ages and to the fact that Mrs. Cressy would be staying home to look after them while Mr. Cressy would have to employ full-time outside help, that it is in the best interests of these children that they continue to live with their mother." Donna felt her eyes welling up with tears. "I, therefore, grant custody of Adam and Sharon Cressy to their mother, Donna Cressy."

Donna didn't hear the rest. The judge was talking about Victor's visitation rights, she knew. She had no problem with that. Victor could see his children whenever he liked. As often as he liked. My God, she had won.

She felt Victor looking at her even as she thought his name. Silently, he compelled her to look over in his direction. She turned and stared into hard, cold eyes. As much as I once loved you, they seemed to be saying, I hate you now. She thought of his earlier admonition—"I promise you," he had said, "that even if you win, you'll lose"—and shuddered.

What would you do to me if we don't work out? She had asked him on their wedding day. Donna felt a cold blade scissor through her insides as she recalled his answer. "I'd obliterate you," he had said simply. Donna turned quickly away from his gaze, but when she looked back at him seconds later, he was still staring at her. And smiling.

Part Two
THE PRESENT

Chapter 15

"Okay, kids, let's get a move on. Daddy's here."

Donna walked back toward Victor, who stood in the small hallway in possibly the most relaxed stance Donna had seen him assume since their divorce five months earlier. He was dressed all in white, which, combined with his dark tan and black hair, made him look better than she ever remembered. And yet, there was no longer any chemical reaction between them. When Donna looked into the deep blue mystery of his eyes, she felt only relief. Let someone else figure out what goes on in there, she thought, then wondered briefly if there *was* someone else.

"Sharon's on the potty," Donna explained with a smile. "Adam's watching her." She had begun to notice, with relief, that she no longer felt her stomach begin to churn every time Victor either phoned or showed up at her door. "Would you like a cold drink or something? It's pretty hot out there."

"The radio said it's the hottest April sixteenth in forty-four years," Victor said matter-of-factly, following Donna into the kitchen. "Ginger ale will be great."

Donna opened the fridge, took out a large bottle of ginger ale and placed it on the counter, deftly closing the fridge door with her foot. It was a very small kitchen, at least half the size of the one she had had when she lived with Victor, and yet it felt much larger. So much more breathing space, she thought, pulling a glass out of the cupboard and pouring him a drink.

The first time Victor had walked through the house, he had said little. Almost nothing. He had satisfied himself, Donna supposed, that she did not have his children living in squalor, and for whatever his reasons, he had saved whatever negative impressions she knew he must be feeling for himself.

The house was certainly small, Donna had to admit. Just the bare essentials—a combination living-dining area, three tiny bedrooms, the master bedroom distinguishable from the other two only by virtue of eighteen extra inches, one bathroom and the minute kitchen in which they were now standing. It's really not as little as it looks, she wanted to tell him every time he came over, but had initially restrained herself and now no longer felt the same necessity. Victor obviously was beginning to feel more comfortable with their situation. With her.

"Here," she said, handing him the glass, noticing a few drops of spilled liquid on the floor close by his feet. Victor said nothing about their presence, but she noticed him deliberately step around the increasingly prominent wet spots as they were about to leave the room.

"I thought I wiped it all up," she said, wishing she didn't still feel the need to always explain herself to Victor. Certainly, Mel never made her feel that way.

"Wiped what up?" Victor asked.

"Adam spilled some apple juice," she explained, her voice trailing off as they reached the living room.

"I didn't notice."

He was lying, Donna knew, appreciating the effort he was making. He'd come a long way in the last few months.

"I'll go see how Sharon's coming along." Donna motioned for Victor to make himself comfortable in the cheap wicker furniture the house had come complete with, and walked down the narrow hallway to the bathroom where Sharon sat, knees touching her chin, on the miniature white plastic toilet. Adam was now sitting on the real toilet, looking very much the little gentleman, even with his shorts pulled down around his ankles.

"Now, they're both busy," she said, coming back into the living room.

"No hurry," Victor said, sipping slowly on his ginger ale, trying his best to look comfortable. Donna sat in the chair across from him and tried not to stare. He was definitely a complicated man, she thought, going over the last five months quickly in her mind. He always made things so difficult for everyone—especially himself. In the beginning, in the months immediately following their divorce, she had thought this would be their pattern for eternity. But in the last few months, he had begun to mellow. Where, at first, he scowled, then he frowned, he now smiled. Or tried to. Where, before, he criticized, now he kept quiet. Perhaps in future months, there might be room for a compliment. Where once was stony silence, now there was polite, even warm, conversation. Perhaps, Donna reasoned, time had calmed him. Perhaps, once he had seen that Donna had no intention of denying him access to his children whenever he expressed his need or desire, he relaxed. Perhaps their divorce had freed him too. The last few years with her, Donna acknowledged, could not have been very pleasant for anyone, especially a man like Victor.

"What are you thinking about?" he asked suddenly.

Caught off guard, Donna blurted out the truth. "Us," she said, then quickly added. "The last few months."

He put his now empty glass on the rounded, heavily fingerprinted glass end table beside his chair. "It's starting to ease up a bit, isn't it?" he asked. She nodded. "I feel it," he continued. "I'm not so uptight about the whole thing anymore, I guess." She looked down.

"I'm glad."

"I fought it, I tell you," he went on, looking back up at Donna. "I really wanted to stay a mean bastard."

Donna laughed. "I'm glad you decided not to."

"Well, there comes a point when you've got to start taking your own advice. You were always telling me I had great theories but that I never followed through on any of them myself. And I thought about it—you see, I actually

did think a lot about some of the things you said—and I
decided you were right. There was no point sitting around
pouting about what was past, what had already been decided. The point was learning to live with it." He paused,
looking directly into her eyes. "I still don't like what's
happened to all our lives. But I have to accept the fact
that it *has* happened. I have to live with it."

"Are you seeing anyone?" she ventured, somewhat
shyly.

He smiled. "Oh, sure. A few people—nothing serious."
He paused. "I take it everything is still going great with
you and Mel. Did you catch that? I actually said his name
without gagging."

They both laughed. "Everything's fine," she said.

He looked around the mostly orange and white room.
He had never liked the color orange, Donna remembered.
"Do you think you'll eventually get married?" he asked. It
was a hard question to ask, she recognized, knowing he
wouldn't, couldn't, look back in her direction until she
had answered him.

Her voice was soft. "Probably," she said honestly. "Mel
has asked me several times. I just haven't felt ready."

"You like your independence," he said, standing up
and moving around.

"Well, the lease on this house still has seven months to
go. Maybe after that—"

They were both starting to feel vaguely uncomfortable
with the topic of conversation. "What's his little girl like?"
he asked, shifting the conversation just enough not to be
too obvious about the fact he was shifting the conversation.

"Annie? She's great. Wonderful. I really like her a lot.
She's crazy about the kids. It's her birthday tomorrow, as
a matter of fact. She'll be eight years old—Mel's having a
big party for her. She even invited Adam and Sharon—"

"Oh, I'm sorry. You should have told me—"

"No, don't be silly. Weekends are *your* time with them.
Annie understands that. Besides, I don't think she'd really

appreciate having them underfoot all afternoon. I think she was just being polite."

Victor smiled. "I can't imagine ever having been eight years old."

"I don't think you ever were," she joked, hoping as the words left her mouth that he would recognize them as such. He laughed.

"I'll tell you what I'll do," Victor offered suddenly. "What time's the party?"

"It starts at two. I guess it'll go till about five. Mel's having a magician."

"Oh, the kids would love that! I'll bring them over around four o'clock. How's that?"

Donna could scarcely hide her surprise. "That would be wonderful," she said, obviously delighted, then added, "but it's not necessary."

"I know it's not," he said. "Subject closed."

"Adam!" Donna called, not wishing to jeopardize a good thing by prolonging its discussion. "What are you doing in there?"

"I'm wiping Sharon's tushy," the small voice yelled back.

"Oh, dear, I better check this out." Donna excused herself and went back toward the bathroom. "Hey, good boy!" she said seeing both her children standing in front of their respective white seats, clothes all properly in place. "You got your pants pulled up all by yourself. Terrific."

Sharon put her arms around Donna's neck, and Donna hugged her little girl tightly against her body.

"Mmm, you're delicious."

The little girl laughed. "See? I pooped," she said proudly, pointing toward the small white bowl.

"Fantastic."

"It looks like the number nine, Mommy," Adam said, also pointing inside the potty. Donna started to laugh. "Next time," Adam asked with great excitement, "can she make a number four?"

"Number Four. Number Four," Sharon laughed, clapping, as Donna adjusted her daughter's sundress, emptied the potty into the toilet and flushed.

Donna walked with the children back into the hallway where Victor now stood waiting. Adam ran into his father's arms. "Sharon made a number nine! Next time, she'll make a number four. Four is my favorite number. Yay!"

Donna handed Victor the bag she had packed with the children's clothes. "There's some Pampers in there if you need them for Sharon."

"No Pamper," Sharon insisted.

"She hasn't had an accident in three days," Donna continued.

"Terrific," Victor said, then looked over at Adam. "Quite a switch."

Donna smiled. "Going anywhere special with them?"

"I thought we might drive over to Lion Country Safari, but it's so hot, I don't know. Maybe we'll just go to the beach. We'll play it by ear."

Donna walked them to the door. "Have a good time with Daddy, sweeties," she said, kneeling down.

"I want to see the lions," Adam squealed, about to run outside.

"Kiss Mommy goodbye," Victor admonished.

"Bye," the young boy said, kissing her quickly on the cheek, then running eagerly outside toward his father's car.

Donna looked at her daughter, at twenty-two months, a chubby little porcelain doll with huge piercing blue eyes that looked right through you, like a little witch about to cast a spell. Eyes that seemed to see everything, absorb all there was to absorb. Aware. So aware. "You be a good girl with Daddy, and have a good time."

The little girl threw her arms around her mother's neck. "Are you coming?" she asked clearly. It was a phrase she had mastered early.

"No, honey. I'll see you tomorrow."

Victor took Sharon's arm. "Let's go, Sharon. The lions are waiting."

"I want Mommy."

Victor bent down and scooped the child up into his arms. "See you tomorrow," he called to Donna as he proceeded down the walkway.

Donna watched them through the door. She watched Adam buckle himself into the back seat and watched as Victor adjusted Sharon into her special infant seat beside her brother. She was still calling out for Mommy. That was strange, Donna thought, watching the car drive off, and then closing the door against the oppressive heat. Victor had been coming for his children every weekend for the past five months. Today was the first time that Sharon had cried.

"Can't we have the magician now?" Annie asked from underneath her pink and red striped party hat.

Donna checked her watch. It was just past three o'clock. She knelt down so that she could talk face to face with Mel's daughter. "Could we wait another hour, honey? Till four? That way Adam and Sharon can see the magician too."

The young girl's face lit into a smile. "Oh, I forgot. They can come!" Donna smiled. "Okay, we'll wait."

"We'll be serving the cake and ice cream in a few minutes," Donna winked, standing up, feeling her knees crack. "Why do my knees always crack when I try to stand up?" she asked no one in particular.

Her friend Susan Reid provided her with an immediate answer. "Old age," she said happily.

Donna turned to face her. "Thanks a lot. I'm so glad I invited you over to help me out."

"What are friends for?"

"I thought most people's knees cracked when they bent down, not when they stood up."

"Yea, well, you were always a bit peculiar. Know any good doctors?"

Donna looked closely at her long-time friend. "Do you ever change?" Susan looked at her quizzically. "I mean, I think that you and I have been exchanging this kind of—

banal banter since we were sixteen. And don't get me wrong, I like it. It's kind of reassuring in a way, knowing that whatever we say, essentially it's all the same thing. Do you understand?"

"No. You been eating funny cookies?"

Donna laughed, looking over at the fifteen noisy youngsters running about the white ceramic tiled patio. "Look at them all," she said, "they're eight years old, maybe nine. Basically, whatever they're going to be is already there. We get older, but we don't really change."

Susan looked from Donna to the crowded patio. "You're trying to tell me you were a peculiar kid too?"

Donna shook her head. "Let's serve the cake."

An hour later, Mel came up behind Donna and put his arms around her waist. "Annie keeps asking me when we can have the magician. It's ten after four."

Donna turned to face him. "Damn. Do you think she can wait for ten, fifteen more minutes? That's all. I'm sure they'll be here by then."

"You're sure Victor said four o'clock?" Donna nodded. "Could be he's changed his mind."

"No, he'd phone if he had. I mean, it was his idea. It's probably something dumb holding them up. I bet Adam's on the toilet or something. You know how long Adam can sit on that thing."

"Maybe you should phone."

"Ten minutes, okay? If they're not here in ten minutes, I'll call them."

"Okay. I'll talk to Annie."

Donna watched Mel as he walked over to talk to his daughter. She smiled with satisfaction. How had she managed to get this lucky? A wonderful man, his terrific kid—and they were both crazy about her. She looked over at the abandoned party table, the young guests having deserted their plates of leftover icing and melted ice cream for the raucous sound of the Village People, a gift to Annie from one of her friends. So this is what they give the eight-year-olds of this world, she thought, looking over at the assortment of records and posters (Kiss, Andy

Gibb, a barechested Erik Estrada—whoever he was) that Annie's peers had showered her with. She looked back at Annie, watching Mel surround his daughter with his arms, and smiled as she saw the child agree to wait another ten minutes. Mel hugged her, then walked back toward Donna.

The last five months had been a revelation to Donna. After six years of convincing herself that her relationship with Victor was symbolic of all relationships, she was constantly amazed to discover that it just wasn't so. After six years of telling herself that another man would simply mean another set of problems, another armload of idiosyncrasies, she was delighted to discover she had been utterly wrong. There *were* men around who were content to let you dress yourself, feed yourself and even blow your own nose. Not everything was worth a major debate. Not every difference of opinion led to all-out war. If anything, Mel went overboard in the other direction. There were a few things that were very important to him—Annie, his work, herself—and everything else was there to arrange or rearrange for their convenience. Almost nothing was worth fighting about. Fighting was a wasteful activity. Playing mind games was destructive. If something made Donna happy, well, then, that was fine with him. If she felt like Chinese food, great. If she wanted to see three movies in the course of one evening, well, why not? If he didn't like something, he said so, flat out. There were no guessing games here.

He walked over to Donna and kissed her on the nose. "What are you standing here grinning about?"

"I didn't think it was supposed to be this easy," she said.

"What?"

"Love."

He laughed. Then he checked his watch. "We have eight minutes before you have to make that phone call," he whispered. "Feel like a quickie?"

Donna laughed. "I love you."

"Does that mean no quickie?"

She nodded. "We can have a whole bunch of quickies later on."

"Umm. Good stuff." He kissed her nose again. "You have a terrific nose."

Donna looked toward the door. "I wish they'd get here," she said anxiously.

After another ten minutes, Donna walked into the kitchen to use the phone. She dialed quickly and waited while the phone rang several times. "Come on, Victor, where are you?" she said to herself, hoping that instead of his voice on the other end of the line, she would hear his brusque knock on the door. The phone made a funny click and a recorded voice suddenly sounded in Donna's ear.

"I'm sorry, the number you have dialed has been disconnected—"

"Oh, rats," Donna exclaimed, hanging up the phone just as Mel and Annie walked into the room.

"They're not coming?" Mel asked.

"No, I dialed the wrong number. 'I'm sorry, the number you have dialed has been disconnected,'" she mimicked.

"Some of the kids have to leave pretty soon," Mel said.

"Can't we have the magician now?" pleaded Annie.

Donna took a deep breath. "Sure," she said. "It's your party, isn't it? I don't know what's happened to Victor."

"Go to it!" Mel said, swatting Annie's behind as she ran from the room. "Sorry, honey, but it's really not fair to keep them waiting any longer."

"Oh, that's fine. Really." Donna paused. "You don't think that anything's happened to them or anything, do you?"

"No, I'm positive nothing's happened to them. Victor probably took them somewhere for the day and he just couldn't get back in time."

"I guess so."

"Come on, let's go see the Amazing Armando."

At five-thirty, all the junior guests had departed and Annie was busy looking over her newest acquisitions. Mel, Susan and Donna sat in the comfortable space that was Mel's living room and had a final cocktail.

"Well, I don't know what to do," Donna said, obviously worried. "I don't know whether to stay here and wait for Victor in case he shows up or to go home."

"What's the usual set-up?" Susan asked.

"He usually brings the kids back between six and six-thirty."

"To your place?"

"Oh, yea. He never comes here."

"Then why would he start today?"

Donna was beginning to feel vaguely sick to her stomach. "I better get home."

Mel stood up. "I'll drive you."

"No," Donna said, also standing. "You promised Annie you'd take her to see *Stars Wars* tonight. Susan can drive me."

Susan got to her feet, quickly gulping down the last of her drink, speaking in Mel's direction. "Sure, I'll stay with her till Victor brings the kids home."

After several minutes, Mel reluctantly agreed. "Why don't you call him before you leave?"

"No!" Donna said, louder than she had intended to. Annie looked over in their direction. "Sorry," Donna explained, trying to keep her voice calm despite her growing sense of panic. What was she so afraid of? "I just don't want to bother him. Things have been going so well lately that I don't want to spoil them by making Victor think that I'm checking up on him. I don't want him to think—I mean, he's changed so much recently—"

"Donna, are you okay?" Mel asked. For a long minute, there was absolute silence.

"People don't change," Donna said numbly.

"What are you talking about?" Susan asked.

"People don't change. I told you that earlier. Victor hasn't changed." Donna began to move frantically about in place, her eyes directed at nothing in particular. "My

God, he hasn't changed at all. I know it. I can feel it. Mel, my God, Mel, Victor hasn't changed at all."

Susan tried to maneuver Donna back toward the over-stuffed beige-and-white sofa. "Come on, Donna, sit down for a minute—"

"No!" Donna pushed Susan away, her eyes still frozen open, seeing only Victor. "Kiss Mommy goodbye," she heard him say. "No!"

"Leave her alone," Mel cautioned Susan. Out of the corner of her eye, Donna saw Annie moving toward her father. "I'll call Victor," Mel began.

"He won't be there!" Donna shouted, the horrible fear that had been gnawing all afternoon at the pit of her stomach finally finding words at the tip of her tongue. "He's gone. I know it, he's gone. He's taken my babies—"

"Daddy—" Annie started, a mild whine of fear in her voice.

"Just a minute, honey," Mel cautioned, turning back to Donna. "Look, Donna, we gain nothing by standing around here worrying about it. Let's just go find out."

"Where will we go?"

"To Victor's."

"You can't," Donna protested irrationally. "You promised Annie you'd take her to see—"

"The fucking movie can wait." Mel turned to Annie. "That's right, isn't it, honey?"

"Sure," Annie said, a mixture of trepidation and disappointment in her voice. "The fucking movie can wait."

"That's my girl," he said, tussling her hair. "Susan, would you mind staying with Annie till we get back?"

"No problem," Susan answered, as Mel put his arm through Donna's and led her out into the front hall. "You'll call me as soon as you straighten everything out?"

"We'll call," he said, opening the front door and leading Donna out into the air of the approaching night.

Donna kept up a steady flow of chatter the entire drive, fearing that if she stopped talking, even for an instant, her worst fears would become an accepted reality.

"He won't be there, Mel. He's gone. That number I dialed, it wasn't the wrong number. I knew it at the time. I knew I hadn't misdialed, but I wouldn't let myself believe it. When he didn't show up at four o'clock, I convinced myself that they still would, that there was plenty of time. I made up all sorts of excuses, when I knew, deep down I knew. I had this sick feeling in my gut. I had it from the middle of the afternoon when I was talking to Susan, telling her that people don't change. I was trying to tell myself something then, only I wouldn't listen. Why wouldn't I listen? I listened to Victor! Christ, I almost had to convince him it was all right for him to take the children for the weekend. He sounded so genuinely disappointed that the kids wouldn't get to go to Annie's party." Donna took a pause only long enough to swallow her accumulation of saliva. "Why did I believe him? I was married to the man for six years. I remember the things he said to me, that no court of law would ever take his children away, that even if I won the custody suit, I'd lose—that he'd fight me till there was nothing left of me! How could I forget he said those things? How could I forget that he'd already packed up and left one life back in Connecticut? What made me think he wouldn't do it again?"

Mel looked sadly at Donna. "What could you have done?" he asked. "There's no way you could have foreseen any of this, Donna. There's no way you could have stopped it even if you had."

Donna felt the first tear starting to fall down her cheek. "You know I'm right, don't you?" she asked.

"We'll find out in a few minutes."

Mel pressed down harder on the accelerator. Donna continued her verbal stream-of-consciousness. "How could I let myself be so fooled? I don't understand. I remember how he was introduced to me—'This is Victor Cressy, the best insurance salesman in the Southern Hemisphere.' How many times did he tell me he could sell sand to the Arabs, for God's sake? Don't you see, Mel? He sold me a desert full of sand! The whole thing was an act. He let us think he'd mellowed—very gradually, of course, that's why we fell for it. He started out bitter and angry and then he started easing up a little every week. Just enough to always be believable, to make us accept him. And I did. Just like he planned. Like he knew I would. Oh, God, Mel, how long do you think he's been planning this?"

Mel said nothing. They both knew the answer. Victor had been setting his scheme in motion from the day of the judge's decision, if not earlier. It was quite possible he'd made up his mind on the evening of Donna's initial departure. He waited only long enough to make whatever arrangements he deemed necessary. Until everyone was perfectly relaxed. Even happy.

"Annie's birthday was a little bonus for him," Donna said quietly, "the salt for the wound."

They drove past Donna's rented house in Lake Worth, but it was as Donna had left it and Victor's car was nowhere around. "He's not there," she said, crawling back into the car after a brief look around. Mel threw the car into gear and they continued their drive toward Lantana.

Suddenly, Donna's voice turned cold with terror. "You don't think he's hurt them, do you? Oh God, Mel, you don't think he's done something awful to them?" She started to shake.

Mel pulled the car over to the side of the road and quickly hugged Donna to him. Then he moved away from her and forced her eyes to look deep into his. "Look at me," he commanded gently. "You're getting panicky. Calm down. We don't even know that there's anything out of line here at all. Victor could be at home getting the kids ready to bring back to you right now. To start imagining that Victor's done something to hurt them is nonsense, honey. No matter what kind of man Victor is or isn't, no matter what he might do or not do to try and hurt you, the one thing I am absolutely certain of is that he would never—never—hurt his children. He loves them, Donna. He may not always be a very nice man, but he's not inhuman."

Donna burst into tears against Mel's chest. "Cry it out, baby," he said.

After several minutes, Donna looked up and moved back into her previous position. Mel started the car again and they continued along their way. Donna wiped her eyes with a Kleenex. "Wouldn't it be something if I'm all wrong?" She started to laugh. "Here, I get myself all worked up for absolutely no reason whatsoever—Victor always used to say that I got myself all worked up for no reason—and we'll get there and he'll be there with Adam and Sharon and a perfectly logical explanation for why they ruined Annie's birthday, made her miss the movie—"

"Would you stop worrying about that movie—"

"And he'll be there. And he'll say, 'What happened to your eyes? Your mascara is running.' " She laughed again, a laugh of desperation, hoping she was right, praying he would be there. Oh God, please be there.

The house was dark.

"Oh, God."

"Take it easy, Donna. They could be in the back. Or we might have just missed them."

Donna and Mel opened their doors simultaneously, unbuckling their seat belts and running out of the car toward the house. Donna frantically tried the door, but it was locked. She no longer had a key. "Goddamn," she shouted, throwing her weight against it. Mel ran around to the back of the house while Donna walked around trying to peer into the various windows.

"No one's out back," Mel said, upon his return.

"There's no one here," Donna said, with quiet resignation.

Mel walked over to the front window and peered inside. "Furniture seems to be all there."

"That doesn't mean anything," Donna said. "He'd leave it." She stood lifeless in front of the doorway. "He's gone. He's taken my babies."

"We'll find him, Donna, I promise you, we'll find him."

"Donna?" The voice caught them off guard. They had not seen her approach, had not felt her presence. "I saw you from my garden, and I thought it was you. The old eyes are really starting to go, you know." Donna turned abruptly to confront Arlene Adilman.

"Where is Victor?" Donna asked, hearing the panic behind her words.

"Oh, he left yesterday," the woman replied casually. "Got eighty-five thousand for the house. Sold it with the furniture and everything. Some nice, young couple. They'll be moving in tomorrow. Apparently they bought the place over three months ago. Paid all cash from what I understand. Didn't even know he'd had it up for sale till he came over to say goodbye and to give me this." She held out a small white envelope. "He said you'd probably come by tonight."

Donna grabbed the envelope from the startled woman's hands. She fumbled around impotently for a few seconds, unable to open it, her hands shaking almost uncontrollably. Mel took the envelope from her and quickly tore it open, handing it back to Donna immediately without looking inside. "Where did Victor go?" Mel asked, as Donna quickly perused the few short words Victor had written.

"I have no idea," Mrs. Adilman said. "Don't you know?"

A low wail began to slowly fill the surrounding air. It started as a hum, became stronger, a definite tone, growing, growing, getting higher and higher until it thrust itself into the open air and exploded. Mel quickly threw his arms around Donna, holding her neck tightly against him, but nothing could muffle the intensity of her cry. The final, agonizing death wail of an animal caught in a hunter's trap. The sound had no beginning and no end. It sprang from the belly like a newborn infant and escaped into the air a full-grown demon.

Mel reached down and prodded the note away from Donna's tightly clenched fist. Holding the note up behind

Donna's back, he read the brief message that Victor had earlier penned:

The point is learning to live with it.

Mel crumpled the note in his hand and threw it angrily to the ground.

Chapter 16

"What were they wearing the last time you saw them?"

Donna stared into the golden-flecked eyes of the moon-faced police lieutenant. He was a short man, intensely muscular but surprisingly neutral in appearance, as if the exaggerated curve of his chin and jowls had wiped out any remaining traces of a character that might have earlier existed. It was a face that betrayed nothing. Probably the ideal face for a police lieutenant, Donna thought absently.

She was so weary. They'd had no sleep the night before, the police having asked them to come back in the morning, Sunday night being no time to cope with anything other than the kind of dire emergencies that Palm Beach County seldom had. Their phone calls—to Danny Vogel and other of Victor's friends and acquaintances—had proved useless. Each knew nothing or claimed to. Donna suspected it was the former. Victor would take no chances. Never having been one to confide in his friends, he would not be about to start now. His disappearance would be well-planned, clean, and total. They had called both Ed Gerber and Mr. Stamler. Neither lawyer was able to be of much help, though they had appointments set up with both men for later in the day.

"Adam was wearing a white-and-blue striped jersey," Donna said softly, picturing her little boy as he sat proudly on the toilet, beaming over in her direction. "And white shorts. No socks. Blue sandals."

"And the little girl?"

The tears immediately began to fall down Donna's cheeks, her eyes already swollen almost shut from crying. "She was wearing a red-and-white checked sundress," she said slowly, trying to keep her voice from cracking. "With matching underpants with ruffles. And white sandals." She stopped, feeling her daughter's small arms around her neck. Mmm, you're delicious, she had told the child. "And a white ribbon in her hair," she added. "Her hair is very curly."

"Yes, we have their photographs," the lieutenant reminded her gently, holding up the pictures she had brought in. "They're beautiful children."

"Yes, they are." Donna reached over and grabbed Mel's hand. They sat side by side across from the police lieutenant. The small sign on his desk identified him as one Stan Robinson. Donna estimated his age at around fifty. He was staring at her, probably trying to organize what he was about to say, but Donna got no clues from the set of his features. She felt only that whatever he was about to say, she was not going to like it.

"I hate cases like this," he began. Donna caught her breath. "We're seeing more and more of them lately. Like an epidemic. One parent gets custody; the other runs off with the kids." He shook his head. "It's about the meanest thing you can do to somebody." He paused. "And there's not a lot we can do about it."

"What do you mean there's not a lot you can do about it?" Donna demanded.

"There's a term for what your husband's done," Lieutenant Robinson said evenly. "It's called legal kidnapping. A parent kidnaps his own kids. It's not really kidnapping because it's a parent. There's no ransom. The object isn't to hurt the child. There's no law against it. They keep talking about bringing in a law but," he shrugged, "frankly, even if they do, it would be a pretty hard law to enforce. I can't see it doing much good."

"But he's in defiance of a court order," Mel argued.

"Yes, that's true. So, we got something there. You find him, we'll slap him with a court order."

Donna felt a strange buzzing sound behind her ears. "You won't help us?"

"We'll help you as much as we can," the lieutenant said, "but I don't think it'll do you a lot of good. Look, Patty Hearst disappeared for how many years? And we had the whole country out looking for her. You're talking about a man and two kids who nobody knows and nobody cares about except the two of you, and you're talking about a whole globe he could be hiding in. The kids got passports?"

"What?"

"You got the kids registered on either you or your ex-husband's passports?"

Donna looked frantically at the ceiling, then back at the police lieutenant. "I have them on mine," she said with some excitement. "When I went to have my passport renewed last year, I had the kids registered on it, I don't know why."

Mel's free hand reached over and squeezed their already interlocked other hands.

Stan Robinson stood up and moved around the desk. "Well, then, at least we know he can't leave the country." Donna let out a deep breath. "That leaves fifty states and probably Canada." He paused long enough to let the hopelessness of his words sink in. "I don't think you need a passport to get into Canada," he continued. "We can check with immigration, but I doubt it'll turn up anything."

"What else can you do?" Mel asked.

"Basically, just tell you what you can do."

"Which is?"

"Call all the airlines, see if they have a record of Mr. Cressy and the kids on any of their recent flights. I'd also call the Tampa and Miami airports. That's a hell of a job because there are so many airlines and thousands of flights he could have taken, if he took a plane at all. Probably he did, but then he probably also used a phony name and paid cash for the tickets. You could check with whatever banks Mr. Cressy used, see if he closed out or transferred any accounts, but I doubt they'll tell you anything. Check where he worked. Maybe he got a transfer. Call your lawyer. Call anyone who knew him. Any relatives. Send pictures to all your friends and family who live out of state, if you have any. You can hire a private detective, but that gets pretty expensive, and usually they don't turn up much unless you can give them lots to work with. Try and remember any place he might have mentioned that he'd like to live. What does he like to do? Any particular sport?" He leaned against the desk. "We had a case here not too long ago where the mother got custody and the father took off with the kid—a little girl. Six years old, I think. The mother hired lawyers, detectives, the works. Couldn't find her. Took a year. They finally found them in Colorado. Husband liked to ski. But it wasn't the lawyers or the detectives or even the wife who clued in. They got a phone call one day from a friend who lived in South Africa, of all places. He'd been to Aspen skiing on a holiday and he saw the guy lining up at one of the slopes."

"Victor doesn't like to ski," Donna muttered numbly, hearing the buzzing sound once more behind her ears.

"The point is—" Lieutenant Robinson said.

Mel cut him off. "She got the point, Lieutenant."

Stan Robinson walked back behind his desk. "Yea, well, I'm sorry. I really wish there was more we could do."

"So do we," Mel said, standing up and helping Donna to her feet.

The buzzing sound grew louder. Before they had walked several steps, Donna felt her legs buckle beneath her, was aware that Mel's arms had prevented her from falling, but was aware of nothing else except the persistent buzzing. Then she fainted, and the buzzing stopped.

The woman had Victor's eyes and full mouth, but aside from these two features, there was little to connect Lenore

Cressy with her son. The woman was blonde, although this was undoubtedly aided by artificial coloring, and was quite short, where Victor was tall and dark. She was somewhat top heavy but she dressed tastefully, even meticulously, and her makeup was cleverly, almost artfully done, to disguise the unwanted wrinkles and creases of age. Donna looked hard at the woman, estimating her age, from what she knew of her background, at close to seventy, although she looked easily ten years younger. Except for the sadness around her eyes, she was still an amazingly attractive woman.

"I haven't seen my son in over eight years," she said with simple directness. Donna felt her heart sink. It was a feeling she had become increasingly familiar with in the last five days.

She and Mel had called every friend or acquaintance Donna could ever remember Victor so much as mentioning—no one knew anything. No one had any ideas. Victor never talked about his plans to anyone—his office had been stunned by his sudden departure. They had no idea where he might have vanished. The airlines had been initially very uncooperative, unwilling, until the police stepped in, to go over the previous Saturday's passenger lists. When the situation was formally explained to them, they grudgingly acquiesced, but after several days, each airline had come back with nothing. No Victor Cressy was anywhere on record. And there were simply too many single parents traveling with children to try to run them all down. Sharon, of course, would not even have required a ticket. If Victor had not used his real name, and he obviously had not, there was no hope in finding them through the airlines.

The bank where Donna had shared an account with Victor was likewise of no help. They could release no information, she was told, though as Donna was about to leave, a sympathetic teller had informed her secretly that Mr. Cressy had closed his account there months ago.

None of this came as any surprise to Donna, but it did come as a constant disappointment nonetheless. Ed Ger-

ber had been kinder than Donna had prepared herself
for—he seemed genuinely surprised by Victor's actions—
but he claimed he knew nothing that could be of any
help. Mr. Stamler said he had various contacts in various
states whom he said he would get in touch with immediately. He also arranged for the hiring of a private detective, who so far had turned up nothing except the fact
that Victor had sold his car—for cash—to Ben's used car
lot on South Dixie. He had apparently dropped it off just
after leaving Donna. The private detective had also called
all airline limousines and taxis but no one remembered
anything substantial. One cab driver thought he remembered taking a man and a couple of kids to the airport either Saturday or Sunday, but he couldn't remember what
airlines, and even if he had, there had been nothing to
stop Victor from then proceeding on to another terminal.
It was all futile anyway, since the airlines had no record
of any Victor Cressy. Knowing Victor, Donna thought, he
had probably changed planes several times in several cities, enjoying every minute along the way.

They had sent pictures of Victor and the kids to everyone they knew who lived out of state, including Mel's four
sisters, two of whom lived in the L.A. area, and two who
lived on the East Coast, and his two brothers, one in the
state of Washington and the other in Hawaii. They sent
similar pictures and information to Donna's sister, Joan,
who was currently living in England, just in case Victor
had managed to somehow get the children out of the
country.

And finally, they had come here to Connecticut. To see
Lenore Cressy.

The woman's eyes filled with tears as Donna poured
out her story. With each new fact, the woman seemed to
grow increasingly fragile. When she finally spoke, her
voice was barely audible. "I never knew that I had grand-
children," she said, making no move to stem the flow of
her pain.

"I'm so sorry, Mrs. Cressy," Donna said with genuine
feeling. "I asked Victor many times in the first years of

our marriage to let me call you, but he was very adamant. I kept hoping you would call, but you never did."

"I called for almost two years, but he would never speak to me. Finally, I stopped calling."

Mel's voice immediately trailed the older woman's. Donna was startled—she'd almost forgotten he was there. "How did you find out Victor had gone to Florida, Mrs. Cressy?" he asked.

"A friend of mine, Mrs. Jarvis, a widow, she went down to Palm Beach to spend the winter. She ran into Victor at a movie one night. He pretended he didn't know who she was, but she knew."

Donna lowered her head. Another accidental sighting like the man skiing in Aspen, Colorado. How long unti¹ they had a similar accident? A month? Two? A year? Five years? Ever? The thought made her start to tremble. She looked around the well-appointed living room. The furniture was obviously old but, like its owner, meticulously maintained.

"Mrs. Cressy," Donna asked, leaning forward in her seat toward the woman who sat across from her. "Can you tell me anything at all about Victor that might help me find him?"

The woman shook her head. "He always took things so to heart," she said, remembering. "Even as a boy, you had to be so careful about anything you said to him, be careful he didn't take it the wrong way. His feelings were always so easily hurt. You had to be so careful." Her voice trailed off, then continued. "He always worried about doing everything exactly the right way. He could never accept responsibility if something went wrong. It was always somebody else's fault. He used to make himself sick with worry the first day of school every year—he was always worried that he wouldn't go in the right door, of all things. Very concerned that he wouldn't find the right door." Again, she stopped.

Donna stared long and hard at the woman who was obviously lost in her own memories. "Mrs. Cressy," she persisted, "would you please call me if you ever hear anything from Victor? Please."

Lenore Cressy's voice was quiet. "No," she said, simply and quietly.

Donna felt as if the word had been loudly shouted in her ear. For a second, she thought she had not heard correctly or that the older woman had misinterpreted her request. Lenore Cressy caught the confusion in Donna's eyes. "You have to understand," she said hesitating, obviously debating with herself whether or not she should call Donna by her first name or as Mrs. Cressy, and then deciding not to call her anything at all, "that eight years ago, I lost my only son because of something stupid that I did. I'm not about to make that same mistake again." Once more, she hesitated. Donna substituted the word Donna for the pause.

"You won't help me?" Donna asked, incredulously.

"For eight years," the woman answered, "I have been praying for another chance. I won't lie to you. If Victor called me, gave me that chance, I'd never betray him again."

"But you never betrayed him to begin with!"

"He thinks I did." She stopped, her head moved slowly from side to side. "Funny, how sometimes the harder you try to do the right thing, the worse it turns out. I tried so hard with Victor and Janine never to interfere in their lives, to always listen to both sides if they ever came to me with a problem, not to judge them. I tried always to be fair. Look where it got me." She looked back directly at Donna. "I'm sorry," she said with great finality. "I won't be able to help you."

Donna felt the frustration rising in her voice, felt the tears edging up behind her eyes. "But they're my children!"

The woman's voice was calm. "He's my son."

"He's a shit, what else can I tell you?"

Donna stared hard at the young woman who sat across from her amid the plethora of cushions on her bright cherry-and-pink flowered sofa. Janine Gauntley Cressy McCloud was perhaps a year or two older than Donna, her face full of interesting angles, her body lush with the early months of pregnancy.

"I spent three years on the couch because of that creep," the young woman was saying. "It took me another three years after that to like men enough to marry one of them, and here I am now, almost thirty-six, finally about to have my first child. You know, even hearing that crud's name still makes me angry, even after all these years."

Donna compared herself silently with Victor's earlier wife. Physically, there was a mild, superficial resemblance. They were both the same approximate height and coloring, the same general age range, but that was really all. Intellectually, Janine McCloud seemed more street-smart, less bookish. Emotionally, she seemed tougher, more coarse. Not really what Donna had expected at all.

"We were married for two years, the most miserable two years of my life. Don't ask me why. I honest-to-God have no idea. I tried—I really did. I wasn't a child-bride or anything. I'd been around a bit. But I'd never met anybody like Victor. I didn't know what to do for him—to make him happy. Nothing I did was right. I busted my butt trying to accommodate him, and you know what he does? He walks out! Announces he wants a divorce. I couldn't believe it."

"And Lenore?"

Janine McCloud stood up and walked to the window. It was night. Her husband was off playing basketball at the local Y. "Oh, her. She's a real case. As bad as he is."

Donna looked surprised. She remembered Victor's assessment of his ex-wife's relationship with his mother.

"I tell you," the woman continued, "that whole family's nuts. All two of them. You wanna know, I made a real effort to be friends with that woman. I was never very close with my own mother and Lenore seemed like a nice enough lady, although, at first, I tell you, she didn't think I was good enough for her little boy and she made that very clear. If there's one thing that lady is, it's honest. But

I was pretty persistent because it seemed important to Victor—I wanted him to be happy. So, I called her every day, I took her to lunch, I visited her all the time. I don't think she ever really accepted me, but she tried—listen, she wanted Victor to be happy too. That was the main thing. Make Victor happy. He was her golden boy, all right. Victor Cressy could do no wrong. She always took his side, no matter what the argument. No matter how badly he behaved. She was always there to make excuses for him. He worked too hard, she'd say, he was under so much pressure. I shouldn't take everything he said so seriously. She was blind as far as he was concerned. She would do whatever he told her to do. I guess 'cause his father died when he was so young and Victor kind of took over, made all the decisions. And she likes that. But underneath it all, she's a very tough little lady. You know what I used to call her? Not to her face, of course, just to myself. I used to call her Mighty Mouse!" She stopped, grimacing and shaking her head. "Hey, I'm not being very nice. I mean, when Victor walked out, she was really very sweet to me. I was in a bad way. Lenore was always there for me. Suddenly, Victor gives her some sort of ultimatum, and I guess it caught Lenore a bit off guard, she took too long to answer—I don't know, and off he goes. Disappears. Wow! Really messed her up." She stopped, walking back from the window to where Donna and Mel sat on the red-and-white striped love seat. "So what does she do? She cuts *me* off—right off. Same as him. Exactly. Just in case he comes back, he's gotta see she's no longer consorting with the enemy. Or something. Beats the shit out of me."

Donna heard Victor repeating the same phrase during their first incredible dinner together in New York, undoubtedly borrowing an expression of his ex-wife's, making it sound so charming because it was so incongruous.

"I really can't help you any," Janine Cressy McCloud continued. "I mean, the only thing you can predict about Victor is that he'll never do what you predict." She sat down. "Wow. I'm beat. Talking about him is almost as bad as living with him." She ran a hand through her shoulder-length hair. "I can't believe how much anger I still have inside me, after all these years."

I can, Donna thought, and stood up to leave. There was no further point in staying.

Donna sat silently for a long minute before she found her voice.

"He won't come here," she said. "It was a dumb idea."

Mel looked around the dimly lit interior of the small, crowded New York restaurant. "Good food, though," he said, trying to joke her out of her increasing gloom. "You should eat something."

"I'm not hungry. Please don't patronize me."

Mel was instantly apologetic. "I'm sorry. I really didn't mean to be patronizing."

Donna shrugged her shoulders, reluctant to look at him.

"We'll find them," Mel assured her. "I promise you."

"How? When?" Please, someone, give me some definite answers.

"Someone's bound to see him. A week from now. A month from now—"

"A year from now—"

"Possibly. Possibly more."

"Oh, God, Mel." Donna felt needles of panic pricking at her sides.

"The important thing is for you to stay well. To stay healthy and on top of things. You can't let this destroy you. You have to keep going on, trying to live a normal life—"

Donna looked at him angrily, knocking over a spoon from her side of the table, hearing it fall noisily onto the floor. What was the matter with Mel all of a sudden? What was he talking about? Living a normal life?! Her children were gone! "What kind of normal life—"

He cut her off. "You're reacting exactly the way he wants you to, Donna. And I understand it. Believe me, I understand it. But you have to stay strong because, don't kid yourself for a minute, this is going to be a long struggle. You have to keep hoping; you have to keep looking. But most of all, you have to keep living!"

"What are you talking about?" she hissed. Several heads turned in their direction. "My ex-husband kidnaps my babies! The police won't help. Nobody can help. We fly up to Connecticut and waste a day talking to two women Victor hasn't seen in at least eight years, hoping they'll be able to tell us something—anything—"

"Did you really think they'd know anything?"

"Yes!" Donna blurted, admitting the truth to herself for the first time. "Yes, I really did! Every time we go anywhere, like coming here, I think we'll see him; every time we ask anyone anything, I always think they're going to tell me exactly what I want to know!"

Mel reached across the table and covered both her hands with his own. "Oh, baby—"

"I can't help it, Mel. I just can't believe any of this is happening."

A waiter walked over and replaced her spoon. Donna glared at him. "Look, Donna," she heard Mel's voice continue. Why didn't he just keep quiet? She didn't want to hear any more words of encouragement, of discouragement, of hope, of despair. Words, words, words. "We're doing everything we can. We have detectives out, ads in the newspapers—"

"I know what we're doing," she said curtly.

Again he was apologetic. "I'm sorry. Of course you do."

"I don't need you to tell me what's being done." She stopped abruptly. "Oh, Mel, I'm sorry. Listen to me, for heaven's sake! The one person who never lets me down, who's always there when I need you—"

"You don't have to apologize."

"You take off work, you leave Annie with the housekeeper, you rearrange your whole life to come with me to Connecticut, to drive me into New York because I still haven't got enough guts to get behind the wheel of a car myself—"

"Donna—"

"You come with me to some dumb restaurant Victor probably hasn't set foot in since he brought me here years ago, so that I can sit here and yell at you!"

"It wasn't such a dumb idea coming here, Donna. One of these days, Victor may very well come back for a meal. We'll leave a picture of him with the maître d'. Something may turn up."

Donna closed her eyes, seeing Mel before her. "I can't picture my life without you," she said.

"You won't ever have to."

"You promise you'll never leave me?"

"I promise." There were several seconds of stillness between them. Then he spoke. "Marry me, Donna."

Donna stared at him in stunned disbelief. He was proposing? Now? Now, of all times, when her children were the only things that really concerned her. What was the matter with him?

"Marry—?"

"I know it probably sounds like a hell of a time—"

"A hell of a time," she repeated, growing increasingly angry, instinctively feeling that any mention of the future would carry her farther away from her past—from her children.

"I love you, Donna, you know that."

"Why are you proposing to me *now?*" she asked, almost desperately.

"Because I think that *now* is a good time to make a commitment. To me. To yourself. To a life together. To life—period."

"A life without my children?" Her voice was becoming shrill.

"I didn't say that."

"What are you trying to say?" An accusation, not a statement.

"Just that life goes on—"

She was beginning to panic. "I really don't want to talk anymore, Mel. Can we please get out of here?"

Mel signaled for the waiter. A few minutes later, he

paid the bill and walked over to where Donna was already standing by the door. "Regardless of whether you marry me or not," Mel was saying as they left the restaurant, "I think that when we get back to Palm Beach, you should move in with me. You shouldn't be alone."

Donna said nothing, was, in fact, grateful for the offer. She needed Mel, especially now. No, she thought, not just now. Always.

"You'll never leave me?" she asked again plaintively, as she got inside the rented gray Thunderbird.

"I'll never leave you," he said. "That's a promise."

Chapter 17

"She'll be down in a minute," Donna said to the very attractive woman dressed in casual summer whites. "She's just packing a few of her favorite toys."

Donna watched the woman settle herself comfortably into one of the beige overstuffed living room chairs. She probably picked out these chairs, Donna realized suddenly, remembering that Mel had told her he hadn't bothered changing anything when she left.

"Can I get you a drink of anything?" Donna offered, wondering what was taking Annie so long, thinking how two ex-wives in as many months was really too much to expect anyone to cope with, no matter how nice or attractive the ex-wives in question were.

"No, thank you."

"I guess Mel got delayed with a patient. He *said* he'd be here when you arrived."

"That's not unusual," the ex-wife named Kate replied with uncomfortable familiarity. "Besides, it gives us a chance to talk," she continued, and then neither woman said a word.

"Annie's a lovely little girl," Donna said, at length, looking through the hallway in the direction of the stairs. Lovely, but slow. Where was she?

"Thank you. I think Mel's really done a terrific job with her."

Donna smiled, why she wasn't sure. The compliment had nothing to do with her. "It's hard," Kate went on reflectively, "seeing her only summers and holidays, and sometimes when I'm pounding the law books I think about how nice it would be to have her with me all the time—" Donna caught her breath. "Oh, I'm so sorry," Kate said sincerely. "That was a very stupid thing for me to have said. I obviously wasn't thinking." She looked anxiously toward the hallway. Annie was still nowhere in sight. "Mel told me about what happened," she said, reluctantly continuing the conversation. "There's been no new developments—?"

"No," Donna said sharply, putting an end to this topic of conversation.

Donna got up and moved out into the hall. She walked to the foot of the circular stairway and yelled up. "Annie, hurry up, honey."

"I'm coming," the child shouted down, but remained upstairs. Why was she hurrying the little girl? Donna asked herself. They weren't going anywhere until Mel got home. Where *was* Mel anyway? She walked back into the living room and over to the white-and-gold French phone.

"I'll phone and see if he's left yet," Donna explained.

She did and he had, so the two women sat in similar chairs facing each other and waited for the other to break the silence.

"I hadn't realized you were actually living with Mel," Kate said, after several seconds, sounding interested rather than upset. "He told me, of course, that he was seeing someone very seriously and that he hoped you'd eventually marry—"

"I moved in a few months ago." She hesitated, not sure what to say. "Things have been very hectic here lately. It must have slipped Mel's mind." Why should she have to speak for Mel? Where was he? Why should she have to be the one who had to explain anything to this woman who was no relation to herself, ex or otherwise? Of course, the woman was entitled to some explanations. Anything that affected her daughter concerned her in some way. At least you know where your daughter is,

Donna thought bitterly, feeling an increasingly familiar resentment rising inside her.

Kate stared hard at Donna. Donna felt momentarily that she was back in court on the witness stand. When Kate spoke, however, her voice was soft. "You do like Annie, don't you?"

"Oh, I love her," Donna answered quickly, hoping her words carried more conviction than she actually felt. She did indeed *like* the precocious little girl, had actually started to love her until, irrationally perhaps, she had become convinced that any commitment to Annie meant she was abandoning her own children. That if she allowed herself to love this little girl, she would lose forever the son and daughter she had created. Her feelings toward Mel's child were an increasing mass of contradictions; she loved having Annie around because it gave her someone to care for, to busy herself with, but she also resented the child because of that very presence. Every time she looked into Annie's eyes, she felt the eyes of the daughter she might never see again. Every time Annie pleaded for a few minutes of her time, she heard her son's pleas for yet another story. "Tell me a story about a little boy named Roger and a little girl named Bethanny . . ." She felt weighed down by an ever-increasing load of guilt every time she tried to be a part of her new family, to proceed with her life, to *make anything* of her life. How could she just ignore what had happened to her? Her children were not teeth to be nurtured, extracted and then forgotten, the numbness gradually overtaking the pain. She felt her body ache.

"I'm sorry, I didn't hear you," Donna said, realizing Kate had spoken.

"I asked if you worked . . . outside the home, that is."

"Oh. Oh, no. I don't."

"Oh."

It was one of those awkward moments when Donna always wished she smoked so she could ask for a cigarette. That, at least, would give her something to do. Something to do. If she really wanted something to do, she should go upstairs and help Annie. No, she couldn't do that. Annie didn't want her upstairs. She'd made that quite clear. Her mother—her real mother, she had emphasized—was coming over today to take her for the summer. There was no room for two mothers. Especially Donna.

She couldn't blame the child. Donna had been increasingly short-tempered with her of late, distracted when she was with her, irritable and uncommunicative. At first, Annie had tried hard to be understanding, but ultimately, she couldn't help but produce a resentment of her own.

"Do you think you'll enjoy being a lawyer?" Donna asked, trying to escape her thoughts, then immediately wished she hadn't. What a stupid thing to ask. I sound like I'm interviewing her for the high school yearbook. Why don't I also ask her what her favorite color is, what her choices are for this year's Oscars, and whether or not she sleeps in the nude?

"Will you specialize?" she continued, not sure if Kate had, in fact, answered her first question. Was there no end to the number of stupefying questions she could ask this woman? Still, just what did one talk to an ex-wife about? The government really should provide a list of topics for conversation between ex-spouses, she decided, hearing Kate mutter something about family law. With divorce assuming epidemic proportions across the country and the percentage of stepparents drastically on the rise, it was really the least the government could do. It wouldn't require a whole lot of effort, she concluded, to throw in a handy little guidebook for dealing with future ex's along with the final divorce papers.

There was a general silence again as Kate and Donna continued to look each other over. Donna felt suddenly over-exposed in her bright pink halter top and white shorts which, in the last several weeks, had begun to stretch ludicrously out of shape. Or perhaps, more likely, it was Donna, herself, who was responsible for their recent ill-fit. She hadn't eaten very much lately—she had no appetite—and the weight she had put on since her divorce seemed to be disappearing again. Where did it go? she wondered. Kate, with her fine bosom and efficient body, must think I'm some sort of anorexic, Donna thought, realizing how much medical terminology had lately crept into her vocabulary. Kate, on the other hand, looked very cool and healthy, her dark hair pulled back sharply into a ponytail, making her look a little like Ali McGraw in *Love Story*. She probably thinks that I look like Don Knotts, Donna decided. The ex-wife named Kate looked like she was about to start talking again. Donna turned her attention to the woman's mouth.

"Mommy!" came the shriek from the hallway. Thank God, Donna said silently. Kate immediately rose to her feet and held out her arms for the little girl, her dark pigtails flying behind her, her ever-present white and pink blanket clutched tightly in her right hand.

"Oh, it's so good to see you," Kate said, kissing the child loudly. Donna stood up. She wished she could be anywhere but here. Annie clung to her mother's neck. It was several very long minutes before the two extracted themselves from each other's arms. "You look wonderful."

Annie beamed. "You look beautiful," she said, instinctively returning the compliment.

"Still have your blanket, I see."

Donna interjected. "She never goes anywhere without it."

"I don't take it to school," Annie informed her coolly, abruptly putting Donna in her place.

"Be polite, Annie," her mother said.

"Well, I don't take it to school," the child insisted.

Kate looked over at Donna. "A friend of mine gave Annie that blanket when she was born."

"Yes, I know. Mel told me."

"It's amazing what good shape it's stayed in," Kate continued.

"Yes." Where *was* Mel?

Annie looked from Kate to Donna and then back again. "Donna's ex-husband took her children away," she said suddenly.

Kate's eyes shot quickly over to Donna's. "Yes. I know that, honey."

Donna turned away, trying to control the anger she was suddenly feeling toward the youngster.

"Daddy says they're going to find that fucking bastard if it's the last think they do."

Where was Mel? Did she really have to go through this now?

"Daddy says he's a no-good prick—"

"That's enough, Annie," her mother said abruptly. "You know I don't approve of language like that."

"Like what?"

Kate smiled at Donna. "They're always testing."

"Yes." I wish Mel were here.

He was. As soon as the wish was out of Donna's head, the front door opened and Mel walked quickly inside, full of apologies. "Sorry," he said, kissing Donna first and then moving over to kiss his ex-wife. A definite pecking order. "I was out of this cream," he said, producing a small brown paper bag from his pocket and opening it. "So I had to stop at the drugstore and pick some up." He handed it to Donna. "For your rash."

Donna took the cream and looked guiltily at the tops of her hands. "Thanks," she said.

"Doesn't Mommy look beautiful?" Annie asked.

"Your mother always looks beautiful," Mel said, seeming to mean it. "How was the trip down?"

"Fine. Uneventful," Kate answered.

"You all ready to leave?" Mel asked Annie.

"My suitcases are upstairs."

"I'll get them in a minute," he said.

"I thought we'd drive up to Disney World for a few days before heading back to New York," Kate said to her daughter who was by this point quivering with anticipation and delight. "I rented a car."

"I *thought* that red job was yours," Mel said knowingly.

"Well, I always did like red."

Donna thought immediately of their bedroom, with its red-and-white checkered wallpaper and matching bedspread and drapes, its red broadloom and ivory lamp with the red shade. The entire room, she decided abruptly, would have to be changed.

"Let's go!" Annie shouted.

"I'll get Annie's things," Donna offered. It was Mrs. Harrison's day off and besides, this way she could avoid the prolonged farewell at the door. When she returned with Annie's two suitcases and an additional bag of selected toys, the hugs and kisses were just concluding. Mel took the luggage from her; Kate relieved her of the bag of toys.

"You going to kiss Donna goodbye for the summer?" Mel asked.

"No!" the child responded quickly.

"Annie!" Her mother.

"Annie!" Her father.

"No!" Annie.

"It's all right," Donna. "Really."

Mel led the way out of the house and over to the red Plymouth. Kate and Annie followed close behind. Donna remained in the doorway. "Have a nice summer," she called after them. No one bothered to turn around. She walked back into the entranceway. Little brat, she thought, feeling her anger growing. It wouldn't have killed you to kiss me goodbye.

It was about five minutes before Donna heard the car back up out of the driveway and disappear down the street. Mel was undoubtedly waving them out of sight. He walked back inside a minute later. By that time, Donna's anger had grown into a minor rage.

"I'm going to have to get back to the clinic—"

"Don't you ever do that to me again!" she shouted.

"What—?"

"I didn't need this stupid cream! Not right this minute, anyway. It could have waited!" She threw the ointment across the white ceramic tile. Mel said nothing, waiting until Donna had finished. "What's the matter with you? You don't think I've been through enough lately? I should have the added pleasure of entertaining your ex-wife for half an hour?! Why didn't you tell her I lived here? What gave you the right to discuss Adam and Sharon with her? Have you any idea what it was like for me to have to deal with all that? How could you do that to me?!"

Mel waited until the anger had drained from her face. Then he walked over and put his arms around her. "I'm sorry," he said softly, shaking his head. "I just didn't think. I'm really very sorry."

Donna burst into tears against his chest. "Why didn't she want to kiss me goodbye, Mel?" she asked in a hoarse whisper. "Why wouldn't she kiss me goodbye?"

The first phone call came precisely at three minutes after two o'clock on a Friday afternoon fourteen weeks after Victor's disappearance.

"For you," Mrs. Harrison said, holding the phone in Donna's direction.

Donna walked lazily over to where the housekeeper stood waiting. She had weeks ago given up hope that it might be someone calling with some useful information. Mel had discontinued the detective Mr. Stamler had previously hired—nothing new had turned up in months. All roads led to nowhere. "Hello."

"I thought I'd find you there."

Donna froze. She felt the color drain from her face and an ache beginning to build at the pit of her stomach. She forced herself to speak. "Victor?"

"You remember. I'm flattered."

"For God's sake, where are you?"

"Always asking for more than I can give you," he said with resignation.

"Where are you?"

"If you ask me that again, I'll hang up."

Donna felt herself panic. "Please don't hang up!"

"You have exactly sixty seconds to ask how your children are." Donna could see him looking at his watch.

She tried to keep her voice from cracking. "How's Adam? How's Sharon?" she asked, obeying his instructions.

"They're fine," he said coldly. "Sharon doesn't miss you at all." Donna thought of her little girl, saw her soft brown curls and pale blue eyes. Those extraordinary eyes which registered everything like an instamatic camera. She will not forget me, Donna thought. She will not forget me. "Adam asked about you."

Donna's heart was beginning to race. "What did you tell him?"

"That you didn't want to see him anymore. That you'd found another family you liked better."

"Victor, you didn't say that! My God, you didn't really tell him that!" He knew. He always knew her worst fears. If she let herself love Mel, his daughter—another family you liked better—she would lose her own children forever.

"Your sixty seconds are up, Donna. Goodbye."

The phone went dead in her hands. "No!" she cried. "Victor! Victor!" She could feel him smiling at her through the phone. She slammed the receiver down hard against its gilded carriage. Mrs. Harrison walked back into the room, her gentle black face looking appropriately alarmed. Donna brushed her aside and moved to one of the overstuffed beige chairs, collapsing inside its oversized arms. She sat there, not moving, saying nothing, until Mel came home from work.

They asked the police about putting a tracer on the phone, but once again they were informed that this was not a police matter. They were also told it was an extremely expensive procedure and one that would be of no value if Donna was unable to keep the caller speaking for at least several minutes. Donna knew that Victor would never take the risk of being traced, if, indeed, he ever called again. Somehow, she knew he would call again. It had been too much fun that first time not to do it again.

They left the police station feeling frustrated and depressed.

"At least we know they haven't left the country," Mel said, as they walked toward the car.

"We knew that already."

"I guess we did." They walked several paces in silence. "What did you think of Annie's letter?" Donna recognized the question as an obvious attempt to turn her attention in another direction, to get her thinking of other things. She understood what Mel was trying to do, but she resented it nonetheless. She did not want her attention diverted. She was not ready.

"I didn't have time to read it."

"You've had two days," he smiled.

"I didn't have time."

"She's sounding very grown-up," he continued, ignoring the edge to her voice.

"Good for her."

"Apparently, Kate took her to a few Broadway plays."

"That's nice."

"You don't sound very interested."

"I'm listening, aren't I?"

They came to the parking meter beside which the white MG was stationed. A yellow parking ticket clung to its window. "Expired," Mel said, checking the meter. "Great." He took the ticket and put it in the pocket of his navy blue pants, removing his car keys from the same pocket in one flowing gesture. He opened first her door and then walked around to open his own. She was already seated, her seat belt secure, when he lowered his body inside. "Where to?" he asked.

She shrugged.

"Feel like a drive?"

"Sure."

"We could drive down to Lauderdale for a sandwich."

"Long way to go for a sandwich." `

"Nice drive though. We'll go along the ocean."

Donna shrugged again. "Whatever you want."

He started the car. They drove in silence until they reached the ocean, then Mel turned the car south. "Do you want to talk about what's bothering you."

Donna couldn't believe her ears. Where was Mel's brain these last few weeks? "About what's bothering me? What do you think is bothering me, for Pete's sake? The weather?"

"Take it easy, Donna."

"Well, what kind of question is that? I get a call from Victor, the police tell us it can't be traced, that there's no way we can trace any future calls, and you ask me what's bothering me? You expect me to talk about Annie's letters! We are no closer to finding my children than the day Victor ran off with them, only I'm just supposed to carry on like they're away in boarding school or something! I'm supposed to carry on like I'm some dumb Pollyanna! What do you want from me, Mel? I'm not Super Woman."

"Nobody wants you to be."

"Then what is it you do want?"

He shook his head. "Nothing. Let's just drop it. I'm sorry if I said the wrong thing."

"You're disappointed because I didn't read Annie's letters?"

"I just thought you might have found the time."

"The letters are all addressed to you."

"She knows you'll read them."

"If she wanted me to read them, she'd address them to both of us."

"You know how kids are."

Donna turned abruptly in his direction, a path of ice between her eyes and his.

"Sorry," he said quickly. "I just meant I'm sure she means them for you as well."

"And I'm sure she doesn't. Mel, has she even mentioned my name in any of her letters? You know, love to Donna, that sort of thing?"

"No."

Donna laughed haltingly.

"Have you ever written to her?" he asked.

"You expect me to write to her?"

"I just asked if you had." He paused. "Look, Donna, the two of you just got off to a bad start. Well, no, actually, the start was fine. Those first five months, you were beautiful together. It wasn't until—this whole thing started—that things started to fall apart between the two of you. She understands what you're going through, but she's a kid. She also understands that you don't pay very much attention to her, that you're preoccupied, that she's—an afterthought—"

"Neat turn of phrase, Doctor," Donna cut in.

He ignored her interruption. "She's very sensitive, Donna. She's already lost one full-time mother. She doesn't want to invest a lot of feeling into somebody else unless she's very sure she's going to get something back. She has strong defenses. Right now she's very aware that you'd trade her twenty times over to get your own children back."

Donna let out a deep breath of air. Everything he said was true. "What is it you think I should do?" she asked sincerely. What on earth was the matter with her? She loved this man; she could easily love his little girl. Why was she so mean to her? Why couldn't she accept her? She wanted to. She wanted to love the little girl. And yet, something kept stopping her. Something that kept telling her that should she open the door for Annie to come inside, she would be forever closing out her own children. "She's found another family she likes better," Victor had said to her. She shook the thought out of her head. No, my babies, she said silently, seeing Adam before her, hearing his small voice say the words with her—never. Never ever.

"I think it would be a nice thing if you wrote to her. I think she'd really like that."

Donna nodded her head. "Okay. I'll write to her." She leaned her head back against the car's black interior. Her hair blew against her cheek as the wind raced in from the open windows, filling the small area with the sound of the surf and the smell of the ocean. Donna let her body relax against the sound of the water's flow, feeling the muscles in her neck give in to the natural rhythm. It was better than a good massage, she thought, wondering how anyone who had ever lived near the ocean could ever bear to live anywhere else.

"Feeling better?" Mel asked after a silence of almost half an hour.

She looked over at him and smiled. "Yes." He always knew when to leave her alone. "Are we there yet?" she asked, childlike.

"Another five minutes."

Donna reached her hand over and let it rest on Mel's thigh. "I guess I've been pretty preoccupied as far as you're concerned too."

"I can wait."

Donna shook her head in bewilderment. "What makes you such a nice man?"

"Good genes."

Donna laughed and for the first time in weeks found herself thinking of her mother. How would she have handled all this? she wondered. They pulled off the highway and started west toward Manny's delicatessen. "I'll write to Annie as soon as we get home," she said, with fresh resolve. Her mother would have written to Annie.

But when they got home at five P.M., she looked over at the telephone in the living room and suddenly felt very tired. She told Mel she was going to lie down for a while, to wake her up when he wanted some dinner. But he didn't, and when she suddenly found herself awake at three A.M., he was sound asleep beside her.

Donna got quietly out of bed, realized Mel had already undressed her, threw a housecoat over her body and walked down the stairs into the kitchen. Then she switched on the radio Mel had recently purchased for her and started to absently wipe at the kitchen counter. After fifteen minutes, she actively sought out the Fantastik and other assorted cleansers. It was almost half past four when she switched off the radio, turned off the lights, and went back upstairs to bed.

Chapter 18

Donna sat in the bedroom she shared with Mel and stared at the red-and-white checks of the wallpaper. Mel had told her that she could do whatever she wanted to with the room, change it however she liked. And so every afternoon, just after Annie came home from school, Donna would come up here and sit cross-legged on the floor trying to come up with some fresh ideas. It was becoming something of a ritual. In the last few days, she realized, she had simply let herself get lost in the monotony of the checkered pattern. Her thoughts, if there were any, had nothing to do with redecorating.

The phone rang four times before Donna realized it was ringing and ran to the night table by the bed to answer it.

"Hello."

The voice was quiet. "You sound out of breath."

"Victor?"

"Sharon's crying."

He hung up.

"Victor? Victor? Hello! Hello!" Donna desperately brought her finger down on the carriage, clicking it up and down, knowing already that the line was dead. Slowly, she lowered the receiver down and stood perfectly still beside it.

"Another phone call?" the small voice asked from the door.

Donna turned and watched Annie walk into the room. She nodded. In the last three months, Victor had called four times.

"What did he say this time?" the child asked.

"Nothing."

"You can tell me." Reaching out.

"Don't you have homework?" Slapping back down.

"I'm only eight years old, for Christ's sake."

"Don't swear."

"Don't tell me what to do!"

"Don't give me a hard time, Annie. I'm not in the mood."

"You're never in the mood. For anything."

"Where's Mrs. Harrison? Why don't you go bother her for a while?"

Donna watched the child's eyes cloud over with soft mist. "She's out doing the grocery shopping," Annie said, her lower lip quivering.

Donna looked away, feeling intensely guilty. Annie had Mel's big brown eyes and her mother's way of holding herself erect. Goddamn her and Goddamn me! she thought. Why does she make me feel so guilty? She's just a child. Mel's child. Yes, Mel's child. Not *my* child. My little girl is God-knows-where. Victor said she was crying. If Sharon's crying, you can damn well cry too! She looked back at Annie.

Annie stood motionless, refusing to let the tear that had formed in her left eye fall. Donna sank down to her knees and extended her arms toward the child. "I'm sorry, Annie," she said softly. "Really, I am. I just get so upset whenever Victor calls. It takes me a few minutes to get my head back on straight. Come here, honey, let me hold you."

The vehemence of the child's response startled Donna. "Stop telling me what to do!" she yelled, letting the tears flow freely. "You're not my mother! You're a rotten mother! No wonder Victor took your children away! I hate you!"

Donna steadied herself against the floor as Annie fled the room.

"You're not dressed yet?" Mel asked, walking into the bedroom, its starkly bared walls still a shock after more than three weeks. Donna had painstakingly removed all the old paper by herself. So far, she had done nothing to replace it.

She watched from her position at the edge of the bed as Mel walked over to look at himself in the mirror over the dresser.

"I don't know what to wear," she said blankly.

"Anything. Rod said it was going to be very casual."

"I spilled coffee on my white pants."

"So, wear the blue ones."

"What blue ones?"

"Whichever ones you want."

"You're a big help."

"Sorry, honey, I just don't know what to say."

"I ask you for one little thing, one simple, little thing, and it's too much for you."

"Hey—"

"I'm obviously having trouble deciding what I should wear—it's a party, you think it's important enough to insist that I go—"

"I think it's important that we start to get out more—"

"You're interrupting me—I asked you a simple favor, help me decide what to wear, only you don't feel it's important enough to bother with."

"It certainly isn't important enough to fight about."

"Maybe I think it is."

"Do you?"

Donna covered her face with her hands.

Mel walked quickly to her side, sitting down and putting his arm around her. "What's the matter, Donna? Did Victor call today?"

She shook her head. "No." It had been five weeks since the last phone call. "I thought he might. I actually sat by the phone for a few hours and waited."

"That's not good."

"Gave me something to do."

There was silence. "Donna, you can't just sit around like this month after month. It's not good for you. It's not good for any of us."

"I can't go anywhere. Victor might call."

"And he might never call again. You can't sit around waiting for the phone to ring."

"What do you recommend?"

"Why don't you get a job? Go back to work."

"You make it sound so easy. I've been away from the work force for a long time."

"I know."

"I haven't worked in seven years."

"Nobody's saying it'll be that easy, but why don't you give it a try, it might not be that difficult either."

"Oh sure, I'll just pick up the phone and call Steve McFaddon."

"You could."

"Oh, Mel, don't be so naïve."

"Oh, Donna, don't be so negative."

"Fuck off." She said it almost casually and was surprised to see he treated it that way. He simply shrugged, removed his arm from around her, stood up, and walked toward the dresser. "Besides," she added hastily, "I thought you liked the fact that I'm home for Annie."

"It was a good idea." His voice underlined the word "idea."

"What does that mean?"

"It means that I think we'd all be a lot better off, Annie included, if you would get out of the house more."

"Has Annie said anything to you?"

"Annie hasn't said more than ten sentences in the last month."

"You think that's my fault?"

"I think you should get dressed so we can get going."

Donna remained exactly where she was. "I told you that I don't know what to wear."

Mel walked over to the closet and pulled out a pair of

mauve pants and a matching mauve-and-white striped top. "What's the matter with this outfit?"

Donna shrugged. "It's all right."

"Well?" he asked.

"Do we really have to go to this thing?"

"Yes," he said simply. "We do." He looked at his watch. "Now, I'm going to spend a few minutes with my daughter. When you're ready, come into her room and say good night."

Donna saluted. "Yes, sir."

Mel stopped. "That wasn't an order, Donna." He walked to the doorway and then turned around abruptly. "Look if you feel that strongly about not going, then maybe you shouldn't bother."

"You'll stay home?"

"No. I'm going to the party."

"You don't want me to come?"

"I want you to do whatever you'll be most comfortable in doing." He didn't give her time to respond. "I'll be in Annie's room."

Donna remained where she was for several minutes, then she stood up and started getting ready to go out.

Donna could see the look of surprise on Mel's face when he opened the car door and found her inside. He said nothing for several minutes although she could tell he wanted to. Instead, he gritted his teeth, stared intently out the front window and started the car. Without looking at her, he backed the car out of the driveway and onto the street. Donna could never remember seeing him look so troubled.

I'm so sorry, Mel, she wanted to say. To reach out and touch his cheek. To reestablish the warmth she knew she was taking away. I want so much to be able to love your daughter, to be able to show you all the love you know I feel for you. Please understand. Understand what it's like for me. He's taken my children away. No matter what I do, where I go, what I say, that fact never leaves me. I see Victor's face everywhere, laughing at me, taunting me.

I see my children reaching out for me, crying for me. Every time I look at Annie . . . I look at her and all I see is the little girl I might never know when she reaches Annie's age. That's why I avoid her. Why I just couldn't go in there to say good night to her. Can you understand what it's like for me? I wait every day for Victor to phone. It's more upsetting now when he doesn't call than when he does. I know that sounds crazy, but when he does phone, I feel my children are closer to me somehow. Please, Mel, tell me that you understand.

"Better put your seat belt on," he said, after they'd been driving for about five minutes.

Donna buckled herself in. Why were they going to this stupid party? What possible good would it do? She'd be off somewhere when Victor might be phoning. Mrs. Harrison would say that Mrs. Cressy was out for the evening; Victor would hang up, perhaps never to phone again. Why had she bothered getting dressed? Why wasn't she at home waiting in case Victor called? In case he told her where her children were.

"Aren't you going awfully fast?"

Mel checked the speedometer. "Maybe a little," he said, slowing.

Donna fidgeted. "How far is this party?"

"Just over in Boynton."

"Are they all doctors there?"

"Some, I guess. Why? You sound like you don't like doctors."

"Well, you know how they are at parties—they only talk to other doctors. And all they ever talk about is medicine."

Mel's voice was filled with obvious impatience. "Well, let's see," he said, taking imaginary stock of the situation, "medicine is out as a topic of conversation because it's boring; children are out because it's too painful; movies are out because we haven't been to one in months; I don't think you've read a book or even a magazine in at least that long, so we can forget about that, and you're not interested in anything anybody else has to say on just about anything. Which brings the conversation around to you. But we can't talk about what *you* do because you don't do anything—"

Donna stared at Mel with a mixture of surprise and fury. "Where has all this been hiding?" she asked.

Mel let out a long blow of pent-up breath. Then he raised and lowered his head as if he had reached some silent accord with himself. "This isn't the time," he apologized. "I'm sorry. I was out of line."

"You're damn right you were," Donna shot back, angrier now that he had apologized and thereby effectively ended that discussion.

Suddenly, she gripped the door handle on her side of the car.

"What's the matter?" Mel asked, looking over at her for the first time since he had started the car.

"Nothing," Donna replied. "I just get a little unnerved when you turn corners that fast, that's all."

"Relax, Donna. The worst I could do is get us killed."

"Great."

"I thought you'd like that."

"What's that supposed to mean?"

"Absolutely nothing."

"No, tell me what you meant."

"Let's drop it, Donna."

"I don't want to drop it."

"But I do."

"So we always do what you want, is that it?"

"Sounds good to me."

"What about how it sounds to me?"

Mel continued to drive, staring straight ahead, saying nothing for several minutes. "I asked you what about how it sounds to me?" she pressed.

"And I asked you to drop it. This is a ridiculous conversation."

They drove for another fifteen minutes before Mel pulled up into the large driveway of an oceanfront condominium in Boynton Beach. He stopped the car in the area indicated for Guest Parking and unsnapped his seat belt.

"I think we should get this settled before we go inside," Donna said.

Mel looked over at her. "Donna, do you even seriously remember what you're trying so hard to be angry about?" Donna looked quickly away from him. "Now, what's it going to be? Are you coming inside or would you rather I drove you back home?" Donna silently unbuckled her seat belt and opened her door, jumping quickly out of the car. "I guess you're coming inside," she heard Mel say to himself just before she slammed the car door shut.

Donna stood by herself in a corner of the room and watched Mel who stood on the sun-colored patio looking out at the ocean. He had his arm around a tall, voluptuous redhead and had been talking with her in a fairly intimate fashion for the better part of an hour. Donna caught sight of her own reflection in the mirrored bar. Mel had always said he liked her hair when it was red—

She looked across the beige-and-yellow room, felt its warmth reaching out to her, and then rejected it, as she had rejected earlier any polite overtures of conversation that had been advanced in her direction. As she had similarly rejected Mel. Her eyes returned to the patio. The redhead was moving her body closer to Mel, laughing at something he had said. Oh, Mel, she thought, why did you bring me here?

"Excuse me," she said, approaching her host. "Could I use your phone?"

"Sure. There's one in the bedroom that might give you a little more privacy."

Her host pointed to his right and Donna edged her way through the medium-sized gathering and into the dark greens and grays of the master bedroom. She sat on the bed, pushing aside the geometrically designed comforter, and picked up the velvety gray phone. Mrs. Harrison answered almost immediately.

"Has anyone called, Mrs. Harrison?"

"No, Ma'am. It's been real quiet here. Annie read for a bit, then she fell asleep."

"But no one has called?"

"No one."

Donna slowly placed the receiver back on its hook. "No one," she repeated. "No one." Then she got up and walked back out to the main room.

The roar of the ocean came rushing over to greet her as soon as she walked back inside. The room was large and its patio doors opened directly over the water six floors below. With the doors opened the way they were now, the only sound that seemed to have any meaning was the ocean's persistent rush to the shore.

She looked for Mel, didn't see him, although the red-head was still there. He's probably getting her another drink, she thought. Where *was* he? It was almost eleven o'clock. She wanted to go home.

"Are you ready to leave?" he asked, coming up behind her, not sounding anything like he usually did.

"I've been ready all evening," she said.

"So I noticed. About the only thing you didn't do was dangle the car keys in my direction." Her eyes shot to his. "Don't ask me what that's supposed to mean because this time I just might tell you."

He took her arm and moved her angrily toward the door. "What are *you* so angry about?" she whispered under her breath. "I'm not the one who spent all night flirting with some tacky looking redhead."

"No, I am," he said, waving a final goodbye in his host's direction. "And in case you hadn't noticed, that's not usually my style. To tell you the truth, the person I'm really angry at and disappointed in is myself. I haven't resorted to that sort of trick since I was in high school and I was ticked off at my girlfriend so I took out her best friend."

"Are you saying your behavior tonight was my fault?" They waited for the elevator. It came almost immediately. They went inside and stood at opposite ends.

"I'm saying it was my fault," he said. "You can't be responsible for my actions."

They got off the elevator at the main floor and walked

to where their car was parked. He walked over to his side of the car, opened it and got inside. Donna thought for a minute that he might just drive off and leave her there, but he reached over and pulled up the button on her side of the car, and then twisted the inside handle, opening the door for her, but just barely. Donna pulled it open the rest of the way and got inside. Lately, it felt that all she ever did was get in and out of cars.

"Well, what is it that you want to say?" she asked as he hit the highway.

"Let's not say anything until we get home, okay?" It was more a statement than a question. "Right now, I'm so angry I need all my concentration just to drive this car—"

"I don't know what *you're* so angry about—"

"You will," he promised.

Except for the outside light, the house was dark when they got home. They walked inside and Mel flicked on the hall light, then abruptly shut it off again. They stood in the semidarkness, figures frozen in the camera's flash, only the light from the moon and stars streaking through the windowed top of the door to illuminate the gloominess of their features. It was eleven-thirty. Neither one spoke. Donna realized, with a bit of a start, that she was almost afraid to speak. She had never seen Mel like this before; he was usually so slow to anger. Donna watched his face, so still, solemn, his profile flickering white and shadow. She was not sure where his beard left off and the darkness began. She wanted to reach over and caress the soft face she saw beside her, but she couldn't bring herself to move.

"Let's go into the back room," he said, and moved, not looking at her, in the room's direction. Donna followed wordlessly. The room at the back of the house had originally been intended as a sewing room for Kate, but in recent years, it had been mostly ignored. When Donna had first seen the room, she had thought what a fine playroom it would make for the kids. She stopped at its entrance.

Why was he bringing her back here? He knew she had always pictured it as a playroom for Adam and Sharon.

"Why can't we talk in the living room?" she asked from the doorway.

Mel, who now stood in the middle of the room, turned in her direction, locking his eyes into hers for the first time since they had left the party. "Because I don't want to chance waking either Annie or Mrs. Harrison."

"You planning on doing some yelling?" she asked, almost playfully, hoping not to have to play the scene she knew she had been almost totally responsible for creating. It had been months in the making, she recognized, wishing simultaneously to back away from it and to rush headlong into its core.

"I'm not sure what I'm planning." No time for games. Too late for games.

"I don't want to come in this room."

"Figures." He stopped. "Why not?"

She hesitated. "You know what I always planned for this room." She held the hook of guilt in his direction.

He wouldn't bite. "Let's not get silly about this, Donna. Come inside and close the door. You can't have memories for something that never was."

"My children were!"

"Your children still are! If there are ghosts anywhere in this room, Donna, they're standing in your shoes!"

Donna felt her anger beginning to grow. It pushed her inside and closed the door behind her. She looked around the large, book-lined room which contained two matching green sofa-beds and a long, low coffee table. "Do you want to start talking in English, Doctor?"

"Do I really have to spell it out for you, Donna?"

"You really do."

"You have no idea what I'm trying to say?"

"Stop speaking in riddles, dammit, you're the one who wants to talk!"

Mel began angrily pacing back and forth.

"I still can't figure out why you're so angry," Donna continued, not waiting for him to speak, afraid now of letting him speak. "I went to your stupid party, didn't I? Only to watch you disappear after the first hour, so that you could spend the next hour flirting with every girl in the room before spending your final hour—your finest hour—all over that redhead with the tits. I didn't throw myself over any of the available males. I didn't embarrass you."

"No, you didn't do anything wrong! You went to the party with me. You said hello to Rod and Bessie. You may have even smiled once. I'm not sure about that last bit—it may just be wishful thinking on my part. And that's all you did—except check your watch every three minutes."

"This is beginning to sound very familiar," Donna interrupted. "In a minute I know it's going to be all my fault that you acted the way you did—"

"No!" Mel's voice dropped like a hammer into the space between them. "I told you before that I am the only one responsible for my behavior. And you want to know something? I'm really sick about the way I acted tonight. I used people. It's been a long time since I used people that shamelessly."

"High school," Donna said curtly. "You told me."

"I realize now why it was so important to me that we go to the party tonight. Oh sure, I thought we needed to get out, but that wasn't the main reason. My main reason was to avoid the scene we're having now, to put off the next few minutes for a couple more hours. But it didn't work out the way I hoped it would, because I've been holding it back for so long that if my anger didn't express itself one way, it was certainly going to come out another. So, Dr. Mel Segal suddenly turned into the highly eligible Dr. Mel Segal. There wasn't a woman at that party tonight who didn't feel my arm around her. And a few of them actually responded to me. You know that redhead had something else going for her besides a pair of nice boobs, and it's a very simple thing—" He stopped talking, swallowing, moving in a slow circle around the coffee table. Donna watched him. She said nothing. "You used to have it," he continued. "I remember." He paused for effect. "A sense of humor," he said simply. "A sense of fun, even when everything around you was falling apart." He raised his hands in the air as if he had just been advised that a gun was pointing at the back of his head. "That's it. Just a little . . . life." He stopped, then continued. "I talked to her and she talked to me, and for the first time in months, I realized that I wasn't apologizing for anything. I listened to her, and wonder of wonders, she actually listened to me. She thought I had something to say that might be interesting. She even laughed at a few of my jokes. I mentioned I had a daughter and this redhead actually smiled at me. What's more, she even expressed an interest in her. Of course, I knew that her interest in my daughter was part and parcel of her interest in me, and I knew that I didn't return that interest because I still happen to be in love with you—" Donna could see that Mel was starting to cry. He made no attempt to either hide the tears or stop them. "And I realized what a louse I was being—to you, to the redhead, whose name is Caroline incidentally, and to myself." He paused, finished one full circle around the coffee table and then started another. "Tinka Segal, you remember her, I've told you about her, well, she was a lovely lady, full of motherly clichés, of course, but that's part of what mothers are for. One of Tinka's favorite sayings was from Shakespeare, that glorious font of so many of today's better clichés. 'This above all,' she used to say, 'to thine own self be true!' " Donna caught her breath. It was an expression she remembered her own mother using. "Well," he went on, "I realized that I was obviously getting to a point in our relationship where I was no longer being true to myself. Or at least a point where I can no longer continue being true to myself and be a part of this relationship."

Donna felt her body go cold. None of this was happening. She felt her throat begin to constrict.

"I love you, Donna. I really love you. I know, believe me, I know all you've been through and all you're going through now. I understand. Maybe if it were just me, I could stick it out a little longer. I'm not sure. I really don't know. It's a moot point because it isn't just me. There's an eight-year-old girl up there who's going to celebrate her fortieth birthday soon, if I'm not careful. Six months ago, she was the happiest kid on the block. Now she's afraid to move. She spilled her milk the other night, you took after her like she'd deliberately engineered the whole occasion just to get on your nerves. She's afraid to say anything around you because it's always the wrong thing to say. She's afraid to do anything around you because it's always the wrong thing to do! Donna, listen to me, isn't this ringing any bells?! Doesn't any of this sound achingly familiar to you?"

Donna tried to speak but couldn't.

"Think, Donna," Mel continued, "stop and think for a minute what you're doing to my kid!" He looked helplessly around the room. "And to me! Yea," he bellowed, widening his circle, "we might as well get it all out while we're at it. I feel like I'm always walking in a mine field—one wrong move and whammo!—we all go up in flames. I have to censor every bloody thing I tell you—if an interesting case at the clinic has anything to do with children, well, then, I can't tell you about it because talking about children upsets you, which makes it doubly hard on me because I happen to enjoy talking about children. I happen to enjoy my child, for God's sake. I guess I've been operating these last few months under the misapprehension that the Donna I fell in love with was going to come back to her senses in just a short while. I remember *that* Donna, you see. I remember the first time I saw her; I remember the first time I kissed her, the first time we made love, when she looked like a boy scout; I remember what she was like those first months after her divorce; I even remember her with fondness when she was a desperately unhappy married lady, because at least then, she was a fighter. Not an alley-fighter like she's become, but someone who was fighting for her survival. Now you just fight to destroy." His voice was suddenly very tired. "Victor did just what he said he was going to do, Donna—he obliterated you. You're nowhere to be seen." He stopped, then abruptly started again, his voice picking up greater speed, greater urgency as he went on. "What I can't understand is why you've let him. You ran away from him when you were married rather than let yourself be destroyed. Now, it's like you can't run fast enough the other way." He shook his head. "You know, my mother once said something else—it was when I had to tell her that Kate and I were splitting up, just about four months, I guess, before she died. I was trying to explain it to her, about Kate's need to find herself, that sort of thing, and you know what she said to me? She said that all this modern business about finding yourself is a lot of crap. She said that you are what you do, you are the way you behave." He paused. "She was right." He ran a tired hand through his hair. "You were married to Victor for six years, Donna. I figure that's enough for both of us."

Donna stood numbly in the center of the room. For several minutes, there was absolute silence. "You're telling me you don't want me around anymore?" Her voice was like a child's.

"I'm telling you that I love Donna Cressy. But I can't live with who she's letting herself become."

Donna began frantically moving her head from side to side. "So, you just desert me too? I mean, my children are gone, why not finish me right off? Is that the idea? Let's all get Donna."

"This isn't the way I want it."

"You are what you do, Doctor!" she snapped. Mel lowered his gaze to the floor. "You said you'd never leave me! You promised me you'd never leave me!"

Slowly, he raised his face to hers, but no words came. Only pain. Anguish.

"You promised me you'd help me find my children!"

"We tried, Donna. We did everything that was humanly possible. But how long can you live your life waiting for the phone to ring? How many times can you stop little children on the street because they're the same height as your son? How many strollers can you run after because it might be Sharon inside? I'm not saying you have to give up hope—"

"No!" She was starting to scream, no longer listening to him.

He continued speaking. "I'm just trying to tell you that regardless of whether or not you find your children, *you,* Donna Cressy, have a life of your own."

She was hysterical, beyond calming down. "You lied to me," she cried. "You lied!"

"Donna—" He moved toward her.

"Liar! Liar!"

"Donna—" He raised his arms to try and comfort her.

"No!" she shouted.

"Try and calm down." He started to move toward the door. "Let's just cool off for a few minutes. I'll get you a drink of something—"

"I don't want anything from you! I just want to get out of here." She moved in his direction.

"You're not going anywhere tonight."

"The hell I'm not!"

"Donna, you're not going *anywhere* now. Let's try and get some sleep—we'll talk in the morning—"

She tried to push past him to the door. "I am not sleeping here! You can't make me stay here!"

She began shoving her body against his.

"Donna—"

"Get out of my way. I don't need you. You're just a liar! Let me out of here or I'll wake up the whole bloody house. I promise you!"

Mel again tried to raise his arms toward her, but she slapped them down with her hands. "Get out of my way! Don't touch me!" Then the words gave way to sounds, pure sounds, gutteral howls that seemed to shoot straight from her heart. She was screaming as if he were killing her, an already wounded animal, her foot helplessly caught in a steel strap, the hunter approaching with his knife.

Mel's hand shot to her mouth, trying to stifle her screams. The action terrified Donna, stopping her breath, suffocating her. She bit down hard on his hand. He cried out with the sudden pain, trying to surround her body with his larger bulk. She was everywhere, all over him, scratching, kicking, pounding at him. "Get out of my way!"

He stood firm, not bending to her blows. "I hate you, goddamn it," she bellowed. Then she slapped him full and hard against his cheek.

Instinctively, his right hand rose up and slapped her back with equal force. Then each recoiled with the sudden horror of what they were doing.

He was the first to speak. "Donna, I'm so sorry—"

"No," she cut in. "I don't want to hear anymore." She looked into his worn brown eyes. "You're worse than Victor," she said quietly. "Victor was many things, but he never hit me."

Mel moved out of Donna's way as she walked to the door. His voice was soft behind her. "Sometimes, it's easier to kill someone without ever having to lay a hand on them."

Donna opened the door and walked out without looking back.

Chapter 19

She had been coming to this playground every day now for four weeks. She wasn't sure just how the whole thing had started, at what point a chance occasion had turned into a well-worn ritual, but every afternoon from the hours of three to five, Donna found herself sitting on the same low green bench on the same side of the small narrow playground off Flagler Boulevard watching the children play.

It seemed a fitting way to end each day, days that were spent filling time with empty thoughts until it grew dark enough to get into bed again and go to sleep. She woke up between seven and eight each morning, took an endless amount of time washing, brushing her teeth, doing whatever else was required before getting dressed, wearing whatever was closest to the bed until it was too dirty to wear anymore, then going for a walk, sometimes by the ocean, sometimes all the way over to Worth Avenue, avoiding the looks of the well-dressed tourists who poured in and out of Gucci's and Van Cleef and Arpels as if they were the local five and dimes. Sometimes she walked up toward the Palm Beach Mall or over toward Southern Boulevard. Sometimes she stopped for lunch; more often she skipped it altogether. Always, she ended up here, in this narrow playground. No matter what direction she started off in, all roads led to here.

It had been one of Adam's favorite places, perhaps because of the numerous animal-shaped swings and slides that galloped, jumped and generally cavorted about in place. Not that she really thought he would be here, she told herself. Still, there was the remote possibility that Victor had never taken the children out of Palm Beach at all, or that he had returned after a brief absence. She shook the thought out of her head. No, Palm Beach was too small a county. There were too many people who might spot them, too many chances they might be discovered. Besides, the detective had combed the entire state, checking real estate offices, nurseries, housekeeping agencies. Victor was definitely not in Florida. Or hadn't been, her mind persisted. He might have come back—

Donna's eyes trailed after a small dark-haired boy as he ran from the entranceway of the park to one of the brightly painted jungle gyms. She watched him as he climbed to the top and hung by his ankles upside down. Where was his mother? she wondered angrily. You don't let small children play unattended in a potentially dangerous environment. The boy was no older than Adam. It was sheer irresponsibility to let him run free without supervision. She looked harder at the child—he even looked a bit like Adam, she thought, at least from this distance, and facing into the sun as she was. If she squinted just slightly, she could almost believe—

"Todd, where are you?" a woman's shrill voice called out. The woman ran into the playground area and then angrily walked toward the boy. "How many times have I asked you to wait for me and not run so far ahead. You know I can't run so fast any more." Donna looked at the woman's body. She was perhaps six or seven months pregnant, five or six years her junior. Then she looked down at her own body. She was the thinnest she'd ever been, her slight frame accentuated by hair that was just a touch too long to be attractive.

"God, I don't know how I'm ever going to manage with two," the woman said, ambling over to Donna and sitting down beside her. Donna was surprised to find she appreciated the woman's presence, the chance to converse. It had been a long while since she had actually talked to anyone, uttered more than a necessary hello or goodbye.

"You'll manage," she said, smiling. "It's hard at first, you don't think you'll ever get organized, but you do, and then it's really nice."

"Yea?" the woman asked, straightening her blonde hair under her bandana, her black roots protruding about half an inch into the sunlight. "I hope so. We can't afford no help or anything. And Todd, he was such a rotten baby, cried all the time. I don't think I could go through that all over again."

"My first was the same," Donna said. "Adam cried for three straight months. But then he stopped and he was terrific. Sharon never cried at all. Maybe you'll be just as lucky with your second."

"I sure hope so." The woman looked over at the playing children, a total of ten now that Todd was among them. "Which ones are yours?"

The question caught Donna off guard. She found herself stammering her reply. "They're—they're not here." The woman looked surprised. You don't have to have children with you to sit in a playground, Donna wanted to tell her. Instead she said, "They're with their father. He took them to Disney World."

"Oh, that's nice. We were there last year. I liked it more than Todd." Donna smiled. The woman looked at her questioningly. "You're not spending Christmas together?"

Donna stared at the younger woman in surprise. How could she have forgotten it was Christmas in just a matter of days? She looked around her, at the palm trees, the green grass, felt the warm December air around her shoulders. It was easy to forget it was Christmas, she decided. The weather was the same as it always seemed to be, sometimes hotter, sometimes less so; there was no one around to shop for, no one to ask daily, is it Christmas yet? No one had sent her any Christmas cards—how could they? No one knew where she was.

She had taken up a quasi-permanent residence at the

Mt. Vernon Motel on Belvedere. At first, it had been intended as transitional, a sort of half-way home between
Mel's house and a new apartment of her own. The lease
on her rented home had expired, its owners returning to
reclaim their territory. And so, she had moved some of
her more portable belongings into the Mt. Vernon Motel
and put the rest into storage. After the tourist season was
over, she'd see about finding a regular apartment. Probably.

"I forgot it was Christmas," Donna said, and immediately wished she hadn't.

The younger woman withdrew, a look almost of fear
crossing her eyes. Donna suddenly remembered the large
Christmas tree at the end of Worth Avenue, saw it lit up
and glowing against the night, saw the store windows all
filled with Christmas trappings. It was amazing what the
mind could block out, she thought. She had actually managed to make Christmas disappear. A not altogether small
accomplishment.

The woman smiled feebly in Donna's direction, pushed
herself into a standing position, mumbled something
about helping her son, and then walked with relative
speed, for a woman in her condition, to where the boy
was dangling. When she concluded whatever it was she
had thought up to say to him, she proceeded to another
bench on the other side of the narrow, elongated park and
sat down, pulling a book from her purse, and not once
looking back in Donna's direction. What kind of a lunatic
forgets it's Christmas? Donna asked herself again; then
she stood up and slowly walked in the direction of the
exit.

The man was tall and skinny and didn't look anything
like John Travolta, she decided, wondering why she had
thought he had in the first place. John Travolta was dark
and had elastic hips. This boy—he was just a boy, she
could see now, despite the dim lighting—had only average
brown hair coloring, a mildly sensual look about him as
opposed to one that was overwhelming, and his hips were

only eager. What was she doing here? No, that was wrongly phrased. What was *he* doing here? They were in her motel room, after all. She was sitting on her own bed; he was standing over by the dresser combing his hair in the mirror. He wore tight black jeans and high-heeled boots. No shirt. Quickly, Donna checked her own body—she was still wearing the light blue velour shorts and matching top she'd been wearing for the last several days. Had they made love already? Was she dressed again and waiting for him to finish preening and leave?

She looked back over in the youth's direction. That was a good word for him, she decided. Youth. Slightly more than a boy, not quite a man. At least ten years younger than herself. What was he doing in her motel room? Where had she found him?

"What day is it?" she asked him suddenly.

He turned slowly in her direction, a look of puzzlement crossing his face. "Friday," he answered. His voice was strange to her; she couldn't remember whether or not this was the first time she had heard him speak. "Be with you in a minute, babe." He was studying his profile in the mirror, much more interested in his own perfection than in her.

"What date is it?" Her own voice sounded strange to her as well. As if she were listening to it on tape. In fact, the whole scene felt like something she was watching from across the room: two strangers, one partially clad and standing, absorbed in his own image, the other still dressed, sitting on the bed and waiting. Waiting for what? For him to leave? To approach her? Make love to her? Who was this boy? How had he gotten into her motel room? What day was it? "What date is it?" the voice asked again, almost feverishly.

"Hey, babe, you keep asking me that. What's the matter? Are you all right?"

"What date is it?" So they had spoken before.

"It's still Friday, December thirty-first." He turned back to the mirror, then checked his watch, which she had noticed he had removed and put on the dresser.

"Like I told you in the park, I can't stay long. I got a date tonight." He smiled sheepishly. "New Year's and all."

Had they already made love? Was that why he was here? She watched from somewhere outside of her body as he expertly kicked off his boots, walked away from the mirror and moved to within two feet of the confused woman in blue who sat on the bed. Both women now watched as he teasingly unbuckled his belt and inched his black jeans down over his hips. He wore no underwear.

"You have a nice body," she heard the woman's voice say. He kicked free of his pants and then took a few dancing steps back toward the mirror, examining his now naked body from all angles.

"Great, huh?" he said, more than asked. "I work out in a gym every day. Just around the corner from the park. Gotta keep in shape," he said, moving back in the woman's direction, "you know, for the chicks."

The scene was moving too quickly, Donna thought from her position across the room. Would the projectionist please stop the film for a few minutes, roll it back, start it again from the top? I missed the opening credits. I don't know who these people are, what this boy is doing in this woman's room. Why does she look so confused? I'm the one who doesn't have a clue as to what's going on here. I always hated coming in in the middle of a picture. Would the projectionist please start the film again? Tell me who these people are?

"A little old for this sort of thing, aren't you?" she heard a woman's voice ask. He was hanging upside down from the top of the jungle gym, the knees of his black jeans wrapped around the bright green bar, his black T-shirt falling up and away from his pants, the button in the middle of his belly almost smiling at her. He quickly scrambled to his feet, turning right side up and facing her. He looked like John Travolta, she thought.

"You a park superintendent?" he asked, chewing furiously on a stick of gum.

She shook her head. "No. No. I just come here sometimes."

"Yea?" he asked, disinterestedly. "You got kids here?"

"No," she answered, shaking her head.

He nodded and looked around. There were a few kids playing nearby. When he looked back at the woman, she was still staring at him.

"So, uh, you just come here, huh?"

"Yea."

"Yea, I know how it is."

"How what is?"

He shrugged. "I don't know." He looked back at the jungle gym.

"My name is Donna."

"Yea?"

"Yea."

He smiled guardedly. "Nice to meet you, Donna."

"What day is it?"

"What day? Uh, Friday. It's Friday."

"Friday the what?"

The smile started to fade. "Friday, December thirty-first. New Year's Eve."

"Now?"

"What do you mean, now? It's only a little after three o'clock in the afternoon. Later. In a few hours, it'll be New Year's Eve. You want to know what year?" The voice was a mixture of sarcasm and bewilderment.

She shook her head. The year was unimportant. She continued to stare at the young man.

"Look, I gotta go. Got a big date tonight. You know how it is."

"How what is?"

He started to move away from her. "Well, Happy New Year." He turned and started to walk away.

The woman took a few tentative steps in his direction. "Wait!" she called.

"I really can't stay," he said, turning.

"Would you like to go to bed with me?"

My, my, but this woman was bold, Donna thought, watching the scene replay.

"Is this some sort of joke?" Walking back toward her.

"No joke. Would you like to go to bed with me? I'm living over on Belvedere."

"Freaky chick," he said, starting to laugh. "Sure, I'll give you a tumble. But I can't stay long."

"You have a car?"

"Down the street."

Donna watched the boy's hand fall across the woman's rear end as they walked together out of the park.

"Don't you think you should take this off?" he was asking, pulling at the woman's blue velour top. They were back in the motel room. Donna watched as the woman lifted her arms into the air like a child and the young man—the youth—pulled the top over her head. "Hey, a bra!" he said, laughing. "I haven't seen one of these things in years." He studied it as if it were material from another planet, moving his hands across her back to undo the clasp.

"It unclasps from the front," she muttered.

"Yea? How about that? Told you it's been a long time since I've been around one of these." He found the hook and undid it effortlessly. "Haven't lost the touch though," he said, his tongue twisting the gum in his mouth. He pulled her bra off, letting it fall to the floor. "I guess this is like one of those zipless fuck fantasies, huh?" he asked, pushing her down on the bed and pulling off both her shorts and her panties in one adept motion.

"I gave up on fantasies a long time ago," the woman's voice said. Donna squirmed from her position across the room. The voice had sounded just a bit too familiar on that last utterance. "I was on an airplane once," the voice continued, "a long time ago. A nun took the seat I'd been saving for Warren Beatty. So much for fantasies."

Donna laughed. The youth didn't. He stopped chewing his gum and straightened up his body, which had been bending over the woman. He was staring down hard at her, examining her with an almost clinical eye. Donna noticed his erection was diminishing.

"Something wrong?"

"What's this?" he asked.

"What?"

"This. Looks like some sort of scar." His fingers traced the vertical line which ran from her navel to her pubic hair.

Donna felt the woman pulling her toward the bed. "My babies," the voice said, haltingly.

"Babies? You got babies?"

"Two of them," she said slowly. "They had to come out by Caesarian."

The youth sat back away from the woman. "That's too bad. Nothing you can do about the scar, huh?"

Donna was back inside the woman's body. It didn't quite fit. She wanted to get out, to get away from this place, this boy, whoever he was, and this ridiculous conversation, but she seemed stuck inside this strange woman's skin, a virtual prisoner of a less-than-perfect, noticeably scarred body. "I never thought much about it," she said. Her own voice. It was true. Victor had always treated her scar as some sort of badge; Mel had never mentioned it except to comment that it was nicely done and to plant kisses up and down it. She stopped. She would not think about Mel. She looked back at the boy, the distaste he felt obvious in his eyes. "You don't like scars, I take it."

He shook his head. "Don't exactly turn me on. But I guess things like that don't bother you 'new women'—"

"New women?" What on earth was he talking about?

"Well, you don't shave under your arms, you don't shave your legs—"

Donna looked down at her legs, felt her underarms. He was right. How long had it been since she remembered to shave? She had no idea. "I guess I'm quite a sight."

He laughed. "Look," he said, getting up off the bed and walking back toward the mirror, "maybe we'll do this some other time. It's gettin' kind of late. I have this date and all."

Donna nodded wordlessly. So even a stray park pickup was turning her down.

"You divorced?" he asked, hopping into his pants.

"Yes."

"Yea, well—" He pulled his T-shirt down over his head. "Maybe the two of you will get back together one of these days." Obviously no one else would be crazy enough—

"Maybe," Donna said, her voice starting to sound comfortably strange again. "Maybe it wasn't really as bad as I thought it was." She looked slowly around the room. "Was it really that bad?" she asked herself. At least she'd have her children back again. When she looked back toward the dresser, the youth was gone. She fell asleep wondering if, in fact, there had been anyone there at all.

She woke up abruptly twenty minutes later and walked into the bathroom. She opened the medicine cabinet, removed her Lady Schick razor, threw out the old blade and replaced it with a new one. Then she soaped her underarms and shaved away any traces of the "new woman." She nicked her skin in a few places, ignored the cuts, and moved on to her legs. She lifted one leg into the sink, ran a wet washcloth down it and then applied the soap. Then she steadied the razor and started to take gentle strokes down her legs.

The first cut was an accident; she had simply borne down too hard—the blade was new, there was no need to press. The second cut was careless. The third was deliberate. As were the fourth, fifth and sixth. She changed legs and repeated the process, watching as she small cuts released long rivers of blood which flowed into one another, tracing imaginary map lines across her legs, twisting and turning and stinging against the soap and water. Oddly enough, she thought, the pain felt good. Victor wouldn't approve, of course, and he would be right. As he was usually right. About everything. If only she could find him and tell him. Maybe he would take her back. Think about it, Donna, she told herself, walking out of the bathroom and getting back into her blue shorts and top. It wasn't really as bad as you made it out to be. Be truthful with yourself now, she said. Was it really that bad?

"My God, what happened to your legs?"

Donna looked from the face of the startled hairdresser to her own legs. "I cut them shaving."

"What did you shave with, an ax?" the woman asked.

"When can you take me?"

The young woman with the purple streaks across the front of her hair looked around the busy shop. "I don't know, Mrs. Cressy," she said. "It's New Year's Eve. We've been booked solid for weeks."

"Please—"

"All right, look, come back in an hour. I'll see if I can fit you in."

"Oh, thank you."

"What is it exactly you want done?"

Donna looked hard at the woman whose shop she had frequented so often in the year following Sharon's birth. The woman's hair was short, very geometrical in shape and a sort of brassy red in color, with large purple streaks running across the front. "I kind of like yours," Donna said.

She wasn't sure what she was doing here except that she had an hour to kill before Lorraine could take her. But why here? She hadn't been here since the funeral, never feeling that the cemetery, the actual tombstone, brought her any closer to her mother. Why did she choose to come here now?

Donna walked between the rows of white tombs, the fresh flowers—no artificial flowers, please, the sign said—spilling over the tops of the actual graves. So peaceful here. She remembered a joke from her childhood—look, there's a new cemetery; people are just dying to get in there! She walked quickly through the rows of graves until she found the row and the headstone she was looking for.

SHARON EDMUNDS
1910–1963
Beloved Wife of Alan
Beloved Mother of Donna and Joan
"A gentle soul; a kind spirit"

Donna stood for several very long seconds in front of the tombstone. Slowly, her fingers worked themselves in and out of the lettering, as if she were reading in Braille. She traced each word several times over and then ran her hand across the rest of the smooth alabaster surface. I don't know what to say, she thought. I don't know how to talk to you. Then she let her knees give way, slowly falling to the ground beside the earth, sitting beside her mother's grave, looking blankly at the headstone. I don't know what to say to you, she repeated to herself, knowing that if there was any possible way, her mother would hear her, even without the spoken word. Please tell me what to do. Please tell me who I am. What have I done to my life? What have I thrown away? She stared deep into the carved lettering. Was my life with Victor really so bad? Please help me, Mother, I need some answers. I need you to tell me what to do!

There were no voices, no strange flutterings, no mysterious signs that spoke of supernatural forces. Nothing. Only stillness. Donna's eyes drifted across the symmetrical rows. Nothing disturbed them. No ghosts rose from them. No slender, translucent figures in white flowing robes. Nothing. Suddenly, she heard Mel's voice. "If there are ghosts anywhere in this room, Donna, they're standing in your shoes."

She pushed thoughts of Mel out of her head, as she did each time such thoughts intruded. This time, they stubbornly pushed themselves back in.

"Are you ready to leave?" Mel.

"I've been ready all evening." Donna.

"So I noticed. About the only thing you didn't do was dangle the car keys in my direction."

Go away, Mel.

"You're telling me you don't want me around anymore?"

"I'm telling you that I love Donna Cressy. But I can't live with who she's letting herself become."

Donna leaned her body against her mother's headstone. Mel's voice was right behind her.

"You were married to Victor for six years, Donna. I figure that's enough for both of us."

Donna's mind began racing like a film gone amuck, backward and at more than triple its normal speed through six years of life with Victor. Words. More words. Endless series of words. Corrections. Suggestions. Orders. Half-truths. Just enough truths. Enough truth to snare the fish. Turn her from an adult to a child. Send her sprawling through the looking glass. Make her small again.

A poem by Margaret Atwood suddenly raced before her eyes and froze. More words.

> you fit into me
> like a hook into an eye
> a fish hook
> an open eye

The right words. She thought suddenly of Victor's mother, saw the waste of almost a decade. His ex-wife. Three years on the couch because of that creep, the woman had said. Still angry after all these years. And herself? The melody of Paul Simon's song wafted past her ears. Still crazy? What was the letting Victor do?

SHARON EDMUNDS

Donna stared at her mother's name. "Yes," she said aloud, the last images of her life with Victor sticking on the reel and scratching to a sudden halt. "It was that bad."

She stood up. A vision of Mel was beside her.

"Are you saying your behavior tonight was my fault?" Donna. The night she had slapped him and walked out on their life together.

"I'm saying it was *my* fault. You can't be responsible for my actions." Mel. Can't you understand what I'm trying to say?

She understood. Why were the simplest truths always the hardest to understand?

Victor was no longer responsible for her life. She would get no answers from anyone else. *Could* get no answers from anyone else. Only from inside herself. She was the only one responsible for her life, for whatever she chose to do with it. For the stranger in her motel room, for the cuts on her legs, for what she, herself—no one else—was letting happen.

Donna gazed around the cemetery. "There's just a lot of dead people here," she said aloud, feeling her mother quickly agree.

There are no answers, she thought, looking over the rows of death. There's only life.

The point is learning to live with it.

Mel was working late so that he could take off the holiday the next day.

Donna felt her heart racing as she climbed the stairs up to his office. Like a kid, she thought, aware of the increased palpitations, recognizing that there was a good chance that he might not want her back, that too much time had elapsed, that she had put him through too much. She stopped midway up the steps, feeling a shortage of air, taking several deep breaths. If he didn't want her back, what then? More endless walks to nowhere? More strangers in children's playgrounds? More blood in her bathroom sink? No, she said silently, resuming her climb. She had punished herself enough. No more blisters. No more blood. She'd already paid.

"Be with you in a minute," he called from inside his inner office when she had entered the waiting room. The receptionist was gone. "I'm just finishing off something for the lab. I'll be right there."

Donna stood in the middle of the room and waited. I will survive, she said to herself. If you send me away, I will still survive. You are not responsible for me. I am the only one who can do that particular job.

"Sorry, I didn't realize I had any more appointments—" He stopped the minute he saw her. Donna saw the tears immediately come to his eyes, felt her own tears forming.

Her voice was clear and very much her own. "Please let me say everything I came here to say before you say anything." He nodded silently. "I've been a real jerk and whatever else you can think of to call me," she began. "I've wasted the last nine months of my life trying to force that damned rock over the top of the hill when we all know it can't be done. It just rolls back over me and anyone else who happens to be standing around me." He said nothing, knowing there was more she wanted to say.

"I've had quite a day today," she continued. "I picked up some kid in the park, I nearly amputated my legs, I almost dyed my hair purple." She stopped. "I went to see my mother." She stopped again. "I've been thinking about that book all the way over here. The book about Sisyphus. And I think that that's the way I have to be. That the only way I'm going to survive what Victor has done is if I recognize and accept the fact that there's just no hope I'll ever get my kids back again. The more I hope, the more I despair. I have no more room for despair."

They were both openly crying now. "I don't know how you still feel about me. I do know that I love you, that I want very much to be with you, to be your wife and a mother to Annie. I also know that I will not fall to pieces if you say it's too late." She laughed through her tears. "I'll be as upset as hell," she said, "but I won't fall apart. I promise you." She paused. "That's all I have to say. It's your turn."

He smiled sadly. There was a long silence before he spoke. "Purple hair?"

She shrugged. "Does that mean you love me?"

"It means I love you right out of my mind."

In the next instant, the space between them disappeared and there was no more need for words.

Chapter 20

Donna sat over a large stack of receipts and unpaid bills, trying to arrange them into alphabetical order. Whoever the last girl had been, she'd certainly made a fine mess of everything. No wonder they had asked Kelly Girl to replace her.

The phone chimed some barely recognizable tune. Why couldn't they have a phone that rang like everybody else's? She picked it up. "Household Finance," she said clearly. "His line is busy. Could you hold for a minute? Fine, I'll connect you as soon as I can." She pressed the appropriate buttons and went back to the stack of receipts and unpaid bills. Another set of chimes. This time the door. A tall, well-dressed, deeply tanned gentleman of about forty-five approached her.

"Mr. Wendall?"

"Just a minute, please." She pressed the appropriate button. She was always pressing appropriate buttons. "Your name, please?"

"Mr. Ketchum."

"Mr. Wendall, there's a Mr. Ketchum to see you. Yes. Fine. I will. Have a seat, sir. He'll be right with you." She released the button.

The phone began to chime. Someone else walked through the door and approached her. More buttons. More chimes. My God, no wonder the last girl had left things in such a mess—she never had a chance to get to them. In the two hours since she'd started to work, she had barely managed to separate the A's from the B's. Not a promising beginning.

She now had three people holding, two sitting on chairs waiting, and a desk full of neglected receipts and unpaid bills. The phone sounded again. "Household Finance," she said pleasantly, breaking into a wide grin at the sound of a familiar voice. "It's a madhouse here. It's almost lunch and I haven't accomplished a thing. How are you? Oh, just a minute, Mel, someone else just came in." She attended to business. "Now there are three people waiting to see Mr. Wendall. I don't know what he's doing back there. Yea, I'm enjoying it. It's kind of fun. Different from the bank."

In the last three weeks since she had joined Kelly Girl, Donna had worked for one Savings and Loan, one accountant and one bank. For this week and possibly the next, she was to serve as receptionist-bookkeeper for the West Palm office of Household Finance. As a Kelly Girl, the jobs she was assigned were mostly nondescript-short-on-responsibility-and-initiative, heavy on clerical duties. Still, they got her back in the work field, kept her active and yet gave her time to think about the type of job she might want to pursue in the future. Her friend Susan had told her she had some new ideas for her. They'd talk it over at the party on Saturday night.

"Okay, thanks for calling, honey. Oh, you remember that I'm meeting Annie at Saks later and then we're having a bite to eat afterward. No, you are not invited. Annie said this is just girl-talk. I'm a nervous wreck. Yea, I will. Okay, hon. See you later. Bye-bye."

She hung up the phone in time for it to ring again. By noontime, she had four people on hold, six more waiting to see Mr. Wendall, who had just informed her by intercom that he was going out for lunch, and a desk full of unsorted receipts and unpaid bills. She also had a whale of a headache. What did Annie want to talk about? she wondered.

Everything had been proceeding very well so far. Since her return to Seabreeze Drive, they had reestablished the trust and regard Donna had managed only a few months ago to shatter. For the first few days, they had stalked each other like leery cats, but soon they had abandoned the cumbersome claws and territorial gestures for the more familiar hugs and laughter, glad to have each other back. Annie seemed genuinely delighted that Donna and Mel were planning to marry, and was thrilled when Donna suggested she accompany her to Saks to pick out a dress for their upcoming engagement party. Then she had thrown out the little bomb about wanting to talk to Donna privately, without Mel around. Was this the old I'll-give-you-a-million-dollars-to-get-out-of-town-and-leave-my-pa-alone routine? Before she had time to think of a possible response, the phone chimed again and two more people walked in the front door.

"It was quite an afternoon, I'll tell you."

"Tell me."

Donna smiled at the young girl who sat across from her in Doherty's restaurant trying to put an entire pastrami sandwich inside her mouth in one gulp. Annie's eyes were wide with a child's curiosity. Day by day, a little at a time, the lines of the skeptic-beyond-her-years were beginning to disappear. Donna was feeling increasingly grateful she'd been given this second chance. She could see how much it meant to the child to be taken into her confidence, to share in the information of daily life, which meant she was an accepted part of that life.

"Well, the place never stops," Donna continued. "I had no idea there were so many people in this neck of the woods who were so much in debt."

"What does that mean?"

"They borrow money and then they have to pay it back," Donna explained. Annie nodded comprehension. "And this Mr. Wendall is a real case. I think he borrowed a few brains from someone to get to his position, but then

returned them too early."Annie láughed. "He's so slow—
he moves like a snail. His appointments get all backed up.
People sit and wait for hours. They keep bugging me
about when will he be ready. I'm the one out front, so I
take all the—"

"Shit?"

"Yea, That'll do. Thank you." She laughed.

They both took bites of their sandwiches before Donna
continued. "Well, this afternoon, things got really ridiculous. He must have had ten people out there waiting for
him, including a few who didn't have appointments. So, I
kept buzzing him. No answer. I finally left my desk and
went back to his office. He's not there. Nobody's there.
I'm walking back to my desk, I hear this voice say, 'Mrs.
Cressy?' I stopped; I looked around. Nobody. I'm just
about to keep walking, this voice says again, 'Mrs.
Cressy?' So I said, 'Mr. Wendall?' And the voice says
'yes.' But he's not anywhere around. Would you like to
know where he was?"

The child was already giggling. "Where?"

"In the closet! He was hiding in the closet!" Donna
shook her head in disbelief. "Apparently, one of the
people who came in without an appointment was some
woman he didn't want to see. She's always bugging him
and has even been known to storm into the back offices
looking for him. When he saw her come in, he made a
bee-line for the closet. He'd been standing in it for half an
hour."

"Did he come out?"

"Yes. And the minute he did, she burst through the
door and cornered him. It was wonderful. I can't wait till
tomorrow to see what he does next."

The child's laughter subsided and her face grew serious. "Are you happy now, Donna?"

Donna looked at Annie with tender regard. "I'm getting there."

"You like me better?"

"I like *myself* better. I've always liked *you*."

Annie smiled. "Do you miss Adam and Sharon?"

"Yes."

"Do you think about them a lot?"

"I try not to."

Annie looked down at what was left of her sandwich, then up at Donna, then back at her plate. "You won't leave again, will you?" she whispered.

Donna's hand reached across the table and covered the child's. She shook her head. "Who would help me choose my dresses if I did?"

"Seriously," the child admonished.

Donna's answer was appropriately solemn. "I'm here to stay, Annie."

Annie's face broke into a wide grin.

"Is that what you wanted to talk to me about?"

Annie shook her head. "Not really. I just wanted to make sure you were really staying before I asked."

"Asked what?"

"It's about sex."

"Sex?"

"Yea, you know."

"Oh, yea, sex. Sure, I know. What about it?"

Annie looked around to make sure no one was listening. "Well, I mean, my dad's explained it and everything, and so has my mother. I know all about the penis and the vagina and things—" Donna tried to concentrate on Annie's mouth, afraid that if she looked into the eyes of this earnest little girl that she would start to laugh. "What I don't understand is how the penis gets into the vagina in the first place."

"You want to know how the penis gets into the vagina?"

"And don't tell me that the man and woman lie very close together because I already know that, and it doesn't answer the question."

It was Donna's turn to look around and make sure no one was listening. "You have to have an answer for that right now? I mean, I don't suppose you'd consider waiting till summer vacation and asking your mother?"

"You're kind of my mother now too, aren't you?"

Donna smiled broadly. "I love you, Annie," she said.

"Will you tell me how the penis gets into the vagina? Does the man use his hands to push it in?"

Donna's mind flooded with highly graphic visual images. She tried to answer honestly, without laughter or condescension. "Well, he could if he wanted to, I guess. It's not necessary. You see, the penis fills up with fluid from the testicles. You know what the testicles are?"

"Of course." Nothing like eight-year-old disdain, Donna thought.

"Well that fluid makes the penis hard—so the man can just—"

"Shove it in?"

"That about sums it up." Donna took a long sip of water.

"Does it hurt?"

Donna shook her head. "It feels nice."

Annie looked around her, a flush of guilt creeping across her face. "I already knew all that," she confessed after Donna had ordered her a chocolate sundae.

"You did? Then why did you ask?"

"I wanted to hear what you would say," she answered slyly.

"Passed the test, did I?"

"That part about it feeling nice, though," she added, ignoring Donna's question, "I didn't know that." Long pause. "I love you, Donna."

I passed the test, Donna thought wondrously, her eyes filling with tears. One down. How many more to go?

"You look fantastic."

Donna did a well-practiced turn around the room. "It's nice, isn't it?"

"Gorgeous. That's the dress Annie helped you buy?"

"She was terribly pleased with herself."

Mel walked over to Donna and put his arms around her. "She did a good job." They kissed.

"What are you going to wear?" she asked him.

"I don't know. Why don't you pick something out for me."

"Okay." Mel started toward the door. "Where are you going?" she asked.

"I promised Mrs. Harrison I'd adjust the fine tuner on the TV in time for the Saturday night movie."

He started down the stairs. "Don't take too long," she called after him. "We're the guests of honor, remember."

"Be right back," he called.

Donna did another turn in front of the mirror, satisfied herself that everything was where it should be and then walked over and sat on the bed, newly recovered in a soft blue-and-cream Laura Ashley print which matched the newly recovered walls. Yes, everything seemed to be falling into place—the room, herself, her life. Everything was definitely where it should be. There were only two things missing, two things out of place. She stood up and looked at the clock. Seven P.M—Mothers, do you know where your children are?

She walked to the dresser and picked up the brush she had purchased on her last outing to the hairdressers—just a few inches off, please. Nothing drastic. She began to furiously brush her hair, angry that she had allowed a glimmer of hope to invade her thoughts. She would not think about Adam and Sharon. She would not allow herself to get upset. Tonight was her engagement party. Donna Cressy—this is your life! she heard the announcer say, the horns blasting around her, the bells ringing triumphantly. Louder. Louder.

It was the phone. She wasn't used to ringing anymore—she was used to chimes. She walked over to the end table and picked it up. "Hello?"

"How've you been?"

She hadn't expected him to call. Somehow, with her fresh resolve, she hadn't prepared herself for his intervention. She was making a new life for herself—they didn't—couldn't—include his sadistic phone calls.

"Don't call me anymore, Victor," she said, about to hang up the phone.

"Donna, wait—there's someone here I thought you might want to say hello to. Sharon, come on over here. There's a lady here who wants to say hello."

Donna could picture him holding up the phone in the child's direction and while she wanted to slam the phone against his ear, she couldn't move. My baby, she thought. I can talk to my baby. Maybe— She could hear the laughter of children playing, familiar sounds lingering in the background, filling the distance between them.

"She doesn't want to talk to you," Victor's voice said, returning unpleasantly to her ear. Involuntarily, she felt the tug of the fisherman's line in her mouth—the fish realizing, too late, as always, that it has swallowed the bait—felt the hook ripping down her cheek as she tried to wriggle free. He had done it again. So effortlessly. As always.

Donna steadied herself against the bed. "Don't call me anymore Victor," she said feeling her mouth fill up with blood, finally shaking loose of the predator's hook, lowering the phone swiftly back into place. Everything now back in place.

When Mel came bounding up the stairs seconds later, she was sitting quietly on the bed.

"I picked up the extension," he explained, moving toward her.

"He won't call anymore."

"Are you all right?"

She nodded.

"What happened to your mouth? It's bleeding!"

He grabbed a Kleenex and hurried over to the foot of the bed.

Donna moved her tongue around in her cheek. "I bit on the inside of my mouth," she said. "It's all right. It doesn't hurt."

"You feel like screaming and kicking your feet?"

Donna took the Kleenex from Mel's outstretched hand

and wiped at the side of her lips. "No," she said standing up.

"It would be all right if you did, Donna. It would only be natural—"

"I'm all right," Donna said numbly, her mind still on the phone call. Then she stood up and walked toward Mel's closet to get him something to wear.

They were all congratulating her, coming over to her and kissing her on both cheeks, shaking her hands, smiling warmly, complimenting her on her dress, her hair, her appearance. You look beautiful, their voices echoed. Donna was only vaguely aware of them.

"Donna, wait—there's someone here I thought you might want to say hello to. Sharon, come over here. There's a lady here who wants to say hello."

Damn you, Victor, she thought, trying to fight the anger, to force it down beneath her toes where she could suffocate it with her foot. I will not let you spoil any more parties. I will not think about you.

Sharon.

Adam.

My babies.

"Congratulations, Donna. You look marvelous."

"Oh. Oh, thank you."

"You're getting a good man."

"Yes. Yes. I know."

The sound of children playing.

"Congratulations."

Something else.

"Hasn't anyone told these people that they're not supposed to congratulate the woman? Only the man. He's supposed to be the lucky one to have found you."

Donna looked over at her hostess, who had just finished speaking. Bessie Milford was a nice lady. Her husband Rod was a nice man. It was very sweet of them to host an engagement party for her and Mel, especially after the way she had acted at the last party she had attended here. Donna looked toward the balcony, remembering that last party. There was no redhead present tonight, however. Just a small gathering of their close mutual friends. A shame Donna couldn't join them, she thought, her mind fastening, despite her attempts at denial, on earlier events.

Something else. The sound of children playing. And something else.

Something familiar.

"Donna, are you all right?"

Donna turned to see her friend Susan. "Fine," she said, absently.

"You look gorgeous."

"Thank you."

"You just look like you're in another room, that's all."

"What do you mean?"

"I mean you're not here. Where are you?"

"What time is it, Susan?"

Susan checked her watch. "Nine o'clock. Ten after, actually. Why? You have a cake in the oven?"

"He called at seven."

"Who called?"

"He called at seven and said the children were playing."

"Victor called?"

"He held the phone up for me to hear."

"Was it Victor who called?"

"What were they doing up at seven o'clock playing? Sharon is always in bed, lights out and everything, by seven o'clock. Victor's a fanatic about it."

Susan said nothing.

"Unless it wasn't seven o'clock."

"I don't understand."

"Unless it was a different time zone."

"The West Coast?"

The sound of children playing. And something else.

Something familiar.

Donna moved away from Susan and over toward the patio doors. "Could we open these, please?" she asked.

Mel was suddenly at her side. "Need some air, honey?"

The doors parted like the Red Sea, she thought, stepping out onto the sun-colored tile and leaning forward against the black wrought-iron railing.

Something familiar.

She stared into the darkness. There were no stars out tonight. The weathermen were predicting a 60 percent chance of rain for the next morning. She couldn't see it, but she knew it was there—the ocean, roaring its continuing disapproval of the approaching inclement weather. She didn't have to see it to feel its presence, know its power. Background. And yet, much more than mere background. So much a part of one after a while to be almost taken for granted, indistinguishable from the air. Yet stronger than the air. A life force.

A force that was capable of propelling itself through a phone wire over a distance of three thousand miles. The familiar sound. The something else. The ocean.

She turned to Mel, who was now standing beside her. "They're in California," she said.

Annie sat beneath the yellow canopy above her bed and stared vacantly ahead of her. She refused to look at Donna, speaking when she spoke at all, only to her father.

"It's just for four weeks, Annie," Donna repeated for what felt like the hundredth time. "If we don't turn up anything at the end of four weeks, we come home. I promise." Annie said nothing. Donna continued, fighting back the tears, trying hard to reach her. "This has nothing to do with my love for you. Do you understand that?" She knelt in front of the child. "I love you, Annie. I really love you. You're my little girl."

"I'm a big girl."

Donna nodded. "My big girl," she agreed aloud. "I love you."

For the first time in over an hour, Annie looked in Donna's direction. "Then why are you leaving me?"

"Only for four weeks," Mel interjected. "And Mrs. Harrison will be with you——"

"Because Sharon and Adam are my children too, and I want them back with me," Donna answered over Mel's voice, knowing now that the child was not concerned with time or Mrs. Harrison. "Because I tried to do too much and it just won't work. I can't deny my children. They exist. I love them. I want to see them again. I can't live without the hope that I might. I tried, but I'm just not built that way, I guess." She paused, taking a deep breath. "It won't be like it was before, Annie, when I was consumed with them, with finding them. When I shut everything and everyone else out of my life. I'll never let that happen again. I swear to you." Annie looked at the floor, trying hard, Donna could see, not to cry. "I love you. I love your father. I'll never let either of you go. You just try and get away from me——"

Annie flung her arms around Donna's neck and the two hugged each other almost ferociously, stopping their breath, burying their faces in each other's hair.

"I hope you find them, Donna," the child said when they finally released each other.

"I hope so too," Donna acknowledged.

Mel moved toward the door. "We better get going. The plane leaves in less than an hour."

Annie waved them out of sight as their car sped down the road.

"What are you thinking about?" he asked her, thirty-seven thousand feet in the air.

"That this could all be a wildgoose chase," she answered. "Oh God, there goes the fasten your seat-belt sign! Why is there always turbulence just when they start serving the food?"

Mel shook his head. "It's probably some drunk in the aisle."

"What do you mean?"

"A friend of mine was going on a trip once," he began

explaining, leaning close to her, "and he happened to know the pilot. In the middle of the flight, the announcement came on that they were experiencing turbulence and would everyone please fasten their belts and stay in their seats. A few minutes later, the stewardess came over to him and asked him if he'd like to see the cockpit—the pilot was inviting him. Well, he protested. No, he said. There's turbulence. I shouldn't leave my seat. Apparently, the stewardess was fairly insistent, so he finally went up to the cockpit. His friend, the pilot, was jovial as could be, showed him around, asked him if he wanted to sit in the driver's seat, the whole bit. My friend couldn't believe it. What about the turbulence? he asked. Oh that, they said. There is no turbulence. We just do that to clear the aisles so the stewardesses can get the wagons through."

"You're kidding."

"Apparently, they also do it if someone's being very rowdy or drunk and they want to settle things down a bit."

"So, all these butterflies in my stomach are for nothing—"

"Some of them."

She smiled. "Why am I so sure they're in California?"

"Deductive reasoning. Actually, I'm very proud of you. You were just like Nancy Drew."

"California's an enormous state."

"We only have to worry about the Coast."

"The Coast is pretty big."

"You want to turn around?"

"What happens when we get there?" she asked, ignoring his question.

"We rent a car."

"I feel pretty guilty about that."

"About what?"

"You having to do all the driving."

"It's supposed to be a beautiful drive."

"That's not what I mean."

The stewardess approached with their lunches. Like

Pavlov's conditioned dogs, Donna and Mel immediately lowered their trays. Donna began unwrapping her salad, picking at it with her fork.

"When we get back," she said with determination, "I'm going to start driving again. It's a belated New Year's resolution. Whatever we find, or don't find, in California, I'm going to start driving again."

"Good." Mel bit into his hard roll. "Meanwhile, you can be the keeper of the keys."

"What's your sister like?"

"Nice lady. You'll like her."

"It's very sweet of her to let us stay at her place."

"She's thrilled to death. I haven't seen my nephews in two years. It'll be nice for everyone."

"I hope they like me."

"I don't think I'd worry about that."

Donna put her fork back on her tray and looked straight ahead. "The turbulence sign's gone off."

"The drunk must be back in his seat."

"Mel—"

"What?"

She stopped. "I don't know."

He looked over at Donna. "You worried about what will happen if we don't find them?"

Donna turned and focused her eyes directly on Mel. "It's been eleven months," she said. "Adam will be almost six; Sharon will be almost three. They might not even remember who I am. They might not want me anymore. And Victor. Every day for almost a year now, I've been praying for that man to die. Every goddawful disease or accident that could possibly happen to anyone, I've wished on him—the more horrible the better. What happens if I see him? What do I say? What do I do? Mel—"

"What?"

"This is really crazy. I'm not worrying about what will happen if we don't find them. I'm worrying about what will happen if we do."

As if on cue, the plane gave a sudden lurch and the pilot's voice came back on to announce more turbulence—would everyone please fasten their belts and stay in their seats.

Chapter 21

If anything, the scenery was even more spectacular than the books described, the Pacific Ocean on one side, the Santa Lucia Mountains looming large, pushing close, on the other. Donna looked out the car window, letting her eyes feast along the ninety-mile stretch of rugged and awesomely beautiful coastline, known as Big Sur, that ran between San Simeon to the south and Carmel to the north. It was as breathtaking a sight as anything she had ever seen—rugged yet somehow intangible, spiritual almost. A rough spindle of land that had managed to remain apart from the rest of this most populous state, it reminded all who traveled into its often dangerous terrain that there were still areas in this world where man had not been entirely successful in leaving his mark.

According to the guidebooks, the name Big Sur was derived from the Spanish *el pais grande del sur,* meaning "the big country of the South." Donna ignored this interpretation. The name she told herself, sprang from a feeling, an almost drug-induced rush—the rocks, the ocean, the mountains, the incredible sight and sound of the surf.

Donna let out a slow, deep breath of air. Mel looked over at her.

"Everything okay?"

"Fine," she said. "It's so beautiful here."

"Yea, it is," he agreed. "Getting hungry?"

"A little." She looked out at the narrow strip of highway on which they were traveling, and smiled. "Do you think there are any good restaurants around?"

"We should be approaching that little gallery soon," he reminded her. One of the real estate women they had conferred with while in San Simeon had told them to be sure to stop at a little art gallery hidden in the woods along the coast. The people who ran it were very friendly, she had told them, kept a ready supply of sandwiches on hand, and had a good memory for faces and bits of overheard gossip. Donna and Mel kept a sporadic lookout for the small rustic gallery. They didn't expect much from it—perhaps only the sandwiches and use of the telephone. It was time again for them to check in with Los Angeles.

The gallery was even smaller and more hidden away than they had expected, so secluded in fact, that they almost drove right past it. Only the odor of smoke emanating from a wood-burning stove gave it away. Mel drove the rented white Buick up into the gravel driveway which was almost submerged by the surrounding foliage, and both he and Donna jumped instantly out of the car, Donna pulling her sweater tightly around her. She hadn't been fully prepared for how cool it was up in the mountains. Los Angeles had been warm, much like Florida. Donna had only been persuaded to take a sweater at all by Mel's sister, Brenda, who argued that she would need one, especially in the early mornings. Donna thought fondly of Brenda, whom they had left exactly one week ago today. She had been very helpful, very supportive, always there with a good word and a hot meal at the end of one discouraging day after another.

They had spent ten days in Los Angeles, had driven through every hamlet and borough, combed the beaches of Malibu and Pacific Pallisades, walked the streets of Newport Beach and Long Beach, talked endlessly and tediously with the residents of Palos Verdes and the other ocean communities. It was an impossible task. There were too many variables—it had been a Saturday when Victor had called, after all; it was entirely possible he and the kids had driven to the beach for the day, possibly the weekend, or to visit friends who lived there. They could be living anywhere, perhaps in Westwood or Beverly Hills, or even the San Fernando Valley. To that end, they checked with all the major realtors in greater Los Angeles—had anyone of Victor's description either purchased or rented a house approximately a year ago? Here again, there were too many variables—too many agents, too many houses, not enough time, not enough interest. They checked with all of L.A.'s insurance companies did anyone of Victor Cressy's description work in any of their offices?

They spent ten days pursuing every available course of action, checking all elementary and nursery schools, visiting all parks, playgrounds and local tourist attractions. Nothing.

Several times, Donna thought she saw a child who might be either Adam or Sharon. In each instance, she was proved wrong. Finally, at Brenda's urging, they agreed to hire another private detective who could aid them in their search, and they themselves took off for their slow crawl up the coastline, visiting every small town along the way, checking daily with the detective, whose name was Marfleet. Had he turned up anything new? Similarly, they reported on their own progress, kept the detective posted as to where they were, where they were headed. If he had any leads, any sources, he directed them in the proper direction. So far, Mr. Marfleet, Dr. Segal and Mrs. Cressy were all tied at zero.

"Hmm, it smells good here," Donna said, stuffing the car keys Mel had handed her inside her purse, feeling the dampness through her cardigan. Mel walked several paces ahead of her toward the two-story log cabin. "Oh, look, Mel," Donna called. Mel turned to her in time to see a large German shepherd lumber up to her side and thrust his nose against her palm, indicating a great willingness to be stroked, which Donna immediately obliged him with. "Oh, you're a nice dog," she purred, nuzzling him close. After several seconds, Donna gave the dog a final pat and followed Mel inside.

It was as Donna had always imagined such houses would be—a genuine log structure, both inside and out, with irregular wood planking across the floor and a high wood-beamed ceiling from which hung several large, circular wood lamps. The scattered rugs were woven and oval in shape, the furniture all colonial and pine. It would have perhaps been even more interesting, she thought, had the occupants worked against the natural setting, done the interior with chrome and plexiglass—modern man versus the elements and so forth, but perhaps such a decor would have taken away from the number of paintings and sketches that hung at neat intervals around the room. At the bottom of each drawing was a price tag, the scale seeming to range between a low of sixty dollars and a high of two hundred. The paintings themselves were unexceptional, obviously deriving most of their appeal from that of their setting.

"Like anything?"

The voice was friendly, almost plump. The woman from whom it emanated was likewise, a large woman of perhaps forty, with an almost mannish build and long brown hair worn plainly, deliberately so, and pulled back into a careless ponytail. She wore no makeup and her skin spoke of teenage acne and still abundant freckles. It was a kind yet very determined face, one that continued the mood of the wilderness and the home she had built in it. In the background, Donna could see a man of approximately the same age, in jeans and cowboy boots, still living the myth of the Western man.

Mel was the first to speak. "This is a lovely place," he said. Donna let him do the talking. She was becoming increasingly poor at small talk, preferring to let Mel amble along gently, almost stumbling into the areas they wanted explored. People were suspicious of strangers, of too many questions. It was necessary to get to know them first, in however superficial a manner. Not so much what you did, she thought, but what you appeared to be doing.

"We don't get too many people stopping here," the woman said. "Our own fault, I guess. We're kind of hidden away. Can we get you anything to eat? Some sand-wiches? Coffee?"

Over sandwiches and coffee, Donna and Mel learned that this couple, David and Kathy Garratt, had run this little gallery from their house—the bedroom and another room were upstairs—for over fifteen years now. The paintings were either their own or those of friends, and they made just enough money to keep themselves going. David also working at various odd jobs—he was a car-penter by profession—in the surrounding territory. They had hit upon the idea of opening their house to interested tourists because they liked people and it gave them the chance to keep in daily contact with the outside world. Because not too many people stopped by on any given day, it usually provided them with about as much outside human company as they wanted. On days they preferred to be alone, they merely hung a closed sign on the front door.

Donna listened with an intermingling of impatience and interest. Only when the former began overtaking the lat-ter, did she interrupt. "Would you happen to remember any of the people who have stopped here?"

Kathy Garratt regarded her with curiosity. "Anyone in particular?" she asked, knowing there was.

"A man. His name is Victor Cressy. He's thirty-nine, tall, dark—"

"Handsome?"

Donna nodded with a measure of defeat. She pulled a picture of Victor from her purse. "Here he is. This pic-ture is a few years old, mind you. He may have grown a moustache or a beard—"

Kathy and David Garratt converged on the photograph. Donna continued speaking. "He probably had two chil-dren with him, a little boy, Adam, he was about five and a little girl, Sharon, about two. This is close to a year ago, I'm talking about."

Kathy Garratt stood up and walked to a tall pine lec-tern. "Let's check the guest book. If he was here, he signed it. When did you say—"

Donna felt her heart starting to speed up, her knees beginning to noticeably weaken as she got to her feet. "Last April—but check May and June too. In fact, could we check it all since last April?"

The woman moved away from the lectern, letting Donna in behind it. "Be my guest," she said.

"Can I use your phone?" Mel asked. "It's to L.A. I'll have the operator ring back with the charges."

Wordlessly, David Garratt led Mel toward the old-fashioned pine wall-phone at the other end of the room. Donna's eyes quickly perused the length of each page for Victor's name.

"It's not there," she said some fifteen minutes later as Mel walked up behind her.

"I just checked with Marfleet," he said, a note of encouragement in his voice. "He said he may have something. Apparently up in Carmel. He's waiting to hear from one of his sources. I told him we'd be there by tonight, so I'll call him then."

Kathy Garratt was walking back and forth in front of them. "I'm trying to remember," she said, more to herself than out loud. "I remember there was a guy here about last April or May with two kids—" She turned to her husband. "You remember, David? The little girl was terrified of Muffin, that's our dog—"

Donna thought of the great German shepherd outside the cabin. She remembered that Sharon had just lately developed a fear of dogs, especially large ones.

"Oh, yea, I remember him. He bought a painting!"

"Didn't he have two kids?"

"I think he did. I can't remember if the other one was a boy or a girl."

Mel interjected. "Wait. You said he bought a painting. Do you keep records?"

"Of course we keep records," Kathy Garratt said, somewhat testily. "We're strictly on the books here. We're not interested in trying to defraud the government of a few extra pennies. We show it all."

Mel was instantly apologetic. "I'm sorry. I really didn't mean to imply—"

"It's just that we've been looking for such a long time—" Donna added.

"Think nothing of it," David Garratt said, walking toward the sofa with the book in which he obviously kept his records. "This is kind of a sore spot between Kathy and myself. It has nothing to do with you. You see," he continued, opening the book, "if it were up to me, I wouldn't be quite so honest about the whole operation—"

"And you'd be in jail," Kathy volunteered as everyone gathered around her husband. "And we'd be no help at all to these people." The plumpness was back in her voice. She turned several pages. "Here," she said, a note of triumph unmistakably in her voice. " 'Solitude'—that was the name of the painting he bought—paid eighty dollars for it on May the twenty-first." She put the book down. "But the name's not the same. Victor Cressy, you said?" Donna nodded. "No, this man's name was Mel Sanders."

"Mel?" Donna asked. "*Mel* Sanders?" She turned to Mel. "Do you think he'd do that? Use your name? S—Sanders instead of Segal? A kind of final cruel joke?"

"He'd certainly enjoy that sort of thing," Mel agreed. "Even if he was the only one to appreciate the irony of it all."

"More so in that case." Donna walked back toward the lectern. "May twentieth?"

"Twenty-first."

Donna quickly located the twenty-first of May in the guest register. "Here it is. Mel Sanders."

"Does it look like his writing?"

"It's hard to tell. It's kind of scribbled. It could be."

Mel walked to her side and checked the signature. He read the information aloud. "Mel Sanders, 1220 Cove Lane, Morro Bay. 'Great setting, great hospitality.' "

"We just came from Morro Bay," Donna muttered.

"It would only take an hour or so to go back and check it out."

"I thought we'd combed every square inch of that place."

"It's up to you."

"It's a chance. I think we have to take it."

"A pretty weak chance," Mel cautioned. "A man with two kids, one possibly not even a boy, who drops in a month after the disappearance—"

Donna turned back to David Garratt. "Did he pay by check or cash?"

David Garratt checked his records. "Cash."

"He looked like that picture," Kathy Garratt said, her memory seeming to grow stronger, "and I remember that little girl of his was crying because of the dog, and she started yelling she wanted her Mommy. Remember that, David?"

He shook his head. "No, I can't remember any of that."

"Sure," the woman persisted, "and he tried to calm her down, and he held her and said that Mommy couldn't help her anymore but that he was there and that everything would be all right. You don't remember that?"

"No," he repeated, then turned to Donna and Mel. "But my memory's nothing like Kathy's. She remembers everything anybody ever said or did. You never want to get into an argument with her, that's for certain."

Donna and Mel settled with the Garratts for the sandwiches and the phone call, signed the guest register, complete with the appropriate superlatives, and walked back toward the car. Donna threw Mel the keys. It was becoming warmer. Before opening her door, Donna took a last look around and then removed her sweater.

The house was neither big nor small, white but in need of a fresh paint job. It was situated on a small square piece of land, as were all the houses on Cove Lane, and it was almost as if each home-owner had taken a pledge to do nothing out of the ordinary that would disturb the outside symmetry of the dwellings. Their charm, their appeal, their very uniqueness, lay in their uniformity. The same little flower boxes lining the front windows, all filled with the same red and white flowers, the same hedges, even identical mailboxes. Donna wondered aimlessly if all the houses on the street needed a similar touch-up with the white paint brush.

"What do you think?" Mel asked.

"The house looks like something he might buy—"

"But?"

"But?" she repeated.

"There was a definite but at the end of that sentence."

She laughed. "I guess there was." She paused, shifting in her seat. They sat parked on the south side of the road, just a few houses down and across from 1220 Cove Lane. "But," she emphasized, "I just can't picture Victor living here. It's so—quiet."

"Palm Beach isn't exactly one of your noisier cities either," he reminded her.

"I know, but—I *don't* know. It just doesn't feel right."

Mel checked his watch. "It's two o'clock. The kids would get home from school in another hour, maybe two—if they came right home, that is. We can wait, or we can take the photographs around to the neighbors—"

"No. He may have made friends here. Someone might alert him. Let's just wait. We only lose a few hours if we're wrong."

"Feel like stretching your legs?"

Donna leaned her head back against the red plush of the car's interior. "No. I'm kind of tired. Actually, I don't feel so hot. Tension, I guess."

Mel put his arm around her. "You'll be okay. Just don't get your hopes up too high."

Donna closed her eyes. For several minutes there was silence.

"You asleep?" Mel asked quietly.

"No," she said, her eyes still closed. "I was just thinking about what I might like to do with my life when we get back home. As far as a career goes, I mean."

"And what's that?" She felt him kiss her forehead.

"Well, I really enjoyed redoing our bedroom," she began dreamily, "and that gallery we visited, I had all sorts of great ideas for it the minute I saw it." She opened her eyes and looked up at Mel. "I think I have a good eye for that kind of thing, but I've just never exercised it. I've always lived in places that, for one reason or another, were already furnished. I guess I always looked on it as one less decision I had to make." She sat up straight. "And now I'm realizing that I like to make decisions." Mel smiled. "So I've decided, right now, this very minute I have decided, that no matter what happens with my children, whether we can bring them home or not, that I am going to take some courses when we get back to Florida and I'm going to go into interior design. What do you think of that?"

"I think you're the most beautiful woman I've ever seen."

Donna laughed, then grimaced. "What's the matter?" Mel asked quickly.

"I don't know. When I laughed just then, I had a pain in my side." She squirmed, laughing uneasily. "Now, it won't seem to go away."

"Where?"

"Here." Donna pointed to her left side just above her waistline. "You don't suppose I'm having a heart attack, do you?"

"That's what I like about you, Donna," Mel said, maneuvering himself around so that he could examine the problem better. "You don't think small. What kind of pain is it?"

"Kind of burning. Like a sting or something."

"Let me see."

"What do you mean?"

"Lift up your sweater."

Donna did as she was told. "Well? See anything?"

"Just a mole" he said, pulling her sweater down again and sitting back.

"What do you mean, just a mole?"

"A mole, what else can I say?"

"I don't have a mole there."

"Yes, you do. I just saw it."

"Have you ever seen it before?"

Donna's eyes watched Mel's. "No," he answered, pulling her sweater up again and touching the round black spot.

"Ow!" she said as his fingers pinched at her side. "What is it?"

"It looks like a tick!" he said wondrously.

"A tick?! Where would I get a tick from?"

"I haven't got a clue. But that's what it looks like."

"Well, how do I get it out?"

"With a sterilized pin and either boiling water or a match, neither of which this car seems to come equipped with."

"Then it'll have to wait."

"We shouldn't wait very long. Ticks can be dangerous. You can get pretty sick from one of these little fellows. It'll bury itself deeper and deeper inside you the longer you wait."

"Are you trying to make me throw up?"

"I'm trying to make you understand that the earlier we get this thing out of you, the better."

"How would I get a tick?" she asked with growing frustration. "The dog! That miserable dog! Muffin!" she said, spitting out the words.

Mel moved back into his position behind the wheel and turned the key in the ignition.

"What are you doing?"

"I'll drive us to a pharmacy and get some ointment, then we can get this out—"

"No!"

"Donna—"

"Not now."

"You don't understand—"

"I know, these things can be very dangerous. I *do* understand, Mel. But an hour or two—I'm not going to die, am I, if we wait an hour or two?"

"You won't die."

"Please, Mel."

"All right," he agreed reluctantly. "But you tell me if you start to feel lousy."

"Okay." She kissed his cheek. "Thank you."

"You might not," he said, adding, "we wait two hours, tops."

"Two and a half," she smiled stubbornly.

"Two," he said forcefully. "End of discussion."

They waited two hours and twenty minutes before the brown Ford station wagon pulled up into the side driveway of 1220 Cove Lane.

"Somebody's home," Mel said, nudging Donna awake. In the past hour, she had grown increasingly lethargic and uncomfortable, yet she refused to leave.

"Is it Victor?"

"I can't tell." He opened his car door. "Do you want to wait here?"

"Are you kidding?" She opened the door on her side of the car as well.

"Will you be all right?"

"I'll be fine."

Donna felt her foot touch the sidewalk, realized instantly how weak she was feeling, how very nervous she was, and only prayed she wouldn't pass out before they reached the house. They arrived at the driveway of 1220 Cove Lane just as the occupants of the car were coming out of the garage and walking up to the front of the house.

A man. Tall, dark and not unlike Victor. But not Victor.

Just a man.

His two children—just children.

Donna collapsed onto the freshly mowed green grass of the front lawn.

She had never seen colors quite like these before, Donna realized, regarding them intensely, wondering only briefly where she was, how she had gotten here. Greens, lush greens, and rain-darkened browns and blacks. Like a

painting by Georges Rousseau. It *was* a painting by
Georges Rousseau, she decided, except that that was bla-
tantly impossible. What, after all, was she doing walking
around in a painting by Georges Rousseau?

She stepped down into the moss and felt her foot instantly beginning to sink, the sudden slime worming up
her shin, feeling cold and strangely wet against her leg,
sticking to her like dozens of thirsty bloodsuckers. She
pulled her foot up, horrified to find a bright royal blue
snake coiled around her ankle. She tried to shake it loose.
It clung to her as if its royal blue skin were her own.

The jungle—it was a jungle, she could see that now—
began to draw closer around her, the branches from the
trees all straining to touch her, the branches suddenly
possessed of suction cups at their outermost tips, the suction cups opening and closing obscenely.

When she looked at her feet again, the blue snake was
gone. The surface of the ground was clear and transparent. Beneath her, she could see fish swimming, eels
wriggling just under her toes, faunas swaying out to
her provocatively, inviting her to swim. Suddenly, she was
up to her neck, swimming through the jungle, watching
the lower half of her body as if it belonged to someone
else, seeing her bare legs treading in the stillness, seeing
the vibrant flesh-colored animal—what kind of animal,
was it? She wondered briefly, watching as its snaillike
body and humanlike hands approached her, found her,
wrapped itself around her and pulled her. Down. Down.

Beneath the surface. Her head disappearing below the
renewed slime, her nostrils filling with quicksand. I can't
breathe. I can't breathe.

Voices. She was aware of distant voices. Coming to res-
cue her. You're all right, it's just a dream.

She opened her eyes.

A large blue snake, coiled and ready for her, sprang at
her from the beam just above her head, wrapping itself
around her neck, slithering its constant pressure tighter
across her throat.

"No!" she sat up, screaming, pulling at the snake.

"Donna! Donna!"

Once again, Donna opened her eyes. Mel's face was in front of hers, his arms moving to control hers which were shooting furiously out into the air around her. "Oh God," she sobbed. "What's happening?"

She let Mel lean her back against the pillows, feeling her body soaking with sweat. She was in a bed in a strange but comfortable room; a television was on across from her.

"You're okay now," he said. "You were kind of sick for a few hours though."

"A few hours? What time is it?" She took several deep breaths.

"A little after midnight." Donna looked at the television. She recognized Johnny Carson. A young and pretty blond woman was stuffing a large boa constrictor into a box. Mel watched her as she watched the TV. "It's been an interesting show," he laughed. "Lady from the Zoo, some starlet who said she was baptized in Pat Boone's swimming pool, claimed he held her head down too long under water—instead of being born again, she thought she was going to die." He felt her head. "You had your eyes open every so often, but you kept drifting in and out. Fever's broken."

She suddenly felt her side.

"Careful. There's a bandage there."

"The tick?"

"Long gone."

She ran a hand through her damp hair. "How much of my life have I missed?"

"Before or after you scared poor Mr. Sanders half to death by fainting into his begonias?"

"Oh, God. Tell me."

"He was very nice about it, actually. He called an ambulance for me and we got you to the hospital."

"Hospital? Is this a hospital?"

"No. This is a motel. The hospital only kept you long enough to remove the tick and give you suitable medication."

"So, Mr. Sanders was—"

"Mr. Sanders was Mr. Sanders. Period. Wife died eighteen months ago, left him with two little girls to look after."

"Both girls?"

"All two of them, as Janine Cressy McCloud would say."

"So much for Kathy Garratt's wonderful memory—"

"And her dog!"

"Who was it that told us to go to that stupid gallery anyway? That lady from San Simeon—she was probably working for Victor!"

Mel laughed. "You feel better, I can tell." He flipped off the television. "You want some tea or anything?"

She shook her head. "I'm just tired. Will I be all right to travel in the morning?"

"I think so. Something tells me I won't be able to stop you anyway." He paused dramatically. "I called Marfleet. He said they may have something definite in Carmel. A man with two children fitting the general descriptions of Victor and the kids bought a house there six months ago. He was going to drive up there tonight and check it out, meet us there tomorrow."

"Oh, Mel—" Donna said, feeling her whole body starting to tingle.

"It might not be them, Donna—"

"I know, I know," she repeated, sinking down under the covers, feeling Mel crawl in beside her. "I know."

Chapter 22

The minute U.S. Highway 1 wound its way into Carmel, Donna felt all her senses begin to come alive. Her nostrils flared with the omnipresent scent of the ocean, her eyes widened with the sight of the houses, some more like gingerbread cottages, doll houses rather than homes; her ears opened to the sounds of the surf and the contradictory nature of the bustling tranquility around her. Every tissue in her body seemed to tighten, to go on red alert. He was here. She could feel it. This was the place he had brought her children.

"Take it easy, Donna," Mel warned.

"I know they're here, Mel. My whole body tells me they're here."

"Your whole body, beautiful though it may be, has been wrong before. Remember, it told you to marry Victor in the first place."

"They're here, Mel," she repeated, as they turned the car east onto Ocean Avenue, a street which actually ran perpendicular to the ocean. Donna watched the street names pass them by—Carpenter, Guadalupe, Santa Rita, Santa Fe, Torres, Junipero—increasingly more and more certain of her conclusions. They passed the large Spanish-style structure the sign identified at Carmel Plaza, 67 shops, and continued down to Dolores Street, where they turned left.

"Where exactly are we meeting Marfleet?"

"A restaurant called A Little Pizza Heaven."

"Pizza at this hour?"

"It's lunch time," Mel reminded her, checking his watch.

"Why'd you let me sleep so late?"

"I wanted you in fighting condition," he winked.

She smiled. "I know they're here, Mel. Can't you feel it?"

"What you're feeling—and yes, I feel it too—is a certain familiarity. This place isn't all that different, in a sense, from Palm Beach. Pine trees instead of palm. But it has that same—rhythm."

Donna nodded. It was the perfect word. "Only better," she added. "And Victor was always looking for better." She suddenly spotted A Little Pizza Heaven to her right. "There it is, Mel."

Mel pulled the car into the parking area and he and Donna got out, Mel throwing Donna the car keys to keep in her purse. Keeper of the keys, he had said on the plane, and obviously meant.

"Don't forget that Victor also lived in Connecticut for most of his life."

"I know," Donna said, putting her arm through Mel's, "but it's hard to go back to ice and snow when you've gotten spoiled by the sun and the ocean."

They were about to walk in the front door of the restaurant when Mel spun around and stopped her. She looked at him questioningly. "Look, Donna," Mel began, "if Marfleet has struck out, if we don't find the kids here, remember that I love you, and that there's still Monterey."

She laughed. "Anything else you want to say?"

"Yes," he said solemnly. "How many psychiatrists does it take to change a light bulb?"

"How many?" she asked, her smile a crooked grin.

"Only one," he answered, "but the light bulb has to really want to change."

She was still chuckling when the waiter led them

through the restaurant and out onto the wind-sheltered patio where Mr. Marfleet sat waiting.

"We missed them," Mr. Marfleet said as soon as they sat down. Donna couldn't believe her ears.

"What? What do you mean?"

"I mean, they were here. But we lost them."

"What do you mean, you lost them?" Donna could hear the shrillness creeping into her voice. No, please, no. She wasn't hearing this.

"I had a man up here," the detective explained, "asking questions. I guess Mr. Cressy, or Mr. Whitman, as he was calling himself, found out about it somehow and skipped. At any rate, he's gone. I had someone watching the house, but Cressy must have skipped out in the middle of the night."

Donna was shaking her head from side to side. She wouldn't accept what her ears were telling her. To have come this far, come so close, to have missed him by one night, the night that she spent sleeping in some motel room in Morro Bay because she had been bitten by a tick! No. It wasn't fair.

"Can you trace his car?" Mel asked, assuming Victor had one.

"We already did. He dumped it at the L.A. airport sometime early this morning. He could be anywhere by now, but we'll keep looking, I promise you. We found him once—we'll find him again."

His voice drifted off. Donna found herself looking at the detective closely for the first time since she had sat down. He was tall, though his height seemed all in his upper torso, and almost rectangular in shape, possessing a square jaw, square shoulders, and a prominent Adam's apple that protruded from the top of his open-neck shirt. His complexion was sallow, as if he rarely got much fresh air, and when he did, that it rarely agreed with him. He had looked much more comfortable amidst the stacks of files that filled his otherwise sparsely furnished office in downtown Los Angeles, where he had at least blended in with his setting.

"He changed the names of the kids," he said abruptly.

"What?"

"The little girl—he called her Carol, not Shannon."

"Sharon," Donna said, correcting the detective.

"Yes, Sharon. And the little boy, he called him—" He glanced down at his notebook. "Called him Tommy."

"You're sure it was them?" Mel asked.

The detective shrugged. "Fit the descriptions, dead on. Look, why would they skip if they're not the ones we're looking for?"

Donna nodded. "Where were they living?" she asked, her voice dull and distant. What did it matter where they had lived? All that mattered was that they didn't live there now. They had gone. Crept away in the night. Vanished. Again. For how long this time? Another eleven months? Eleven years?

"Not far from here." Marfleet laughed the laugh of someone trying to fill some empty space. "Actually, nothing's very far from here. The house was on Monte Verde," he said, checking his notes again. "147 Monte Verde."

Donna got up from the table. "I want to see it," she said.

"It's empty," Marfleet said. "And locked." He made no move to stand up.

Mel got to his feet. "I'll drive Donna over. We'll take a look around."

"Oh, sure," the detective agreed, as his pizza—everything on it—was laid before him. "You don't mind if I eat this first?"

"Take your time," Donna said, hating this man for his callousness, but, most of all, for the hope he had held out to her, only to pull away again with such fierce abruptness.

No, she thought, walking out of the restaurant, Mel behind her, it wasn't Marfleet's fault she had let herself get so worked up. She had done that little deed all by herself.

Just as she had screwed up the timetable with a little help from a big German shepherd named Muffin. She threw the car keys over to Mel. She couldn't go through much more of this. They were gone. She had let them get away. For whatever perversity of motives, she would visit the home her children—Carol and Tommy, he had renamed them, so strange, so foreign to her—had lived in for the past six months. Perhaps, like a psychic picks up vibrations when fingering appropriate articles of clothing, she would tune in to some vague feeling—

She got into the car, thinking enough was enough. From now on, she would leave the detective work to the professionals—don't call me until you have my family behind bars—and as soon as she had satisfied herself that Victor and her children were truly gone, so would she go. Back to Florida. Back to Annie. Back to pushing great boulders up an ever-increasing number of hills.

They decided to stay the night and then start back for Los Angeles the following morning after they got a good rest. Donna had said nothing for the rest of the afternoon, nodding silently in agreement to all of Mel's suggestions. If it had been any other way, she kept thinking, if it hadn't been them at all, even that would have been better, but to have come so close only to miss them by one day. She just couldn't accept it. They could be anywhere by now, she thought. We're back to square one. Farther back because now Victor was on the alert.

She and Mel had spent an hour at the house on Monte Verde. It was obviously empty—they had peered in all the windows, waited in vain for any neighbors to come home. Everything spoke of a hasty retreat. There was no ocean in the backyard, but it was close enough. What was it Marfleet had said? "Nothing's very far from here." Victor had called her from Carmel, of that she was absolutely certain. And now he was gone. He had stolen her children—again.

"Where are we?" she asked, looking out the car window for the first time in what felt like hours.

"We're up in the Carmel Valley. I thought it might be pretty to see. We can get a nice little motel—the guide-book says there's one along Carmel Valley Road, The Hacienda, that supplies little hibachis. I thought we could pick up some steaks, get ourselves a fine bottle of wine at this place called Yavor's Deli and Wines, head back to the motel, eat and maybe yell and scream a little bit."

She smiled wearily. "Sounds good. What time is it?"

"Almost four," he said, checking his watch. "Here we are." He turned the car into the parking area of the Haci-enda Motel. "You want to stay in the car?" She nodded. "Okay. I'll see if they have a room." She watched him walk inside the office and return minutes later, dangling a long room key. She realized that in those minutes, her mind had remained a total blank. "Room 112," he indi-cated, "around the corner there, small private patio, our very own hibachi."

"Good." It was the weakest good she had ever heard.

"You feel like lying down while I go get the wine and the steaks?"

She shook her head. "No, I'll go with you."

"Okay. This wine place is right up the street a few miles. And there's a shopping center there where we can pick up the steaks." She put the room key inside her purse.

"Terrific." Terrific sounded only marginally better than good.

"I love you," Mel said quietly. "I'm very proud of you."

"Why? Because I'm not acting like a blithering idiot?"

"Who said you aren't?"

She smiled feeling the tears she had been holding back start to cascade down her cheeks. "Damn," she said, burying her head against Mel's chest. "Goddamn."

"That's my girl," he said soothingly. "Don't keep it bottled in. Let it all out, honey."

Mel found a parking spot in the already crowded parking area of the shopping plaza. He maneuvered the car into place, pulled the keys from the ignition, handed them to Donna and then got out of the car. "Coming?"

"Why don't I go get the steaks while you get the wine?" she asked, joining him on his side of the car.

"Sure. You have money?"

Donna checked her wallet. "Plenty," she said.

"Okay. I'll meet you back here." They kissed gently. "You all right?"

She nodded. "I'm okay."

They walked in opposite directions. When Donna turned to see him, he was already gone, disappeared into the front door of Yavor's Deli and Wine. The thought crossed her mind that when she got out of the grocery store, he would not be there. Vanished—like everyone else she let become a part of her life. Dead—or simply gone. No, she reassured herself, tapping her purse, unless he intended to walk back to Florida. She was the keeper of the keys, after all. He would be there. He would always be there.

The store was beautifully appointed, large outdoor murals lining the walls, fruit trees seeming to spill their colorful produce directly from the pictures onto the cleverly arranged trays that were placed in front of them. And so it was throughout the store, a careful, loving blend of style and substance. The best of all worlds. It took a large dose of talent, she found herself thinking as she walked aimlessly up and down the aisles, to turn what was essentially an everyday grocery store into something as pleasant as this place was, to make it as unique as this place was, to make people want to come here from all over Carmel, as this place obviously did. The store was crowded with shoppers—women, a surprisingly large number of men, quite a few children.

She first saw the little girl as she was walking up one aisle and the child, sitting in the small front seat of a shopping cart, was wheeled by at the far end of that aisle. The child had been staring at Donna. Even at a distance of approximately fifteen feet, there was something extraordinary about that child's eyes.

Donna felt her heart beginning to race. Her legs seemed frozen to the floor. Stop it, she told herself. This has happened before. So many times, so many children who looked like either Adam or Sharon. So many mistakes. So much wishful thinking, as this was. Victor was no longer in Carmel; he had taken her children and fled in the night.

"Excuse me."

"Pardon?" Donna asked, turning around to face a young, pleasant looking woman, a baby wrapped in a cotton Snugli around her chest.

"Can I get by?" the woman asked.

"Oh, of course, I'm sorry." Her voice trailed off. "I hadn't realized I was blocking the aisle."

But perhaps it hadn't been Victor, she thought suddenly. Perhaps it was someone else who had fled. Someone in the same predicament as Victor; someone in his own kind of trouble. It didn't matter. What mattered was that Marfleet could be wrong! What mattered was the child she had just seen wheeled by directly before her eyes.

Her feet suddenly released her from the floor, pushing her forward so that she all but crashed into the young woman she had only seconds before let pass. "Sorry," she muttered, reaching the top of the aisle and walking slowly, so as not to attract unwanted attention, past the next aisle. The child in the shopping cart was not there. Had she been an illusion? Donna dismissed the thought and walked toward the next row of canned goods.

They were there. The child, clutching a small packet of Jell-O instant pudding to her chest as if it were a prized teddy bear, and the woman. Donna looked hard at the woman while pretending to be looking equally hard at the shelves. Donna had never seen her before. She was darkhaired and tanned, though not overly so, and Donna estimated her age at around fifty-five. Too old, obviously, to be the child's mother. A grandmother, perhaps. Or a house-keeper.

Donna focused her attention on the little girl. It had been eleven months since she had seen her, but eleven months can only alter, not completely change, a person's face. While the little girl who sat singing in the shopping cart had thinned out in places and matured (an odd word for a child not yet three years old) in others, she still had the same basic little features—the small, upturned nose, the mouth that formed a natural pout just like her father's, the curly hair, now longer though no less curly, and the enormous witch's eyes that looked right through you. Donna caught her breath as the child looked over in her direction. There was simply no mistaking that face. In the year since she had last seen the little girl, the child had come to resemble even more than before the woman she had been named after. My mother, Donna thought. My mother—my daughter.

"Oh, darn," she heard the woman say to the child. "I forgot the potatoes."

"Tatoes?" the child asked.

"I'll just be a second," the woman said. "Don't worry. I'll be right back."

Donna kept her head lowered and directed at some canned fruit, as if carefully assessing each tin's individual merits, as the woman walked past her up the aisle. The second she was gone, Donna rushed toward the child. What do I do? she wondered furiously. What do I do? Do I just pick her up and run? What if she fights me? What do I do? What about my son? Where is my son?

"Hello," she said quietly.

The child looked at her warily, her eyes penetrating Donna's skull. Can you see me? Donna asked silently. Can you see who I am? Do you remember me?

The little girl smiled. "Hi,"

I found you, Donna thought incredulously. I found my little girl!

"Sharon?" she asked tenuously.

The child's face hardened into a frown. "I'm not

Sharon," she pouted. Donna's heart sank. "I'm Big Bird."

"What?"

"I'm Big Bird."

Donna felt her body starting to shake. "Oh. Oh, I see."

"Please, can I be Big Bird?" the child pleaded, her voice suddenly soft.

"Of course you can. Big Bird is a lovely name." She touched the child's hair. "You have beautiful curly hair, Big Bird."

"No," the child whined, the threat of tears suddenly close. "Not hair. Feathers!"

"Uh, feathers, of course, they're feathers." Donna's mind was running around in circles inside her head. She didn't want to scare the child; she didn't want to cause a scene; people here, the cashiers, perhaps they knew this woman who was looking after her child, perhaps she came here often with Sharon. If she tried to grab the girl and Sharon resisted, then others might restrain her, hold this mad raving lady while the other woman fled with her child. She couldn't allow that. Better to confront the woman once she had left the store, with Mel hopefully at her side, force her to tell them where Adam was. Get both her children back.

Donna heard footsteps approaching and instantly withdrew, returning once again to the stack of canned pineapples she was pretending to examine. Out of the corner of her eye, Donna watched the woman put a five-pound bag of potatoes in with the rest of the groceries.

"You father would be very upset if we forgot the potatoes again," the woman said, checking inside her basket. "I think that's everything." She took a small piece of paper out of her purse and ran through the items she had listed on it. A list, Donna thought with some wonder, a list. "Okay, that's it. We'll go pick up your brother and go home."

"I want an ice cream."

"After supper."

"A pink ice cream."

"After supper."

Donna followed a few paces behind the woman to the front of the store. The woman had to wait in line. Donna, having made no purchases, walked ahead to the front of the store and stood waiting by the front window. From where she was, she could see the wine store—was Mel still inside? Had he returned to the car? Please Mel, be there. She looked back at the woman—she was third in line but another cashier looked like she was about to open her line, and so Donna was afraid to run out and try to find Mel. She couldn't afford to lose her child again. My God, she thought, I've found her. I've actually found my little girl! It's over. The nightmare is over.

Not quite, she thought. Nightmares weren't over until you woke up. She wouldn't be fully awake until she had both her children under her protective wings and was flying out of California.

The other cashier opened her line, and the woman moved directly to it, quickly unloading her items onto the moving countertop. Donna looked back and forth between the woman and the window. Where was Mel? What was taking him so long?

She looked through the maze of cars, and after several seconds was able to spot the white Buick they had rented in L.A. Mel was not there. She looked back toward the wine store. Nothing. Back to the woman. The cashier was still ringing up items. Hurry up, Mel. You have to help me!

And if not, she thought with sudden terror, if Mel didn't return from the wine store in time. The store was supposed to carry all sorts of rare and exotic wines—it was entirely possible he had gotten caught up in the wonder of it all. He was unaware of any urgency—Victor and the kids had fled to the Los Angeles airport early this morning!

Except that whoever had fled had not been Victor. Carol and Tommy, whoever they were, were definitely not her children. Her children were here in Carmel. One of them was here in this grocery store. Right in front of her. And she would not let her get out of her sight. No matter what. No matter if Mel was there to help her or not. If need be, she would confront this woman alone, scream for the police. She would not let this stranger get away from her if she had to single-handedly take on the entire combined force of all who shopped and worked at this shopping center.

The checker loaded all the groceries into bags until four were filled.

"Could I have someone help me carry these to my car?" the woman asked.

Donna felt renewed fear breaking into her fresh resolve. She hadn't been prepared for anyone else being part of the initial confrontation. Again, she looked toward the window. Mel was nowhere in sight.

The woman walked past her holding tightly onto the little girl's hand. As they were going out the door, the child turned abruptly to Donna and stared up at her, wordlessly.

"Come on, don't dawdle," the woman said, pulling on the child's arm. The grocery clerk followed close behind her with the cart full of newly bagged groceries. Donna took a final look around and followed the teenager, a mini-parade gone hopelessly out of step but still persisting gamely.

The woman walked slowly, the child an obvious encumbrance to what Donna guessed was her usual brisk style of walking. Still, this woman looked at her child with great tenderness. She was not simply a caretaker; she was obviously a woman who cared. Donna was, at least, grateful for that.

The woman's car was parked in the next row and at least six cars up from where Mel had parked the white Buick. Donna watched the grocery clerk from a safe distance as he loaded the four bags of groceries into the trunk of the beige-and-green Volare, license number NKF 673. She made a mental note of the number—NKF, NKF—Nikita Khrushchev Fucks, she said to herself, supplying her memory with the necessary key.

The keys. Keeper of the keys. She had the car keys.

The woman tipped the clerk, who subsequently held her car door open while the woman tucked Sharon into her infant seat in the rear. Oh God, Donna thought, they're going to get away! She moved forward just as the boy held open the woman's door, and watched the woman maneuver her body behind the wheel before the clerk then closed the door. My God, they were going to get away! Was she just going to stand there and let them go?

Donna looked frantically over in the wine store's direction for Mel. He wasn't there. Goddamn it! The woman started the car.

No! Donna thought, suddenly grabbing at the keys inside her purse. She would not let them drive away from here. She would not let them get away. Instantly, she ran through the rows of cars, her eyes still glued on the beige-and-green Plymouth. She found her row, found the car, took one last desperate look around for Mel, then thrust the keys into the lock, opened the door and jumped inside.

The woman was having trouble angling herself out of her parking space. Donna felt her whole body trembling, as if it had been newly invaded by thousands of ticks. She felt simultaneously sick and euphoric. She couldn't stop the shaking.

It was as if the whole scene had taken place that very afternoon and not almost four years ago. The night of the party. Getting ready to go out. One word flowing into another. One nightmare becoming yet another. All of it so intricately interwoven, one thread of the design inseparable from any of the others. Your face Donna it looks like Emmett Kelly your dress strictly bargain basement look out for Christ's sake you almost hit that trash can where are you going Donna you passed the turnoff three blocks ago how fast are you going anyway watch out you almost missed that stop sign what the hell are you trying to kill us you drove through a red light you drove through a red light get out of the car Donna I'll drive I don't know about you but I'm going into the party and have a good

time and what about Adam do you intend on divorcing
him too I'll have you committed blow your nose Donna
shut up Donna just shut up for a change his body pounding against hers invading her insides invading her sanity I
am a dead woman I will not fight you anymore.

She watched the beige-and-green Volare as it made its
final maneuver to freedom, watched it angle into its
proper position, watched it proceed cautiously down the
aisle.

Victor's face seemed to jeer grotesquely at her from her
front window. Her child was disappearing with each passing second. The car was almost at the exit.

I am not dead, Donna heard a voice say from deep inside her. She touched the bandage on her side. I am not
dead *yet*, and you have been inside me long enough! Victor's image feigned surprise. "Get out, Victor Cressy!" she
screamed, her hand pushing the key into the ignition and
pulling the driving shaft into reverse. She pushed her foot
down on the gas pedal, backed the car deftly and quickly
out of its temporary home and threw the Buick into drive.
As the car sped to a halt behind the beige-and-green Volare, she caught sight of Mel through her rearview mirror,
his arms loaded with undoubtedly vintage wines, a dazed
and puzzled look on his face. I'll explain later, she
thought, her eyes returning to the car directly ahead of
her. Right now, I haven't got anymore time to wait.

A second later, staying several feet behind the car
ahead, she turned the white Buick onto Carmel Valley
Road and started heading west back to U.S. Highway 1.

Chapter 23

The woman proceeded north along U.S. Highway 1 with Donna right behind her. Several times the woman checked her rearview mirror. Each time Donna lowered her head and held her breath. Was this woman aware she was being followed? Did she recognize Donna from the supermarket? Had Victor shown this woman her picture? Told her to be careful if she ever thought she saw her?

Donna checked her own rearview mirror. Although she was doing just over the speed limit, a chrome-colored sportscar was trying his best to pass her, first on the outside, then on the inside lane. After several seconds of cat and mouse, Donna angrily gave him the finger, and watched him instantly slow down with surprise. She relaxed only to find he had merely slowed for a second wind and was now determined to pass her even if it meant going right through her. Damn you, she shouted to herself as he suddenly roared past her on the inside, quickly maneuvering his small, sporty bulk between Donna and her child. Then he slowed down. Deliberately. Painfully. He slowed right down to a crawl.

Donna swore, first silently, then aloud. She wanted to blow her horn, but was afraid of attracting the Plymouth's attention. She could still see the car—as long as she could see it, she told herself, it would be all right. But the Plymouth seemed to be picking up speed while the sportscar seemed to be constantly reducing his. "Move it, you bastard!" Donna yelled, bursting with frustration.

As if he had heard her, the driver of the sportscar suddenly picked up speed, stepping hard on the accelerator and throwing the car into fourth gear, easily overtaking and then zipping by the Volare, leaving a huge cloud of dust and a raised middle finger in his wake. "Jerk!" Donna muttered, once again filling the space between herself and her child.

The woman's left signal suddenly flashed and Donna followed the car ahead onto the by now familiar Ocean Avenue. The woman then continued west on Ocean to Casanova where she turned left and proceeded along Casanova for five more blocks. Donna followed at a distance of half a block. She saw the woman pull the car into the driveway of a large yet unassuming house.

Was this where they lived?

The woman honked the car horn, first once, then again a moment later, with less patience. This was not their home, Donna concluded, remembering the woman's earlier words—"We'll go pick up your brother and then go home." There was no response to the woman's beeping. Leaving Sharon strapped securely inside her infant seat, the woman got out of the car and proceeded to the front porch. Just as she did, the door of the house opened, and several youngsters came spewing out, one on top of the other, all boys, all approximately the same height, one perhaps slightly chunkier than the others. They were laughing and wrestling, falling all over each other as the woman moved with determination to the center of the melee and pulled one of the struggling boys free.

Donna strained to see his features more clearly, but she was too far away. She watched him break free of the woman's hand and madly circle the car several times in an effort to get in at least one or two more parting shots. The woman finally secured him into the back seat beside his sister and then opened her door, waving a final goodbye to another woman who seconds ago had come out onto the porch. Donna improvised their parting dialogue—"Goodbye, Mrs. Smith and thank you for letting

Adam play here after school." "My pleasure, Mrs. Jones, anytime at all."

No, thank you, Mrs. Smith, Donna thought. No, thank you, Mrs. Jones. There will be no more times. No more times.

The woman backed out of the driveway and out onto the street, Donna again following from a comfortable distance behind. Both her children were there in that car now. She was separated from them by a distance of maybe twenty-five feet. Twenty-five feet of steel and glass and chrome and concrete. How much longer until she had them with her? She tried to project ahead until the evening. In another few hours, this would all be over. All the pain and fear and longing she was suffering now would be part of her past. Everything would be resolved—one way or the other.

The woman continued down Casanova several more blocks till Thirteenth Avenue where she signaled and turned right, heading toward the ocean. She drove for three more blocks to a street named San Antonio, whose backyards directly overlooked Carmel Bay. It was a breathtaking sight, the beach, stretched out before the fading sunlight, only a stone's throw away. The woman continued for only a few dozen feet before pulling the car into the driveway of one of these oceanview cottages and then stopping. Donna continued driving past several more homes and then pulled her car to a halt. She quickly got out of the car, shutting her door gently, not locking it, and walked over to where she could observe the woman with her children and yet not be observed herself. The woman opened the front wrought-iron gate and the children scrambled inside. "You can play in the backyard till dinner's ready," the woman called after them, opening the trunk of the car and lifting out one of the large brown bags.

Dinner! Donna thought, realizing it must be after five o'clock. Victor could be on his way home any minute. There certainly didn't appear to be any sign of him around. Donna watched a few cars passing her by, thought for a moment of Mel, stranded up in the Carmel Valley, and then directed her attention back to the woman, now lifting the second bag of groceries from out of the trunk.

Hurry up, damn it, she wanted to scream. We don't have all day!

But the woman was in no such hurry. One by one she unloaded her bags of groceries and carried them through the gate and into the soft-brown painted wooden house with its white clapboard shutters. When the last parcel had been disposed of, and the woman had disappeared inside, Donna moved with great speed toward the house. She was almost at the gate when the front door opened and the woman appeared again. Donna ran quickly to the nearest shrub and hid behind it breathlessly, feeling for some unknown reason, like Jim Rockford of the "Rockford Files." Oh, please, don't see me, she prayed. Not now. Not yet.

The woman walked back to the car and opened her car door, pushing some sort of remote control unit attached to one of the car's sunblinders which obviously served to open the garage door. Then she drove the car into the now opened garage. Seconds later, she walked out again and back through the gate toward the house. Donna sat for several interminable seconds behind the shrub that had shielded her, and then stood up. Just as she did so, as if the woman inside the house had been aware of her presence all along and was scheduling her actions to coincide precisely with Donna's, to arouse her maximum fear quotient, the garage door noisily came lowering back down. Donna stopped, her heart pounding. Nancy Drew, Mel had called her. No, she thought conjuring up a mental image of the teenage sleuth, no. Nancy Drew was definitely out of her league, not to mention Jim Rockford. She belonged more with Sherlock Hemlock, the fumbling detective of "Sesame Street." The thought immediately wiped away her fear. Her own little Big Bird was in the backyard waiting for her. There was no more time for fear.

She walked slowly and carefully toward the front gate. What if Victor were to pull up right now? What if his car came barrelling up beside her? She heard footsteps. Oh God, no, she thought, feeling him walking up behind her. Abruptly, she turned. A young man walked past her without acknowledging her presence. Maybe she wasn't really here, she thought. Maybe this was all a dream—like the snakes. Well, if it's a dream, she said to herself, turning back to the gate and opening it with great delicacy, we might as well see it through to the end. The gate opened easily and noiselessly. Once inside the pleasant front garden, she brought the gate closed with her hand and then stopped, listening to the sounds of her two children playing in the backyard.

The cottage had a large glassed-in front porch. Donna stared at it for a minute, her mind trying to decide exactly what to do. She would steal quietly around the side of the house, get into the backyard, see her children, explain who she was, and then run with them to her car. Donna peered inside the glass windows of the front porch. If only she knew where the woman was. She was most likely unpacking the groceries and trying to get things organized for dinner. That meant she was undoubtedly in the kitchen, and the kitchen was very probably at the rear of the house overlooking the backyard. Damn, Donna thought. Somebody help me. You've got no one but yourself, a voice suddenly told her. Her own voice. A voice she was hearing more and more from in the past few months. Stronger. Louder each time. Get moving, Donna, it said. Donna took two tentative steps toward the side of the house, and immediately found herself tripping over a large yellow beachball she had somehow failed to see. Recovering quickly, she tossed the ball off to her side, watching as it came to rest just below the front steps.

A concrete pathway of reasonable width lay before her and it led straight to the rear of the house. Donna, keeping one eye on the side wall for any unexpected windows, moved slowly along the pathway toward the backyard. The ocean was roaring its encouragement; Donna was

feeling tingly and light-headed. She came to the first window and peered inside at a neat and conservative living
room, a few toys scattered with almost deliberate precision at regular intervals. There was something so organized about even this amount of disorder. Donna
continued along the wall. The next set of windows looked
into a bedroom, probably the housekeeper's—it looked
too small to be Victor's, too colorless to be for the kids—
followed fast by the windows of the kitchen. Donna felt
her stomach beginning to churn. Surely, the woman would
see her here. Donna slid her body up along the side of the
exterior wall.

The woman was at the opposite side of the room, still
unloading the various groceries, putting them in their appropriate places. The room was large and square, all
white with occasional splashes of yellow and green. It was
surrounded on two sides by windows, another side led in-
ward to the rest of the house, and the last side, the most
westerly side, led into a combination breakfast nook and
sunroom, which, in turn, overlooked a patio, the backyard
and the ocean. If the woman remained busy in the kitchen
and didn't come out into the sunroom, Donna felt she had
a fair chance of getting to her children without attracting
the woman's attention.

Donna remained frozen for several seconds at the side
of the house. Then, her shoulders straightening instinctively, she thought, I didn't drive this far to leave here
empty-handed! She moved softly to the corner of the
house where she could now see her children playing.

They were playing ball—a small, bright, multicolored,
rubber ball—tossing it back and forth. Or more correctly,
Adam was tossing and Sharon was running back and
forth.

"No!" the small male voice yelled over at his sister.
"No, I keep telling you—keep both hands up—Not like
that!"

Donna stared hard at the little boy, quite tall for his
age, slender, beautiful. So much a little man. Unmistakably her son. Adam, she mouthed silently. My baby.

"Are you going to listen this time?" the boy demanded impatiently. "I'm not going to keep telling you." He walked quickly toward his sister and grabbed her hands. "Like this. Now, keep them like that." He brought his head up and stopped.

He had seen her. Was staring right at her. Not moving.

The little girl did a slow turn in Donna's direction.

They all stood staring at each other from their respective positions.

"Hi," Sharon spoke.

"Daddy said never to speak to strangers," Adam admonished. Donna felt the tears spring to her eyes. Damn, she did not want to cry. Adam looked warily toward the back door.

"I'm not a stranger," Donna whispered.

"What?" he demanded. "I can't hear you."

Donna raised her voice just slightly. "Don't you know who I am?" she asked. He was old enough. Surely, he must remember, even a little.

"Who are you?" the boy asked, a protective arm draping instinctively across his sister's shoulder.

Donna swallowed hard, lowering herself till she was crouching at their eye level. "I'm your mother," she said. "I'm your mommy."

Sharon's eyes opened wide with curiosity; Adam's opened with fear. He took several steps back. Sharon remained stubbornly where she was.

"You're not our mommy!" Adam said defiantly. "Our mommy left us. She didn't want us anymore!"

Donna stared into the boy's frightened eyes. How could Victor have told you that? she asked him silently. How could anyone be that mean? How could anyone hate that much?

"That's not true. I never left you. I have always wanted you. I have been searching for you ever since your daddy took you both away from me."

"Liar!" the little boy shouted. Donna immediately looked toward the window but the woman was still busy, by now undoubtedly used to the constant shrieking of her young charges.

"You know I'm not lying, Adam," Donna said softly. "You're old enough to remember me. You can't have forgotten me completely. You know I'm your mommy!"

"You're not my mommy!" He was starting to cry now.

"Oh, please, honey, I don't want to make you cry. I just want to hold you. I want to kiss you. Take you home with me. Back to Florida."

"I live here! You're not my mommy!"

"I *am* your mommy. I want you more than anything in the whole world."

Adam just stood staring at Donna through his tears, which were now streaming down his cheeks. Suddenly Donna became aware that Sharon was no longer standing still, that she was moving slowly but with great determination in Donna's direction. Donna kept her eyes on both children as Sharon moved closer and closer toward her, her large eyes burning into Donna's.

She walked to within a few inches of where Donna sat crouching. Slowly, she raised her right hand into the air and gently reached over and stroked Donna's cheek. "Mommy?" she asked softly.

Donna's arms shot out from her sides and wrapped themselves around the small child with an urgency she had never known. "Oh, my baby," she cried. "My beautiful, beautiful baby!" She smothered Sharon's cheeks with kisses. "Oh God, I love you. I love you so much."

"She's not our mommy!" Adam screamed, a note of hysteria now obviously present in his voice. "Our mommy didn't want us! She didn't want us!"

Donna heard a car door slam shut from the front of the house. Good God, Victor! Scooping Sharon up under one arm, she raced at Adam and brought her hand around his mouth just as he was preparing to scream. He kicked at her, biting her hand, trying to pry her hand away from his mouth.

She heard the front door close. Victor was inside the house.

Her only hope was to run toward the front of the cottage as Victor was walking toward the rear.

Not realizing she had such strength, Donna pitched the struggling boy under her other arm and started to run.

"Daddy!" he screamed. "Mrs. Wilson!"

Mrs. Wilson heard her name, recognized the intensity with which it had been shouted, and looked toward the sound. She saw Donna, a child under each arm, just as Victor walked into the kitchen. Victor turned toward the window. Everything froze—a photograph suspended and enlarged. In the split second that followed, Victor's eyes locked with Donna's, once two matching shades of blue, now jarring, unforgiving oceans of hate.

Donna raced down the side path, feeling Victor running in a parallel line inside the house. Adam kicked frantically at her legs; Sharon offered no resistance. She could see the gate just feet ahead of her, could hear Victor's frantic footsteps as he pushed open the front door and jumped down the few steps, his arms reaching out to grab her as she ran past. She felt his hands brush against her shoulders, his fingers straining to catch onto the back of her blouse, and then losing their grip as his feet shot out from under him, the yellow beachball escaping from under the weight of his body as he fell, sprawled out against the grass. Donna reached the gate, pushing it open just as Victor recovered and got to his feet.

Adam screamed loudly the second they reached the street. But if anyone took notice, Donna was too preoccupied to care; if any passing cars were pulling over, they would have to line up behind Victor. Nobody was going to stop her. Her only thought was getting to her car—she had just seconds now. She heard the front gate slam; she knew Victor was right behind her.

The car seemed further down the road than she remembered parking it. Her body was starting to tire, starting to ache. No, not yet, she told herself, readjusting her son, reaching the car, opening the door, throwing her children inside, first her daughter, then her son, hurling herself in after them, slamming the door, locking it just as Victor reached for the handle.

Again their eyes locked, seared, and parted. Donna had seen enough of his hatred. She started the car, feeling Victor's fists pounding against the windshield, feeling Adam's fists pounding about her face.

"Adam, please, honey—"

"You're not my mommy! You're not my mommy!"

Victor moved his body directly in front of Donna's car, daring her to move.

Don't tempt me, Donna mouthed. The car idled, waiting to go. Donna stared straight ahead into Victor's face. She could see his resolve, knew the stubborn mind she was dealing with. He would die right there in front of his children before he would move even one step out of the way. Carefully, deliberately, imperceptibly, yet with great speed, she checked her rearview mirror. There was no one there. Moving her eyes back to Victor, she struggled free of Adam's hands, and using her right arm to shield and protect the small bodies beside her, threw the car into reverse, pushed down hard on the accelerator and raced backward toward Thirteenth Avenue.

She allowed herself only an instant of self-congratulations, knowing Victor would be quick to recover. By the time she was able to stop the car and change directions, heading west onto the wide scenic oceanside road, Victor had jumped into his own brown car—somewhere between a sedan and a more sporty model—and was only one car behind her. She wound the car furiously along the beach highway, the cross streets receding with ever increasing rapidity—Tenth Avenue, Ninth, Eighth, Seventh. A sign ahead directed her to Pebble Beach and the Famous 17-Mile Drive. Not now, she thought. She had no time for seventeen miles of scenery, however spectacular. Ocean Avenue suddenly appeared. The familiar name gave her a rush of needed confidence. She made an abrupt right turn and headed east toward the main highway. What then? she thought frantically.

The blue car between her car and Victor's had long

ago gone its separate way, and Victor was quickly narrowing the space between himself and Donna. She pressed down harder on the accelerator. Victor reciprocated. Throughout it all, Donna continued to wrestle with her son, the sounds of his fear and anger serving almost as a sort of surrogate radio, the a cappello rantings of the latest in Punk Rock. She pressed down harder on the gas pedal, making another swift, unplanned turn at the next corner. She heard the squeal of tires behind her, knew Victor was still directly on her tail. She caught a quick glance at the terrified faces of nearby pedestrians, saw their bodies arch and stiffen as she approached, withdrawing as far from the street as they could.

The noise level inside the car was reaching deafening proportions. Donna's head was pounding. Where are the cops in this town? she wondered frantically. Isn't anyone going to stop this insanity? She saw herself spending the rest of her eternity in a rented white Buick, her son pounding his fists against her brain, her daughter absorbed in the quickly passing scenery, being chased in an endless maze through the streets of picturesque Carmel. As far as hell went, she decided, it beat an eternity of doing the dishes!

This strange thought brought with it its own calm. I'm going to be all right, Donna said to herself, recognizing in the seeming absurdity of such thoughts, traces of her former self, the pieces of the jumbo puzzle that made up Donna Cressy assembled in their entirety for the first time in many years.

"Things are going to be okay, kids," she said aloud. "We're going to be okay. Everything's going to be fine."

Suddenly, they heard a bang, felt the car lurch and bounce. Again, Donna frantically spun her head around. "Jesus Christ," she swore, seeing Victor moving closer for yet another premeditated rear-end collision. "Are you crazy?" she shouted. "Your kids are in here!"

Victor brought his car crashing into the back of the Buick yet another time. This jolt sent both children flying forward against her arm which shot instantly out to shield them. Another such jolt and she might not be able to hold them back—they could go flying right through the window. Both Adam and Sharon were now starting to cry. Adam, for the first time, stopped fighting with his mother and looked toward the rear of the car at his father.

Donna's voice was frantic and loud.

"Can you get your seat belts on, kids?" she yelled.

Sharon was crying. "I'm scared," she whined.

"I know, honey. But please, do you know how to buckle your seat belt?"

"I don't know how," the child sobbed.

Donna looked at her daughter, silently measuring the space between them. There was no way she could lean over Adam, adjust the child securely in place, and continue driving this car. Her only hope was her son. She looked over at his frozen face. He sat on his knees, staring wildly out the rear window at the face of his father. "Adam," she said with as much soft urgency as her voice could impart, "please, honey, can you help us? Put your sister's safety belt on and yours too. Please."

She watched Adam's eyes enlarge with terror; Victor was about to ram the car again. Donna pressed harder on the accelerator, got temporarily out of his reach, and looked back at her son.

"No, Daddy, no!" he started screaming. "Stop it! Stop it!"

"Adam, please," Donna yelled over his screams. "Sit down. Help us. Please. Help us!"

Suddenly the boy turned around in his seat, reaching over and pulling on his sister's seat belt and then adjusting his own. Donna swallowed hard, feeling the perspiration on her face and underarms, quickly turning another corner—where was she? She'd lost all sense of direction—and continuing on up the street. The children were whimpering with fear, their hands, she noticed, now tightly interlocked.

After a few more frantic turns, she found herself back on U. S. Highway 1, although nothing looked familiar. Where were the cops? She had the court order right in her purse. If only someone would stop them. Please stop us, she cried against the steering wheel, before he kills us.

She felt another bang, but this time the crash came not from the rear but from her side of the car. He was gaining on her, pulling up beside her, ramming the side of his car against the side of hers.

"Oh God!"

Adam became increasingly hysterical. "Stop it, Daddy!" he was screaming. "Please, Daddy, stop it!"

Donna hung onto the wheel as if her hands had been welded to it. What was the matter with Victor? How could he do this to his own children? How could he put them through this?

She looked out her side window at Victor's car, saw his face, recognized he was aware of nothing at this moment but his hatred for her.

"Daddy, stop!" Adam yelled again as Victor once more brought his side of the car against the white Buick.

Donna lost control of the wheel for several seconds and careened off the pavement for a number of yards before being able to right the automobile back onto the highway. The children reacted hysterically.

"Stop!" Adam screamed, starting now to sob like his sister. "Please stop! Mommy! Mommy! Please stop!"

Donna turned abruptly to the word, staring deeply into the tear-soaked faces of her children.

"Oh my God, my babies!" she cried. "What am I doing to you?"

She slowed the car as quickly as she could directing it over to the side of the highway, and then stopped, pulling the children tightly into her arms. Within seconds, Victor had pulled over and stopped just slightly down the road, and was now racing angrily over to where the three sat huddled and crying together.

Chapter 24

Donna's face was sore and bruised, scratched bloody by her son's nails, punched red by his sturdy fists; her legs were stiff and bore many small brown blotches, evidence of the force of her son's well-placed kicks; her arms ached; she could barely move her fingers; her stomach was in worse knots than she could ever remember, and her throat was hoarse from screaming.

"You okay?" he asked her.

Donna stared over at Mel. "Never better," she smiled.

Mel got up from his seat against the wall and walked over to where Donna sat in the center of the large room. "I'll say this for you, lady," he began, "for someone who hasn't driven a car in four years, you do all right. Might even make it to Indianapolis—providing, of course, they don't take away your driver's license."

"You think they will?"

"Well, they'll have to find it first, I guess."

Donna ran her hand through her hair. "What a mess! I don't believe it! But who thought, you know, I haven't driven in so long, why would I bother renewing my license?"

"Exactly."

She brought her hand across her forehead, looking up at Mel. "You think they'll charge me?"

Mel shook his head. "For what? Driving without a license? Driving a stolen car? Going eighty miles an hour in a twenty-five-mile-an-hour zone? Creating a public nuisance? Reckless driving? Why would they charge you for anything as silly as that?" He knelt down beside her and smiled.

"Thanks a lot."

"Not to mention kidnapping—"

"I showed them my court order!"

"I think they were more interested in the papers you were lacking."

"Oh, so what if my name wasn't on the rental papers!"

"You tell 'em, kiddo."

"Oh, Mel."

"I love you."

For the first time since Mel had been ushered into the large police room by two equally large policemen, they embraced.

"I was so afraid you wouldn't be there," she said, leaning against him. "I thought, you know, they'll give me this one phone call and he won't be there."

"Where else would I go?"

"I had the room key!"

"They had others."

"Were you surprised when I took off like that?"

"Surprised is an interesting choice of words."

She smiled. "Did you explain everything to them?"

"I tried."

"So did I. Do you think they understood?"

"*They* tried."

She looked sharply into his face. "Did you see the kids?"

"I looked in at them. They look okay. Tired. They're with the housekeeper, a Mrs. Wilson."

"And Victor?"

"I didn't see him."

Donna moved restlessly around the room. "I wish they'd come back in here and tell us what's going on." She paused, thinking back to just two hours ago. "You know, they came out of nowhere. One minute there was only Victor and me; the next minute I think the entire Carmel police force was beside us." She walked back over to Mel. "And now they all disappear again. What time is it?"

"Almost eight."

"I've been sitting here for an hour. The kids should be in bed by now."

Mel rumpled her hair. "You did it!" he said proudly. Donna smiled.

The door opened and the room suddenly filled with police, four men in total, two in uniform, two in plainclothes.

"Sorry things took so long," the man in charge said, taking what was obviously his regular position behind the desk. "It's just an inconvenient time to check things out, especially with the time difference between here and Florida. Not many people up this late working—" He stopped. "Everything checks," he said finally. "You can go get your kids. Take them home."

Donna burst into tears; Mel's arms went immediately around her, hugging her close in silent celebration. "You're not going to charge me?" she asked, wiping her eyes.

"And have every newspaper in the country label me the new Simon Legree? Lady," he continued, disarmingly, "if I tried to press charges against you, I'd be the one the courts would throw in jail. Not to mention, my wife would probably murder me as I slept. Go on, take your kids and get out of here. Don't look a gift horse—wherever."

Donna and Mel began walking toward the door. Donna stopped. "What about Victor?" she asked tentatively.

"Him, we can charge," the man said.

"Can I see him?" Donna asked, surprising even herself.

"If you want."

Donna nodded. One of the uniformed officers led her through the door and out into the corridor. Mel indicated silently that he would wait for her where he was. The officer led Donna down the hallway a few feet to the next room.

The room was much smaller than the one Donna had been held in. Victor was standing by the far window, looking out onto the street. He turned immediately when the door opened. Donna could see he had been crying.

"Come to gloat?" he asked.

Donna lowered her head. What had she hoped to accomplish by seeing him? What had she sought? His assurances that he would leave her alone? Not come after her and the children? It was pointless to ask him. Pointless to have come. She turned to leave.

"Donna—"

She stopped, looking back in his direction. His voice was ineffably sad.

"Would you please tell the kids—tell them how sorry I am that I frightened them the way I did." She nodded. "I really love my kids, you know."

Donna remembered a time much earlier in all their lives when he had said the same thing. When she spoke, her voice was calm, in command. "I guess you have to decide what's more important to you—your love for the children or your hatred for me." She paused. "I'm taking them home now."

Victor lowered his head; Donna turned and walked out of the room.

Both children were curled up against the folds of Mrs. Wilson's skirt, fighting sleep, when Donna and Mel walked into the room. Adam sat up immediately upon their entrance, backing into the curve of the housekeeper's arm.

"If you want," the woman said quietly, "I can pack their things and bring the suitcase around to your motel tonight."

"Thank you," Donna said. "I'd appreciate that. We'll be leaving first thing in the morning."

They all spoke in whispers, as if afraid to disturb the sudden peace.

Donna walked over and picked up her half-sleeping daughter. The child stirred momentarily awake, her eyes smiling in recognition, her hand reaching forward and stroking her mother's cheek. Then she let her head lower to Donna's shoulder, and her eyes closed in instant slumber.

Donna looked down at her son. "Adam?" He hung back, still clinging to Mrs. Wilson. Donna moved to Mel and transferred the sleeping youngster from her shoulder to his, then she walked back to Adam, and knelt down in front of him.

"Once upon a time," she began, not sure exactly what she was going to say, "there was a little boy named Roger and a little girl named Bethanny, and they went to the zoo to see the giraffes. And they took some peanuts with them. But the sign said—" She stopped, feeling her throat catch.

Adam was staring at her wide-eyed and breathless.

"The sign said 'Do Not Feed The Animals,'" he uttered softly and then stopped.

"Oh, Adam, I love you so much. Please come home with me!"

Suddenly, he was in her arms, his hands tightly around her neck, the sobs openly pouring from his body.

"Oh, my baby. My beautiful little boy. How I love you!"

She stood up slowly, carefully, Adam's legs wrapping themselves around her lower torso, clinging to her as tightly as he knew how. At first she thought his mutterings were just sounds; soon the sound became more distinct. A word. Over and over. Mommy.

Donna and Mel walked with the two children in their arms to the doorway. Donna turned to Mel and smiled through her tears. "Let's go home," she said.